Esther Freud was born in London in 1963. She trained as an actress before writing her first novel, *Hideous Kinky*, which was shortlisted for the John Llewellyn Phys Prize and made into a feature film starring Kate Winslet. Her other novels include *The Sea House* and, most recently, *Love Falls*. Her books have been translated into fifteen languages.

LUCKY BREAK

It is their first day at Drama Arts for each of the nervous students huddled in a circle: Dan, serious and driven; Nell, already convinced that she is going to fail; fiery, rebellious Jemma and careless, glamorous Charlie. They are told, in no uncertain terms, that here, they will be taught to Act. To Be. To exist in their own world on the stage. But outside is the real world — a pitiless place in which each of them hopes to excel. So what comes next? Facing a multitude of difficulties, these young actors will grapple with sleazy directors, desperate competition, dreary tours, unobtainable agents, rocky relationships and endless tempting jobs . . .

Books by Esther Freud
Published by The House of Ulverscroft:

THE SEA HOUSE
LOVE FALLS

ESTHER FREUD

LUCKY BREAK

Complete and Unabridged

CHARNWOOD
Leicester

First published in Great Britain in 2011 by
Bloomsbury Publishing
London

First Charnwood Edition
published 2011
by arrangement with
Bloomsbury Publishing
London

British Library CIP Data

Freud, Esther.
   Lucky break.
   1. Acting- -Fiction. 2. Actors- -Fiction. 3. Ambition- -
   Fiction. 4. Success- -Fiction. 5. Large type books.
   I. Title
   823.9′2–dc22

   ISBN 978–1–4448–0748–6

Published by
F. A. Thorpe (Publishing)
Anstey, Leicestershire

Set by Words & Graphics Ltd.
Anstey, Leicestershire
Printed and bound in Great Britain by
T. J. International Ltd., Padstow, Cornwall

This book is printed on acid-free paper

For my friend Kitty Aldridge,
who was there on the first day.

Hamlet's advice to the players.

'Speak the speech I pray you, as I pronounced it to you trippingly on the tongue. But if you mouth it as many of our players do, I had as life the town crier spoke my lines. Nor do not saw the air too much with your hand, thus. But use all gently. For the very torrent, tempest, and, as I may say, whirlwind of your passion, you must acquire and beget a temperance that may give it smoothness. O, it offends me to the soul to hear a robustious periwig-pated fellow tear a passion to tatters, to very rags, to split the ears of the groundlings, who for the most part are capable of nothing but inexplicable dumb shows and noise. I would have such a fellow whipped for o'erdoing Temagant. It out-Herods Herod. Pray avoid it.'

William Shakespeare

Advice to a young actor starting out.

'It's not fair, and don't be late.'

Michael Simkins

PART ONE

1992 – 1994

The Chosen

Nell dressed in the same clothes she'd worn to the audition. A large blue, cotton-knit top over faded jeans, with her hair tied high, so that when she turned her head the pale ends of it swished against her face. Yes, she thought, as she checked herself in the mirror, smudging a line of black under each terrified eye, that's good, and she held tight to the thought that however plump and freckled, she was the same girl who, six months before, had stood before the board of Drama Arts and performed a Shakespeare monologue and a modern.

'You off?' It was her landlord, leaning over the banister from his rooms above. Nell forced herself to smile up at him, unshaven, a mug of coffee in his hand. It embarrassed her, this unexpected involvement in her life. 'First day,' she told him, and heaving her bag on to her shoulder, she swung out through the door.

The bus was packed. Nell squeezed on and spiralled up the stairs, and pushing her way towards the back, she clung to a pole as slowly, haltingly, the bus moved forward along Holloway Road. Beside her a man jammed an elbow into her side as he wrestled with a newspaper, and a woman on a nearby seat struggled with a small boy. 'Shh,' the woman said, 'stay still, why don't you,' and she tried to slide the slippery weight of him up on to her knee. No one knows, Nell thought as she looked down on the hurrying heads of the people below. No one knows that I've been chosen. And she almost flew forward as the bus came to a stop. The doors swished open, passengers streamed off, and one girl clattered up the stairs, breezy and beautiful, a silk scarf wound round her neck. Nell's heart clamped tight. What if she'd been chosen, too? Nell knew it was crazy, but this was exactly the kind of girl that should be starting drama school, and she imagined them arriving together and being told, sorry, we're over-subscribed, only one of you can stay.

The bus swung into the middle lane, and turned right by the prison. Nell watched the open plains of the triple-width road as the engine heaved and churned, and gathering speed, thundered up the hill. Large houses lined the way, flaking, dirty, with makeshift curtains, a sign for bed and breakfast beside one yellow door. Her parents had lived on this road once, right here, at the top of Camden, and then, when Nell was a baby they'd moved to Wiltshire, to a tidy, leaf-green village, where, after only a year, her father had declared that he was stifled. Nell began to count the roads, marking them off on her fingers, straining for the junction with York Way when the bus would slide under a bridge. She glanced at the girl, her face turned into sunlight, and pressed the bell. She didn't move, didn't even look round. And flooded with relief, Nell squeezed past her, and ran down the stairs.

The Oracle

Dan wasn't sure why he packed the letter, but at the last minute, along with black tights, white socks and a pair of flattened, size-eleven ballet shoes, he slipped it into his bag. Maybe he'd need it as a pass to gain entry to the college, maybe he'd be asked to present proof. He imagined a cloaked figure — a highwayman with a scarf over his mouth, leaping out to bar the way. 'Who goes there?' 'It's me,' Dan would protest and he'd point to the signatures of the directors of the school. But no one apprehended him. No one tried to keep him from his destiny as he made his way north along the busy road, short-cutting through an estate of flats with narrow, olive-green front doors, into a Victorian terrace, and up the wide, shallow steps of Drama Arts.

The building had originally been a hospital, although now there was nothing left but the façade, and the foyer — with its domed ceiling and stone-tiled floor — still held an air of urgency and panic. Students whispered as they milled about, some watchful of the door as it swung open, while others stood staring in silence at the noticeboard on which was pinned a list of names. Dan scanned the list until he found his own name, and reassured, wandered into the narrow corridor of the canteen where a hectic woman in an apron, grey hair trailing from a bun, was slicing mushrooms for a soup. 'I'll be open at first break,' she told him. 'Best to have breakfast before you come, I can't open any earlier, it's just not . . . '

'No, it's fine . . . ' Dan retreated, and catching sight of a girl in a lace dress pulling open another door, he followed her and found himself in a large, oval hall. There was a circle of chairs arranged in the centre, with several people already sitting at odd intervals, alone. Dan and the girl looked at each other, and, shrugging, they sat down.

'Hi,' she said. She had dark gold curling hair, and her legs under her dress were bare. 'I'm Jemma.'

'Dan.' He put out his hand, and instantly regretted it. Clumsily their fingers touched. 'Actually,' he admitted, 'I've no idea what I'm doing here.'

Jemma smiled, and a dimple dented her cheek. 'At my audition they asked me to imagine I was a snowman and I was melting, slowly. I nearly didn't come.'

Dan sank lower in his chair and watched as, one by one, the seats filled up. There was a tall red-headed girl biting her nails, and a boy with unnaturally green eyes. Dan could see, even from across the room, that his face was smeared with beige foundation, ridged in grooves around his nose. He turned to Jemma, hoping to share a smirk, but she was watching a group of long-legged blondes already chatting in a row. He let his eyes linger for a moment on her creamy skin, visible beneath the stretched wool

6

of the dress, but when she turned to him he looked away.

There was one older student, a man in a striped city shirt. He sat with his arms crossed, his face deep red as if already prepared to be embarrassed. Beside him was a black girl of intimidating beauty, her hair cropped short, her cheekbones sharp, her almond eyes half closed with boredom.

'This free?' A boy with a Scottish accent slumped down on the other side of Dan.

'Sure.'

He stretched his legs. 'I'm Pierre.' Pierre had a gold hoop in one ear, and on his fingers a collection of tarnished silver rings. 'You'd think there'd be someone here to greet us, on our first day.' He tipped back his chair and Dan followed his gaze to a gallery above their heads where lockers stood like sentinels around the edge.

'They're probably spying on us from up there.' Pierre smiled widely to show he didn't care. 'Start as they plan to go on, I guess.'

'What do you mean?' Dan frowned.

'They have a theory here. Break them down to build them up.'

'Really?' He could feel Jemma listening. 'Break us down how?'

'Oh, I don't know.' Pierre shrugged. 'Strip away all our pretensions, get to the raw emotion, the bones. I've got a friend who was here a couple of years ago. She said it was intense.'

'I came and saw a graduation show,' the red-headed girl on his other side leant over, 'and how they got there I don't know, but it was bloody brilliant. As far as I'm concerned it's the only drama school worth bothering with.'

The door creaked open and a girl looked in. She was wearing a blue jumper that came almost to her knees and her eyes were wide with fear. She spotted the last empty chair, and on tiptoe, as if she could avoid being noticed, she made her way towards it.

Dan looked round. There were thirty students here now, fifteen girls and fifteen boys. They seemed an odd, assorted group.

'But is it true . . . ' Jemma was leaning over him to get to Pierre, 'that people get asked to leave, just like that, for no reason at all?'

'It does happen,' Pierre lowered his voice. 'I mean, you know they're a couple, the men who run this place? Well, if they like someone . . . sometimes they get . . . a wee bit protective. There was one boy who was a real favourite, actually you may have heard of him, Ben Trevelyn, he's gorgeous, and he's doing really well, but anyway, every time he got a girlfriend, that was it. Two weeks later, she was gone.'

The room was full of chatter. Students discussing their auditions, their re-calls, what other drama schools they had applied for, whether or not they'd found anywhere to live.

'They threw them out?' Jemma looked shaken. 'Didn't anyone complain?'

Pierre laughed. 'My friend said the girls were pretty useless anyway. Actually, I think one of their dads did write a letter, but Patrick Bowery wrote back to say they were doing her a favour. Not encouraging her in this misguided choice of career when she was utterly devoid of talent.'

'God!' Jemma snorted. 'That's awful.'

'But I thought . . . ' the redhead whispered, 'I mean, don't gay men usually love women?'

'Sure,' Pierre agreed, lifting one shoulder. 'But sometimes they love pretty boys more.'

The door at the far end of the room slammed. Everyone looked up and a hush fell as Patrick Bowery himself, taller and thinner than Dan remembered from the audition, strode across the room. He stopped at the edge of the circle, and slowly and carefully, with raised eyebrows, he looked them over, one by one. When he had scrutinised them all, he drew a pack of cigarettes from his pocket. It was a foreign pack, soft and unidentifiable. He tapped it against his palm and, releasing a cigarette, put it to his lips. He flicked a lighter, and inhaled deeply. There was a relaxing among the students. Pierre grinned, and a slight, fair girl began to rummage in her bag. Patrick exhaled airily. 'I smoke.' He said it loudly, cutting into the K. 'You don't.' The effect was startling. Everyone sat up straighter. There were no smiles now. Patrick took two more drags and ground the cigarette out under his foot. 'So,' Patrick remained standing. 'I'm going to start today with the first baby steps of your education, by initiating you into the marvels and sophistication of the earliest documented era of theatre. The reason for this, and I know that it's not usually considered polite to mention it, but you young people who drift towards acting as a profession usually do so because you're God-damn Fucking Useless at anything else.' There

9

was a thinning of the air as every student in the room breathed in. 'But here, at this school, I will not, do you hear me? I will Not tolerate ignorance.' Dan noticed the mature student shift uncomfortably in his chair, and Jemma dipped her hand into her bag for a pen. Dan had nothing to write on except the back of his acceptance letter, and as Patrick Bowery launched into an elaborate description of the sixth-century BC cult of Dionysus, of orgies, outsized wooden phalluses, men who drank so heavily that they passed out on the hillside and were treated to miraculous visions of fornicating gods, Dan scribbled across the worn folds of the paper. Soon he ran out of space and looked round nervously, and Jemma, without meeting his eye, ripped a sheet of paper from her own pad and handed it over. Thanks, he mouthed, and he attempted to catch up.

Patrick talked of the significance of the Greek chorus and the dancers, the musicians and the instruments they played. He talked of his favourite playwrights, Aeschylus and Euripides, and he waited, watchful, as the students grappled with the spelling. 'Of course,' he continued, 'as you know, three tragedies were performed during just one day, followed by a comedy, and the most famous of the theatres where these spectacles took place was the theatre at Epidaurus. Now for any of you, really truly passionate about your craft, a visit to this ancient monument should be at the top of your list.'

Visit Epidaurus, Dan wrote, and the thought of azure skies, of history, of ancient, fallen columns, momentarily distracted him. Where were they? He glanced over at Jemma's page, her writing, blue and beautiful, spanning out in legible lines. Comedy, he read. Bawdy, satirical, razor-sharp. By the time he'd copied it down, Patrick had moved on to college rules. 'Punctuality.' He looked ready for a fight. 'Is Vital. Anyone who arrives late will be sent home again. Late on more than three occasions during the course of one term and you can expect to be called into the office for an interview. Now,' he lowered his voice to a more thoughtful tone, and it occurred to Dan that everything he did and said had been rehearsed, 'not everyone in this room will stay the course. I want to warn you. Not everyone will have what we consider the suitable requirements to enter the third year. And the quickest way to find yourself Out,' the tempo was lifting again, 'is to fail to actually come In.'

There was silence while Patrick Bowery looked at the circle of students. Some of their eyes were fixed on him, their pale faces turned up like wilting flowers, while others stared down at their hands, appalled.

'It's not a game.' His mouth was twisted, his own face white. 'Out there. In the world. It's ruthless, harsh, competitive, the hardest profession to break into, and if you can't even manage yourself to be on time, there are no second chances. You'll be replaced. That's one of the things that you'll learn here.'

It was an hour and a half before he set them

free. They gathered themselves up and fled to the canteen, where Becky, the grey strands of her hair newly bound up, her polka-dot apron pulled in tight, plied them with tea and sausages hot from the oven.

'Honestly,' Pierre rolled his eyes, 'ruthless, harsh, competitive. Anyone would think we were joining the SAS.'

'I Smoke. You Don't,' someone else tried, not a bad impression.

Dan took his tea and squeezed his long body into a corner, his back to the wall, listening to the shrieks of outrage, the accents, adopted and real, the gasps and splutters of laughter as his fellow students dissected the day so far. He took out his notes and flicked through them, closing his eyes as he imagined himself centre stage in the vast stone auditorium at Epidaurus, his every syllable razor-sharp, his words booming out across the terraces where a thousand stunned spectators sat transported by the power of his voice.

★ ★ ★

After the break, Patrick Bowery was softer. He asked each student to introduce themselves and then, handing out slips of paper, he told them to choose one person in the room and write down three words to describe them. Keep it secret, he told them, one day we'll hand them back out, and see if first impressions are really what they seem to be.

'Is that what you do with us?' The red-headed

girl smiled flirtatiously. 'Label us, and see if we evolve?'

'No. It is not,' Patrick snapped. His eyes were icy. He turned away and to Pierre's delight asked him to collect the slips of paper. The whole class watched him scamper round the circle, scooping them into a bag.

'So,' Patrick adjusted his pose, 'I'm going to let you into a secret. I'm going to tell you something that you may not know. At Drama Arts you'll be learning to Inhabit your Characters. You won't be performing. You won't be prancing around in fancy dress. There will be no public shows until the third year, and in the first year you'll only be seen by the staff. In the second year, if we think you're ready, we'll let the other students watch your efforts, and no one else, and this is because we want to do everything we can here to rid you of the desire to perform. We want you to learn to Be. To exist in your own world on the stage.'

Patrick shook his head. 'Now I'll let you into another secret. At other drama schools, however renowned, they don't Teach anything. At other drama schools they put on a series of plays and hope that somehow, through pot luck, something will Sink in. But Here, and I hope you all realise how lucky you are to be here, You will Learn. You will be taught Stanislavsky's method of acting. You will learn to create a fourth wall. When you walk on stage you will have an Objective and a series of Actions, and these will be the secrets of your trade. You will be clothed with these tools, and you will cling tight to them like treasure.

13

Never will you go ahead without them. Just as in life you walk into a room for a reason with all your thoughts and needs, your vices, your weaknesses and strengths. So you will walk out on stage. If you go to the theatre tonight, or on any night,' he continued, 'in our famous West End, you will see no end of vacuous performances, actors with no idea where they are, or where they're going, really just attempting to speak and not bump into the furniture, but a student of Drama Arts will stand out from this colourless troupe. A student from here will have a purpose, an energy, that will drive him forward, so when you are still here, rehearsing late, night after night, complaining you're cold or hungry or tired, remember how lucky you are. You are actually learning something. You are being Trained!'

Patrick looked around. All eyes were gleaming at him. Every face was on fire. Yes, Dan thought, this is what I came for! And then to his surprise, Jemma put up her hand. 'I wanted to ask, I mean, I do sometimes see really good plays, with actors, well, not from here . . . and so, is that just luck then, that they're good?'

Dan saw the girl opposite him — Nell — look up as if she too had seen actors she admired, and might be about to name them. But Patrick Bowery was frozen to the spot.

He took a deep breath and held it like a child in shock. 'LUCK?' he bellowed.

Jemma visibly began to shake.

'No. It is Not luck. It is your inability to tell what is art and what is interpretation. And in future if you have nothing intelligent to say then PLEASE, unless you're asked, keep quiet.'

There was silence in the room. No one moved or spoke.

'Right.' Patrick Bowery had recovered himself. 'If there's nothing else, no other questions . . . you are free to go.'

★ ★ ★

That afternoon Dan changed, with the other boys, into ballet clothes, forcing his legs into the unfamiliar tightness of tights, hopping and laughing, and attempting to avert his gaze from the awkward bulges and dents revealed by Lycra. Eventually when they were all ready, they shuffled out to meet the girls, their ballet slippers scuffling, hoping for camouflage in the matt-black studio at the back of the building. 'Please,' Silvio Romano's voice was gentle, his dancer's body moulded into muscled planes. 'Please, tell me your names.'

He nodded as each one spoke, his eyes running over them, drinking them in, gliding in his whispery dance shoes up and down the rows. He was older than Patrick, with a worn face and dusty, dyed brown hair, but when he moved he was agile as a boy. The slight, fair girl with the broad Manchester accent was called Hettie, the quiet Canadian in full make-up was Eshkol. The French girl, one of the three blonde beauties, Dan forgot as soon as she'd spoken. But the redhead was Samantha. Then it was Dan's turn. Silvio smiled at him. 'Daniel, of course,' and Dan

15

felt a melting as if he'd been touched. Jemma was beside him again, defiant in a low-cut leotard, and on the other side was the black girl, Charlie Adedayo-Martin. 'Ahh, Charlie,' Silvio paused. 'I remember you,' and Charlie, colt-thin and awkward, her skin smooth caramel, held his stare with a wry smile.

To Nell, dumpy, in a T-shirt pulled over her leotard, he simply nodded, perfunctorily, moving on to Susie, Tess, Mikita. The boys were grouped together too. Pierre, whose real name, Dan now knew, was Pete. There was the mature student, Jonathan, newly gay, newly free from a life as an accountant, and Jermaine, lithe and powerful, his hands over his crotch.

'Now,' Silvio said, when each student had introduced themselves. 'I want you to greet our accompanist, Miss Louise Goeritz.' A tiny, ancient woman was crouched behind the piano, her head nodding rhythmically to music only she could hear. 'Miss Goeritz, would you play us something? Miss Goeritz?' But it wasn't until Silvio touched her shoulder that she came to life, her fingers trilling automatically up and down the keys, running together, crashing down in a crescendo of surprising force. 'Thank you.' Silvio bowed, motioning for the students to applaud, and the old lady sank down once more on her piano stool and drifted into a reverie of her own.

Silvio waited for absolute quiet. Not a sigh or a shuffle in all the rows of black. 'What I am about to teach you will be difficult,' he looked small and mournful suddenly in his woollen trousers and black top. 'Impossible even for

16

some to understand, but if you can take it in, then, instead of nothing, there will be something, on which to base your art.' There was a general stir, a shifting of bodies. It was harder than it looked, standing still. 'Now, I want you to think about the four concepts,' Silvio spread his arms as if he might fly, 'of Sensing. Thinking. Intuiting and Feeling. These four concepts are revealed in our movements by the motion factors of Weight, Space, Time and Flow.'

Dan glanced around him. The faces of his fellow students were expectant, anxious, baffled. 'There is much to learn,' Silvio continued. 'But let me tell you first about character divisions. All humanity,' he explained, 'is divided into six character types. And each character is made up of conscious states. Now, I do not expect you to remember everything. There will be many other opportunities to learn . . . '

In front of Dan, Pierre started to droop, and then as if to save himself, he began slowly rotating his head, emitting a series of sharp crunches which made Dan wince.

'Now, each of these conscious or subconscious states,' Silvio continued in his silky voice, 'can be activated by bodily movements. We'll take one character type at a time, and work on it and by the time we've examined them all, you'll have six basic characters, each with its own rhythm, on which to base any part you're given.' He let his eyes peruse them for a minute as if to ensure that they were worthy of his effort. 'So for example, Number 1, which I call Close . . . ' he roused himself, 'is light and quick, a not very deep-thinking or complicated person, whose rhythm is made up of quick, dabbing strokes.' Silvio adopted the voice of a young girl, ''I will not go down to the shops for you.'' But his flowery Italian accent blunted the effect. ''You can bog off with your demands,'' he continued, jabbing with his finger for effect. And relieved to have something to smile about, the whole class smiled.

'And now,' Silvio stretched his body into a star. 'We will begin our movement. Keep your heads entirely still, and look with your eyes to the right. Only eyes. Now left. Lower left, upper right, right forward, lower right. And left.'

Dan thought he might be going to faint. He'd spent the night before on a friend's too-short sofa, a boy he'd met at youth theatre. They'd sat up late, toasting his new beginning, his new life, only pausing to jeer at the TV news which showed John Major, white-faced and coldly sweating, reassuring the country that even though billions of pounds had been sold in order to keep Britain in the ERM, interest rates wouldn't rise above 12 per cent. 'The man who ran away from the circus to be an accountant,' Dan's friend laughed. 'I bet he regrets it now.' And then just when he'd been ready to sleep, three flatmates, eager for a party, had come stumbling in and opened up more beer.

'This is how we mark our thought processes in time.' Silvio's eyes were alive with wonder, and he explained how by looking up, and to the right, you could take your audience with you into the future, or back through time into the past. Dan's body ached. There was nothing to lean against, and he wondered what would happen if he lay down on the floor. And then Silvio was dancing. He bent his knees, his body upright, and stamped his feet fast. The stillness and the force of him was startling. He moved in parallel planes, Cossack style, with his arms crossed, stamping, up and down and side to side. Miss Goeritz, awakening, caught up with him, and Silvio sprang on to his toes. He leapt and twisted, twirled and arced, holding his body, pulling against air, pressing himself into the ground, and then releasing, spinning, free.

How old is he? Dan wondered, and humiliated, he shook his tired limbs.

'And so you see,' Silvio came to a gentle stop, unfolding from a perfect pirouette, 'nothing comes from nothing. Everything in this life, it comes from dedication and work.'

There was an awed silence.

'We will meet again tomorrow, and the day after, and the day after that.' Silvio let his gaze wash over them. 'And in each of you, if it is there to be discovered, we will find the kernel of your talent. Now . . . ' he looked as if he might be about to let them in on a final secret. 'You may get changed.' And, an old man again, he shuffled from the room.

The Lesson

Babette's method acting class took place in the large, oval hall. A stage had been set up at one end, built from hollow wooden blocks, and one by one, the students were expected to step up on to it and present their understanding of Stanislavsky's Action and Three Activities for her discerning eye. 'Oh Nell . . . ' Pierre leant over to her and nudged her in the ribs. 'I have to tell someone . . . '

Nell kept her gaze fixed on the stage where Samantha was shrugging off her coat.

'It's agony,' Pierre tried again, his large eyes threatening to overflow, and Hettie, who was sitting on his other side, hissed, 'Save it for your improvisation.'

'I cannae.' Pierre's voice rose to cod-Glaswegian. 'I think I'll die . . . '

Nell turned towards him and pretended to be stern. 'What is it?'

Pierre gave a wide slow smile. 'I'm in love.'

'Really?' Nell was unable to resist. 'Who with?'

'Shhh.' A Swedish girl spun round in her seat. Pierre ignored her. 'Go on,' he grinned. 'Try and guess who it is.'

Nell glanced round the room. The students were scattered across the hall, some singly, others in groups. Babette, their teacher, sat at a table in the centre, her possessions strewn around her, coats and scarves, an overflowing

20

bag, a dog with a matching mop of faded yellow hair. She gave the impression that she must be involved in some multi-fabric task, weaving, or knitting an enormous shawl, but she was in fact keenly watching each exercise, making notes, giving her verdicts in a slow, throaty, American drawl. Nell's eyes settled on Jonathan, who, at thirty-one, had a car and his own terraced house in Fulham, where, last week, he'd invited a group of them to supper, serving up a stew he'd left all day slow-cooking in the Aga. Or could it be Stuart, short and stocky with a perfect alto, who tramped off every evening in his motorcycle boots to seek new thrills, or the same thrills possibly, on Hampstead Heath? These were the only two, apart from Pierre, who were openly gay, although there were others who may well be about to come out — soft-spoken Cecil, who spent extra hours practising his pliés in the movement studio, and Giles and Kevin, who recited poetry at every opportunity in plummy, competing voices. Nell ignored Rick with his leather jacket and quiff. She didn't linger on Billy or Jermaine, a couple of chancers, both of whose names had gone up on the board for lateness, whose lives at Drama Arts were already under threat, even though Jermaine could triple-flip across the movement studio and had mastered Silvio's Cossack dance in less than a week. Nell looked over at Dan, dreamy, distant Dan, his dark hair tufted into peaks, but even as she looked, Jemma leant towards him and whispered something into his ear. Nell sighed, a small knot of longing tightening her gut, and

21

turned back to the stage. Samantha had hung up her coat and was standing before an imaginary mirror. Nell knew it was a mirror, because both Hettie and Charlie had already peered into it, but Samantha wasn't brushing her hair, or applying make-up, Samantha was unbuttoning her shirt. The room fell silent. Every murmur and shuffle cut short as button by button, Samantha's fingers fumbled, until her shirt fell open to reveal the bright purple lace of a bra. Next she unzipped her skirt. Her knickers were purple too. She must have planned this.

'Bloody hell,' Pierre hissed as she unclasped her bra. 'Typical. That's upped the ante. Whose turn is it next?'

'Yours,' Nell told him.

Samantha turned away and flung her bra on to the bed, and then, in one swift movement, peeled away her knickers. Her body, from behind, was strong and white, with a scattering of orange freckles on each shoulder. Nell held her breath. Would she turn to them? Would she examine herself in the invisible mirror like any normal woman? But no, Samantha was running in a sideways crab towards the wardrobe. She was searching for something she'd hung up, a grey silk slip, which she pulled over her head, where it stuck, just for a moment, but long enough to give the room the luxury of examining her unseen. Her large white breasts with their unexpectedly small nipples, the narrow triangle of flaming orange hair. And then the silk of the slip fell, and with a communal sigh Samantha was covered, her poise regained, and she ran back across the room and slid into bed.

There was a pause, in which Pierre clutched Nell's arm.

'Well done, Samantha.' Babette nodded. 'So tell me, what was your Objective?'

'To get a good night's sleep.'

'And your Action?'

'To prepare myself for sleeping. To get undressed. To put on my slip. To get into bed.'

'Very good. That's excellent.' Babette turned and shot a swift look around the class. 'Next?'

Pierre stood up. 'Keep guessing,' he told Nell as he hurried on his skinny legs to the front of the room.

Pierre waited a few moments before leaping on to the stage. He ran forward, almost tripping over a corner of the bed, and set down a cassette player on the floor. Then he turned away, his back to the audience, and struck a pose. The class could hear the grind and hiss of the tape turning, but no sound came. Hettie and Nell exchanged a glance. The tape hissed on. Pierre waited. Eventually, red-faced, he turned, adjusted a dial and suddenly the music burst up to the ceiling, startling everyone, even the dog, who sat up and gave a bark.

Pierre threw himself into the dance, wiggling and strutting, twirling and tapping, striking sudden idiotic poses until the audience of Year I was united in compulsive, convulsive laughter and Babette was forced to rise from her nest of wool and call a halt.

'What are you doing?'

Pierre looked jubilant. 'Dancing?'

'And your Objective? Your Action?'

'To . . . um . . . entertain you all.'

Babette paused. 'But you're not telling a story, not showing us anything. Pierre, honey, you're just showing off.'

Pierre slunk back to his seat. 'Bitch,' he hissed, 'just because I didn't get my knob out.' But Nell knew he was ashamed.

★ ★ ★

The pub adopted by Drama Arts was warm and dimly lit, with tassels on the curtains and heavily upholstered seats.

'The thing that worries me,' Hettie said, once they'd slipped in behind the much-coveted corner table, 'I have to decide who Thea is by tomorrow. Apart from being a wallaby, I mean. Well, obviously, she's a girl, but the animal I've chosen for her is a wallaby. So, anyway, I've done her back story, which is fine, but the real problem is, I'm still not sure which of the Inner Attitudes she has, and our scene's coming up before Patrick Bowery tomorrow.'

'OK.' Pierre flipped over a beer mat. He prided himself on being Silvio's most assiduous student. 'What's the first Inner Attitude?' Nell and Hettie leant forward as if he might be about to perform a trick. 'It's Close.' He sunk his biro into the soft cardboard. 'Which is sensing and intuiting. And aren't all children Close? I mean, Thea's a child really, isn't she? I mean, more so, say, than Moritz, who's probably number 6 — Adrift.'

24

'Do you think?'

'Well, Adrift is sensing feeling. With Inner Participations of Intending and Adapting. Motion Factors are Weight/Flow and Inner Quests — What/Why?'

Hettie frowned and Nell caught her breath. 'I wish I understood it like you.'

'Yes,' Hettie agreed. 'You're amazing. So, if Moritz is Adrift what are his elements?'

'Light and strong, free and bound,' Pierre came back.

'That's brilliant.'

'So if Thea's Close,' Pierre said reassuringly, 'her elements will be light and strong, sustained and quick.'

'Right.' Hettie blinked. 'Sustained and quick. And while we're on the subject, who fancies another drink?'

'I'll get them,' Nell said. 'Same again?'

Nell stood on the metal footrail and used her extra height to attract the barman's attention. But for all her efforts the man beside her, more recently arrived, was served first. He was stocky, dishevelled, in an overcoat and a paisley scarf. No one she recognised from Drama Arts. A paperback novel, the title of which she couldn't read, protruded from his pocket. He ordered his Guinness and walked over to a table not far from theirs, where he proceeded to roll himself a cigarette.

'We're so lucky,' Hettie was saying, when Nell slid the dented metal tray of drinks on to the table, 'to have all this to work from. Honestly. I don't know where I'd start otherwise.'

'We are lucky.' Pierre winced at the first bitter taste of beer. 'My back story has given me so many insights into Moritz's character, and each time I rehearse, just having my Objective — I know I was bitching about Babette today — but really, it's like having a coat to keep you warm.' His eyes went misty. 'A magic cloak of confidence. To think some people just wander on to the stage, without any idea where they're going.'

'Yes.' Hettie was excited. 'You know in that skipping scene, with the other girls, well, I'm actually meant to be visiting my Grandma, and then I get distracted, but all the time . . . ' Her face was flushed, and her voice rose in pitch. 'I'm feeling guilty, I'm actually thinking, shit, Grandma's waiting for me. And of course none of that is in the script.'

'Yes,' Nell agreed. 'That's brilliant.'

'And if Thea is Close,' Pierre added, 'then you've got her rhythm for nothing. Her Shadow Moves are punching, slashing, floating, gliding, pressing, wringing, dabbing, flicking.'

'My God.' Hettie tore open a packet of crisps. 'Yes. I can work out every single one of her lines. Well,' she laughed, 'not that there are that many.'

'Whereas Moritz,' Pierre squeezed his hand in for a crisp, 'is Adrift, and the Shadow Moves for Adrift are punching, pressing, floating, flicking, wringing, slashing, gliding and dabbing.'

'Bloody hell! Does Silvio know what a genius you are at his work?' Nell asked. She didn't know how he'd memorised the lists, especially when so many of them were the same.

'I'm not sure, but I thought I'd better make an effort. In the third year we have to create whole characters from his Six Tables.'

Hettie looked alarmed.

Pierre sighed. 'I think I'll do my Mum, everything she says sounds as if she's wringing out a sheet.' He began to twist an imaginary piece of cotton, his face contorting with the effort. 'For Christ's sake son,' his voice was strained, 'when are you going to get a proper job and stop messing around?'

'You're a genius.'

'Yeah. Well. I thought I'd better start making plans. I mean, what are they going to do? The ones who haven't bothered really listening? I guess they'll be out on their arses, doing walk-on parts in Panto, if they're lucky.' He drained his glass. 'Actually, I feel sorry for my mate at Guildhall, not learning what we know. All they teach them there is tits and teeth. Maybe we should try and explain some of Silvio's theories.'

'I'm not sure.' Nell felt doubtful. 'What if we get it wrong?' She imagined attempting to reproduce Silvio's work, the intricate multi-coloured charts, the graphs and tables, the three-dimensional drawing of a cube with abbreviated directions for the angles of your thoughts.

'True.' Pierre tore open another packet of crisps. 'Maybe we're not ready yet. Anyway, you still haven't guessed the identity of my beloved.'

'It's me.' Hettie licked her salty lips.

'Warm.' He put an arm around her narrow shoulders and laid his head against her fine, pale

27

hair. 'If you were a boy, you'd be perfect.'

'I wonder if we'll ever all work together?' Nell watched them. 'I mean in the future. When we get out.'

'It will be odd to be on stage with people not from Drama Arts,' Pierre said. 'I guess we'll stand out. Or they will. Our training will put us on a whole other level.'

Yes, Nell thought. She took a last sip of her whisky mac and felt entirely happy. There would be actors, acting, and then *them*, inhabiting their actual characters, an entire psychological life, both physical and mental, all mapped out. 'It's going to be so strange. Maybe we should set up our own company. The three of us!'

A shadow loomed over their table. They all looked up. It was the man from the bar, the man in the overcoat and paisley scarf. 'You lot,' he gave a little rueful smile, 'you know something . . . ' He leant further down towards them and dropped his voice. 'You're full of shit.'

Nell felt herself flush. Beside her, Pierre's mouth fell open, but he didn't say a word. The man raised his eyebrows, in derision, in warning, and pulling on his roll-up, he pushed his way out through the swing doors of the pub.

None of them spoke. There seemed nothing to say. What a horrible, bitter, cynical man, Nell thought. But she felt dirty, as if she'd been caught doing something obscene.

'He's probably a failed actor,' Pierre rallied.

'Yeah.' Hettie looked pale. 'Maybe he trained at the Guildhall.'

Nell laughed, but she felt unnerved, right in

the pit of her stomach where up until a minute before the whisky had been.

'He's in the second year,' Pierre said eventually.

'Who?'

'My discovery. Look out for him. Gabriel. He's going to be a major star.'

'Really?' Nell glanced up at the clock. She was ready to go home, but the thought of the note, propped as it was most evenings against her door, inviting her upstairs for a nightcap and a chat, dissuaded her.

'Don't forget, you heard it here first. The Angel Gabriel. Gabriel Grant.'

'OK.' Nell had never even noticed a Gabriel. 'If you say so, then I'm sure you're right.'

The door swung open and a horde of students burst in, Dan and Jemma at the head of them, Charlie just behind.

'Make room for the others.' Pierre and Hettie shifted along the bench away from her, and Nell lost sight of them in the crush.

The Rehearsal

Charlie Adedayo-Martin was the most beautiful girl in their year. There were other girls, some more obvious, more perfect — the French girl, Marvella, with her sultry, bee-stung mouth, Jemma with her tangle of blonde curls — but Charlie had glamour. She was tall and angular, with toffee-coloured skin and peroxide hair cropped short against her head. There was a rumour she was the daughter of an Abyssinian princess but Nell had discovered she was in fact the child of a legal secretary from Cheltenham and the Nigerian businessman she'd married.

'That bastard, Rob.' Charlie's dark eyes welled up with tears. 'He's in love with someone else.'

'No!' Nell took her hand and led her out on to the blustery steps of the college, where Charlie told her in gulping tones of outrage that she'd been flicking through her boyfriend's diary when she'd found a poem — a love poem — in several tortured drafts.

'No!' Nell said again, although what she really wanted to ask was whether Rob wrote poems often, and if he'd ever written one for her. But under the circumstances she knew these questions would sound heartless. 'The bastard,' she said instead, 'how could he?' And she put her arms around Charlie and breathed in the cool, flowery smell of her skin.

'He's moving out. He's borrowing a car this

weekend and taking his things.' Her nose grew red and her eyes, already swollen, spilt over with new tears. 'I'll be living on my own.'

Nell looked away. It gave her an unexpected flash of pleasure to see that even Charlie, the enviable Charlie, could look unattractive when crying. When Nell cried her whole face puffed up, her neck turned blotchy, her ears grew red, and she'd do whatever it took to hide herself. Unless, of course, she was acting, when her tears, unreal, were made of lighter stuff and would trickle, just one or two, down the side of her face. This wasn't always what was wanted. 'You're a milkmaid,' Patrick had bawled. 'Not a Lady. Get a hanky out. Let's see some snot!' Nell had blushed deep red, right down to her cleavage, which was shown to great effect in yet another square-cut bodice trimmed with white. Among the many beauties in their year Nell felt small and plump as a pony, and so far, six months into the course, she'd been given nothing but wenches, children and servants to play, although once when she'd complained, she'd been cast as someone's aged mother.

'Nell?' Charlie had hold of her arm. 'Listen, I've got an idea. Why don't *you* move in?'

'Me?'

'Please! It will be fun. You can move in on Sunday, right after Rob takes his things. Or before. Or anytime. You can have the spare room.'

Nell bit her lip. She'd have to give notice where she was. Although not much, and at Charlie's she wouldn't have to endure those

31

late-night talks outside the bathroom with her landlord, always inexplicably wandering round the house in his open dressing gown whatever time she came home.

'OK,' she said. 'I will. I'll do it. The week after next.'

'Thank you.' Charlie wiped the tears from her face and Nell watched as with one small smile her beauty was restored.

★   ★   ★

Charlie lived on the top floor of a house in Willesden. From the outside the house looked unexceptional, the window frames peeling a little more than most, the glass in one panel of the front door boarded up, but once you were inside, the full scale of the dereliction hit you. Damp, decay, and a deep heady stench of rotting wood. Charlie ignored it. She kicked shut the front door, swept up the two flights, past the abandoned flats on each landing and on to her own floor, where the radio was playing low, the battered sofa was draped in creamy shrouds of cotton, and bunches of dried flowers stood on low tables among scattered photographs and abandoned mugs and the occasional beautiful object — a blue glass bottle or a carving of a Nigerian god.

Nell had visited several times. Had gone back with Charlie after college to go over lines, had sat on the foam comfort of the armchair, encased in its white throw, with the gas fire blasting and Charlie, even in midwinter, slouching in a pair of combat trousers, her bare feet tucked under her, her smooth brown arms and prominent shoulder bones shown off to their best advantage in a boy's school vest. Until now she'd never really noticed the spare room — had only seen the room Charlie shared with Rob — its low white bed, always unmade, the layers of antique lace at the windows, the clothes — flea-market dresses and a dun-coloured trench coat, hanging from pegs on the wall. But today Charlie continued up the stairs to a small room in the attic. It had a window that looked out to one side with a view over the garden, and a gas fire built into the chimney breast, cracked across the middle. There was a bed and a cupboard and the raised pattern of the wallpaper just visible through a coat of magnolia paint.

Nell dropped her bag and sat down on the edge of the bed. Charlie crouched on the floor and lit a match and the fire fluttered and flickered and attempted to catch. 'Are you sure it's safe?' Nell asked, remembering vaguely some warning of her mother's about the dangers of gas, but Charlie blew on it a little to spread the flame and said she'd slept in here often after rows with Rob and she always left the fire on all night.

'Bastard. Bastard.' She crawled across the bed and lay stretched out. 'Thank God he's gone. You wouldn't believe what a wanker he was. You know, he was so vain? He was obsessed with his ears. Said they stuck out too much. He was always holding them back and asking what I thought.'

Nell pictured Rob and laughed. She'd met him three or four times but he never remembered her. He was one of those men who only noticed women who were beautiful. 'Fuckable' is what he'd probably have said. 'Now you mention it I did notice his ears,' Nell said, revenging herself. 'Has he considered surgery? You could offer to re-set them yourself,' and they lay on the bed, laughing up at the ceiling, their fingers entwined.

'So . . . ' Nell added after a while, 'what now? You're free and single. It's been two long weeks. Anyone you've got your eye on?'

Charlie sighed and rolled towards her. The flames from the fire threw shadows over her still face and then suddenly she was crying. Her face creased up, her fists against her eyes as if to stop the tears. 'Bastard,' she said. 'How could he? I thought we were so in . . . ' She choked and flicked the tears angrily away, while Nell watched her, intrigued, thinking all the time, if I was a man I'd never leave her. What's the point of anything if men leave girls as beautiful as that?

'He's an idiot,' Nell said gently. 'He'll regret it, that's for sure.' And impulsively she put her arms round her friend and kissed her cheek. Charlie, sniffing, pushed herself against her. Her face, still damp, nuzzled into Nell's neck, her shoulder pressed hard against her breasts, and they lay like that, breathing shallowly, until the room was almost dark. Eventually they got up and moved into the kitchen, where wordlessly Charlie set a pan of water on to boil.

'Can I do anything?' Nell looked around.

'No, no.' Charlie was chopping an onion. 'This is your welcome dinner, go and sit down.'

Nell went into the sitting room and waited, listening to the radio, which spun out drifty, catchy tunes, interspersed with a murmur of chatter, too low to catch. The fire was on in here too, hissing soporifically, and Nell sat down in the soft foam of the swathed white armchair and closed her eyes.

After twenty minutes or so Charlie came in with two plates of rice. The rice had been fried with slices of bacon and green pepper and a few scratchy sprigs of parsley. She put the plates on the floor and came back with a bottle of white wine and two glasses.

'Cheers,' she said, 'here's to freedom,' and she filled the glasses to the top.

The food was disgusting. Oily, and a little undercooked. 'I'm so sorry.' Charlie winced. 'Please don't eat any more, I'm the most hopeless cook,' and she put her plate as far away as she could get it and took a huge gulp of wine as if to drown the taste. Nell ate two more mouthfuls, out of politeness, and also because she was ravenous, and then abandoned hers too.

'You know who I do quite fancy, if I had to choose someone from college . . . ' Charlie lit a cigarette. Nell lit one too and curled into her chair. This was definitely better than her old room, where, once she was home, there was no one to talk to except the gloomy landlord or his spotty teenage son.

'Who?' she said, picturing the entire year seated in a circle.

'Well, if I had to choose someone, just for a fling . . . I think, if I was forced . . . I'd go for Dan.'

'Dan Linden!' Nell felt her stomach falling. 'You're joking!' Heat rushed to her face. 'But you know how I feel about Dan. You know I've been besotted with him since day one!'

'Oh my God!' Charlie put her hand over her mouth. 'Of course. I forgot. I'm so sorry. Forget I said anything. Please.' She looked at her and creased her eyes, pleading, and just in case that didn't work, she poured them both more wine.

'Anyway,' Nell said gloomily, thinking how Charlie could get Dan with one quick look. 'He's back with Jemma. God. Why are there no decent boys in our year?'

Her stomach still felt hollow but the blood had drained away from her face and she was cold. She wrapped her arms round her legs and stared into the fire.

Charlie stretched out on her sofa. 'I really am sorry.' She looked over at her. 'I suppose I've spent too much time thinking about myself.' And when Nell didn't respond she said, 'Hey, why don't we make a plan. To seduce him. For you, I mean?'

Nell frowned. 'But how? He's with Jemma. They're always together.'

'Well . . . Hang on, I'm going to run a bath. I always think better in water. Come on.'

The bathroom was in the corridor beside the kitchen, and when the bath was full and the strawberry smell of the bubbles had filled the room, Charlie slipped off her vest. She had no bra on and her breasts were small and high, the same smooth colour as the rest of her. She had no knickers on either. She just stepped out of her trousers and kicked them to one side. 'Ow, ow, ow,' she said happily as she climbed in, 'it's hot.' And soon a deep red flush had spread across her face and chest and the damp curls of her hair clung prettily around her ears.

Nell sat on the edge of the bath and trailed her hand in the froth of bubbles. Charlie closed her eyes and lay back. 'Hmmm,' she said, and when she opened them she caught Nell looking. 'Get in, why don't you? It's lovely in here.' And she moved her long legs to the side as if to show her how much room there was.

Nell turned away to take off her clothes. She had on tights and a jean skirt, boots and several layers of vests and T-shirts. She struggled with them in the narrow room, the steam making the walls and floor shimmery with wet, until she was naked and uncomfortably aware of the heaviness of her thighs, and the great weight of her breasts as they released from her bra. There seemed so much of her, although she was shorter than Charlie by five inches at least. Charlie bent her knees against the bath edge and Nell slunk down into the water. It felt good. The heat and the pink sweet smell, and the shiny feel of her friend's thigh up against hers as she slid in. She leant back against the end, propped her head between the taps and smiled.

'So.' Charlie grinned. 'How do you get Dan into your bed?'

Nell didn't answer. She had no idea. It had

never occurred to her that it was up to her. Fate, she'd always imagined, would decree.

'How about . . . ' Charlie mused. 'We ask him back here to rehearse a scene. After college. Then we'll go to the pub to discuss, come back here for supper, I'll open wine, you can show him round the flat, and when you get to your room . . . pounce! Hang on.' Charlie rose from the water, her body gleaming, dotted with foam. 'I'll be right back.' She stepped out of the bath, and naked, ran from the room.

Nell heard the music turned up loud from the sitting room and Charlie appeared again with a new bottle of wine. She slipped back in. 'So?'

Nell lifted her glass and took a quick cold slug. 'Let's do it.' She grinned, and although her head was spinning she raised the glass again and drained it.

'You know something?' Charlie was smiling at her. 'You're gorgeous.'

'No!' Nell protested, disbelieving, thrilled. But she didn't repay the compliment, because she couldn't have said it without blushing, couldn't have watched Charlie while she skimmed the foam off the water and rubbed it gracefully across her neck, under her arms, and up over her chest.

★ ★ ★

Dan Linden was tall and lanky, with a dark tousled head of hair. He had a slow, lopsided smile — which was his charm really, and the fact he was faced with almost no competition from

38

the other boys in their year, who were either obsessed with perfecting juggling skills or quoting Shakespeare sonnets in low, sonorous voices. Most of the girls had boyfriends in the year above, unfairly populated with heterosexual, effortlessly talented men, or like Charlie, they'd looked outside college for their love affairs. But since the first day of the first term Nell had been in love with Dan. She'd waited, smiling occasionally, brushing past him in the queue for lunch, until one afternoon she realised she'd waited too long, because there was Jemma, holding his hand, standing at the bus stop with him, wearing his scarf. Occasionally, it was true, they split up, but within days there was a stormy reconciliation and there they were again, sheepish, dishevelled, late for college.

'Dan . . . ' Nell caught him in a corridor.

'Hello.' He gave her that wide soft grin, and shuffled slightly. He wore his trousers low on his hips and when he stretched or yawned, which he did often, he showed a glimpse of flat smooth stomach.

Nell spoke fast before she lost her nerve. She told him about the scenes she and Charlie were rehearsing, how they needed a man for the . . . she hesitated, male parts, and she suggested Tuesday. Next Tuesday. After college.

Dan shrugged. 'OK.'

'A friend of Charlie's might be going to film it,' she threw in, to make it more enticing. Dan nodded as if it was all the same to him. 'See you then,' and he moved off along the corridor.

'The deed is done!' Nell hissed to Charlie as

39

they stood at the bar for ballet, risking the hawk eyes and vicious tongue of Olinka, the teacher, who'd once tapped Nell's stomach with her stick and loudly requested that she pull it in. Nell's cheeks still burnt when she thought of it and she would have liked to have taken that stick and beaten Olinka with it, and shouted into her ear, 'I want to be an actress not a fucking freak of a ballerina,' but instead she'd stood at the bar with tears of humiliation in her eyes, dreading the moment when they'd have to leap diagonally across the room.

★ ★ ★

On Monday night Nell and Charlie lay in the bath. Nell had dotted the room with vanilla-scented candles, and Charlie added some-musky essence, twice the recommended amount. 'So what will we rehearse?' Nell asked. 'Shouldn't we have pages or something?'

Charlie sank under the water and came up sleek as a seal. 'Oh, we can read a few pages of . . . ' she hesitated. 'I'll find something. Don't worry.' She rubbed shampoo into her hair and sank down again, pushing her body hard up against Nell's end of the bath, her legs bent, her thigh against her shoulder. There were tiny bubbles shimmering in the tight curls of her pubic hair and it occurred to Nell she could move her hand a matter of inches and slide it between her legs. No! The thought was painful, sharp as knives, jolting such a spasm through her that she gasped.

'Sorry,' Charlie laughed, as she came up, and Nell slid down too to wet her own thick hair and hide her scarlet face. She kept her body pressed against the bottom of the bath but there was nothing she could do to submerge her breasts, which hovered above water. To feel Charlie's hand just graze against them, she allowed herself to think, to feel her mouth cover each nipple in turn, but she came up as if nothing was different and vigorously rubbed in shampoo. Before she had time to slide down again, Charlie was standing above her, glorious, blazing, steam rising off her thighs as she stepped out. She wound her hair into a towel and left the room. Alone in the bath, Nell felt deflated. She washed under her arms and between her legs, desultory and workmanlike, and with the day looming so close, she began to dread it. The ridiculous idea of the pounce.

⋆　⋆　⋆

Nell and Charlie stood on the steps of college, pretending not to watch, while Dan and Jemma said goodbye. Jemma clung to Dan and Dan whispered, at unnecessary length, Nell thought, into Jemma's ear. Nell turned her back and shook her head, and wished she could think of something to say to pass the time, when eventually there he was, loping towards them, his bag hanging carelessly from one shoulder, his trousers lower than ever on his hips. Just then a bus swung round the corner. 'Quick,' Charlie yelled, and they ran

41

towards it, shrieking and free.

They raced up to the top deck and sat in a row at the front, where Charlie, her dark eyes glittering, began to sing in perfect imitation of Samantha, whose ambition it was to go into musical theatre. 'I'm just a girl who can't say no. Can't seem to say it at all.'

'Agony.' Dan was laughing. And Nell reminded them of hulking great Kevin and his rendition of 'Somewhere Over the Rainbow'.

'I thought I was going to die.' Charlie clutched her stomach, and they dissected every minute of that afternoon's music class, every flat note and clumsy move, weaving themselves tight into a net of their own superiority until they were on the corner of their road and they clattered down the stairs. 'Stop, wait!' They leapt off the end of the bus as it slowed.

'A drink first? Or rehearse?' Charlie asked, and without waiting for an answer she pushed open the door of the pub. They started with lager, a pint each for Charlie and Dan and a half for Nell, who sat between them at a corner table and explained about the scene they would rehearse and how when they were ready, a film school director would film it, and show it, probably, to anyone and everyone who was important in the business, so that basically, the three of them, before they'd even finished college, would be stars! As Nell talked, Charlie pressed her arm against hers, and then as they drank, drink after drink, moving from lager to spirits, she wove her arm around her shoulder and twined her finger in her hair as if to present her to Dan as a tender, longed-for thing of beauty, or possibly, Nell found herself hoping, to claim her as her own.

It was almost eleven when they tumbled out through the door of the pub. 'Which way?' Dan said, unsteady, and Charlie linked his arm and snaked her other round Nell's waist. 'Isn't she lovely,' she whispered to him loudly, 'isn't she fucking gorgeous?' and when Dan stuttered and mumbled she pulled Nell in towards her and kissed her on the lips. Nell's mouth opened in surprise and Charlie's tongue slid in, firm and narrow, hot as whisky, her lips as soft as down. As she kissed her, she pulled Dan round to shield them, and used her free hand to slide it up under her jacket and rub it, hard, against her breast.

'Bloody hell,' Dan muttered.

Nell was reeling. She wanted Charlie's hand against her skin, she wanted to unclasp her bra and push her breasts into her mouth, to kneel on the floor and slide her tongue along the length of her perfect thigh, but Charlie had taken control and was leading them both towards the house.

'Bloody hell,' Dan said again, as the door slammed shut behind him and the splintered boards and broken banisters revealed themselves. He covered his nose against the smell of damp and gas, and paled a little as he followed them up. At the first landing he took hold of Nell's hand, but her passion for him had faded, and the touch of his skin, so longed for, felt clammy and foreign.

'Boys and girls,' Charlie called from the

43

kitchen, 'wine or beer?' and she appeared with both and led them towards the sitting room.

A pale face loomed out at them from the landing.

'My God.' Nell started back, pressing herself against the wall.

'Hello.' It was a man's voice, low and amused. 'What time do you call this?'

'Rob!' Charlie stood and stared at him. 'What . . . I mean . . . ' but with one hand Rob reached out, and taking hold of her wrist, pulled her roughly into the room. The door clanged shut behind them and Nell and Dan stood alone in the hall.

'My room's up here,' Nell said, cold suddenly and nauseous from no supper, and she led him up the small flight of stairs to the attic.

Dan sat on the bed while she attempted to light the fire, blowing on it as Charlie had done while the flame guttered and ran and refused to catch. 'Is that safe, do you think?' Dan asked. 'Gas can be dangerous.' And Nell threw him a withering look before giving up. Their backs to each other, they took off their clothes, or as many of them as they dared, and climbed into bed, where they lay side by side until eventually Dan said, 'Do you mind if we don't . . . it's just Jem . . . she'll mind.'

'No, it's fine. Sorry.' And they turned away from each other and tried to block out the moans and cries of Charlie and Rob as they crashed about in the room below.

The next day Charlie's door was firmly closed when Nell and Dan got up for college, and later

44

when she arrived home — having endured a day of searing headaches and accusing looks from Jemma, and Jemma's closest friends — Charlie was lounging, smoking, on the sofa. 'Can you believe it?' She tossed over her pack of cigarettes. 'He's back for good! I hope you don't mind, I mean you can stay till the weekend, of course, but then, you're going to have to find somewhere else.'

Nell stared at her. 'But . . . '

Charlie crawled across the carpet to her. 'He's dumped her. Isn't that great? He's said he's sorry.' She grinned. 'Said it about ten times in fact. But anyway, how was last night?'

'Last night?'

'Dan? How was it?' Her face was starry with expectation.

'Great.' Nell gathered herself. She even smiled. 'Really good.'

'So aren't you going to thank me?' She put her head on one side. 'For getting you two together?'

'Oh yes. Of course. Thanks.' Hurriedly, Nell got up and went into her room, where, unsure what else to do, she kicked her foot so hard against the fire that the cracked pieces fell out on to the floor, leaving nothing but the gas pipe and two camel humps of wire.

The Festival

It was hot in London, dense and languid, but in Edinburgh the sunshine was glassy, spiked with ice. Nell shivered in her summer clothes, her sandals clacking against cobbles as she scrutinised the festival map. She turned it round, traced the emerald oblong of the park, the straight avenue of Princes Street, the Royal Mile in narrow parallel above it, and then, no clearer, she folded it into her pocket and prepared to climb the steep grey hill that led up towards the castle. By the time she reached the top the breeze had turned her legs to goosebumps and her heels were nicked and torn. She pulled the map out again, puzzled over it, attempted to fill in the missing, theatre-less streets, even asked directions from a passer-by, a man in a tartan beret, who turned out to be Danish. 'It's all right, don't worry,' she called, as he began to unfurl his own unwieldy map, and she hurried on, cutting between the houses, dragging her bag down a steep gulley of steps and then hauling it up again until she emerged in a crescent of tall houses. It was cooler than ever amidst so much stone, and the air smelt sweet and bitter as if something were being brewed up in a giant pot. Below her fell another flight of steps and from here she could see the gauge of the railway line she'd left behind, with trains like glinting streams, the rails as sleek as silver. Carefully she made her way towards it, thinking she'd start again, and found herself unexpectedly in the road that she'd been searching for, and there, halfway along, was the venue — MacDillons.

MacDillons looked closed and shabby, its neon sign switched off, but when she leant against the door it opened. Inside were shapes and shadows, and the pale moon of a woman's face, rushing towards her as the door fell back. 'Shhh,' her hands flew up as wood and metal crashed, too late, and then noticing her bag, the woman softened. 'We're about to start the runthrough. You must be Nell. Come in. Sit down.'

⋆ ⋆ ⋆

There were four actors in the play, two men and two women, and they were all American. They circled around each other, flirting, worrying, caught up in lies and misunderstandings and occasional simulated acts of sex. There was a tall, lolloping actor and a short neat one, and each time they stood beside each other, it was impossible not to laugh. The women regarded these men with pity, confiding in each other that they might have married the wrong people, but all the same, when one woman tested out this theory with the other's husband, it led to a mighty scene of retribution which involved the small actor huddling naked in an oversized bed, while the two women hurled objects at each other, and then, when he tried to intervene, at him. A cushion, a book, and a lethal-looking stiletto, which he managed to dodge before being rescued by his friend — a frilly pink nightie hiding his vanity as he was carried swooning from the stage.

'Well done. All of you. Well done!' The beaming director stepped out of the shadows, the lights came on, and applauding people uncurled from the darkness.

Nell stood beside her bag and clapped, and when that no longer seemed appropriate she pretended to be transfixed by the set. 'Aha, can this be Nell? Our budding actress?' The director had spotted her. He was a short, balding man, with a warm handshake. 'I'm Dominic, we spoke on the phone.'

'Yes.' Nell imagined he was comparing her to Hettie, who'd had this same job the year before. Handing out leaflets, running the box office, charming them all, Nell imagined, with her filthy sense of humour and her brazen smile. They'd asked her again, but Hettie's mother was ill and she'd gone back to Leeds to help take care of her.

'So . . . ' Dominic looked round. 'You haven't met your partner in crime yet, have you?' and he called to a pale blonde girl, tall, in sneakers and white jeans, talking to the lolloping actor. 'Cath. Over here a minute.'

The two girls greeted each other, and even while they smiled, Nell felt a pang of fear that she and Cath had not a single thing in common.

'Right.' Dominic rubbed his hands. 'This man here will tell you what to do.' He pointed to the stage manager, who nodded gruffly. 'If you listen to him, you'll get along fine. We need you to drum up business, hand out leaflets, put up posters, walk the streets, sell your bodies if you think it'll help.' He gave a snorting sort of chuckle. 'Basically, do whatever it takes to get bums on seats.'

Nell and Cath both nodded. 'So . . . ' Nell began, but Cath had turned away.

★ ★ ★

The actresses had changed out of their costumes, and now they moved breezily across the room, their long boots swishing under skirts, their arms weighed down with bags. 'Sorry we can't stay and have supper.' They embraced their director — so self-assured and professional, and neither of them in fact American. 'But we're going back to our digs to work on that monster of a bloody scene.'

'You'll be marvellous.' Dominic kissed them both. 'You are marvellous,' and once they were gone, he looked round for the men. 'Snakeskin should be here in half an hour,' he told them. 'Once they arrive we'll go and find somewhere to eat. Make them feel welcome.' He eyed Nell and Cath: 'I hope you girls will come along too, but in the meantime, if you could stack the rest of those chairs, and if there's a broom somewhere . . . this place turns into a nightclub in an hour.'

The stage manager handed Nell a broom and went back to his clipboard, checking items off with a pencil as he collected up the props. She and Cath glanced at each other and together they trailed the room, gathering up the scattered chairs, stacking them into the corner, sweeping the dust-black floor. Dominic and the short, neat actor, Kyle, sat at the bar and opened wine. They hunched together and talked in great earnest about what worked and what didn't about the play, while Nell wondered what training Kyle had had and if he knew about the six basic character types, the conscious and unconscious states, and why so far at Drama Arts, no one had mentioned the importance of learning to do an American accent.

'Girls,' the tall actor, Richard, was calling to them, 'if you're finished, come and have a drink,' and so they went and stood over by the bar while Dominic poured out warm white wine. 'Here's to us.' He raised his glass. 'Cheers.'

Snakeskin didn't arrive till late. They'd called in from a service station to say their engine had overheated not far from the border. If they were careful they'd most probably make it without having to stop again.

'Where will we eat?' Richard asked, concerned. 'They're bound to be starving.' But Dominic waved his glass and said they'd find somewhere. 'There's a little Italian on the corner. We can go there.'

They opened more wine and waited, perched on red velvet seats, watching as the nightclub staff arrived and adjusted the lighting, bathing the room in pools of pink. They tested the strobe above the dance floor, dimming the spots around the bar, so that finally, when the music blasted on, Dominic conceded defeat, and heaving himself up, bustled everyone out.

It was freezing on the street, the sun long gone, the sky grey with fading light. 'Smell the sea air.' Dominic pointed his nose east, and they all turned to stare into the distance where the sea apparently lay. Nell shivered. All she could smell was the baking of potatoes from a Tasty Tatty booth at the end of the road. Her stomach contracted with hunger. 'Shouldn't be long now,' Dominic said, and Nell wondered if she should unzip the bag at her feet and pull on a jacket and a pair of socks. I'll hold on, she decided, and she tucked her hands under her arms for warmth.

★   ★   ★

The mini-van hooted as it turned the corner. It rattled slowly over the cobbles, its windows rolled down, heads and hands stuck out. 'Yoohoo,' voices called. 'We're here! We made it.' 'Well done!' Dominic strode towards the van. 'Welcome,' and he yanked open the door. A tall boy staggered out, his legs stiff at the hips. He stood for a moment, grinning, and then he leant back in and pulled out two grey crutches. Next came a girl, delicate, in a delicate pink shirt, pushing a white stick before her, its fine end feeling for the pavement, sending small vibrating messages up to her white hand. The driver was unpacking a wheelchair from the back, and when he had it ready, he lifted out a man. The man seemed older than the others, with a proud dark face, long arms and huge, strong hands. The driver lifted him under his arms, and as he

51

swung free of the van, Nell saw he had no legs. Instead of legs there were two bare feet protruding from a rolled-up pair of shorts. The feet were twisted, set at an odd angle, their soles turned upwards like palms.

'Anish, my friend,' Dominic exclaimed. 'Good to see you.'

Anish swept the welcoming party with his large black eyes. 'Good to have finally fucking arrived.'

'Are you all starving? What a journey that must have been.'

The driver was unpacking another wheelchair, and this time Dominic helped him as they shifted an older girl on to the stretched seat. 'Helen,' he said. 'Welcome.' And white-faced with exhaustion Helen nodded her thanks.

Now everyone was out they set off along the street, the driver pushing one wheelchair, Dominic the other, the tall boy lunging forward, the girl beside him, nosing her stick over the stones.

★ ★ ★

'Shit.' Dominic held open the door to the Italian restaurant, behind which was a steep flight of steps leading into a basement. 'Wait one minute. I'll see if there's any other way in.' He appeared a moment later. 'Sorry, folks. Onwards. No wheelchair access here.' The party rolled downhill, craning their eyes for somewhere open. They found a bistro, its menu up in the window, and they crowded round, reading it for the blind girl, Amelia, and for Anish and Helen, neither of whom could see that high. 'Anything vegetarian?' Amelia asked, but when they pushed open the door, a waitress hurried out to say that no, it was impossible, they were about to close, and anyway they didn't have the . . . amenities. She drew back, appalled, her eyes swerving away from the huddle of figures, taking one more look, despite herself, as she caught sight of Anish's bare brown flipper feet resting on the canvas seat of his chair.

'Don't feel bad.' Anish shrugged as the door chimed shut. 'We're used to terrifying the non crips,' and he spun his own wheels in his hands, and led the party on. They attempted two other places, a pub that was already full, and a fish and chip restaurant, the door of which was too narrow to fit a chair through.

'Anyone fancy a baked potato?' Dominic asked, embarrassed, but Anish screeched to a stop. 'Now you're talking!' And he began to heave back up the hill, while the others, heady with enthusiasm, hurried along beside him, chatting, laughing, telling jokes, flanked by the members of Dominic's company, mindful of the tangle of grey metal, the wheels and the thin white stick. 'On me, on me, ladies and gentlemen.' Dominic was the first to arrive at the counter. 'Whatever filling you like. Don't hold back, caviar, foie gras . . . ' An air of supreme satisfaction settled over the party as, warm from their hike, they ate out on the street, scooping prawn cocktail and egg mayonnaise, cheese and beans, salad and tuna out of the hot buttery baked potato cases.

Nell's flat was up by the castle, on the top floor of a house whose front door opened, sideways, on to a sheer drop of steps. It had an unlived-in feel — with bare boards, cheap, undersized furniture, and in the sitting room, a row of curtainless windows facing the castle ramparts, through which shortly after eleven a burst of fireworks exploded into the sky. It was the culmination of the Edinburgh Tattoo, a spectacle of Scottish military might, kilts and sporrans, and bagpipe-players, marchers and drummers and flag-wavers, which took place every night. Nell stood at the window and watched the night sky crack open with a volley of rockets, their red and green flares ascending, the sparks falling into the ravine below. New flares went up, silver and blue, leaping like fountains, hissing and whirring, and then the rockets cracked again, shivering the window panes, echoing in the near empty rooms.

Nell waited till it was over before going to bed. She and Cath were sharing a room, and as she lay reading, she watched Cath undressing out of the corner of one eye. Perfect, flawless, a head girl in white knickers and sports bra, a Snoopy on her thigh-length T-shirt, the faint smell of peach as she folded her clothes. Nell turned away. They had to be at the theatre by 10 the next morning. The show was opening for its first performance at 5. She let the book fall from her hands and just as she drifted into sleep she saw the horrified face of the waitress rushing towards her. 'We don't have the amenities.' The woman's voice was high, and then there were Anish's blazing eyes as he spun away from the closed door.

★ ★ ★

Armed with bundles of slippery new leaflets, Nell and Cath trawled the city, jostling with jugglers and stilt-walkers, clowns, contortionists and fire-eaters, to thrust adverts for *A Hell of a Marriage* into the hands of passers-by. They walked from the Castle down to Hollyrood Palace, across to the Grassmarket and along the high terrace of shops that curved into the hill. They walked across to Princes Street and found to their surprise that here, in this shopping street, there were people, local people, real people, who hardly knew there was a festival on at all. They stared in surprise at the proffered leaflets, exclaimed over the early starting time, and muttered that they'd be at work then, or fixing tea. Nell and Cath walked back through the park, stopping to admire the clock of flowers, its face planted with pansies and primulas, its large hand clunking heavily as it ticked. They passed the railway station, pushing leaflets into the newly arrived hands of visitors, watching them pityingly as if they'd lived here all their lives.

As lunchtime approached, they took a short cut to the theatre, climbing a cobbled ramp that led into the street above, and as if the city really was theirs now, and everyone in it, they saw the bright-shirted figure of Dominic, walking towards them. 'Girls!' he called, 'good timing,' and he pointed out a group of figures above them on the corner, turned in on themselves as if in consultation. 'Why don't you join Snakeskin for lunch? They're going to try The Stag.'

'Oh.' Cath blushed. 'I said I'd . . . ' she looked back towards MacDillons. 'That I'd meet Richard . . . '

Nell and Dominic both looked at her. That was quick. But neither of them said it. 'Nell. You free?' Dominic patted her distractedly on the arm, and he nodded in the direction of the pub.

Nell swallowed. What would she be expected to do? To say? Her heart hammered high up in her chest, but even as she neared the group, she saw Anish turn and wheel himself through the double doors of the saloon bar, bursting them open like a cowboy in a film. Nell began to run, entering the pub just in time to see a solitary man pick up his pint and shuffle to the back of the room.

Snakeskin settled themselves around a cluster of small tables, adjusting their wheelchairs, laying down crutches and sticks. Nell sat on a spare stool. 'Get us a pint of Guinness, would you?' Anish pressed some money into her hand.

'Anyone else?' Nell could feel the place where Anish had touched her, the strength of his cool fingers, the callus on the pad of his thumb.

Amelia felt for her bag. 'I'd love a lemonade, and a cheese toastie.'

'I'm on toasties,' David, the tall boy, insisted. 'Toasties can't spill,' and leaving his sticks under the table he staggered to the bar.

56

There weren't many people in the pub, but Nell could feel every inquisitive eye on them. Whenever she looked up, heads quivered and glances swerved. Snakeskin seemed oblivious. Their show was opening in three days. 'I can't see,' Amelia started, 'I mean I know I can't see, God,' the others giggled, 'but what I mean,' she was choking on her lemonade, 'is how it's going to work.'

'It's not going to,' Anish cut in. 'Unless we all make a superhuman fucking effort.'

'I'm trying.' David was defensive.

'Yeah. Not hard enough.' Anish stared him down. 'Who says we do extra rehearsals from now on, every evening?'

Helen, a heavy girl, welded to her wheelchair, nodded. 'I'm in.'

'And me.' Amelia tilted her head. Her blind blue eyes were opaque as cloud, wide-spaced and plaintive in her heart-shaped face. She had the look of an old-fashioned minstrel, a lute-player from a ballad. Nell found herself wondering if she knew that she was beautiful. If she sensed with her fine fingers the clothes she was choosing were the right light colours for her skin. David leant into her and whispered in her ear, his thin legs bent at an odd angle. 'All right,' he conceded. 'If you think it'll help. But I don't want a repeat of *Backerjack*. I was ill afterwards for a month.'

'You'll be fine.' Anish shrugged. 'Be a man.' And he held up his pint. 'Cheers. Here's to a

Fringe First. Here's to us.'

'Cheers,' the others agreed.

The toasties, when they finally came, were delicious, or maybe it was simply that there'd been nothing for breakfast in the Castle Terrace flat. Nell bit into hers, burning her tongue, soothing it with the cool swirls of cucumber arranged on a scattering of cress.

'So,' Nell looked up, 'what's your show about?'

Anish wiped the froth of Guinness from his top lip. 'That's a very good question.'

'To be honest,' David said, 'we're not quite sure.'

'To be really honest,' Helen added, 'no one has any idea.'

'Now children,' Anish shook his head, 'enough of that. There's still time to re-cast rebels. There are plenty of other wannabe Snakeskins out there who'd kill for your jobs.'

'Sure,' said Amelia, 'but it's just getting them up here. It's taken us most of the morning to find this pub.' And she, David and Helen shook with laughter.

'OK.' Anish took another swallow of Guinness and turned to Nell. 'It's a sort of philosophical meditation . . . a soul-wrenching, but entertaining extravaganza, a rollercoaster journey . . . '

Nell nodded solemnly. 'Right.'

'Is it fuck.' He grinned at her, and he drained the last of his Guinness. 'Oh, I nearly forgot to give you these.' He leant down and retrieved a brown paper package from a bag attached to his chair. 'We're relying on you now, for our audience.'

Nell saw that they were leaflets, at least 500 of them. She slipped her hand in and drew one out.

'I don't know about you lot,' Anish stretched, 'but I need another drink.'

'Right.' Nell stood up. 'Anyone else?'

The others shook their heads.

'Oh and another toastie, go on then.' Anish smiled.

'Greedy pig,' Helen goaded him.

'I'm a growing boy. What's that expression? Oh yes.' He winked at Nell. 'I must have hollow legs.'

Before she could stop herself she laughed. 'That's terrible!' She clapped a hand over her mouth, and turning away, hurried to the bar. As she waited for her order she glanced down at the leaflet.

Like nothing else you'll see all year.
A new play by Snakeskin.
Don't Look Away.

'How was lunch?' Cath asked her as they waited in a queue at the Fringe Office to collect any unsold tickets.

'All right. How was . . . Richard?'

'Nice.' She frowned. 'He wanted me to run through his lines. He's really nervous about tonight.'

'Really?' Nell couldn't imagine any of the cast of *A Hell of a Marriage* being nervous. They seemed so assured. She wondered if any of them had even needed drama school, or if they'd been born like that, swishing through life, saying

59

darling, running over lines.

'I'm definitely going to see Snakeskin when they open,' Nell said.

Cath shivered. 'What will it be like? I can't imagine.' She lowered her voice as the queue moved forward. 'Just think.' She wrapped her arms around herself. 'If we'd been born a few years earlier . . . '

'Yes.' Nell exhaled. 'My mother was sick as a dog when she was pregnant with me.'

'They might have given her that pill too. Thalidomide.' Cath's face paled. 'If she'd asked for it. Or even if she hadn't.'

Yes, Nell thought. How odd that even if they had, she might still have wanted to be an actor. They shuffled forward in silence.

Fifty-five tickets had been sold for that night's performance of *A Hell of a Marriage*. The venue held seventy and they might sell more on the door. 'Wouldn't it be great if we sold out on the first night?' Cath said, and buoyed up with this thought they thrust spare leaflets into people's hands, gaining in confidence, hollering as they went: 'First night tonight. Be there or you'll regret it. Only one hour long.' With every leaflet they handed out, Nell included another one for Snakeskin, *Don't Look Away*. And under the title, the picture of a snake, its mouth open, and out of its mouth, a perfect naked child.

★　★　★

Nell met up with Snakeskin again the next day for lunch. 'How are rehearsals going?'

'Bloody awful.' Anish shook his head. 'The show's going to be a disaster.'

'That's not true,' Helen put in. 'You're just such a perfectionist.'

'Listen,' Anish spat back. 'People will be paying to see us from the day after tomorrow. It's not a charity. It's a theatre company. I don't know about any of you, but I'm not after pity.'

They sat in silence. Nell wondered if there was anything she could do to help. She shook her head. She could offer to go through his lines?

'Sweetheart,' the touch of his hand startled her, 'would you mind getting me a juice?'

'No Guinness today?'

'No, not today.' He looked at her sadly.

David came too and ordered more toasties. 'Don't mind him, he's . . . ' David paused. Nell waited expectantly. A frustrated genius? In terrible pain? David sighed. 'A self-indulgent twat.'

Nell set the drink down in front of Anish. 'You'll be there on the first night, won't you?' He leant towards her, and she felt her heart quicken as his fingers grazed her hand.

★　★　★

Snakeskin were performing at a hall on the other side of the Grassmarket. Their show started at seven. Dominic and the actors headed off as soon as they were changed, but Nell and Cath had to stay and tidy up. Props had to be put away, chairs stacked, floors swept, the theatre left ready to be transformed into a nightclub.

'Done?' Nell called optimistically, but the stage manager wasn't finished. He took a last look round, knelt down for a fleck of dust, found the weapon of the stiletto hidden behind a pillar and then, finally, reluctantly, let them go.

Nell ran, stopping occasionally to wait for Cath, glancing at her watch, dreading the thought she might be late. 'Where are we?' They'd reached the Grassmarket but there was no sign of the theatre. She looked round for someone to ask, consulted her flimsy, disintegrating map, and then remembering it was above the Grassmarket, they set off, climbing up towards the main road, pounding along the pavement, until they found themselves outside a church hall, a ramp over its steps, a large poster pasted across its noticeboard.

The hall was half full. Richard turned to wave at them, to wave at Cath, and he moved along the row of chairs to make room. The lights dimmed. There was silence and then Anish wheeled himself on. Slowly he circled the stage, a showman, sombre in his ring, his short broad body, his powerful arms, his face austere in the dim light and then, he spun around, straight on to the audience and grinned. The lights came up. The audience smiled back. It was audible. The relief. 'Welcome, ladies and gentlemen.' There was a dangerous glint in his black eye, a cruel twist of his mouth, and everyone sat back. It was clear he was in charge. Behind him, in a pool of light, Amelia began to sing. She let her eyes roll upwards as the pure high song poured out of her. Anish put one finger to his lips and slipped into the shadows and Helen, who'd appeared silently, slid from her wheelchair, and using her hands and the strong muscles of her shoulders she began to dance. She danced unlike any other. She rolled and arched and slithered. A mixture between break dance and ballet. David swung himself on. He stopped, and letting his crutches fall, he braced his legs and held his hands out to Helen, who lifted herself up like a mermaid. They danced in slow motion, their fingers interlinking, slipping, catching, turning, while Amelia stood behind them, her voice filling the hall, an angel singing, until just when the audience had fallen into a trance, Anish uncoiled a circus master's rope and flicked it across the floor. It snapped, cracking, and the actors froze, a tableau of tenderness and beauty, just for a moment before the lights blacked and the low harsh thud of the bass began.

★　★　★

There was a party afterwards at Snakeskin's flat. Dominic had provided beer and Ellie the wardrobe mistress was in the kitchen making sandwiches, pouring crisps into bowls.

Nell had to work her way through a crowd of admirers to get to Anish.

'You were fantastic.' She knelt down beside his chair and emboldened by the rapturous clapping and the glass of lager she'd gulped down, she took hold of his hand.

Anish almost crushed her fingers in his own. 'Bloody amateurs, did you see David? He

63

messed up a line in the car chase scene, just before the end.'

Nell stared at him. 'You're mad. Really, it was brilliant.'

'No.' He lifted her hand to his lips. 'I'm not mad. I want it to be good.'

'But it was good!'

He looked at her. 'You're very kind. But if I haven't done my best, if I know the show isn't as good as it can be, I can't care about anything else. Not really.'

Nell felt her eyes fill with tears. 'Right,' she said, untangling her fingers. 'Of course.' And leaving him, she struggled through the crowd to get herself another beer. She pressed the cool bottle against her face. But it *was* good! She looked round at the animated people, enlivened and invigorated by what they'd seen, and she remembered Patrick Bowery telling them how the long-ago actor Henry Irving had sacrificed everything that stood between him and his passion for the theatre, cutting himself off from his disapproving parents, abandoning his wife when she failed to mask her irritation as she waited, pregnant, for him to be done with his repeated curtain calls after the first night of *Hamlet* at the Lyceum. 'Are you going on making a fool of yourself like this all your life?' she'd asked him, later, in the carriage, and without answering he'd ordered the driver to stop, and gathering his cloak around him, he'd stepped out into the night. From then on Henry Irving had devoted every moment of his life to the theatre, re-popularising Shakespeare, commissioning new plays, overseeing the design of elaborate scenery, taking his company across America, through blizzards and snowstorms, the sets for up to seventeen productions in wagons attached to the actors' train. He'd lived a long and fruitful life, dying finally without ever having seen his wife again, only minutes after performing Becket on a tour of the north of England which his doctor had warned him not to undertake.

It was almost midnight before Nell arrived back at the flat. As she put her key in the door the fireworks began to burst. She ran up the stairs and rushed to the window as a cascade of red and orange petals fell from the sky. Babies crying, she found herself thinking, inexplicably, and she imagined cut glass shooting from their eyes. As the flares melted away, Cath appeared on tiptoe in her Snoopy T-shirt. 'Hello,' she mouthed, and she disappeared into their shared room. 'Night.' She blushed as she appeared again, and on pale, bare legs she ran in the direction of Richard's room. Nell turned back to the window. The sky was dark. The night was silent. And then a volley of gold rockets scorched up through the blackness and cracked open the sky.

The Interview

'You know they're only planning to keep four girls for the third year?' Samantha's eyes were wide with fear as she shuffled along the bench towards Nell.

'Who said? How do you know?'

'I heard it from Charlie. But everyone's talking about it. Patrick knows what he wants to direct, apparently, and there are only parts for four girls. The interview times are up, have you seen?'

Nell abandoned her lunch and dashed to the front of the building. Traditionally, information was pinned to a notice-board inside the main doors, and there it was — one white A4 sheet of paper on which, in two columns, was printed the names of the twenty-two remaining students. Nell traced the list with her finger. She was in the second column. Near the end. She was before Jonathan, and after that freak Eshkol. She felt herself go pale.

'Look,' Samantha pointed to the list, 'I'm second.' She laughed nervously and a red flush appeared on her neck.

'But what does it mean?' Pierre joined them. 'Why have they put us in that order? It's not alphabetical. It's not by date of birth . . . is it some sort of code, do you think?'

'Probably,' Nell said gloomily. Instinctively she glanced up at the balcony where, rumour had it, Patrick hovered between the lockers. What could he hear from there? Gossip, exhilaration, bitter grievous tears?

'Right,' Samantha chewed on an already chewed-up fingernail. 'Well, they'll obviously keep Charlie. And Hettie? What do you think?'

'Probably.' Pierre agreed. 'And Marvella's popular.' Only last week Silvio had praised her 'inner tranquillity'. Inner docility, more like, Nell thought now, but it was hard for a man, even a gay man, to see beyond those suntanned limbs and the natural wave of her blonde hair.

'Yes. And . . . and . . . who else?' Samantha's broad shoulders were bent forward, her large oddly bare face, gaunt.

'They like you,' Nell assured her. 'They won't throw you out.'

'Really? Do you think so?' Blood coursed through her, revealing pleasure and a new brief belief. 'And you!' Politeness overcame her. 'They'll keep you. They'll have to. You were amazing last term in *Othello*. No one could have done Emilia better.'

'Really?' Nell felt her stomach sinking. 'But that makes five.'

'You know they're only keeping ten boys,' Pierre shook his head. 'Just think how awful it'll be, for the only one to go.'

Both girls turned to him but neither could summon up the necessary sympathy. 'It's bloody ridiculous,' Samantha wailed. 'Most of the boys in our year are useless, everyone knows that.'

'Yes.' Nell hoped Patrick *was* listening. 'It's not as if there aren't any plays for women. You just have to look a bit harder. Show some imagination.'

A door slammed and Jemma hurried through the foyer. She kept her head low, as if distracted by the large bright orange tutu cradled in her arms. She pushed against the door on to the street, and stood there for a minute silhouetted against the day, dust mites dancing round her curly head, each strand picked out in sunshine.

'Does *she* know the list's up?' Pierre mouthed.

Samantha sighed. 'And what about Tess and Mikita? And Susie? What if they throw Susie out?' Susie was a vegan, moved to tears by the sight of the sausages for sale in the canteen at first break.

Nell turned away. Maybe it wasn't true. Maybe Charlie had made the whole thing up. But why would she? She imagined attending a debate on the likely reasons. Voices were raised. Outrage expressed. Sheer, unparalleled disbelief. 'We're talking about Charlie Adedayo-Martin,' Nell cut through the rabble. 'She'd do it — why? Because she can.'

Nell's soup was cold, her bowl of salad wilted, but she set about eating it all the same.

'Sweetheart,' it was Samantha again, tapping her on the shoulder, a sympathetic tap, she was sure of it, a tap that told her she was number 5. 'I'm going to walk down to Woolworths to get more glitter. Do you need anything?'

Nell smiled mildly at her. 'No. Thank you. I'm fine.'

That afternoon was the dress rehearsal for *Grease*. Everywhere girls ran back and forth, assembling costumes, practising dance moves, taking photos, marvelling at their transformations, not the inner transformation they'd been trained to produce, using Silvio's series of instructions, but the revelation of a high pony tail, of hair smoothed back behind a lemon-yellow hair band, of bare brown legs in bobby socks and a tightly belted waist. Nell was playing Sandy — well, some of Sandy, the part was divided between her, Charlie and Marvella, and she had the first song, a duet. 'Summer lovin', had me a blast,' she sang between mouthfuls of salad, 'Summer lovin', happened so fast.' It was the first time in her two years here Nell had been given a chance to play a lead. It was a good sign, she'd imagined, but now, of course, she wasn't so sure. And then a thought occurred to her: maybe they hadn't decided. Perhaps this production was the final test. Nell felt the truth of this ring through her. 'Summer days, drifting away,' she forced herself on, 'bu-ut oh, those summer nights.'

By three o'clock everyone was dressed. Their director, a diminutive Australian, hired by the school for one term, was giving them a last high-octane talk. 'OK guys. This is it! Do you hear me? I want focus. Got it? I want energy. Yes?' He clicked his fingers. 'And I want to see you having some fun. Yes. Fun!' And his muscles bulged in his neat arms as he shimmied his shoulders and boxed the air. What he didn't know was that Patrick Bowery had opened the far door and was approaching from behind. 'And what *I* want . . . ' Patrick's voice was cruel with amusement. 'Is a quick word.'

The Australian blushed and, half bowing, moved to one side. Patrick took his place. Come on then, Nell thought, let's hear it, but Patrick remained silent. Instead, he surveyed them from on high, raising his eyebrows at the slicked quiffs of the boys, finally handsome in white T-shirts and jeans, the girls, in pastel cardigans done up with one button, their bras pushing their blouses out in peaks.

'So,' Patrick began, quietly, ominous. 'There's been an awful lot of talk recently about people being Thrown Out, and I would like to assure you, before this goes any further, that no one is being Thrown Out.' There was an audible sigh of relief. Jemma clutched hold of Dan's arm, Samantha spun around and stared triumphantly at Nell. 'But I would like to remind you of the contents of the prospectus, which I'm sure all of you read before choosing to enrol at Drama Arts. In the prospectus it clearly states that not everyone will be suited to the rigours of the third year, and that some of you, for various reasons, will be more suited to setting off on different paths.' Twenty-two pairs of eyes dropped to the floor. 'And it has come to our attention that some pupils, as predicted, have nothing left to learn from us, and will therefore be released from their obligation to keep studying the art of acting, and will instead be free, as from next week, to wend their eventful ways out into the world.'

No one spoke. They'd learnt from bitter experience that questions or comments were rarely welcome. So we *are* being thrown out, Nell thought, and it was no easier to bear the second time round. She remembered reading that clause in the prospectus and knowing absolutely that it would never, ever, apply to her. It was for people who were late, or unable to learn their lines, who crashed into furniture, or questioned the validity of what they were being taught. There was no one in the room like that. Those students had barely lasted the first term.

'Right.' Even the Australian looked subdued. 'So remember, kids. Have fun.' And they wandered off to take up their positions for the start of the show.

★　★　★

The interviews were scheduled for the following Tuesday. There were no lessons for their year that day, although the year below were still busy, taking ballet class in the studio with Olinka, running through Stanislavsky's method exercises with Babette in the hall. The third year were preparing for their final production, open to the public, where their friends and family, agents and casting directors could come and speed them on their way. Only the music room was free to wait in. It was a mirrored room, that doubled as a stage make-up and dressing room, and it was opposite Patrick's office.

There were three students waiting there when Nell arrived. 'What's happening?' she said, glancing at her watch, and Jonathan looked up

71

and whispered, 'It's Pierre, he's been in there for bloody hours. You can hear him, if you listen, pleading and begging.' They all did listen. A high, hysterical murmur drifted through the door. 'You're wrong, please, come on . . . if you give me one more chance, one term . . . I worked so hard . . . ' But he was drowned out by low, stern words, and the fluting fluttery tones of Silvio. If they throw me out, Nell thought, I won't beg or plead. I won't give them the satisfaction. I'll just walk away. She felt herself go icy cold, and eggy pools of sweat collected under her arms. Just then Hettie appeared in the doorway. 'Hey,' Nell patted the seat beside her. 'What's the news? Did you hear, is Samantha in?'

Hettie nodded, and Nell nodded too, to keep her lip from trembling.

'But it's so awful,' Hettie was close to tears. 'Susie's out, and Tess and Mikita. They're all in the pub. Dan's in, of course, but he's threatening to leave because of Jemma.' Nell glanced at her watch. 'What time are you?'

Just then the door opened, and Pierre drifted across the hall. 'They wouldnae listen,' he said, and he fell on Nell's shoulder.

Eshkol, his green lenses glinting, his face swathed in foundation, swept past them. 'If they keep that weirdo I'll kill myself,' Pierre wept. 'Oh God, what will I tell my parents? They've paid for two years of this place and I have nothing to show for it. No agent. No photograph in *Spotlight*. No contacts. It's as if I was never here.'

Hettie hugged him. 'Babe,' she said. 'I know this might not sound very helpful, but loads of the third year are leaving and they don't have any agents or contacts either.'

'Yes,' he sobbed, 'but at least their mums and dads had an excuse to come to London. Got to see them. Got to clap and read their name in a photocopied programme.' Nell and Hettie laughed, and through his tears Pierre did too. 'Oh, the dreams, the glamour.'

But the door was already opening and Eshkol, his face a mask, his eyes staring, turned and walked away down the stairs. 'Go after him,' Pierre hissed. 'Find out what happened.' And Hettie skittered away.

'It's you,' Jonathan looked up from where he'd been sitting calmly by the window.

'Right.' Nell's heart was galloping, her shirt was clammy with sweat. 'Here goes.'

Nell had never been into Patrick's office before. It was smaller than expected, and two long desks had been pushed together against one wall. Behind it sat Patrick, Silvio and the registrar, Giles. For a moment she was reminded of her audition, but they'd been smiling then, encouraging, whereas now they were steeped in a tragic air of knowledge. Nell sat down, and found herself sinking backwards into the soft cushion of a chair. Flustered, she righted herself and perched uncomfortably on the edge. 'Nell Gilby,' Patrick frowned at his papers as if reminding himself who she was. 'We at Drama Arts feel quite confident . . . ' Nell looked at the three faces, at Patrick, his grey hair thinning, but

73

still spiked vertically at the front, at Silvio, his eyes sadder than ever, and at Giles, who gave her one tight smile, 'that here, among the myriad opportunities to expand one's resources . . . ' Nell looked up at the clock. It was already four. Would they even have time to see everyone today? 'that when a student is ready, and let's face it, courageous enough to truly open themselves to the sensations and sense memories . . . ' Nell listened hard, 'only then can they develop into an actor of exceptional qualities . . . ' There was a pause. All three men looked at her, quizzically, as if she was a specimen of rare interest. 'And, we've discussed this at great length, and we're sorry to say, we do not think you possess these qualities.'

Nell swallowed. She looked at them. Sad, grey, disappointed. Nothing, she remembered. Comes from Nothing.

'And so . . . ' Patrick had clearly only just begun. His head was tilted back, his Adam's apple working. 'We heartily believe . . . '

'I'd better go then.' Nell stood up, and even though she heard Patrick splutter, and Silvio — was he calling her back? — she walked out and firmly closed the door.

'I'm out,' she stood in the doorway of the waiting room — for one short moment, victorious — but, apart from Jonathan, there was no one there.

Jonathan stood up and came across to her. 'Too bad,' he said kindly, 'we'll miss you,' and he leant forward and gave her a quick brotherly kiss on the cheek.

∗ ∗ ∗

Nell walked down the stairs, bracing herself for an assault of sympathy, a barrage of questions, amazement and respect when she described how she'd not even waited for the end. But no one called to her, no one was there. The foyer was deserted, even the canteen, with no sign of Becky, stirring soup behind her hatch, sliding another tray of flapjacks into the oven. I suppose they've all gone to the pub, she thought, unless they've thrown out the whole school, and she laughed and with it came one shaky sob. No. She breathed in, I won't cry, and then Hettie rushed past her. 'Eshkol's slashed his wrists out on the street.'

'Oh my God!'

'It's horrible.'

Nell ran down the steps towards a group of people, soothing and wrestling with Eshkol's kneeling figure. 'Leave me . . . leave me alone,' he fought. Trails of mascara ran down his face and a clear red patch of stubbly skin was visible where he'd wiped his nose. 'Oh Eshkol,' Nell sank down beside him, 'you'll be all right. Really. Don't give up.' But Eshkol looked at her without recognition, and why shouldn't he; this was the first time in two years that she'd offered him a single word.

'I've called an ambulance,' Hettie was back. 'It'll be here in a minute.' But Eshkol pulled away and began to tear along the road. They all ran after him, Becky, her apron flapping, Pierre, Hettie, Samantha. 'Stop, you idiot.' It was Dan,

75

fast, and stronger than he looked, who raced ahead and grabbed him by the shoulder. 'You need help, mate,' he said, and he pinned him against the wall. A flap of tissue paper had unravelled and for a moment Nell saw the raw mess of his wrists. Becky grasped his arm and bound it up again. 'Naughty boy,' she said, 'taking my knife,' and her nose reddened and her eyes dripped tears. 'Bastards,' she shook her head. 'It can't be right.' And then Hettie remembered it was her interview next.

'What shall I do?' She was shaking. But Pierre nudged her sharply. 'Get going. Run.' The ambulance, its siren screaming, turned into the road. 'Over here!' They waved, holding tight to Eshkol, as other students came streaming out of college. 'What happened?' 'Fucking hell,' they clutched each other, and Nell thought — is this drama any more real than the duet she'd sung with Pierre the week before: *Summer dreams, ripped at the seams, bu-ut oh, those su-ummer nights* . . . The long top note had mangled somehow — the harmonies clashed, and she'd sworn it, she'd seen Patrick wince.

Eshkol stopped struggling as soon as he was in the medics' care. They unwound the tissues and examined his wounds. They asked numerous questions, particularly of Becky, who ran back to find the knife which lay abandoned in the yard outside the caretaker's office. People from the pub, unable to resist the lure of the blue light flashing — Jemma, Charlie, Tess and Susie — handed out cigarettes, their faces ashen, beer hanging hotly on their breath.

They watched while Eshkol was led into the back of the ambulance, laid out on the stretcher and belted in. He had new, thick padded bandages halfway up his arms, and his face, with its mess of make-up, was blank. They watched until the ambulance had turned out of the road, and then they wandered back towards their college, where they sat on the steps in the falling sun and waited for the last interviews to be over.

'You all right?' Charlie sank down beside Nell.

'Yeah,' Nell nodded. 'I'm fine.'

'It's such a relief, isn't it? It's crazy, I know, but I was tense as fuck.'

Nell looked at her. 'No. I don't mean that. I'm . . . They're not keeping me.'

Charlie's long body jolted with the shock. 'Oh babe! I didn't realise.'

'I guess some people take it worse than others,' Nell laughed dryly, and she pressed her thumb over the blue veins of her wrist.

'But what will you do?' It was clear, and Nell was grateful, she really hadn't known.

'Try and get work, I suppose. Find an agent. Show the bastards that they're wrong.'

'But will I see you again? What will happen? Will you promise to keep in touch?'

'Sure.' It seemed ironic, such concern, when they'd hardly spoken this last year. 'I'll be here tomorrow. I'll have to clean out my locker.'

'Let's have lunch,' Charlie moved closer. 'Listen. I have to tell someone,' her eyes filled with tears, 'I think I'm pregnant. I know I am. And Rob's gone off to Japan on a British Council tour.'

Nell put her arm around her, she couldn't help it, and breathed in the familiar scent of her hair. 'Does he know?'

'No, and I'm not planning to tell him. Fuck it. Why wait for lunch tomorrow? The pub's open now. Won't you just come for one drink, please, and have a chat?'

★ ★ ★

That night Nell dreamt she was in the interview. Over and over again she walked into the office and sat before the three stern men. 'Nell,' they told her, 'you're not exceptional . . . but,' and this time she stayed to hear them out, 'with one more year, you will be.'

'Nell,' they'd called to her as she was leaving. 'Sit down and listen to us.' She'd waited and Silvio had raised his eyes to her. Just as on the first day, it was his turn to be kind. 'We *want* you to be exceptional, we know you can be, congratulations, please do stay.' Even Giles had smiled. Even Patrick. They'd smiled and smiled until she'd smiled too and sunk back, falling into the empty well of the trick chair.

Nell woke in a tangle of sheets. What time was it? Sun was streaming through the thin curtain. And then she remembered. She didn't have anywhere to go. She closed her eyes and rolled away from the light. And almost immediately she was in another dream. 'Where are you going?' Patrick was chiding her. 'Sit down, you silly girl,' and there were Silvio's eyes again, creased with kindness and regret. 'Shhhhh,' he'd shaken his

78

head. 'Not you. We wouldn't let you go.' She'd choked with relief, warm tears spilling on to her cheeks, and she'd bent her head and felt the healing, almost holy touch of Silvio's broad hand. When she woke again she lay quite still. She could hear her landlord's son moving about upstairs. He was meant to be studying for some extra exam he'd failed, but there was the low drone of the television and the clink of cutlery as he poured himself more cereal.

Very quietly she crept along to the shower. The water was tepid, the timer long switched off, but even so she washed herself all over with lily of the valley soap, and rinsed her hair until it squeaked. She would make a last magnificent entrance. 'Nell?' Patrick might open that secret door that led on to the balcony. 'Come in here a moment,' and she would leave her locker open, her ballet shoes and library copy of Chekhov revealed, and follow him through to where there were party poppers and champagne. Olinka would be there, and Babette, even the voice teacher Steven who had tried so hard to iron out any hint of a west country burr.

'So glad we caught you,' they'd say. 'Yesterday, it was all a misunderstanding. Congratulations.' Their glasses were raised. 'Cheers. Here's to the third year. Here's to you!'

Nell clutched the towel round her and ran back to her room. She rolled her hair into a turban and threw back her head. There she was in the mirror, gleaming, her skin tingling, her features stretched into optimistic arcs. No one would ever know, she thought, that inside, her

79

heart was bleeding, her stomach had been lashed into a knot. Was that because she was a marvellous actor? Or did it prove that she was incapable of showing true emotion on her unexceptional face?

★ ★ ★

An air of desolation hovered over Drama Arts. Even the canteen was empty. There was nothing on the chalkboard menu, just a plate of cold sausages on the counter, and one hardening flapjack. Becky was scrubbing out a pan. Her hair was bound up with a ribbon and she had on her customary polka-dot apron, but when she turned, Nell saw her face was weary, the skin below her eyes puffy and red. 'Any news?' She ran water into the pan, and Nell's heart stopped at the thought that she would have to tell each person she met: they threw me out.

'From the hospital,' Becky prompted her. 'About Eshkol,' and Nell realised that although the knowledge of it had stayed with her through the long afternoon and evening at the pub, where she'd sat in a corner with Charlie, ravelling and unravelling solutions to her predicament, attempting to convince her that she owed it to Rob to at least tell him what she planned to do, she'd forgotten to think once about the details. 'No.' She was appalled. 'I don't even know where they took him.'

'Well, he's probably out by now.' Becky looked sour. 'It just worries me, who will take responsibility. Not those . . . ' she lowered her voice to a whisper, 'so and so's upstairs.'

Becky went back to her pan. 'If you hear anything . . .'

'Yes.' Nell wandered through the empty rooms, pushing aside a chair, glancing into the hall, trudging up to the balcony where costumes from last night's production were racked up on metal trolleys. Many of the lockers had already been cleared out. They hung open, their insides sharp and empty. Nell leant down to hers. She'd brought a bag especially, and without looking at what was there she scooped two years' worth of accumulated dance tights, hair ties, leg warmers and make-up into it. No one called to her. No one opened a secret door. On her way down she took a detour past the caretaker's room. The merry sounds of children's daytime television drifted out. 'Joey?' She looked in, her nose already filling with the familiar sour smell of spirits, but instead of the caretaker's thickened, dark red face, there was Susie, sewing a button on to one of his shirts. 'Hey,' Nell said, and then she saw that Joey was lying on the bed behind her, fully dressed, his head sunk into a stained pillow. 'Guess what?' Susie licked the thread and brought the needle to her eye. 'When Joey wakes I'm going to take him to an AA meeting. He said he'd come. He promised, last night, in the pub.'

Nell nodded. She didn't want to remind Susie that he'd promised to stop drinking many, many times before.

'I mean, once I'm gone,' Susie knotted her thread, 'there'll be no one to take care of him, and he won't last here, indefinitely, unless he sorts himself out.'

Nell looked at Joey's feet, his socks threadbare, his ankles white and bony where his trousers had rucked up. He had a wife somewhere, she knew that. And three kids. But his wife had thrown him out.

'Where is everyone?'

'They're already in the pub. Are you all right?'

Nell nodded. She didn't dare ask Susie how she was. Susie, so kind she would cry on a daily basis for water voles or the plight of Tibetan monks. Only last week she'd been inconsolable when news came through that a Colombian footballer had been shot dead for scoring an own goal during the World Cup. 'See you later then.' Nell couldn't bear to see Susie cry for herself. 'Good luck.'

'And you,' Susie held out a hand to her. 'Good luck.'

Hamlet

Dan hated to admit it, but the atmosphere in the dance studio was electric. Just the twelve of them. The chosen. The ones that had survived. 'Right,' Olinka was actually smiling. 'Who's ready to learn tap?' She gave a sparkling, razor-sharp demonstration, and nodded to the accompanist, Miss Goeritz, still miraculously with them for another year.

'A shuffle, shuffle, shuffle tap. A tap, tap, tap, step.' Olinka clicked her fingers above the shambling piano, and repeated her moves. There was an assumption that they knew what they were doing, that the clumsy, hopeless drifters had fallen by the way. Charlie danced noncha-lantly beside Dan, in black tights and a faded T-shirt, her hair longer now, the tight curls softened to a wave. She swayed her hips, her long legs bent a little at the knee, and marked the steps with brand-new shoes.

'And a shuffle, shuffle, shuffle, tap. A tap, tap, tap, Turn . . . '

Dan swivelled the wrong way and collided with her. 'Sorry,' they both said, overlapping, and they trotted round in a circle, their hands flapping, their toes blunt.

'I didn't think we'd see you back here,' Charlie spoke out of the corner of her mouth, as they rearranged themselves in a line between Kevin and Marvella.

83

'Yeah, well . . . ' Dan flushed to think of his drunken posturing on the last night of the summer term, his adamant announcement that he wouldn't be back, however much they begged him, no, they wouldn't be seeing him again. It was inhuman, that was his conclusion, the way Drama Arts toyed with people's lives. He gave Charlie a shifty smile. 'Here I am.'

⋆ ⋆ ⋆

Dan had woken the following day, his head splitting, his throat parched, and before Jemma could stop him, he'd pulled on his clothes and made his way to college. 'I need to speak to Patrick Bowery,' he'd presented himself at the door of the staff office, nervous and already sweating, but the registrar had told him Patrick wasn't in that day, he was probably working at home.

Dan knew this was his chance — he could leave a message, and slope off — but he'd made a promise and he was going to follow it through. 'I need to speak to him,' he repeated, as much to himself as anyone, and he turned away.

Dan had never been to Patrick and Silvio's flat, but he knew it wasn't far. He set off at a run, his head thudding, his thoughts frozen, until, after a few false turns and one stop for directions, he found himself outside their building, climbing the steps, ringing the bell, hoping, praying even, that no one would be in. He took a deep breath and counted, and just as he was about to move away, he heard the shudder of an interior door being opened. Heavy, familiar footfalls approached along the hall.

'Daniel Linden.' Patrick didn't seem surprised to see him there. 'Good morning.' And with a toss of his head, he stood back to let him in.

Dan walked through a narrow corridor into a living room, spotless, with only a framed photograph of Laurence Olivier to indicate who the inhabitants were. Silvio sat at a table, in dance trousers and a polo-neck top, a glass of water before him, as if he might be about to perform. 'Hello,' he said, and he nodded as Patrick closed the door. The two men looked at Dan, expectant.

'The thing is . . . ' Dan started. He felt crumpled and chaotic. If only he'd stopped for breakfast, or a wash. 'The thing is, I just . . . ' and to his mortification tears forced themselves into his eyes. 'I just . . . ' Dan struggled, 'I don't agree with the way you do things . . . it doesn't seem fair . . . ' His voice rose, childish, complaining, and he looked round angrily, swatting away his tears. 'I mean, what difference does it make, one more year . . . why does it have to be so harsh?' and Silvio handed him the glass of water. Dan drank gratefully. 'Thank you,' he murmured, passing the glass back, and for a moment there was silence. 'I don't see how I can stay.'

Silvio took Dan's hand in his own warm palm and led him to the sofa. 'You are very young,' he said gently. 'And you feel everything, with passion.' He sat beside him, 'which is right and

85

true, but it is different for us, we see things clearly.' Without mentioning Jemma's name, he explained that in some cases they were being kind, kinder than if they offered up encouragement. In time he would come to understand, this great and difficult profession was not suitable for everyone.

'The real question is . . . ' Patrick cut in, impatient, but Silvio quieted him with a look.

'Daniel,' Silvio bent towards him, 'we have been thinking about you, more than you imagine, and we've been considering . . . How would you feel . . . if you *were* to stay with us for another year, about taking on a challenge . . . a play that would stretch you. The pinnacle of most actors' careers.'

Dan frowned.

'Are you willing to be challenged?' Patrick strode across the beige carpet.

'I . . . I'm not saying that . . . I mean, of course.'

'The Dane.' Patrick fixed him with his steely eye.

'Hamlet,' Silvio whispered.

'You're joking?' Dan felt a rush of adrenalin flood through his body, the whole of his future career mapping out.

'Patrick would direct,' Silvio said proudly. 'Of course, *Hamlet* is a play very rarely done at drama school, for reasons of . . . well, maturity, but we feel, with your essential qualities, and the way you have understood my techniques, we could make it into something . . . spectacular.'

'Bloody hell,' Dan ran his hands through his

hair, 'that would be hard to resist.' He frowned as if he was still considering, but even as he did so he knew he wouldn't miss this chance.

'I have been wanting to direct *Hamlet* for a long time,' Patrick stared into the middle distance. 'I've been thinking about the central themes, the haunting, the psychological truths, the relationship the poor boy had with his mother.'

'And of course we have our Ophelia,' Silvio looked shyly towards Patrick.

'No,' Patrick snapped round. 'There is no Of Course about it.'

Silvio pursed his lips as if he'd been slapped. And there was silence. Dan shifted in his seat and glanced round the room. It reminded him of his mother's house in Epping. Neat and beige, with a fruit bowl on the table. There was a varnished trolley with gold detail beside the sofa, on which sat a teapot on a linen doily. From what he'd heard, he'd never imagined it like this. Some of the boys from his year were regular visitors, dropping in for evening drinks, and even on weekends. Kevin, in particular, and Jonathan. Stuart apparently had once gone round for dinner and found himself wrestled by Patrick into an awkward embrace.

'Well, thanks,' Dan shifted. 'I mean, if you really think I'm up to it . . . ' It disgusted him, this need for one more word of reassurance.

'If *you* think you're up to it,' Patrick had caught him and he knew it. 'Well, only you can say. How far you are prepared to delve into yourself, examine your innermost compulsions, your motivations, your sexuality . . . your fears?'

The questions were left hanging there. 'Yes.' Dan nodded like an idiot. He bit his lip.

'So, we'll see you next term,' Patrick pinned him with his protruding eyes, 'and continue the discourse?'

'Right.' Dan moved towards the door. 'I suppose you will.' He turned to Silvio, still sitting by the window, stung. 'Bye then.'

'Of course,' Silvio roused himself. 'Please, enjoy your summer.'

'And you.'

In the hall two wooden masks hung side by side. One tragic, and one comic. He put his hand up and touched the smooth surface of the stained wood. To be or not to be. And he let the door slam hard behind him as he ran down the steps.

★ ★ ★

As soon as Olinka's class was over Dan called Jemma from the phone box in the canteen. 'What are you up to?' he asked.

'Nothing much,' he heard the rustle of sheets, 'just lazing about.'

'Really?' He pressed his face into the receiver.

'Yes. Really. And thinking about you.'

Dan turned to check he wasn't being overheard, but there was only Becky, slicing up a tray of those infernal flapjacks; the others had all gone outside to smoke.

'Hmm. Sounds interesting. So what . . . are you dressed?'

'Actually,' she lowered her voice, 'I've been a bit naughty. You know, downstairs. Well, there was no one there so I snuck down and tried on some of the clothes.'

'Jem!'

'It's all right. I didn't take any. But there are such lovely things. A long silk slip with the most beautiful embroidery, and a white fur tippet. I might surprise you when you come home.'

'Miss you,' he said quietly.

'I miss you too. What are you doing there? Have they dragged you up to the office yet, tried to convince you that you're gay?'

Dan laughed and looked up towards the gallery. 'Just tap. Quite a laugh actually. If you're good later I'll show you my routine.'

'Can't wait.'

'Nor me.' They were both laughing. 'See you later. Or meet me for a drink if you like?'

'No.'

'All right,' he sighed, thinking of the dank comfort of the pub, the cold pint between his fingers, the glass slippery with wet. 'I'll come straight home.'

★   ★   ★

Jemma and Dan had found a flat to rent from a woman who sold old clothes. Dresses from the 1940s and '50s, flowered, with coloured piping, made from crêpe, cotton and silk. There were shoes too, faded silver sandals, a pair of two-tone spats, and a bargain basket of roughly knitted berets, children's jumpers, scarves. The shop belonged to the stepmother of a friend of Jemma's, and by amazing luck they'd heard about it two days before the start of term. It had a small kitchen at the back, and upstairs were two bedrooms, everything furnished in the same spare tasteful style as the shop, with antique lace curtains and a patchwork quilt across the wide brass bed.

'It's so romantic,' Jemma had said, and Dan lifted a corner of the curtain to stare out at the traffic on the Mile End Road.

Jemma and Dan had spent the summer travelling, free for a few months from the tyranny of rent. They'd taken the train to Italy, missing their connection at Calais, ending up in Paris, where, with no French money, they'd fled through the Metro, leaping over barriers, dashing to catch up with the right train on the other side of town. But it turned out not to be the right train, something they only discovered the next day when it deposited them at a small station in Switzerland, where they sat for three hours, huddled together against the mountain cold, rewarded eventually by another smaller train with their destination, Verona, listed on the side. Their plan was to camp on the shores of Lake Garda, in a small town they'd heard was idyllic, but by the time they arrived in Verona it was late at night, and the bus they'd hoped to take had long since gone. They sat in the tiled corner of the station and discussed hiring a taxi, but a taxi was inconceivably expensive. We'll just have to wait here, they agreed, and catch the bus tomorrow, but Dan woke in the early hours to find that Jemma had wandered into the station master's office, and was demanding someone show her where she could wash her hair. 'Sorry,' Dan grimaced at the small crowd of spectators who had gathered, and he took Jemma by the arm and led her back to their bags. 'Hey?' he looked into her face, 'what's going on?' and she giggled and said she must have sleepwalked into the office, but when she woke up she'd been so embarrassed she thought she'd better carry on pretending to be asleep. They laughed so hard, stifling their gasps, that Dan's whole body ached. 'Let's stay awake now,' he urged, 'it must be morning soon,' and itchy-eyed, they leant against each other and dealt out a hand of cards.

It was the following afternoon by the time they reached the little town of Torri del Benaco. They'd boarded a bus, but had fallen asleep almost as soon as they sat down, and only woken, some hours later, to find themselves thundering along beside a lake. Automatically they looked behind them, where the roofs of a cluster of houses were disappearing round a hilly bend. 'Torri?' they asked, and a woman jerked her thumb, back, the way they'd come. 'Stop!' they'd shouted, leaping up. 'Please, *per favore*!' and grabbing hold of their bags, they'd scrambled to the front of the bus, where, with a swish of rubber, they were let out on to the road.

Jemma immediately burst into tears.

'For God's sake,' Dan hissed at her, 'not here,' and he waved cheerily at the driver as he cranked his vehicle into gear.

'Why *not* cry?' Jemma shouted. 'Why do we

91

have to keep pretending it's not all a stupid bloody disaster?' And she sat down by the side of the road and sobbed into her hands. Dan looked left and right along the deserted road and wished he was anywhere but here. The lake stretched before him, as vast as a sea, and behind them, rising steeply, was an inhospitably rocky hill. Great, he thought, and whose idea was this? but he knew better than to say a word. Eventually even Jemma saw the pointlessness of crying and so they began the long walk back, arriving in the town so numb with tiredness they hardly noticed the sun beating down. The first shop they came to they went in, and Jemma surprised Dan by asking in Italian, her voice trilling up and down, for enough food for a picnic. They sat on the narrow strip of beach below the road and tore open the bread, stuffing it with curls of ham, wedges of salty cheese and small sweet tomatoes that squirted pips a metre high as they bit through the skin. In between mouthfuls they gulped warm peach juice, and when they were already full, forced in apricot biscuits, their centres melting into jam. Dan lay back against the pebbles, sunshine dappling his face, the water lapping at his toes, and flooded with contentment he told Jemma he was sorry, she was right, they should have both wailed and beaten their chests when they missed their stop. Jemma said she was sorry too. She was just so tired, and hungry. But it was funny, she started laughing, when Dan smiled so cheerily at the bus driver, and waved him on. 'Don't worry about us, we'll be fine,' she mimicked him, 'we want to stop here, yes, just here, by the side of the road,' and they lay on their backs and howled up at the blue sky until tears ran down the sides of their faces.

They walked to the other end of the town where they found the campsite, and after several false starts they set up their tent and, more than three days after leaving London, they crawled inside, and with small shivers of laughter still rippling through their bodies, they held each other and slept.

They stayed in Torri del Benaco for a week, the days lulling by, swimming, reading, playing cards, walking along the strip of restaurants, gazing in, deciding which one might be cheap enough to eat their evening meal in. They could have stayed there all summer, but they knew it would be cowardly — they'd set off with the idea of seeing as much as possible of Europe, and so reluctantly they packed up, and took the train to Venice, where they were directed to a campsite in a low-lying swamp where that first night Jemma was so badly bitten by mosquitoes she refused to come out of the tent.

'Listen . . . ' Dan coaxed her. 'We're in one of the most beautiful cities in the world, no one's going to be looking at you.' But when eventually she did crawl out into the open, one eye was swollen shut and her top lip was so distorted she looked like a cartoon. 'But then again . . . '

'Come on,' she snapped, 'let's get to St Marks Square, quick,' and she stamped off towards the lagoon.

Occasionally, as they sat outside cafés, or lay

on their backs in the orange light of their canvas tent, Dan took out his New Penguin Shakespeare. 'The Tragedy of Hamlet, Prince of Denmark', it said on the first blank page, and these words reminded him that the play was in fact the story of a man, a family, two families, a whole court unravelling, and not just a chance for him to play the lead. The first time he opened it, Jemma leant over, and with her finger ran down the list of characters. 'Only two women,' she sniffed. 'If they had to do Shakespeare, why couldn't they have chosen *As You Like It*, or *The Winter's Tale*?' And when Dan didn't reply, she sighed. 'Who do you think will get Ophelia?'

'No idea,' Dan shrugged. 'Knowing them, they'll probably cast Kevin.'

'And Samantha will get Lords, Attendants, Guards and followers of Laertes. If she's lucky.'

Dan was determined to get to Greece, but with the war raging in Bosnia, it was impossible to travel through Yugoslavia by train, and so they used Jemma's credit card and bought two plane tickets. 'It's all right,' she told him, 'I'm going to get a job, teaching English to foreign students. There's a course you can do. And anyway, when you're a big star, playing Hamlet at the RSC, you can pay me back.'

'Sure,' he said, 'sure,' but he felt himself grow pale under the mask of his tan.

Athens, when they finally reached it, was stifling. An almost solid weight of heat pressed down on Dan's head, and to get away from it, the next morning at dawn they joined a group of tourists in pressed, clean clothes, with sunhats and expensive cameras, and took a bus to the theatre at Epidaurus. They dozed and played cards and looked out at the scorched countryside, until Jemma scrabbled in her bag for *Teach Yourself Greek* and slid it into her walkman. Dan closed his eyes against the hiss and whirr and found himself instead listening to the woman in front read aloud from her guidebook. *The ancient sanctuary of Aeslepios at Epidaurus is a spiritual place worth travelling around the world to visit.*

But not even the guidebook could prepare him for the spectacular grandeur of the amphitheatre when they eventually arrived. It had been dug out of a hillside and its perfect terraces stretched away on three sides, the limestone seating of its steps dazzling in the sun. For a while he simply stared at it, the cicadas whistling, the turquoise sky blazing down, until, mesmerised, he walked to the centre of the circular stage. He noticed as he did so that Jemma had climbed, taking the aisle that led up to the right, ascending nimbly, heading for the promise of shade provided by a scrag of trees at the top.

'Hello . . . ' he tested out the famous acoustics, 'can you hear me?' and he listened for the echo as his voice rose away from him. 'Hello, hello.' He imagined himself before an audience of thousands and then, unable to resist, he coughed, glanced around and began:

'To be or not to be, that is the question;
Whether 'tis nobler in the mind to suffer

The slings and arrows of outrageous fortune
Or to take arms against a sea of troubles
And by opposing end them.'

He could see people looking at him, some even choosing seats. He took another breath, his chest opening, his voice powerful and low.

'To die, to sleep, no more — and by a sleep
    to say we end
The heartache and the thousand natural
    shocks
That flesh is heir to.'

He paused again and held the silence, cupped against his ear.

'Tis a consummation
Devoutly to be wished.
To die, to sleep —
To sleep — perchance to dream.'

And then from above Jemma's voice came floating down.

'Twas brillig and the slithy toves
Did gyre and gimble in the wabe,
All mimsy were the borogroves,
And the mome wraths outgrabe.'

'Come down here,' Dan shouted to her, high above him in her flowery dress. But she only shouted back.

'Beware the Jabberwock, my son!
The jaws that bite, the claws that catch!
Beware the Jubjub bird, and shun
The frumious Bandersnatch.'

Later that week they boarded a ferry, arriving at the end of a long day, blistered and windswept, on the tiny island of Foligandros. No one else got off, apart from one lone man in hiking gear, who they followed from the port to where a group of small, stout women dressed in black were standing waiting for a bus. When the bus came, already full, the women surged forward, fighting, shoulder to shoulder, to get on. Dan hung back but Jemma joined them, muttering in her few new words of Greek, giving Dan no choice but to follow and receive a barrage of body blows. The bus didn't go far. It rumbled up a hill and stopped at the corner of a village square. The buildings round its edge looked closed, shuttered-up and quiet, and the women who got off the bus disappeared down side streets, into alleys, leaving them in silence. Dan walked into the centre of the square and sat down under a tree — an old, gnarled ancestor of a tree, its branches worn and shiny. 'Whose idea was Foligandros anyway?' It was hard not to think of all the pictures of Greek islands that he'd seen, white houses, beaches, water skiers, young people dancing under the stars.

'We don't have to stay,' Jemma said. 'The ferry comes by again tomorrow,' and they glanced towards the only bar, where two old men, sitting outside, slammed down counters in a violent and accusing way.

Dan and Jemma walked back down to the harbour, where they set up camp in a little wood of pines. As the sun began to set, they sat on a rock above the sea and watched it sink, deep red, into the water. 'I know this is embarrassing,' Jemma said, scrabbling around in the seams of the boulder for pebbles, 'but I have to try something.' She stood up, and mumbling, she hurled a small stone into the sea.

'What was that?'

'Envy,' Jemma flushed. She found another pebble and threw it, watching while it cut into the darkening waves. 'Bitterness.' She threw one more, already in her hand. It made a tiny satisfying plop. 'Regret.'

'Is that it?' Dan put his hand on the back of her knee.

'Yes.'

'Really?'

'Yup. Simple as that. We can go home now.'

Dan pulled her down beside him. He wished he could pick up a whole boulder and hurl it as far as it would go. Doubt.

'I love you,' he said, to steady himself, and Jemma snaked her cool arm around his waist and they sat in silence until the sun slipped below the surface of the water and was gone.

★ ★ ★

Dan sat on the steps of Drama Arts in a communal haze of smoke. They'd just been given the list of plays they would be working on for the next three terms. '*Hamlet!*' someone whistled, 'bloody hell.' And Dan felt himself colour as he purposefully didn't look round.

'I know,' he heard Jonathan cough. 'I'm bloody shitting myself. But at least I've got till next spring before I have to show my arse.'

Dan swung round. Jonathan was leaning back, a deep purple shirt unbuttoned to his navel, a cigarette jammed between his fingers, the last vestiges of his old accountant self, dispensed with over the summer. 'I told them no, it's too much, may be the part should be divided up, but this is the third year, the real thing, and I guess we owe it to the public to give them a good show.' He shrugged and inhaled deeply and Dan, bile rising, threw his own cigarette on to the road.

PART TWO

1995 – 2000

The Call

Since leaving college Nell had been on the books of a firm of solicitors whose offices were in Soho. She worked, filling in for other, more permanent clerks, sometimes a day here or there, and occasionally, if the case was quick, following it from beginning to end. The days were short, from ten to four, which meant, in theory, she was still available for auditions. Sorry, she could say, I can't get to the high court tomorrow, I'm up for a musical touring production of *Phaedra*, but in reality, with no agent, and only a photograph and the most basic information, eyes — brown, hair — brown, height — 5 feet 3½ inches, listed in the actors' directory, *Spotlight*, this rarely happened. Instead, Nell traipsed regularly into Soho to collect her wages, cash in hand, and sometimes, if she lingered, they would give her the details of a new job. A day at a magistrates' court in North London, a week at a county court in the city, and once, a trip to the Old Bailey.

For the last few weeks Nell had been on the case of sixteen South American pickpockets. It was a complicated case, made more so by the fact that each of the sixteen accused, in an attempt to dissociate themselves from their alleged accomplices, had insisted on his own counsel. That week the courtroom was full. Nell sat behind her barrister, Mr Hawley, a broad-shouldered, heavy-limbed man, his black cotton gown carelessly thrown on, as if by failing to arrange the pleats and folds of it, he could continue to look manly. He sat in a row of his friends, all whispering, scribbling, drawing cartoons, passing along jokes, occasionally glancing round to guffaw at colleagues in the seats behind. Nell ignored them. She looked straight ahead at the miserable bent heads of the South Americans who'd been waiting for this trial for nearly a year. Had they noticed that their lawyers were giggling like schoolgirls, that the clerks, or at least one of them, were entirely unqualified for the job? She'd spent the last two years lying on the floor searching for sense memories, or visiting the zoo to study zebra. And now, she thought grandly, a man's very life depends on me. The pickpockets looked oblivious. Their eyes, for the most part, were fixed on the floor, their bodies slumped forward, their heads drowsy with the wait. They were in the ninth week of their case, and they must have sensed it wasn't going well. Last week Nell had gone down into the cells with Mr Hawley and listened to their man's — Estaban's — scrambled English as he'd begged them to find someone who could write a letter to his wife. 'So long time. No one helping. No one.' His hands, which he rubbed together, were stained and stubby. 'You?' he'd fixed his pleading eyes on Mr Hawley, 'you help me? Yes? Please?' And not knowing what else to do, Nell had taken notes.

Later, once they'd been locked and unlocked through a cage of double gates, checked out past a man in a booth, and free, had taken the twisting staircase two steps at a time, Nell had asked, hopefully, 'Will he get off?'

'Doubt it.' Mr Hawley was already striding ahead, his black gown flapping. 'The case isn't looking good at all.'

'But the letter . . . ' she asked, anxious.

Mr Hawley waited for her to catch up. 'All the procedures for correspondence are in place.' He narrowed his eyes at her. 'Hey,' he looked amused, and she had the sudden flashing realisation he saw himself as attractive. 'Don't get drawn in.'

The next day there was much hilarity in the courtroom when several pairs of men's platform shoes were presented as evidence. The shoes were examined by the judge and passed along the line of jurors. 'Now the question arises,' the prosecutor was enjoying himself, 'do these gentlemen wear their high-heeled shoes for vanity, coming as they do from a race of, shall we say, vertically challenged peoples, or, as we are inclined to believe, to conceal stolen items of monetary value?' Shoes were held up, cavities revealed, groans and jokes flung back and forth. 'On my soul,' a balding defence lawyer whispered, 'I do believe I've been shoe-horned into this.'

'It's a job for a free man,' another quipped. 'Freeman, Hardy and Willis.'

'Arsehole,' Mr Hawley sniggered.

A row collapsed around him. 'Our soles. R soles.'

The South Americans watched unblinking as their shoes travelled the length of the courtroom.

105

They didn't smile or glance round, denying themselves even the comfort of friendship in order to keep up the pretence of never having seen each other before.

'Unless they really don't know each other?' Nell worried.

Colin, the clerk beside her, laughed. 'They come from one small village in outer bloody Guatemala.' He shook his head. 'They were rounded up during a single police sweep of the Tube. What do you think they were doing? Making separate trips to the circus?'

At the lunch break Colin asked if she wanted to get something to eat. She had been planning to buy a sandwich and sit in the cemetery, her face in the sun, the trilling of bird song sharp over the traffic, but instead she walked to a corner café with Colin, where they sat at a metallic table and ate sliced white bread sandwiches so tasteless, that, following his lead, Nell opened her bag of crisps and pushed some inside. Conversation became impossible as their lunch scattered and crunched. 'How very civilised,' Colin wiped his mouth, his shirt front and his trousers. 'We must stop meeting like this.'

'Yes,' Nell laughed. 'Actually, I'm on another case tomorrow. Down in Pimlico. At the juvenile court.'

Colin took a slug of Seven Up. 'Shame. Will you be back in time to hear the verdict on this one, do you think?'

'I don't know. I'd like to be.'

'If you fancy . . . ' Colin was searching for

more crumbs, 'I could take your number. Let you know how it ends up?'

'Yes. I'd like that.' She didn't say how much she hoped that they'd get off.

'Softie,' he said, as if he'd heard her anyway, and he passed her his pen.

★　★　★

Nell could hear the phone ringing as she turned her key in the lock of her flat door. It wasn't five yet, and Pierre would still be at the call centre, where he had a job. Nell threw down her bag and ran to answer it. 'Hello?'

'Is that Nell Gilby?'

'Speaking.'

'Ah ha.' It was a man and she could hear the rustle of paper before he went on. 'Now, I got your number from *Spotlight*, and I have someone who would like to meet you. Do you have a pen?'

Nell looked round, frantic. She couldn't see one. She retrieved her bag and pulled out Colin the clerk's pen, which she'd absent-mindedly stolen.

'Right?'

'So . . . ' the man coughed, 'Harold Rabnik would like to see you for his new film. I'm arranging meetings for later today. If you could make, say, 6.45. He was very taken with your photo.'

Nell stared at the paper on which she'd written 'Harold Rabnik'. Harold Rabnik! She and Pierre had been to see his most recent film only the week before. If she was honest she'd found it boring, gratuitously violent and comical by turns, but Pierre had loved it, said the knife-wielding psychopath was ironic and if she'd seen his earlier, edgier films she'd have understood. Nell pressed the point of the pen hard into the paper. 'Today?'

'Well, yes, this evening. For a quick chat? Are you available?'

'Yes.' Nell wanted to suggest he see her tomorrow, when she'd had time to prepare, but then what about her case? She had to be in Pimlico by ten. 'When would the job start?'

'Oh, Mr Rabnik will talk to you about that,' the man said vaguely. 'So, here's the address,' and he began to spell out for her the name of the street. 'Thank you, we look forward to meeting you,' and he put down the phone.

★ ★ ★

Nell calculated she had an hour before she had to leave. She ran herself a bath, topping the lukewarm water up with kettles, searching through her clothes for something to wear. 'Damn,' she told herself, 'I should have asked what kind of character it was for.' She stared at the mess of cotton T-shirts and bobbled jumpers, the jeans and skirts and tights. The only smart things she owned, she was wearing. A black skirt with three buttons at the back before it fanned out. A cherry-coloured cardigan and cream silk shirt. But she needed something new for Harold Rabnik. She began to lift down the clothes she

108

never wore. A black satin shift dress she'd made herself. A maroon velvet coat she could never quite accept was too long. She chose the dress, matched it with long socks and a beaded emerald cardigan. She hung them together on the bathroom door and watched them while she washed. What if the part was for a cleaning woman, or a revolutionary? She cursed herself for not asking. Or a character from history? Maybe she should put her hair up in a bun? But Harold Rabnik had seen her photo. She closed her eyes. He'd been 'very taken' with her photo, and fat tears squelched out from under her eyelids as she allowed herself to imagine that he might be happy with her, exactly as she was.

★   ★   ★

Nell assumed she was heading for an office, with late-working secretaries and a lift, but once she was out of the Tube she found herself in a leafy street of houses. They had canopied front doors, huge windows, and the further she walked, the larger the houses loomed. Number 51, she checked the doors, and to her alarm she saw that number 51 was a mansion in its own enclosed garden, its stone wall, eight feet high at least, topped with iron spikes. Nell stared at the address. Her heart was beating. What if it was just her and Harold Rabnik? And then she remembered the man's voice. 'We look forward to meeting you.' Of course, there would be any number of people there. She glanced at her watch. It was 6.44. She waited a few more seconds and rang the bell. 'It's Nell Gilby,' she spoke into the grate, 'I have an audi . . . ' The door buzzed and she was in.

A covered pathway led through the garden, luscious and visible through glass, to another door that stood open. 'Welcome. Very good of you to come.' An exceedingly smart man came forward to meet her. 'Mr Rabnik will see you in a minute, he's just on a call.' He looked her over, giving nothing away. 'Please, take a seat.'

Nell sat in an old-fashioned parlour, on an ornate wooden chair. There were Wellington boots and raincoats and a pile of *Country Life* magazines. It was so still she felt as if she was in the country. Faintly she could hear a gruff, American voice, unhurried, amused. She imagined a man with his feet up on the desk, a man prepared to give her a chance in his next block-busting film. She remembered to breathe and in an effort to calm herself, she picked up a magazine. A girl stared out at her. Pale-skinned, in pearls, her ash-blonde hair brushed over to the side. 'Sir Anthony and Lady Browne are delighted to present their daughter Alice.' It was a coming-out photograph, in the old style. Alice was leaning against a stone pillar, a spray of pink roses complementing the blush of rouge across her cheeks. 'Alice loves horses and dogs, especially her black and white terrier Minstrel. She is planning to take a cordon bleu cooking course . . . '

'Nell Gilby?'

Nell flapped shut the magazine and stood up.

Harold Rabnik was a short, balding man, his

110

shoulders sloping under a flowered shirt. He put out his hand to shake hers. 'Well, hello,' he said in a transatlantic drawl. 'Welcome to Rabnik Towers.'

'Very nice to meet you,' she said, her hand still caught in his, and when he didn't let it go, she added, 'Thank you. I mean. Great.'

Harold Rabnik looked at her. 'There's nothing to be nervous of.' He let go of her hand. 'Now, come along through and we can have a chat.' He led her into the main part of the house, into the office where his assistant was now on the phone, through into a dining room where a highly polished table was set with candelabra, and paintings of high-tailed horses lined the panelled walls. 'Bought it fully furnished and kept everything the way it was.' He opened the door into another, smaller room. 'Although this here is my favourite.' The room was oval, painted pale blue, with arched windows high up like a turret. A table was laid with a damask cloth, and there were place settings for two. 'I hope you'll be my guest?'

Nell stepped back in surprise. 'Your assistant . . . he just said, a little chat . . . '

'Relax.' Harold Rabnik smiled. 'It's OK. I was down on my luck once too, you know. So I like to share my good fortune.' He pulled out a chair. 'Sit, eat, drink, enjoy.'

Nell flushed. 'Actually,' she was stalling. 'I really have to . . . can I use the bathroom?'

With an almost imperceptible frown, Harold Rabnik directed her along a corridor to a cloakroom the walls of which were lined with

111

photographs of young men, Brideshead fashion, steering punts. Nell looked at them distractedly before examining herself. Her eyes shone glassily, her cheeks were blazing red, and her hair, held back for a day in court, stood out statically around her head. It's all right, she told herself, that man is here, and if we're having supper, there's probably a cook, and even a waiter. She washed her hands, adjusted her clothes, attempting to pull her socks as high as they would go to cover the suddenly suggestive schoolgirl gap above her knees.

'So,' Harold Rabnik was sitting at the table, tearing apart a bread roll. 'I hope you've built up an appetite, or at least a thirst that we can quench.' He rose from his seat and poured her a glass of wine. 'This is a particularly fine full-bodied red.'

Nell put the glass to her mouth and sipped. 'Mmm,' she said, obedient.

Soon there was a tap at the door and the assistant, an apron round his pinstriped waist, appeared with an enormous tray. He set it on the side and brought them each a bowl of soup. 'Thank you, you can leave the rest of the dishes. We'll manage from now on ourselves.'

'Of course.' The man dipped his head, and looked briefly in Nell's direction. 'I'll see you tomorrow then?'

Nell looked up. 'Good bye, nice to meet you,' she said brightly, and to show she was unconcerned she took up her spoon and dipped it into the pale green swirl of soup. Before she'd even raised it to her mouth she knew that it was cold. So there is no cook, she thought. Or if there was one, they've gone home. She laid her spoon down again, and listened, and hearing nothing but retreating footsteps, she took another gulp of wine.

'Well,' Harold Rabnik wiped a streak of green from the corner of his mouth, 'tell me about yourself, why don't you?'

Nell hesitated. What did he want to know? All she could think about was when it would be polite to leave. 'Well . . . ' Nothing that came into her mind — Drama Arts, the sixteen south American pickpockets, the usual procedure for auditions — seemed in any way appropriate. 'Well,' she said again, 'I went to see your film last week.'

Harold Rabnik smiled. 'And what did you think?'

'We . . . I liked it. I missed some of it, I had to keep my hands over my eyes . . . ' She tried to laugh.

'I'll take that as a compliment.' It was clear he was used to more overt enthusiasm. His smile was thin as he stood up to clear their bowls. 'I hope you're not a vegetarian or anything.'

'No.'

'We have a little shoulder of lamb.'

'So,' Nell wrested back the conversation. 'What's your new film about? I mean . . . your assistant mentioned you had me in mind . . . ?'

Harold Rabnik cut into the meat. 'The thing is, Nell, I'm at a very early stage with this film, and when I'm at an early stage I'm constantly looking round for inspiration. To be totally

113

honest with you,' he slid a plate of pale pink meat into place before her, 'your photograph reminded me of someone, a very interesting young woman . . . a talented actress, in fact . . . ' He passed over a bowl of string beans. 'I hope I haven't offended you. Insinuating you're not an original, in your lovely form. But it is uncanny . . . ' He gazed at her.

'No,' Nell said cheerfully, hoping he would stop.

'Actually, this particular actress was in one of my very first films, one of my most successful, so I suppose if you were to psychoanalyse me, which I'm sure you have no desire to do, you might find I was trying to claw my way back to my youth. My days of glory.' He grinned and raised his glass. 'More wine?'

Nell shook her head. She felt a little dizzy, but couldn't make herself eat.

Harold Rabnik's appetite, on the other hand, was hearty. He tore apart another roll, mopping up the gravy with bread, and then, heaping his plate with salad, he pushed the leaves into his mouth, leaning over so that the dressing dripped down his chin. Pierre would be home from work by now, Nell thought, regretting she'd been in too much of a hurry to leave a note. She'd call him as soon as she got out. But Harold Rabnik was pouring them more wine. 'I've always loved the Brits,' he told her, 'and everything British, so as soon as I could I came over here to make movies.' He embarked on a story involving a shoot in the West Country which ran into trouble when two wolves he'd had imported from

Transylvania escaped and the leading lady refused to come out of her trailer. 'Oh Lord,' he stopped, his fork in the air, 'that reminds me, I never called back a certain young friend of mine. Poor sweetheart, she was fretting whether or not to sign up to some dreadful pilot with an option of six years, when of course she mustn't, especially when I haven't decided yet who I'm going to cast in my next film.' He winked at Nell and stood up to open another bottle.

'Actually,' Nell folded her napkin and laid it on the table, 'it's been great meeting you, but I really have to go now.'

'No, no, no,' he looked astounded. 'I never let anyone out of my house without giving them the tour. Come on, we can talk as we walk.' He seized the bottle and topped up both their glasses. 'It won't take long.'

Nell was relieved to be on the move. Anything to get out of that claustrophobic tower of a room, and anyway, as soon as they reached the parlour with its copies of *Country Life*, she'd make her excuses and run. She imagined the door handle, already in her palm, the covered walkway leading to the outside world. But Harold Rabnik was walking the other way. 'Take a look at this,' he flung open double doors that led into a sitting room, where deep, floral sofas were grouped around glass tables, their low surfaces heaped with photographic books, jugs of flowers, vases, lamps already lit. But what Nell noticed most was that outside it was dark. What time was it? She squinted to see the hour on a grandfather clock on the far side of the room, while Harold Rabnik walked to the window and closed a wall of curtains with a swift tug of a cord. 'That's better,' he said, and he threw himself down on a couch. 'Tell me. Do you ride?'

Nell wasn't sure if she'd misheard.

'Am I wrong, or can I see a passion for ponies somewhere in your youth?'

'Yes.' She laughed, despite herself. 'I did ride. I used to help out in the local stables. But not for years.'

'I thought so,' Harold Rabnik shook his head. 'You see, I need my actress to be able to ride, and to have an air of . . . ' he looked at her, 'innocent reticence. Nell Gilby, I'm very excited about you. I may have found what I've been looking for.'

Nell moved forward and sat on the sofa opposite him. 'Really?'

'Let me tell you,' he lowered his voice, 'there are girls out there, ten a penny, who hold nothing back. What you see is what you get, do you know what I mean? But with you it's different. I've been watching you, and I can see it. The old brain working, weighing things up, assessing. You're not impressed by just anything. Am I right?'

Nell took a breath. 'Is the film set now . . . or in the past? Do you write the screenplays yourself, or, or . . . ?' Her heart was beating as she hurtled past his compliments. What would they say at Drama Arts if she overtook the favourites — Dan and Charlie, Hettie and Marvella, before they'd even finished college?

Harold Rabnik put his head on one side. 'Well.

At the moment everything is wide open. So, yes, no, or possibly, to all your questions. Anyway, come on, you want to see the house.' He led her out of the room and to the foot of the stairs, the wine in his glass wobbling as he ascended. 'You're about to see some of the most up-to-date technology on this side of the Atlantic,' he said. 'For anyone interested in film, which I know you are, it's not to be missed.'

Nell nudged her own glass on to a ledge on the landing and abandoned it.

'Now, my girl,' they were peering into a bedroom, the bed's oxblood quilt piled high with cushions, its headboard draped in gold brocade, 'expect to be amazed!' and he moved towards the bed and pressed a button which activated a full-sized screen which slid slowly, noiselessly down the wall behind her. 'Quick, come in and shut the door,' and as she did so the lights dimmed and music poured from every corner of the room. 'Here,' he patted the cushions beside him, 'see this,' and there on the screen opposite them was a girl's back, a coil of strawberry-blonde hair snaking over one shoulder, the soft shape of one breast just visible. She had a cloth wrapped loosely round her waist, slipping a little to reveal her thigh, and then as she leant forward, large letters bled on to the screen. A HAROLD RABNIK FILM. The girl turned, hoisting up her muslin cloth, and Nell gasped as she recognised her favourite actress, the actress whose role in the TV series *Shannon* had prompted her to apply to the National Youth Theatre when she was thirteen.

'Lovely, isn't she?' Harold Rabnik had kicked off his shoes and was stretched out on the quilt, his hands behind his head, gazing up from the front row of his own cinema. 'She'd probably still be working in Tesco's if I hadn't given her a break.'

God, Nell thought, this is ridiculous. But good manners dictated that she watch ten minutes at least. The girl ran through a field, looking shyly back over her shoulder at the camera, her skirt bunched up in her hands, her white calico milkmaid's top laced with delicate ribbon. A shadow darkened the screen, a shoulder, the arm of a coat, and chasing her was a dark-haired man with gleaming teeth. A door flew open, the girl ran through a farmyard kitchen, across a flagstone floor, up a ladder to a loft, and now the man was behind her, and at last, as the music swirled, they tumbled together on to the bed, all oatmeal sheets and rough blankets, her summer hair falling across his face.

'ENRAPTURE,' a trumpet heralded the title, '*written, directed and produced* by HAROLD RABNIK.'

Beside her, Harold Rabnik sighed. 'Now,' his hand moved across and patted Nell's, 'I want you to tell me which of these girls is the one who reminds me of you.' He kept his hand on hers, stroking it absent-mindedly. Nell cleared her throat and tried, politely, to remove it.

'Ah, this scene, it looks so simple, it was actually a fucker to shoot.' On the screen a group of girls were wading into the river. They had

118

their skirts hitched up, the ends already wet, and they were filling wooden buckets and bringing them dripping to the side. 'Can you see her?'

Nell stared at the screen. As soon as she identified her she could go, and then one of the girls slipped, soaking her white cotton chemise, so that the material became invisible. The girl looked down at herself, the blush of her nipples appearing through the cloth, and hearing laughter she picked up her bucket, filled it and hurled a spray of water at her friend. The other woman shrieked. Her shirt was wet through too, and soon there was a frenzy of splashing and giggling, as the first girl peeled off her dripping blouse. 'Her big scene,' Harold sniggered, and Nell leapt from the bed. 'I have to go.' She looked round for the door, but his arm shot out and seized her. 'Did no one ever teach you any manners?' His mouth was small and mean. 'At that pony club of yours.'

Nell swallowed.

'No one likes to be disturbed while watching a film, and especially not their own.'

'I'm meant to be somewhere ... my boyfriend ... ' she stuttered.

'It's your boyfriend now, is it?'

On the screen the girl had fallen and slipped into some mud. The mud had splashed across her chest and now she was dabbing at her quite enormous breasts in a pathetic attempt to wipe it off.

'Actually, we're engaged.' Nell pulled away and stumbled for the door, but with surprising alacrity Harold Rabnik was up and blocking her way. 'Engaged?' He raised his eyebrows as if the whole thing was a joke. 'So then, may I propose a last exquisite fling before you plunge into the banality of marriage?'

Nell tried to laugh. 'No, really.'

'Are you sure?' He moved in closer so that Nell was backed against the wall.

'You may not know this but I never cast anyone unless I've had a chance to get to know them, personally.' He slid his short leg between hers and pushed his face close for a kiss. 'No!' she protested. But the blunt end of his tongue, thick and liverish, slipped inside her mouth. Her stomach heaved. 'Get off me!' She shoved him so hard he tottered back, and she ran to the door, wrenching it open. But it was only a cupboard, a row of bright shirts wavering with shock. 'If you don't let me go right now,' she spat at him, 'I'll call the police.'

'And what will you tell them?' His eyes were tiny. 'That, after an intimate supper and some very superior wine, you found yourself in a certain person's bedroom, only to change your mind?'

'Ooooh,' the screen women moaned. They were rubbing mud into each other's bodies.

'Just let me out and I won't say anything,' Nell changed tack, searching the dim room for another door. 'I promise you. The thing is,' she forced tears into her eyes, 'I'm pregnant.'

Harold Rabnik laughed.

'I am, I really am. I know it doesn't show yet but . . .'

'Is that what they taught you at that fancy

drama school of yours? Pathetic!' And Nell blushed to the roots of her hair.

'I am,' she insisted fiercely, 'I am pregnant!' And as if to illuminate the havoc caused by her hormones she picked up a small statue that stood on its own podium and flung it across the room.

'No,' Harold Rabnik gasped, 'not my Global Globe,' and he careered after it as it slid under a chaise-longue.

Nell seized her chance. She hurled herself against the wall, searching for the door, until embedded in the soft flock of the paper she found a hinge. And there was the handle, disguised as the centre of a flower, and while the screen women moaned, she pulled the door open and slipped through. She ran without looking until she reached the landing, and then glancing back to check she wasn't being followed, she almost threw herself down the stairs. Nell scurried past the sitting room, the dining room, into the office, her blood racing, imagining him behind her, his hot fat hands holding her back. What if the door was double locked? She pulled at the catches, frantic, her nails tearing, sure she could hear his heavy steps, but magically she was out in the cool air, running along the covered corridor that led to the street.

In the distance, travelling towards her, was the orange light of a cab. 'Taxi! she screamed, racing towards it, waving, terrified she wouldn't be seen, but the taxi stopped and the man rolled down the window.

'Where to, love?'

'Archway.' She threw herself into the back.

The cabbie adjusted his meter, flicked off his light and began moving forward. 'Hey, that's where that Harold Rabkin lives, isn't it?' He twisted to look at the wall of metal spikes.

'Yes,' Nell wiped her eyes. 'I was just there. He's horrible. He tried to . . .'

But the cabbie wasn't listening. 'Here,' he was grinning round at her, 'when you see him again, you couldn't put in a word for me, could you? You see, I'm hoping to get into the old acting game myself. This job, this is back-up, while I wait for my big break.'

Nell turned towards the window. It had started to rain, fine slanting splinters that sliced against the glass. There was no film. She felt disgusted. And even if there was, it wouldn't be for her. 'Actually,' the numbers on the meter were rising dangerously, 'you'd better drop me here. I'll catch the bus.'

Tomorrow she'd get up and make her way to the juvenile court. She'd listen to the life story of someone with no chance at their dreams at all. Someone like Nonnie, the sixteen-year-old Turkish girl who'd been caught shoplifting and was in danger of being sent down. 'I'm sentencing you,' the judge had told her, 'to fifty hours' community service,' and he'd added that although he had to take into account the twenty-seven previous convictions against her, he was also keeping in mind the baby daughter she lived with in a hostel in Streatham, and the promises she'd made to reform.

'I'll try my best,' Nonnie had stood out on the

street with Nell and the lawyer. 'Honest guv, I will.' And she'd flashed a mischievous smile, revealing the gap between her two front teeth, so that it had taken all Nell's strength not to run after her as she wandered down Vauxhall Bridge Road and slip her own address into her hand.

Big Heat

Charlie allowed herself a small triumphant smile. 'She took me on.'

'Really?' Rob looked up from his prone position on the sofa. 'Maisie Monck?' He dropped the book he'd been reading, a worn, familiar copy of Bukowski — *The Most Beautiful Girl in Town*. 'But of course she'd take you on. Why wouldn't she? She'll make a fortune out of you.' He sat up and stretched. 'Come to think of it, I should get a cut, dragging her along to that interminable four-hour production of *Hamlet*.'

'It was a work of genius.' Charlie narrowed her black eyes. 'My Ophelia was sublime. And anyway, you do get a cut, regularly.'

'I do?' He grinned. 'Not every night, though, eh?'

The night before, after meeting Rob from his production of *Hedda Gabler*, Charlie had had to wait for thirty minutes, smiling coolly by the bar while Rob dispensed wisdom to a wide-eyed, melting understudy. 'I have a meeting tomorrow morning, in case you've forgotten,' she'd said eventually, trying to keep sweet for the sake of her audience, and nodding goodbye, she'd headed for the door. But Rob didn't immediately follow. Charlie had stood out on the street, bracing herself against the taunts and whistles of a horde of football fans let loose on a night out,

124

cursing him with every minute that passed. As punishment she'd stood stiffly apart on the busy late-night Tube, her mind searching round for evidence of all the grievances she had sustained in the three years since they'd met. 'Wish me luck then, why don't you?' she'd spat, as they stamped up the stairs to their flat, and when he didn't speak, she'd pushed past him into the spare room and slammed the door so ferociously the loose panes of the window rattled.

★ ★ ★

'So tell me,' Rob was pulling her down beside him — he loved a row, it always left him amorous — 'what did Maisie say? I want to know everything.'

'Well,' Charlie slipped out of his embrace and sat, her knees pulled up, at the other end of the sofa, 'she asked me a million questions about what I wanted to do and how I thought I might go about achieving that, and what extra skills I had, you know, singing, dancing . . . swimming with dolphins . . . '

'Sure,' Rob nodded. 'Always say you can do everything and then worry about it later.'

'Then she said she was pretty certain she could get me work, even though the industry is still very narrow-minded about anyone . . . exotic. But it's changing, she said, anything is possible if you're determined enough. And she liked the way I do my hair.' Charlie ran her fingers through her new, dried straight hair, honey-toned and falling to her shoulders.

Rob grinned. 'I knew she'd take you on.'

'No, you didn't.'

'I did!'

'This isn't about you. Why does it always have to be about you?' Charlie wasn't really angry, but she couldn't help it, she found she was hurtling towards another row.

'Anyway,' she continued irritably, 'haven't you got to go in for your matinée?'

'It can wait.' He leant over and nibbled at her ear. 'I've arrived after the half before. They know I'll get there. Come on, we'll be quick.'

'No,' Charlie squirmed. 'But how about I meet you later. We can go out and celebrate. Stage door? Or shall I come up to the dressing room and surprise you?'

'Stage door is fine.' He ignored her taunting tone. 'Unless you want to see Barry and Hugh in the buff. Not a pretty sight. I'll be down. Soon as I can.'

She gave in then and kissed him, and the spark that she'd been fighting ignited in her blood. 'Later,' she breathed, her heart buckling, 'I'll be there.'

★ ★ ★

As soon as Rob had gone Charlie phoned her parents. It was always easier to talk to them when she had something definite to say. 'That's wonderful news, dear,' her mother said, before shouting to her father. 'Udo, dear, take the phone upstairs, it's Charlotte.' She turned her attention back to Charlie. 'Maisie Monck

126

Associates. How grand.'

'Maybe,' Charlie lit a cigarette, 'let's wait and see if I get any work,' and for something else to say she told them about Equity, the actors' union, and how until the year before it had been a closed shop. 'No one could work unless they had an Equity card, but the only way to get a card was if someone offered you a job.'

'That doesn't make any sense, though.' Her mother sounded vexed.

'Well,' her father boomed into the second receiver, 'it does make sense if you're already in the union, then you don't have newcomers flooding the business every year. Now it will be even more impossible to find employment.'

She heard her mother sigh. 'If only you'd kept up with your languages. You could have worked internationally.'

'There are so many opportunities,' her father said, 'abroad.'

'You might have tried one of those big hotels. You were always such a clever little thing . . . '

'Look,' Charlie held the receiver away from her ear. She knew this routine well. 'I'd better go. My agent might be trying to get through.'

There was an affronted silence at the other end, but they couldn't argue.

★ ★ ★

Five minutes later, like a miracle, her agent did call. 'Right,' Maisie said. 'I'm going to be sending over some pages of a script. It's a French — American co-production — *Celestina* — and

127

they're looking for a newcomer, an unknown, so we're going to push you. I'll let you know when I've set up a meeting. How's your French?'

'Umm. Fine.'

'Great. I'll get the pages in the post today. Let me know as soon as you've got them.'

★ ★ ★

Charlie arrived at the theatre early. She nodded to the man who sat inside the little booth, and stood in the narrow corridor, listening to the last scenes of *Hedda Gabler* echoing out through the tannoy. The tension was building, that poor woman spiralling into despair, and then Rob's voice as Tessman, sending a shiver through her, as, once again, he failed to understand his wife. Charlie heard the rustle of skirts as Hedda sat at the piano, and the raucous notes of a polka as she crashed up and down on the keys. There was Tessman again, telling her off, and the false tone of acquiescence as Hedda demurred. 'I shall be silent in future.'

By the time the shot rang out, Charlie felt her nerves ready to snap. For a moment there was silence, then the gasps and shudders of the audience, before Rob began to wail. To hear that sound, that keening wounded cry of sorrow, had Charlie transfixed, her eyes pinned to the mesh box of the tannoy, her breath held, so that it shocked her when the applause rose up and rattled in her ears.

'Good show tonight.' Actors were pounding down the stairs. They must have had their

128

clothes on underneath their costumes, or the lure of the pub was enough to put a spring into their step that was sometimes lacking, at least Rob claimed, when they were on stage.

'That sounded good.' Charlie waited while he posed for a photo with three Italian teenagers and signed an autograph for a lone man who'd not seen the play.

'Fucking rubbish,' Rob huffed, the smile dropping from his face as soon as they were out of earshot. 'God, that little bitch Jessica gets more tricky every night. You should have seen what she was getting up to, some business with a ball of wool, right in the middle of my big scene with Hedda.'

'Well, I only heard the last ten minutes but it gave me goose-bumps, honestly, it was so good, even stage-door Stan looked moved.'

'No?

'Really. He had tears in his eyes.'

'Don't push it.' Rob was laughing, and arm in arm, friends again, they walked through Chinatown and into Covent Garden, not even stopping to discuss where they were going, striding across the square, turning off down a quiet street that Charlie felt was theirs, and in through the secret, thrilling door of Joe Allen's.

'Good evening to you both,' the head waiter welcomed them warmly, and it occurred to Charlie as they breezed after him through the maze of tables, that for the first time, tonight, it was *her* good luck that they were marking.

★ ★ ★

The pages arrived the next day. The first scene was on a train. A young girl, Celestina, off to work as an au pair, meets a French boy and falls into conversation. They talk, they flirt, they are drawn compellingly towards each other. The scene was full of awkward pauses, misunderstood English, flirtatious glances. Just reading through it made Charlie smile. And almost all her lines were in English.

'This is my stop, sorry, I suppose I'd better get off.'

The girl jumps down on to the platform but when she turns to wave, she finds the boy has jumped off after her.

The second scene was very short. The two characters lie by a smouldering fire, their clothes in disarray, the sound of waves lapping on the nearby shore.

'Don't go back.'

'I have to.'

'You don't have to do anything. Except stay here with me.'

They begin to kiss.

'But what about university, my degree . . . '

'What about life?'

He looks at her in the moonlight.

'Yes. Life.'

They kiss again, more passionately. The fire flickers. Big Heat.

★   ★   ★

'You can't do this. It's porn,' Rob said, when he'd read the scenes. 'Don't be fooled by that old

130

euphemism, big heat, it means full-on nudity and fucking.'

'It does not,' she scowled. 'It's art. It's French, mostly, and the director, his last film was about the poet, Victor Hugo.'

'Well,' Rob's face was dark, 'you probably won't get it anyway.' And that night in bed, he kept the light on and read his Bukowski, flicking the pages noisily, until long after Charlie was ready to sleep.

★ ★ ★

The meeting went well. The casting director greeted her enthusiastically, and the director, a small shadowy Frenchman in a polo-necked sweater, watched her keenly as she read. 'Very nice,' he said, nodding, 'very nice.'

Maisie was ecstatic when she called. 'They loved you,' she gushed, 'they want to see you again, for some camera tests, and this time to read with the boy they've cast. Marcel Perez. He's a bit of a star in France. Are you free next week? On Monday?'

'Sure,' Charlie said, and she turned to check that Rob was out of earshot before asking if she could get hold of the whole script.

'I don't know,' Maisie sounded distracted. 'They've only sent these scenes through for now. They're probably still working on it. So, two o'clock on Monday. Same place. Call me the minute you get out.'

★ ★ ★

That Saturday it was Rob's last night. Charlie went in early and sat in the dressing room, listening to the voices, magnified, telling the story with pure sound. She closed her eyes, and felt the whole tragic world of Norway, of Ibsen, of lies, ambition and hopelessness, descend upon her. How could they bear it, these actors, every night, spinning out the same sad story? But even as she thought this she could hear too that they'd found new meaning in the lines. I'm probably not cut out for theatre, she decided, I'll concentrate on film, and snapping open her eyes, she caught sight of her face in the mirror and laughed briefly to imagine for a moment she'd be lucky enough to choose.

Charlie stood up and looked at the cards stuck on to the mirror, the flowers, some fresh, others drooping, the towels and books and assorted make-up, the little pot of black powder Barry used to fill in the bald spot on the back of his head. He had a photo of his children, and a card from one of them, 'Good luck Daddy, break a leg', with a drawing of a man hopping happily across a stage. Every night after the show Barry rushed to catch the train to Brighton, arriving around midnight, cycling his bike through the deserted streets to Hove. It's worth it, he said, just to smell the sea air, and be there when the kids wake up in the morning, and Charlie knew that if she'd had Rob's baby, if she'd moved anywhere for sea air, she'd never have seen him again.

Charlie waited until the famous shot rang out, the audience began gasping, and then she

132

slipped out of the dressing room and down the stairs to stand in the little corridor beside Stan's booth. They both kept their heads down as Rob wept for the last time and when the play ended she imagined the audience up on its feet, exalted, the clapping was so loud it hurt her ears.

There was a party afterwards at a bar in Holborn for the cast, the stage management, the director and assorted friends. The actress who played Hedda, Sally Warren, arrived weighed down with flowers. 'Oh my darling,' she clasped her arms around Rob's neck, and Charlie understood why it was that actors talked with such intensity. How could you not say 'darling' when you'd journeyed through a lifetime with a person, bared your soul, wept tears, exchanged kisses, borne heartache, reached the heights of unimagined bliss? Why would you shake hands sombrely when you'd once died in their arms? 'We'll keep in touch,' they promised each other. 'Yes. We *must*.'

Charlie took a glass of wine from a passing tray. 'Cheers,' she leant in to Rob, 'you sounded amazing tonight. And you too . . . ' Sally Warren was beside him, 'you were incredible.'

Sally raised her own glass. 'Congratulations to you too. Rob tells me you have your first screen test coming up.'

Charlie glanced at Rob. 'Yes . . . I'm not sure . . . '

'That's right,' Rob rested his arm heavily on her shoulder. 'She's going to be a big star.' He looked balefully across at her, and with a knowing smile Sally moved away.

'For God's sake,' Charlie turned to Rob, 'why do you have to tell everyone? I probably won't get it.'

'Everyone will know soon enough.' He had her arm in a tight hold. 'When you're down in the earth by the smouldering fire with your kit off and some French bloke humping you from behind.'

'Rob!' Charlie looked round, but no one seemed to have heard. The room was filling up, a trail of men and women in white shirts was circling, heavy round platters of canapés held aloft. Starving actors descended on them. 'Shit.' Charlie felt her stomach flip. She turned her back to the room. 'Don't look, but it's Gabriel Grant. From Drama Arts. You remember? Pierre was obsessed with him and Patrick Bowery was convinced he was the great white hope of British theatre. He's handing out snacks.' She turned to check, hoping that maybe she'd imagined it, but Gabriel, oblivious, was heading straight towards her.

'Where, which one?' Rob strained to see, and at that moment Gabriel's eyes met hers. A sort of shudder washed over him, the physical embodiment of shame; but it was too late to look away. Rob turned to the bar.

'Hey,' she waved. 'Hi. How are you?'

'Great.' Gabriel lowered his tray. There was one squashed cherry tomato on it, piped round with a swirl of cream. Charlie took it, and with a sigh he let the tray drop to his side. 'I'm . . . I've just been . . . yeah, up for a few things, but it's a fucker, trying to get work worth doing. And the

134

agents. I had a few circling at the end of drama school, but then, maybe I was too choosy . . . I don't know. The whole thing's nonsense.'

Charlie nodded. 'I know, it's ridiculous.'

'And you?' He looked at her, pityingly. 'You're out now, in the big bad world.'

'Yeah, as of last Thursday.'

'You know Nell Gilby got her Equity card, did you hear, playing a penguin in a theatre in education tour?' He made a pained expression.

'That's right,' Charlie refused to react, 'I saw her.' She had an image of Nell, trilling operatically, her arms flapping as she fell forward in a rolling dive, while children, aged from four to seven, lit up with delight. 'Actually, she was rather good.'

'Well, I'd better get going,' Gabriel glanced over his shoulder. 'Work to do.' And grimacing, he set off through the crowd towards the swing door where identical white-shirted figures were emerging with new trays.

Rob was still at the bar, deep in conversation with the director. Their heads were close together and although Charlie stood near by, there was no way in without an interruption. She took another glass of wine and wandered off, keeping her eyes fixed on the middle distance, unable to bear the thought of another agonising chat with Gabriel, until it occurred to her that other people's last-night parties were a club that could not be broken into, a place where you would never belong. She slid her glass on to a passing tray, and stepped out into the street. The night was clear and soft, the pavement, the grey granite of the buildings, breathing warmth. Fuck it, she thought, looking up at the dreary details of the night bus, and she stuck her arm out for a taxi home.

★ ★ ★

Marcel Perez was young and slight, with gleaming jet-black hair. He took hold of Charlie's hand and didn't let it go. 'Let's rehearse,' he said in his beautiful, lazy accent, 'quick, while they set up.'

The director and the cameraman were busy with a monitor, and the casting director was on the phone.

Charlie pulled out her pages. 'You didn't learn?' Marcel looked alarmed.

'Well, yes, I did, I sort of . . . '

'Perfect.' He flung her script away. 'And if you forget, just invent it, no?' He looked round comically. 'It's all right, the writer is not 'ere.'

They rattled through the lines, watching each other, looking away, smiling, in spite of themselves, so that by the time Charlie was ready to get off the train, she would have been surprised to turn round and find Marcel not there.

'It is instant,' Marcel looked intently at her, 'this attraction, non?'

'Oui,' Charlie agreed and they laughed, a shivery, nervous laugh.

The second scene was more difficult. They sat on the ground. 'Ahhh,' Marcel stretched out and warmed his hands on an imaginary fire.

136

'OK,' the director called. 'We'll film this one. When you are both ready.'

'Don't go back.' Marcel took hold of Charlie's hands.

'I have to.' All Charlie could think of was, were they actually going to kiss?

'You don't have to do anything. Except stay here with me.' His hand was on her face, pushing back her hair and he was leaning forward, oh for God's sake, she closed her eyes and felt his mouth, for a brief second, soft against her lips.

'But what about university, my degree . . . ' she spluttered. Had she broken off too soon?

Marcel looked startled. He sat back on his heels. 'What about life?' he insisted.

They stared at each other. She could hear a clock tick on the wall. 'Yes. Life,' she conceded, swallowing. Marcel moved towards her again, and slowly, with his arms around her, began to lean her backwards so that, gently, elegantly they both sank down to the ground. 'Ze Beeg Heat,' he whispered, and she answered in her best, clipped *Brief Encounter* voice, 'I say, you're awfully good. Do you do this sort of thing often?'

They collapsed, shaking and holding each other while the camera kept on running and the director gazed at their laughing, love-struck faces on the screen.

★   ★   ★

'They want you!' Maisie told her. 'And Equity have agreed to give you a card.' She sounded ecstatic. 'Now, we haven't done the deal yet, so

137

don't expect vast riches, it's a low-budget film.'

'All right, I won't.' But even so, when the offer came through it was more money than she'd allowed herself to imagine, more money than Rob had earned in the last year.

'You'll be flying to Paris to do the hair, make-up and costume tests.' Maisie called again. 'They'll film a few scenes there, but mostly they'll shoot on location in the south. They'll organise your travel from there. You'll be based in Marseilles.'

'That sounds fun,' her mother said when she told her, and her father hoped she'd get home to Cheltenham for a night before she went.

'Probably not,' she told them, 'I've got a million things to do before I go, not least of all, learn French,' and before her mother could start on about the money wasted on her education, the letters they'd received from the headmistress, the piano lessons she'd missed, Charlie interrupted, 'There's someone at the door, sorry,' and she rang off.

★   ★   ★

That night Rob made love to her with excruciating care. 'I will be back,' she reminded him, but he didn't smile. Instead he attended to her, stroking and kissing, turning her over, running his tongue down the dents of her spine, as if to leave the imprint of himself on every inch of skin. Afterwards he held her tightly, his limbs leaden over her own, as guiltily she thought about Marcel. She wondered how they'd greet

138

each other when she arrived in France. It is instant, this attraction, non? and for the thousandth time she wondered if he meant their characters, or their own. But soon she'd slipped into a dream that even from within her dream she recognised: the play was starting, and she was miles from the theatre. Fast as she ran, her feet were clay. She tried to call to warn them, but each time she dialled the numbers, her fingers slipped, until she gave up, and seizing a bicycle, she peddled madly until she hit a slick of oil and skidded to the floor. Desperate, she wrenched herself awake. Rob still had his arms round her, his leg was pinning down her own, but he was shivering now, his flesh clammy and cold. 'What is it?' she soothed, clasping his heavy head against her chest. 'Sweetheart, what is it?' but he only held her tight and wouldn't say.

Three days later Rob was offered a job. A small-scale tour of *Macbeth*. Birmingham, Newcastle, Liverpool, Llandudno, and all going well, the Theatre Royal, Bath. Almost instantly he was caught up in preparation, reading and obsessively rereading the play, meeting up for pre-rehearsal rehearsals with the actress who was to play Lady Macbeth, and then, in the evenings, spending hours on the phone to her in all-engrossing discussion. Charlie was left free to prepare for her departure. As she packed she glanced round at the dilapidated rooms of their flat. How much longer would she be living here? Would she actually come back? And it occurred to her, that with both of them away, there would be no sign the building was inhabited. Similar houses in the next street had recently been demolished and surely it was just a matter of time before the bulldozers moved in and knocked this one down? She collected her favourite possessions and packed them into a cardboard box, her winter coat and cowboy boots, a polka-dot teapot and matching cups, one tall glass vase that Rob had given her, just wide enough for a single rose. She took them by taxi round to Nell's. 'Just until I'm back,' she said. 'Is that all right?' And Nell promised that she'd keep everything safe. 'Have an amazing time,' Nell put her arms around her. 'And write and tell me what it's like. And what he's like. Marcel Perez.'

'I will, I promise,' Charlie said, and she hugged her friend and wondered if she actually would.

★ ★ ★

That first night in Paris she was invited to dinner with the director, the writer, two producers, and Marcel. They met at a brasserie not far from her hotel, ornately beautiful, but casual too, as if this was how Parisians effortlessly ate. The director ordered fruits de mer, a tier of dishes so high it was almost impossible to see over it, and on each tier, arranged on beds of ice, were mussels, crayfish, oysters, prawns, the raw slippery meal of it leaving her high-spirited and drunk.

Afterwards Marcel walked her back to the hotel. They walked in silence, their fingers millimetres apart. 'So, it was a great pleasure to

140

see you once again,' Marcel stopped on the steps, 'I hope you sleep well,' and to her surprise he took hold of her shoulders in a businesslike clasp and kissed her lightly on each cheek.

'Good night,' she tried to catch his eye, but he was already turning away.

Charlie lay in her crisp new hotel bed and gazed around her. Everything was so substantial. The built-in wardrobes, the desk with its leather-bound book of information, and the telephone on a table to her right. She should call Rob, she thought, tell him she'd arrived safely, but instead she leafed through the schedule. There had been no time to look at it before dinner, only to change her clothes, examine her face, add a little lip gloss. Now she saw that they would be shooting the train scenes first. They'd be filming outside Paris and then, as soon as they got to the coast, just days from now, they would be doing one of the last scenes in the film. Big Heat.

'Ze Beeg Heat,' she murmured, hoping to revive for herself the air of frivolity created by Marcel at the audition, and as she lay in bed, running over her lines, she imagined herself and Marcel making love by firelight, so easily and fluidly, people would turn to each other in the cinema and whisper . . . is that real?

She fell asleep, the script still in her hand, and woke an hour later with a jolt. A pang of guilt engulfed her as she remembered Rob, sweating and shivering as he'd held her in his arms. I must call him; she reached for the phone, but although she dialled the number twice, even checked with the concierge for the right code, no one answered at the other end.

★ ★ ★

On set Marcel was friendly, but aloof. He flirted during each take, his dark eyes brimming with amusement, but as soon as the director called 'cut', he drifted off and Charlie could see him talking to the producers, larking around with the crew, making himself tea. By the time they came to do the train scene Charlie felt skittery with longing. Now, she thought, now he would have to acknowledge her, and as he moved across the carriage to lean his head towards hers, to hear exactly what she had to say, she found herself gazing into his eyes. 'Where am I going? To Aix-en-Provence,' she told him, 'to work for a family with three small boys,' and then when he pressed her further, 'I'm sorry, je ne parle pas français, seulement un petit peu.' They smiled at each other, shyly, and when she leapt down from the train, she was sure she could feel him, coming after her, linked by an invisible thread.

'Yes, yes, very nice,' the director murmured, and the next day a car came for Charlie early and took her to the airport, where she flew to Marseilles. She expected to see the others at the departure gate, expected to see Marcel, but no one else was there, and at the hotel, although she had all that day to recover, to wander in the gardens, to sit by the blazing pool, she felt self-conscious and alone.

Big Heat was a night shoot and she wasn't

called till six. It wouldn't be dark till after eight but there was hair and makeup and hopefully, some opportunity to meet and rehearse. Charlie's costume was already in her caravan. A pair of minuscule knickers, no bra, a shirt with a tie at the waist, shorts. She'd chosen these clothes with the wardrobe woman, in Paris, in a dumb show of shrugs and smiles, but rather than reassure her with their familiarity they hung on their hangers like a threat. As soon as she put them on — it was inevitable, she would be called upon to take them off. What worried her most was that it had never been made clear exactly how much she was expected to expose. 'Make sure you get some kind of clause,' Rob had told her, and when she'd mentioned it to Maisie, Maisie had sighed and said she could insist on 'no pinky bits' but that usually resulted in the director having a tantrum and bringing in a body double. Did Charlie want that? She could insist on it. Certainly. But with this being her first job she didn't want to push too hard.

'Right. Of course,' Charlie had conceded. Not wanting to remind her that the pinky bits were in fact black. 'Don't worry. I'm sure it will be all right.' And that night she'd stood in front of her bedroom mirror, examining herself. Who cares, she thought, twisting to get a good look at her arse. Not me. I'd walk down the Kilburn High Road naked if someone said they'd give me cash. But now that she was here, alone, with strangers, she didn't feel so sure.

Charlie changed into her costume. The shirt was red and white check and tied above her

143

navel. The shorts were faded blue. A pair of brand new flip-flops stood ready in her size. 'Oh, là là. Très jolie, n'est pas?' The make-up woman smiled as she sat down, and pinning Charlie's hair back from her face, smeared a wash of beige foundation over her skin. As she watched, her cheekbones sharpened, her lashes sprang up, slick with black, and two careful stripes of silver drew out the liquid of her eyes. 'Merci, madame,' Charlie said gratefully. The whole procedure had calmed her. For the first time in her acting life she hadn't set out to create a character. She was determined to prove she didn't need the rigours of Silvio's six psychological divisions, or the straitjacket of Stanislavsky's method. She was opting for instinct and natural attraction. She was going to play this girl as herself.

She moved along to Hair, where a large man abandoned his knitting to smooth and preen and even snip at the dry ends before pulling her newly straightened hair into a ponytail, freeing two strands and wetting them so that they sprang back into ringlets which hung down over her ears. 'Parfait,' he said, kissing his fingers, and Charlie smiled into the mirror.

The location was in a glade of trees high up above the city. The air smelt sweet of thyme and sunshine, the evening light, as it slanted down, bathing everything in a haze of gold. A car took Charlie the five minutes from her trailer to the set, and when she stepped out she found herself in a clearing where a fire — the fire — was already lit. Some kind of sacking had been laid down, with leaves and grasses scattered over it, and Marcel was there, in jeans and a T-shirt, hovering by the table where tea, coffee, fruit and biscuits were supplied.

Charlie wandered over to him. 'Good evening,' he said, holding a polystyrene cup under the spout of the urn. 'I hope you are feeling well?'

His face looked unusually smooth, and his hair flopped silkily forward over his eyes.

'Yes. Thanks.' She made herself tea too. There was an uncomfortable silence. It's like one of those horrible first dates, she thought, when you know you're going to end up in bed but you don't know how you're going to get there. She unpacked a Cellophane-wrapped biscuit, and then found she couldn't eat it. Maybe I should have jumped on him that first night on the steps of the hotel, and then at least I'd know what to expect. If I'd already touched him, I'd know how to touch him now, and Charlie shivered at the unsettling possibility of moles, of back hair, of the new foreign feel of his skin. My Objective, she thought desperately, too late, is to . . . what? What was her Objective? She couldn't think. Surely that was the whole point of her character, she didn't have one. She wants to go back to England, take up her place at university, but she doesn't want to lose him. OK. So her Actions are to love him, seduce him, in order to keep him. But in the script, isn't it him, seducing her?

'Sorry?' Marcel was smiling.

'Oh, nothing. I was just . . . '

'You want?' He held out a stick of gum, and she took it, embarrassed.

145

Maisie had assured her, that for any scenes involving nudity, there would be a closed set. No one who wasn't strictly necessary would be allowed in, but here, in this forest clearing, who was going to guard against it? Anyone at all could be lurking in the shadows — prop-buyers, mechanics, the entire catering staff. Even people who had nothing to do with the film could probably take a look. Late-night ramblers, truffle-hunters, men out poaching pheasants. Charlie stared into the fire. I don't really care, she reminded herself, I just don't want to look a fool, when it turns out that I'm actually in *Carry on Au-pairing* while my Mum is telling the whole of Cheltenham WI that I'm in a charming little arthouse classic.

Marcel stretched out beside her. 'Where are you living in London?' he asked politely.

'In Willesden,' she told him, 'you know it?' He said he didn't.

'And you?' she asked.

'Yes, I live in Paris. In the Marais.'

Conversation between them faltered. They both looked up, hopefully, when the director walked over. 'OK, so . . . ' he crouched down to squat at their level, 'what we want to see is . . . love, tenderness, passion.' He smiled, as if delighted with the clarity of his notes. 'You want to rehearse, or we start filming?'

Marcel turned towards her. 'Sharlie?' He said her new soft name. 'What would you prefer?'

'Me?' And unable to bear the thought of

prolonging the agony any further she opted to start filming.

★ ★ ★

'And Action.'

They both stared into the fire.

'Don't go back.' Marcel put an arm around her.

'I have to,' she turned to look at him.

'You don't have to do anything.' He took her hand, and pressed it. Warmth flooded through her. Sharlie, she thought to herself. Sharlie! 'Except stay here with me.'

She was ready when his kiss came. His lips, as soft as she'd remembered them, his teeth, clean as mint. This time she didn't pull away so fast. 'But what about university, my degree . . . ' She remained in the circle of his arms. He held her there against him and almost whispered, so that the furry arm of the boom swung down above them, 'What about life?'

Charlie remembered Rob, their boarded-up front door, the radio that she'd probably left tuned to Radio I. 'Yes. Life.'

Bereft of any more lines, Marcel leant in for another kiss, his hand, sliding down her side, his body pressing into hers. How big is this heat, she found herself wondering, as together they fell back on to the matting which must have been laid on a path of rocks, because one of them was digging into her spine. In any normal situation she would have shrieked and sat up, but this was serious, this was love and passion. Marcel

147

continued to kiss her and she him. Now what? she thought, beginning to suffocate, and before her lips went numb she broke away and began to kiss his neck, his ear, all the while stroking his hair. If only they could have gone on talking? We need more lines to help us through, and just then, as if his career depended on it, Marcel sat up and tugged off his shirt. Charlie's heart contracted. Not only was he beautiful, clean and strong in the half light, but now it meant she too would have to make a move. He pulled her up against him and they kissed again, her hands on his naked back, his, stroking the stretch of bare, brown midriff below her handkerchief of a shirt. When they could kiss no more, he bent his head to the tie of it and together they fumbled with the knot so that by the time it fell open to reveal her breasts Charlie was so relieved to have succeeded with it that she hardly cared.

'Cut' came the unexpected call. A woman rushed forward with a dressing gown. Marcel turned away and wiped his mouth.

Charlie looked towards the director but he was busy. Instead she pulled her gown around her and tilted her head patiently while the make-up woman patted powder over her flushed face.

'Right,' the director called eventually. 'Great. Let's go again, and let me see, more . . . more urgency, more desire.'

This time when Marcel took off his shirt, Charlie ran her hands over his body, felt the warm flesh, the springy ribs, the muscles in his arms. Her shirt, which she'd re-tied, slipped off her shoulders and he bent down and kissed each

148

breast. She felt her face flame and then grow pale and she remembered Sally Warren telling everyone at the raucous first-night *Hedda Gabler* party how once, during a sex scene, an actor, who she refrained from naming, put his tongue in her ear, whereupon she promptly threw up. To get away from Marcel's mouth she eased him back so that she was straddling him, but now he had his hands at her waist, unbuttoning her shorts. She stopped abruptly and looked towards the camera. She was met with a row of eager eyes, each dropping away as she stared them out.

'What is it?' The director came out from the safety of his camp.

'Am I? Do I have to . . . for God's sake, do you want all my clothes to come off, or what?' The man looked embarrassed. He shrugged and pouted and glanced from side to side. 'I think . . . Yes. The shorts. Off.' Then, he looked away. 'The panties, they can remain. Or not, be playful, express yourself. You were in drama school, no?'

Charlie crossed her arms over her breasts to stop herself from punching him, and she thought of the long hours in Silvio's studio, moving their eyes from left to right. 'Yes,' she mouthed darkly, and she wondered what would happen if she had signed the no pinky bits clause. Where would the body double come from? Would she dash out from between the trees, a huge black bottom wobbling, and throw herself in abandon on Marcel?

'So, très bien,' the director nodded, and they prepared to go again.

This time Charlie wriggled out of the shorts herself, but Marcel didn't remove any more of his clothes. He unfastened his belt, and made a show of tugging at his flies, before rolling her over on to the sacking and pressing himself against her with a groan. For a full five minutes they humped and moaned.

'I'm so sorry,' Marcel said, when it was over. 'Are you OK?'

'Yes,' she winced, feeling underneath her for more rocks. She waved away the dressing gown. What was the point of pretending to be modest, when any minute she would be writhing and gasping again? Marcel snapped up a sharp green blade of grass and stretched it between his thumbs. 'I stayed in London once,' he told her, whistling through it like a boy. 'My father worked for a bank, when he was living, and we used to go to Hyde Park, and row on the little boats.' He sank down on one elbow and Charlie lay beside him. 'I know those boats,' she said, 'it's funny but I've never been on one, and I've lived in London since I was sixteen.' There was silence. 'What happened to your Dad?'

'Oh.' A cloud passed over the surface of his face. 'He was ill, for a long time.' He touched her hand. 'Maybe one day we'll go on the boats. No? Me and you. And I will row.'

'Maybe.' Charlie felt ridiculously pleased.

'Before, have you been in France?'

'Just once, for a weekend.'

'But you have travelled?' It seemed now the act was done, and done and done again, they were free to talk.

'Not really,' Charlie told him. 'My Dad took me to Nigeria once, when his father died . . . to the land of his ancestors, you know . . . but that was hard, it was as if he turned into someone else . . . you know what I mean?' She felt, of all people, he would. 'And when I came back my mother had arranged for me to go to boarding school, in Kent, if you can call that travelling.' An unexpected surge of misery flooded through her.

'You didn't like it?' Marcel looked at her, concerned.

'I fucking hated it.' But when she saw his solemn face she laughed. 'OK, it wasn't that bad. They didn't beat us or anything. I just felt different. And I missed home. And then I hated home because they'd sent me.'

Marcel pressed her hand. 'And now?'

'Now?' She thought for a moment. 'My parents don't know anything about me.'

★ ★ ★

It was light by the time they got back to the hotel. 'You will sleep?' Marcel asked her. They'd travelled in the same car, dressed once again in their own clothes, gazing out at the waking countryside, the old stone of the houses, the stirring dogs, the sudden flashes of sea between the trees.

'Yes,' she said.

'Or would you like . . . we could swim?'

'Now?'

'Why not?'

151

'Will the pool be open this early?'

'The pool?' He grinned. 'The sea!' He leant forward and spoke in rapid French to the driver, who swerved away from the palm fronds of the hotel entrance and veered out on to the road.

Charlie looked at him. 'I was going to say later.' She shook her head. 'I was going to be sensible and say, let's meet up for lunch.'

Marcel grinned. 'Now I'm allowed to talk to you, I don't like to wait.'

Charlie turned her whole body towards him. 'What do you mean,' her voice was low, 'allowed?'

Marcel took her hands. 'To keep the tension, I had to promise, to stay away, but now, the big scene is done, so . . . '

Charlie was open-mouthed. 'You left me on my own all this week . . . ' her heart was pounding, 'you bastard, for the sake of the film?'

Marcel gave some quick instruction to the driver, who veered off the road. Below, across a stretch of rocks and tiny flowering sea-plants, was the curve of a blue bay.

'Wait, attend,' he told the man, and pulling Charlie after him, he ran with her across the rocks and pools and down to the fine white pebbles of the beach.

'I am sorry,' he said, 'it was not easy for me too. Please. Will you forgive me?'

When she hesitated he dropped down on to one knee. 'I'm 'orrible, I know. Just 'orrible.'

'Stop it.' Charlie had to laugh. 'You 'orrible man.' And she tugged at his arm so that he stood up.

'Thank you.' He reached out and touched her hair, tentative, as if the feel of it was new. 'But it worked, no? You were at your best. Exquisite.' And with no one's eyes on them he drew her towards him, finally, for their first real kiss.

Who's Your Agent?

Nell's agency was run by an old woman, with an old woman's name — Ethel Dabbs — but Nell dealt almost entirely with her assistant, Lyndsey. Lyndsey was young and enthusiastic, and she'd taken Nell on after seeing her play the nurse in a production of *Romeo and Juliet* in a theatre above a pub in Chiswick.

'Welcome to Ethel Dabbs Associates.' Lyndsey had ushered her into their office, and Ethel Dabbs herself had looked up from behind a desk, and adjusting her glasses, peered at her unsparingly.

Nell was delighted to have an agent. Instead of scouring the pages of *The Stage* for adverts, or writing off with her photo and CV to every repertory theatre in the country, she sat and waited for the phone to ring. Mostly it was her mother wondering how she was getting on, but sometimes, thrillingly, it was Lyndsey with details of auditions — a play at Leicester Phoenix or a season at the Glasgow Citizens. Once she even called with news of a meeting for a small part in *The Bill*. Nell forced herself to wait for several days before ringing her back, and when she did, Lyndsey was always cheerful. 'Not this time, I'm afraid. It didn't work out. On to the next one, eh?'

'Yes,' Nell agreed, but as the months passed Nell felt increasingly alarmed.

*   *   *

Early in the New Year Lyndsey called and asked if Nell would pop into the office. 'Is anything wrong?' she asked, aware that the word 'pop' usually preceded something unpleasant — an invitation to climb on to a doctor's couch, a request to pop to the toilet — but Lyndsey reassured her. 'Ethel wants to have a little chat, that's all.'

Ethel Dabbs's agency was in the basement of a house in Putney. The basement was as cluttered as a real home — with a sink and a draining board under the window, and three desks arranged around the room. Ethel was busy on the phone. 'Yes, darling. Yes, of course. I'll tell them you can't *possibly*.' She took up a pen and made a note. 'I know, I know, it's one of your peccadilloes. You just can't share a dressing room with *anyone*!' When eventually she was finished she beckoned to Nell. 'Now,' she adjusted her glasses, 'it seems we have a problem.'

Nell swallowed.

'My dear girl, you're not getting any work.'

Nell stammered. 'I know, but . . . '

Ethel put up a hand. 'I'd like you to try something. I'd like you to go and see someone. He used to be an actor himself, one of mine in fact, but now, among other things, he gives coaching in audition skills.' She wrote an address on a piece of paper and pushed it towards her.

Nell felt herself enveloped in a flush of shame. She'd spent three years at drama school — in fact it had been two, but she couldn't always

155

admit, even to herself, that she'd been asked to leave. She shouldn't need any kind of coaching.

'Don't worry about the money.' Ethel mistook her hesitation. 'The agency will pay. We'll consider it an investment.'

'No. It's not that, it's just . . . ' Nell remembered her manners. She folded the address and put it in her pocket. 'Thank you,' she said, and smiling briefly at Lyndsey, she hurried towards the door.

★ ★ ★

The ex-actor lived in Pimlico in a large, solemn apartment. He led Nell through the hall and into a study. 'Please,' he said, indicating the polished parquet of the floor before him. 'When you're ready.'

Nell took a breath. She looked round as if to centre herself, cleared her throat, coughed twice, and then, knowing that really she'd never be ready, she chose a chair, placed it at an angle and began.

'*He thought it was terrible, the idea of women shooting at each other . . .* ' She'd chosen a play by Ian McEwan, a play for television that she'd never seen. '*It is terrifying . . . But it terrifies men for a different reason . . .* ' Nell, although her gaze was fixed on an imaginary colonel from the Second World War, was also watching the actor. '*On the anti-aircraft units the ATS girls are never allowed to fire the guns.*' She saw the actor blink, and scratch his head. He hates me, she thought, he knows I'm useless. Nell had to struggle to remember the next line. *'Their job is to fire the range finder. If the girls fired the guns as well as the boys . . . '*

Nell had borrowed this audition speech from her new flatmate, Sita, who'd got it from a friend. *' . . . if girls fired guns, and women generals planned the battles . . . '* She imagined Sita in their tiny sitting room, her long hair flying, her cat's mouth spitting out the words, and she wondered if she should attempt to sound more like her, less West Country, more East End. *' . . . then the men would feel there was no . . . morality to war, they would have no one to fight for, nowhere to leave their . . . consciences . . . '*

In her imagination the colonel leant forward and put his hand, condescendingly, on hers. *'Take your hands off me!'* she bellowed, flinging away his arm. But immediately she was plunged into doubt. What if the actor was offended by her choice of speech? Thought she was a feminist making a point? She dropped her voice, showed she could be thoughtful. *'When we went to bed it didn't matter that he couldn't . . . I didn't care . . . I really didn't care . . . '* and as she mused about love and shame, and the parallels between the war and sex, she sank down, finally, on to the chair and waited for whoever was judging her to lift their rifle and take aim.

'Thank you,' the actor said, giving nothing away. He motioned for Nell to come closer. 'I want to ask you a question.' He looked at her, kindly. 'And I want you to tell me honestly.' There was a pause. 'What are you thinking when you're doing your piece?' Nell looked at the floor and without expecting it, her eyes filled with tears. 'What am I thinking?' She frowned. 'I'm thinking . . . ' She thought of all the many things that she'd been thinking, but then one clear truth rolled towards her. 'I'm thinking . . . I'm not going to get the job.'

'So what happens?' The man was smiling at her.

'What happens?' Nell's head was so full she could hardly hear. 'What do you mean?'

'What happens when you stand there, laying bare your heart and soul, with that certainty running through your brain?'

'I don't get the job?'

'Exactly,' the man rewarded her. 'Exactly right. Now, I want you to answer me a few more questions. Are you a good actress?'

That was the terrible thing. How was one to know? 'I think so.' She took courage. She remembered her performance as Emilia in *Othello*. 'Yes. I can be.'

'And are you reliable, co-operative, hard-working?'

'Yes.'

'Would you be a valuable member of a company?'

Nell shrugged, but the actor wasn't letting her off. He cupped his hand to his ear.

'Yes.'

'So you may in fact be just what a director is looking for. You may be the answer to their prayers.'

'Well . . . ' It had never occurred to Nell that

158

she might actually be useful. Each time she'd been offered a job she assumed it was a mistake which the director would soon discover and regret.

'Now.' The ex-actor leant back in his chair. 'Will you do your piece again?'

'All right.' Nell grimaced. What if she was just as bad?

'All right!' he challenged her.

Nell found her spot on the floor. '*He thought it was terrible, the idea of women shooting at each other.*' This time she knew who *he* was, and she remembered that she liked him. Loved him, even. She flew through the lines, Sita, a distant memory, working as she was today in Monsoon Accessories, her long black hair tied back with baubles, her ears hung with silver hoops. '*The men want the women to stay out of the fighting so they can give it meaning. As long as we're on the outside and give our support and don't kill, women make the war just possible . . .*' She glared, not at the actor but at the colonel, who was, frankly, scared. '*But I'm withdrawing my support.*'

When she was finished she looked up and it didn't matter to her what the actor thought. What anyone thought. Even whether or not she got the job. Not that there was one.

'Thank you so much,' Nell smiled.

'Thank you,' the actor told her.

Nell reached for her coat. 'Or is there something else?'

'Nothing else.'

'So it's just . . . confidence. Is that all it is?'

'Confidence.' He shrugged. 'And talent obviously, and luck.'

They laughed, and the actor held open the door. He watched her as she ran down the stairs. *'When we went to bed, it didn't matter that he couldn't . . . I didn't care. I really didn't care.'* The words bubbled out of her, transparent, delicious. It was as if she'd thought them up herself. *'He didn't have to be efficient and brilliant at everything . . . I liked him more . . . But he couldn't bear to appear weak before me. He just couldn't stand it. Isn't that the same thing? I mean . . . as the war. Don't you see, the two . . . the two . . .'*

Ecstatic, she leapt aboard a bus and settled herself at the front like a queen.

★ ★ ★

Within two weeks Nell had her first professional job, at Hampstead Theatre. She was to play a singing telegram-a-girl caught up in a shopping centre siege. At her audition she'd had to bark the first verse of 'My Way' as if she was a dog.

'Woof, woof.
Woof, woof, woof, woof.
Woof, woof, woof, Wooooooooooof.
Woof, woof. Woof, woof, woo . . . ooof.'

But nothing had fazed her.

'Congratulations.' Lyndsey was as pleased as if she'd got the part herself. 'I knew you could do it.' And on the first night she sent her a spray of pink and red carnations with a card signed from all at Ethel Dabbs.

'*Who's* your agent?' The lead actress, Phyllida de Courcy, squinted at the card as Nell stuck it on to the mirror, and the director, Timmy, who had sidled into the dressing room for a last quick chat, answered for her. 'Ethel Dabbs. You know, when they sent out her CV it was all round the wrong way. Nell, really, you should have a word with them about that.'

'The wrong way?' Nell didn't understand.

'They'd put everything in order of the date.' He turned to Phyllida. 'Not with her most recent work first, but what she'd done at drama school!' The two of them laughed in an agonised sort of way as if it was just too hilarious and sad to bear.

Nell put her carnations in water.

'Darlings, my darlings, one last note.' Timmy turned and put his spare arm round Nell's shoulders. 'Pace. Pace. Pace.'

'That's three notes.' Phyllida laughed, but Nell saw that under the rouge and the lipstick she was pale.

'It's the half,' the stage manager called from the corridor and Phyllida shrieked. Nell rushed to the loo. Her body felt molten, flaming, slick with fear. It was as if she was about to step out of an aeroplane and plummet into space. She pressed her face against the smooth paint of the door, crouched down and wrapped her arms around her knees. Why am I doing this? she asked herself, and she imagined the shock of her mother, her sister and her sister's boyfriend, of Lyndsey, Sita, Pierre, Charlie, everyone who'd

161

promised they would come, their faces dissolving as she crashed to the floor.

'Fifteen minutes.' Someone was knocking and she roused herself. 'Please God,' she murmured, and she swore that if she made it through the night she'd never, ever put herself through anything so terrifying again.

When she went back into the dressing room she found Phyllida smoking out of the window. 'You don't mind, do you, darling?' she asked and she offered her a puff. The stage manager was back. 'The five,' he said gently. 'Positions, please.'

Phyllida clasped Nell's hand. 'It doesn't get easier.' Her whole body was trembling. 'I feel more nervous now than when I first began. More to lose!' and they stood together, ice-cold with fear, their palms sweating, clutching each other in the wings.

The audience were in, they could hear them shuffling and chatting, happy, innocent, not knowing that only yards away there were people suffering in agony for their sakes, and then to Nell's horror the lights dimmed, the music faded and forgetting everything she'd ever known, even her name, she stepped out into the empty white glare of the stage.

There was silence. The audience, she assumed, were just as panic-stricken as her, and then, as she'd rehearsed them, her lines came out quite normally, as if she was someone else. Phyllida was behind her, humming, bustling, offering her toast, and by the time Howard entered in his security guard's uniform, Nell was able to turn to him, a cup of tea in one hand, a broom in the other, and welcome him as if this was her home.

During the interval Timmy put his head round the door and blew them both a kiss, and when Nell went on for the second half she was skipping, flying, barking out her song with glee. 'Woof, woof . . . woof, woof, woof, woof . . . ' She caught Phyllida's eye and smiled, she waltzed around the stage with Howard and later, when they all hid behind a bunker of jaffa cake boxes, she crouched there, her blood singing, ecstatic as she'd not been since she was a child. And it was over. There was rapturous applause. The three of them gripped hands and bowed, three times, their hearts high as the moon. 'You were marvellous, absolutely wonderful.' Lyndsey hugged her, and over her shoulder Nell saw her mother, tearful, glowing, a look of wonder in her eyes, as if now she understood.

★   ★   ★

That night Nell could hardly sleep. There'd been drinks in the bar of the theatre and then a party back at Timmy's in Brick Lane. His agent had been there, a bright and efficient woman from Dove Coutts, and afterwards Timmy had whispered, 'She liked you. I think she'd take you on if I put a word in.' He topped her glass up with champagne. 'A chance to get away from the dreary Ethel Dabbs?' And by the time she'd finally got to bed her head was spinning.

Lyndsey rang early with the first review. '' . . . as truthful and charming a performance as I've seen this year on the London stage',' she

163

crowed. 'Hang on, hang on, there's more. 'With affecting insouciance, newcomer Nell Gilby . . . ''

Nell didn't ask what insouciance was. Her head thudded too painfully to care. 'Thank you, so much, for calling,' and she crawled back to bed, making ugly faces at herself in the hall mirror as she remembered her introduction to Amanda Jones of Dove Coutts and how she'd smiled and simpered and lapped up her praise.

★ ★ ★

That Sunday there were more reviews, many of them carrying large photos of Phyllida and Nell, and the words underneath. 'Mesmerising'. 'Deeply affecting'. And under one small picture of her, alone, 'A talent to watch'.

Lyndsey called, although she said that really she shouldn't, not on a Sunday, but she just couldn't resist it. 'Congratulations! I hope you're thrilled.'

'Well, yes.' Nell was still in her pyjamas, having walked up to the corner shop with her coat on over the top.

'I'll be coming to see the show again soon,' Lyndsey promised, 'and I hope to bring some casting people with me.'

'That's great,' Nell told her, 'thanks,' but beside her was her diary, with 11.30 a.m. Wednesday — Amanda, Dove Coutts, written in black ink.

'What if she finds out?' she turned to Sita, who

was preparing for her lunchtime shift at Pizza Express.

'Don't worry. You don't have to *go* with her. Just see what you think. Anyway, she might not even take you on.' Sita tucked her red T-shirt into her skirt — she hadn't worked as an actress since a TV play she'd done last year in which she'd played a young Pakistani girl caught up in an arranged marriage. Now she couldn't get seen for any part unless it was specified as Asian.

'Fuck.' Sita was plaiting her long hair. 'I'm going to be late. The manager will have a fit.'

'Bye then.' Nell spread the papers out before her. 'And bring me back some chocolate fudge cake, if you can.'

'Don't get your hopes up. Last time they fined me for eating a slice. They took the money out of my wages.' Sita slammed out through the front door.

★ ★ ★

Dove Coutts had smart offices on Oxford Street. Nell gave her name to the receptionist and looked round warily as she waited to be seen.

The phone rang constantly, and each time the receptionist answered in the same cool tone. 'Dove Coutts? Sorry, her line's busy. Can I take a message?'

Eventually Amanda Jones appeared. 'Hello!' She put out her hand. 'What amazing reviews you've been getting!' But she said it accusingly as if she was a particularly rivalrous friend.

165

'Yes.' Nell was flustered, and then remembering she was here because of Timmy, 'it's great for Timmy. He's hoping the play might transfer.'

Amanda didn't comment. She turned and led her back down the corridor and into an office with one large desk and a plate-glass window, through which could be seen the sharp lines of other offices and the green sloping tiles of a department store roof. Amanda tucked her swathes of cashmere around her and swung into her seat. She pushed a vase of flowers tied up with ribbon to one side. 'My boyfriend keeps sending these ridiculous bouquets!' and she smiled sweetly, as if, finally, she was all Nell's.

'Well,' Nell began, 'I thought this might be a good opportunity to get a new agent. I mean, I haven't actually been with Ethel Dabbs for long, but they're very small, and well, Timmy seemed to think that you might be interested . . . '

Amanda leant towards her and took a good long look. 'Yes,' she said, 'you wouldn't be here if we weren't. The wonderful thing about this agency is, we have so many big stars here, actors and directors, and we have offices in America, obviously, but what it means is . . . when we're negotiating deals we can push our younger, less well-known people forward.'

Nell nodded. She could see how cleverly it could work.

'Now, I've been thinking . . . there's the new pirate film, casting at the moment, and they're making a film about Shakespeare's wife, they need a girl. We could get you seen for those. What kinds of things do you like? Where do you

166

picture yourself, say, in five years?'

Nell was dazzled. 'Well . . . I'm not sure. Mostly I've done theatre, which I love, and I'd like to do some TV, but film,' she took a deep breath, 'I'm really enthusiastic.'

Amanda smiled at her. 'You could still do theatre. They're looking for someone to take over in the Neil Simon play in the West End.'

'That would be amazing.'

'So,' Amanda was leafing through her diary. 'How long does your run have to go?'

'At Hampstead? Another three weeks.'

'Great. We'll get working. Start sending you up for things straight away.'

Nell's breath was shallow. 'I'll need to tell Ethel, and Lyndsey . . . '

Amanda ignored her. She took down a copy of *Spotlight*, Actresses D to G, and leafed through it till she reached Nell's quarter page. 'You'll need new photos.'

Nell looked at herself upside-down, her hair pulled back, her eyes shining clear out of a freckled face. She rather liked the photo.

'We have someone we tend to send our people to.' She handed Nell a card. 'Nicolo Manzini. He's ever so good.'

'I'll have to tell Ethel . . . ' Nell repeated.

Amanda looked towards the door. 'Of course. Well, just let me know when you've done that and we'll get going. See what we can do.' She made as if to get up, and Nell imagined all the messages banked up at reception waiting to come pouring through.

'Bye then, thanks so much.'

'Bye.' Amanda gave her a twinkly smile. 'I'll be waiting for your call.'

Nell walked back along the corridor, past the array of posters, *Ben Hur, Gone with the Wind, King Kong*, all starring, she imagined, exclusively Dove Coutts clients.

★ ★ ★

Nell didn't call Lyndsey that day, she couldn't find the courage, but the next morning, before she'd had a chance, Lyndsey called her. 'Just thought I'd let you know I'm in tonight and I'm bringing a casting agent from Granada.'

'OK,' Nell said. She didn't say anything else.

'Is something wrong?'

'No,' Nell faltered, and then knowing it could only get worse, she let the words rush out, hopeless, as if it was all beyond her control. 'Actually, Amanda Jones at Dove Coutts wants to take me on.'

There was a silence.

'And is that what you want?' Lyndsey's voice was flat and cold.

'I don't know,' Nell lied. 'I suppose it seems such an opportunity and they've got so many big names that are already in films, so many contacts.'

'Well, we have contacts . . . '

There was another silence.

'Listen,' Lyndsey said. Nell heard her swallow. 'Think about it. Really think about it and call me later and tell me what you've decided.'

Nell wanted to shout that she'd decided now.

She couldn't call her again. She just couldn't. 'All right,' she said in a small voice and she put down the phone.

★　★　★

Nell waited until three o'clock before calling back. 'I'm so sorry,' she said by way of explanation.

'Right,' Lyndsey's voice was clipped. 'So you've decided to leave. One minute. Ethel wants to have a word.'

Nell felt herself go pale.

'Well,' Ethel spoke sharply. 'I think you're a very ungrateful girl. We've worked hard for you, young lady. Lyndsey in particular. And now, after all the groundwork we've done, someone else will reap the rewards. I expect you'll go on to do good work. I'm sure you will.' She paused. 'But I just want to say, I think you are being very disloyal.'

'Sorry,' Nell said. She made a face across the room. 'I'm really sorry.'

'Be that as it may,' Ethel Dabbs answered curtly, and when Nell put down the phone she was cheered by the thought she'd never have to speak to her again.

Immediately she rang Amanda.

'Hello, Dove Coutts, can I help you?'

'Yes, it's Nell Gilby, can I speak to Amanda Jones please?'

'I'm sorry,' the voice said breezily, 'she's busy, would you like to leave a message?'

'Oh.' Nell felt deflated. 'Please tell her that I called. Nell. Gilby.'

Nell waited by the phone but Amanda didn't call and by 5.30 she realised that if she didn't hurry she'd be late for her warm-up at the theatre.

★ ★ ★

Timmy and Phyllida thought it was marvellous. Phyllida, fresh-faced with happiness at the successful run, took her in her arms and danced her round the room. 'A real, starry agent,' she told her, and Timmy said he hoped she'd remember him in her Oscar acceptance speech.

Then Nell told them about Ethel Dabbs. 'I think you're a very ungrateful girl!' she mimicked. And they all squealed. She didn't tell them about Lyndsey and the break in her voice when she called back with her decision. She supposed she wouldn't be coming tonight, and neither would the casting director from Granada.

That night the show was flat. 'The audience is terrible,' Howard muttered, 'there's a woman in the third row practically asleep.'

'Brutes,' Phyllida said. 'There's a man in row F sucking a bloody lolly.'

Timmy came in during the interval. 'Pace. What have I told you!' And he stomped out to talk to Howard.

★ ★ ★

Nell tried calling Dove Coutts again the next morning, but it wasn't until late afternoon that she got through. 'Yes?' Amanda said, 'is the deed done?' and she yelped with such excitement when she told her, that Nell didn't like to mention the fact she'd never returned her call.

'Now,' Amanda said. 'We need to get those new photos, and start sending you up for things. I hope you're keeping your days free?'

'Yes. Of course.'

'Great. I'll be in touch soon. Bye till then.'

★ ★ ★

The photographer, Nicolo, was based in Fulham. He had cowboy boots and tight white jeans, and a girl to fix Nell's hair and make-up. But first he looked Nell up and down and asked if she'd brought any other clothes. 'Yes,' Nell clasped her carrier bag, 'but you don't think this will do?' She was wearing a striped blue-and-white T-shirt cut square across the shoulder and she liked the way it made her look, young and a little theatrical.

'Show me what else you have.'

Nell pulled out a black cardigan, bobbled from the wash, and a flowered calf-length dress.

The photographer stared at them. 'Try the cardigan,' he said.

'Over this T-shirt?'

'No. On its own.'

Nell felt self-conscious when she re-appeared. The cardigan wasn't a cardigan she usually did up and those buttons that she had managed to fasten strained across her bust. Nicolo put his head on one side. 'Try undoing one more,' he said unhappily, as if even then, it wouldn't please

171

him, and so Nell let the cardigan bulge open still further, exposing the high curves of her cleavage and the lace trim of her bra.

Nicolo turned to his assistant. 'Hair down, I think, Gina, over one shoulder, and some nice strong colours on the lips and eyes.'

'Actually,' Nell sat down, obedient before the vast array of make-up, 'I prefer a natural look.'

Nicolo ignored her. 'I'll be right back,' he said, and he sauntered from the room.

Gina hovered over her. She picked out some eyebrow tweezers and after a few seconds' scrutiny nipped in and plucked out a hair. 'OW!' Nell screamed. She had never encountered anything so painful. 'What are you doing?'

'I just thought I'd neaten up your eyebrows.' She stood back and waited, arms crossed, as if to say, fine, it's nothing to me if you want to look like a Yeti. Unnerved, Nell capitulated. 'OK, then, do it,' and she sat, her body tensed, trying not to scream as the hairs came out with a tiny audible tear.

Afterwards Gina dusted shadow on to her newly tender skin, smoothed colour into her cheeks and painted her mouth with a slick black paintbrush dipped in red. 'Right,' she said, having fluffed and brushed and blow-dried her hair so that it felt a foot high, and she stood back to admire her.

'Can I see?' Nell asked, looking round for a mirror, and while Gina dug for one in her bag, she assured her. 'You look fabulous.'

The mirror was small and Nell had to squint to see more than one feature at a time, but even so she was appalled. She looked like someone in fancy dress, a harlot from a Restoration comedy. 'It'll look very natural in the photographs,' Gina swore, but Nell began to rub it off. She smeared the lipstick on to the back of her hand and dabbed at her sore eyes, but just then Nicolo came in. 'Wow. You look fantastic. Let's get going straight away,' and he took her arm and led her over to where a large white sheet was hanging from the ceiling. For two hours she stood against it, twisting and turning, smiling and sombre, sultry and cheeky, a hand in her hair, a finger in her mouth, eyes forward, to the side, modestly down, having given up all power to resist.

* * *

'I just *love* the photos,' Amanda told her as she spread them over her desk.

'Yes?' Nell looked at them, once more upside-down, and her heart sank. For all the bright make-up and dazzling lights they were pale and un-arresting. They were printed on ultra glossy paper as if to make up for the murkiness of vision, and Nell imagined how easy it would be to toss one into the bin.

'Trust me,' Amanda told her. 'These are much more commercial. You look young, and sexy and . . . ' she peered closer, 'available.'

'OK.' Nell was willing to be convinced, and she imagined that Amanda was unlikely to be putting her up this year for a season at the Sheffield Crucible.

* ★ ★

The play was in its last week and all the talk was whether or not it would transfer. 'Don't tell Timmy, but as far as you're concerned,' Amanda lowered her voice, 'we don't want it to go on and on . . . we want you to be available for work.'

'But it would be work,' Nell suggested, and Amanda laughed. 'Oh, I was thinking something more high profile.'

There was a party on the last night and although Amanda didn't make the play — there was one empty seat right there in the middle of the third row — she arrived in time for drinks in the upstairs rooms of a club in Soho. She was with a man, a tired-looking banker, and announced that they'd just become engaged. Everyone congratulated them and poured them champagne, and Nell found herself in a corner talking to Timmy's boyfriend about his lifelong passion for embroidery. By the time she extricated herself Amanda was gone.

★ ★ ★

The first few days after the play were glorious. Nell woke each morning, thrilling with the sense of freedom, the lack of fear, the promise of a new day, a new life, but by Thursday she was bored and lonely. Sita had accepted a part in a daytime TV series, not only playing another Asian girl but one whose marriage was being arranged, and she left at six every morning and arrived home late, exhausted. 'It's work,' she said, throwing herself down on the sofa. 'I mustn't complain. But honestly, I feel as if I'm just saying the same lines over again.'

Nell rang Amanda and for once was put straight through.

'Hello?' Amanda sounded snappy.

'I was just wondering,' Nell gulped, 'if there was anything going on?'

Amanda took an audible intake of breath. 'It's only Wednesday . . . ' (Thursday, Nell wanted to correct her.) 'You've been unemployed for exactly half a week.'

'I know . . . it's just . . . '

'Patience. Have patience. I'll be in touch soon.'

Nell called Phyllida and arranged to have tea.

'Darling,' Phyl wailed, 'isn't it awful? These endless days. Oh, I do hope the play transfers. God knows what I'll do if it doesn't. I'll probably never work again.'

'Of course you will,' Nell protested, and Phyllida took her hand in her own — manicured and elegant with one dark ruby where a wedding ring might have been — and asked her how many parts she thought there were out there, good parts, parts worth doing, for a woman of her age?

Nell sighed. They'd told her at drama school that only 8 percent of actors were working at any given time and mostly it was the same 8 per cent, and mostly they were men. But she hadn't believed them.

'And what about Timmy?' Nell asked. 'Have you seen him?'

175

'Oh, Timmy, he's off to New York. Always got a finger in several pies, the slut.'

Another week passed in which Nell heard nothing from Amanda, and then another week, after which she plucked up the courage to call. 'I just wanted you to know,' she said, when she eventually got through, 'that I'm going away for a few days, in case you need me.'

'Going away?' Amanda sounded alarmed. 'Oh dear. Will you be far?'

She and Sita were planning to go to Somerset to stay at a cottage belonging to a family friend. Sita had hardly ever been out of London, only to Bradford and Birmingham, for work, and now she had passed her driving test and had a small second-hand car of her own, she was in a rush of excitement to get going.

'I'll ring in every day and see if there's anything happening,' Nell told Amanda. 'I can always get back.'

'Good,' Amanda sounded relieved. 'I've been working very hard here . . . so don't go far!'

'I won't!' Nell was thrilled. 'I promise.' And she danced around the flat and sang as she packed her bag.

★　★　★

It was May and the Somerset hedgerows were thick with spring flowers. The lawn was a carpet of daisies and the field behind the house shimmered with new grass. She and Sita sat in the garden and looked up at the pale blue sky. 'I could stay here for ever,' Sita said. 'I'm sure if I

176

lived in the country I wouldn't care about anything so much.'

Nell folded over a corner of her book. 'Maybe we could start one of those community theatres in an abandoned barn or something. Never have to wait around for anyone to offer us work ever again.'

'Yes. We could put on plays, have a youth theatre, workshops. Can you imagine? But are there enough people to actually make up an audience, let alone be in it?'

'Probably not.' Nell looked round. All she could see were birds, twittering and scrapping in the hedges, and beyond, a field of sheep. 'But maybe they're all hiding. Just waiting to rush out into the open if there was only something to do. That's what it was like in Wiltshire.'

'Really?'

'Why do you think I moved to London as soon as I was legally allowed?'

They lay back on their bed of rugs and looked up at the sky. 'So maybe it's time to move back.'

'Maybe,' Nell yawned, 'but I don't think so.'

After lunch they walked down the sloping lane to the village. They wandered through the one street of houses, peering into sparse front gardens, at the overgrown churchyard, the pub and the village stores. They bought two tins of soup for supper and a loaf of bread, and then, as they struggled back up the steep hill, they came across an abandoned shop, set back from the road. It must once have been an ironmonger's. There was a pile of old screws and hinges on the window ledge, scattered with dead flies, and on the faded paint above the door, a sign: Knobs and Knockers. Both girls screeched with laughter. 'Maybe that could be the name of our company,' Nell choked, and she laughed so hard, doubling over to hold her stomach, that a tin of Heinz tomato soup fell out of her bag and rolled into a ditch. 'Let's take over this shop,' Sita said. 'Turn it into our café theatre. Can you imagine how perfect it would be, to stop and have some tea and entertainment right here? It's all that's missing.'

Nell pressed her face against the glass and stared through the dusty window. 'We could have round tables and a small stage at the back and we could get all our friends to come from London and do cabaret while people eat scones with jam and cream.' As her eyes adjusted, she could make out a ruined wooden floor, bare bulbs, green and yellow panelled walls dotted with nails. 'Just think of all the unemployed actors we know who could do with a break. Fresh air, a bit of singing and dancing. We'd be providing a social service for everyone involved. We could apply for a grant. Aren't New Labour promising to pour money into the arts?'

'Knobs and Knockers. Complementary rhubarb jam with every ticket sold.' Sita turned to look left and right along the empty road.

'Or we could call it Star Lollies,' Nell suggested. 'And hand out sherbet dips.'

'Café de la crème.'

'Sita and Nell's.'

They linked arms and began to walk uphill, amassing names as fondly as if they were

178

expecting a child, moving on eventually to the menu — meringues, apple upside-down cake, brownies, lemon tart — so that by the time they reached the cottage they were so hungry that they tore open a packet of digestive biscuits and with mugs of tea they sat out on the back porch and watched the sun go down.

'It's brilliant here,' Sita said, breathing deeply, and Nell confided in her how worried she'd been in case she was bored.

'Bored!' Sita huffed. 'You know what I'm really bored of, ringing my agent and hearing: 'Sorry love. Nothing new. Talk tomorrow?''

'Oh God!' Nell put a hand over her mouth. 'I promised I'd call Amanda.'

'Don't worry about it.' Sita collected up their cups. 'Just ring in the morning. I haven't called my agent all week.'

'But it's different for you. You've got work, on and off, until October.'

'True. But all I can think about is when it'll be over. I guess it's not the kind of work I want to be doing. You know the joke about the unemployed actor?'

'No.'

'He gets a job. First thing he does is look through the schedule for his day off.'

They laughed despairingly and stepped into the kitchen. 'Here's another one,' Sita said. 'Why doesn't the actor look out of the window in the morning?'

'I don't know. Why doesn't the actor look out of the window in the morning?'

'So he has something to do in the afternoon.'

179

Nell groaned, although secretly she was thrilled to be making jokes about what was now officially her profession. Sita turned the radio on, filling the room with music, an old-time quickstep from before the war. 'It'll all be different when we get Knobs and Knockers off the ground,' she shouted, and she grabbed hold of Nell and danced her round the kitchen. 'Here's to Knobs and Knockers,' they toasted later with red wine, and they scalded their mouths on the soup which had been left bubbling until it overflowed.

★   ★   ★

It was impossible to hear the phone from the garden, so Nell sat on the sofa in the darkened sitting room, leafing through copies of old *National Geographic*, waiting for Amanda to call her back. 'Right,' she said, when finally she did. 'There is something. Yes. Can you be at the Athenaeum Hotel this afternoon at three o'clock?'

'Today? But I'm in Somerset . . . '

'What! Well, can you get back? I might be able to change it to four.'

Nell hesitated. 'Yes. Sure. What's it for?'

Amanda shuffled more papers. 'It's to see the director for a film they're making in Russia. They need a girl . . . they haven't sent in anything very detailed. Just go in and meet. He's a big director. Raoul Romolkski. Four o'clock. OK?'

Nell looked out of the window. Sita was lying on a mound of cushions, reading a magazine in

180

the sun. 'I don't think I've ever been anywhere so peaceful,' she said, squinting, as Nell came out. 'I did once go to Wales but it rained non-stop, and anyway that was with school.'

'Sita,' she stood over her, blocking out the sun, 'you're not going to believe it but I've got an audition.'

Sita sat up. 'What for?'

'Some Russian film. Raoul Romolsksi? Oh God, the thing is, it's today, at four.'

Sita flopped back onto her cushions. 'That's so bloody typical. Couldn't they see you some other time? Even tomorrow. We've just arrived.'

'You could stay here. You could drive me to a station.' Nell looked round as if there might be a branch line on the other side of the hill. 'And I could come back first thing tomorrow.'

'Are you crazy?' Sita scowled. 'I couldn't stay here on my own. I'd be terrified. Did you see how dark it was last night?' She glanced round at the green wash of the valley, the hedgerows full of voles and birds, the dilapidated roof of one lone building on the crest of the next hill.

'I'm sorry.' Nell picked a blade of grass and tore it into fine green strips. 'The thing is if I'm going to make it, then we'll need to leave . . . quite soon.'

Sita pulled herself up. 'OK,' she said, 'let's get going. I suppose we need to clear everything up.' And dragging the cushions with her, she went into the house to pack.

★ ★ ★

Nell sat on a spindly gold chair in the corridor of the Athenaeum Hotel. Lined up against the walls were at least ten other girls. Blonde and dark, short and tall, all wearing carefully applied make-up, with bare legs and high heels. Nell had on a thick coat with a fur collar. It was hot in the hotel and Nell longed to take the coat off, but underneath she only had on a strappy flowered dress, and anyway the coat, she was sure of it, was Russian. One by one the girls were called in. Theresa. Sheridan. Jade. Nell looked down at her black boots. How many parts were there? And she remembered Phyllida telling her that on average there was one woman cast to every five men.

Eventually Nell was called in. The director stared at her. He was not Russian but American. Big and fat, with lines across his forehead so deep they'd dented into grooves. 'Too . . . ' he shook his head, 'young,' and the assistant showed her hurriedly to the door.

★ ★ ★

A month passed without any more auditions and then another month. Hettie called to tell her she'd been cast as a child in a play about a chimney sweep, and then Pierre phoned to invite her out to celebrate his promotion. He'd been invited on to the managerial team of the cold-calling company for which he'd been working for the last year. Nell took a job at Sita's branch of Pizza Express, working six shifts a week, from five till midnight, taking orders,

182

eating her supper in the kitchen, alone except for the clatter of the dishwasher being loaded and unloaded by Dragan, the silent Croatian. Nell's mother asked if she wanted to come on holiday. She was going to Spain with Nell's sister, a last trip before the birth of her first child, but Nell was unsure whether or not she could risk it.

After another month she rang Amanda. 'If it's convenient I'd like to pop in — (pop in!) and see you, just for half an hour . . . ' and as she spoke she looked at herself for signs of idiocy in the hall mirror.

⋆　⋆　⋆

The first thing Amanda did when Nell was shown into her office was thrust forward her hand. 'Look!' Nell stepped back, confused, and then she saw it — a huge glittering engagement ring studded with stones. 'He finally came up with it.'

Nell smiled weakly. 'It's lovely,' she said, and as Amanda made no effort to do so, she slid the vase of flowers to one side of the desk.

'I'm really worried.' Nell came straight to the point. 'The play finished in April. It's now August and I've only had one audition. I mean, have you been sending out my photos, my CV and reviews? It's pretty clear the play isn't going to transfer.'

Amanda looked amazed. 'Of course we have. Constantly. Now . . . ' She stood up. 'Where's your file?' She began pulling open drawers, and finding nothing she picked up the phone and

183

spoke into it, imperious. 'Please bring in Nell Gilby's file. Right,' she smiled, 'I know it's been disappointing. But I have been talking you up and it's just, over the summer, it's often a slow time. September is when things tend to get busy again.'

'Really?'

There was a knock on the door and a timid, middle-aged woman put her head in. 'Here's Nell's file, but I'm afraid there's nothing much in it.'

Amanda rose up out of her seat. 'Nothing in it?' She glared. 'What on earth is that about?'

The woman looked at her as if she had no idea.

Nell stared at the desk.

'Sort it out. Photos. CVs. Reviews. They must have gone astray. Unless . . . ' There was a pause, 'we've run out.'

Amanda sat down and opened the empty file. One CV fell flatly to the side. 'You'll have to order more photos,' Amanda told her. 'I'd no idea we'd run out. So sorry. Now. If there's nothing else, I've got to dash. I've got a screening. Rupert's in rather an exciting new film.'

Amanda pulled on a gauzy shawl and picked up her bag.

Nell stared at the file. 'But could you have really used 100 photos? Are you sure they're not somewhere . . . I mean.' Nell remembered the sheer cost of having the last batch printed. 'And the reviews I gave you. Wouldn't you have photocopied them?' She saw the long-ago clip

184

from the paper — *A talent to watch* — sliding away into the bin.

'Well,' Amanda did pause, 'I'll talk to my secretary about it. Shall we go down?'

It was awkward in the lift. Amanda, her whole self gleaming, her hair bouncing, her nails buffed. Beside her Nell felt dull — three months of pizza suppers and late nights, of wearing the same red cotton T-shirt and black skirt, of running between tables, mindful of the orders, the side salads and garlic bread, the ever important tips.

'Bye then,' Amanda hailed a taxi. 'Golden Square,' she ordered, and she was gone.

★　★　★

When Nell got home she wrote to Lyndsey. *I've made a terrible mistake. I wish I'd never left. Is there any chance at all of you taking me back on? I understand of course if you can't. Please let me know.* She signed and sealed it, and marking it 'private', ran to the postbox and sent it on its way to Ethel Dabbs's.

Four days later Lyndsey called. 'What happened?' Concern almost masked a whisper of clear joy.

Nell poured her heart out to her.

'I have news too,' Lyndsey told her. 'When you left, I had to admit, I was pretty shaken. I actually went home and cried. And then I thought. It's not me, I know that, I couldn't have worked harder. It's the agency.' She giggled. 'Ethel Dabbs.'

185

Nell pressed the receiver hard against her ear.

'So. I applied for a new job. I'm working for A.G. Blythe. In Covent Garden. They've got a wonderful client list. Much more vibrant, and I love being in town.'

'So . . . ' Nell felt her heart thumping. 'Is there any chance . . . I mean . . . I . . . '

'Oh darling.' Lyndsey's voice was all regret. 'When I got your letter I showed it to my colleagues, and the thing is . . . it's such a problem, but we've got another girl on our books who's rather like you.'

There was a silence in which Nell still allowed herself to hope.

'It just wouldn't be fair,' Lyndsey continued. 'To her. Or to you for that matter. I'm so sorry.'

'That's all right,' Nell managed.

'I mean,' Lyndsey obviously felt bad, 'I do see it's been a disappointment, but Dove Coutts do have an excellent reputation. It may still work out.'

'Yes.' Nell felt like weeping. 'Thank you, Lyndsey. And I'm so sorry to have upset you . . . '

'No, I should thank *you*. Really. If you ever feel like having lunch, as friends, you know where I am.'

'Bye then.'

'Bye.'

Nell phoned her mother and sobbed. 'It would all have been all right. But they've got someone else. Like me.'

'You poor love,' her mother sounded anguished. 'It's just you've been working so hard, that's all,

186

why don't you change your mind and come away with us on holiday? There's still time.'

'Oh, Mum, you don't understand. The thing is, I haven't been working. Not really. And the last thing you feel like doing after no work is going on holiday.'

'But you have been working, in that pizza place . . . '

'No, you don't understand. It's not working really, it's sort of . . . waiting . . . '

Nell sniffed and they both laughed. 'Maybe next year.'

'And Nell . . . '

'What?'

'There's no one else like you.'

★   ★   ★

Nell took the bus to Soho and found a three-day-old copy of *The Stage* in a news-agent's on Old Compton Street. She sat in a café and leafed through the adverts. This was where she'd found most of her work before she had an agent. A children's theatre tour in which she'd played a penguin, the production of *Romeo and Juliet* Lyndsey had seen her in above the Chiswick Arms. Today an experimental company was looking for an actress with physical theatre skills, and a small outfit based in Balham needed a girl who could do an Irish accent for a play by Brian Friel.

Knobs and Knockers, Nell doodled a box of her own. Inventive performers needed for cabaret and improvisation. Singing, dancing, juggling, cake-making, ironmongery . . .

When she got home Sita was lying on the floor. 'Are you all right?' Nell asked, but Sita said she was exhausted. 'I've been screaming at Harish all day. 'I'm too young to be married. Don't make me do it. Don't marry me off to that old man.' By the end I just wanted to fly to Pakistan and have done with it.'

Nell sat down with her back against the sofa. 'Why don't we put on a show of our own. We don't have to go to Somerset. I mean look at this,' she opened up *The Stage*. 'There are adverts here for all sorts of crazy things all over London. We could do Knobs and Knockers. We could have sketches about, I don't know, anything . . . '

Sita pulled herself up. 'I've always wanted to do a show about working as a waitress . . . you know, the first job I ever had, I had to dress up as a giant prawn. It was in a fish restaurant.'

'Yeah, we could both be actresses, dreaming of stardom, and . . . you know a friend of mine worked in a burger bar where she had to rollerskate from one table to the next.'

'Right.' Sita leant over for a pen. 'Let's write it ourselves. What do you want to be called?'

'Ummm.' Nell considered. 'Belle?'

'Right. I'll be . . . Rita. God, we're imaginative. So,' she began to scribble. ' 'Two girls, on rollerskates, one dressed as a lobster, the other as a prawn . . . ' This is going to be so good . . . '

They hunched over the paper. 'We'll start with really dreamy music . . . and then each girl can have a monologue . . . about their hopes and

188

aspirations . . . and then . . . loud voice over. 'Table ten is waiting. Hop to it.''

'Yes.'

Just then the phone started ringing.

'It's probably my evil agent,' Nell said.

'Don't answer it,' Sita challenged her.

'OK, I won't.' And they sat, pens poised while they waited for it to stop.

'That's better. Right, where were we? 'OK, Hop to it, prawns, Table ten is waiting.' Then what?'

'I know.' Nell held up her hand. 'A kind of mad rollerskating dance between the tables with more and more plates. Can you juggle?'

'Not really.'

'Fuck it, we'll learn.'

The phone rang again. Nell didn't look at it. 'So,' she said, leaning over to flick on the answerphone. 'Prawns. Lobsters. Juggling. Music. Right, what next?'

'A glitter ball.'

'Really?'

'Yes, we have to have a glitter ball, and then the lights will dim and the whole black stage will be full of tiny silver reflections.' A woman's voice began to talk, nonchalantly into the machine. Sita twisted down the volume.

One glitter ball, Nell wrote, and she sat back and admired her work. 'How about a sketch with all the worst chat-up lines we've ever heard.'

'You're Taurus. I'm Aries. Just think. Two horned creatures in the same paddock.'

'Oooh, I remember him. Creepy.'

189

'But, as it turns out, a source of good material.'

'And how about, 'You're looking tired. An all-over body massage might do the trick?''

'The manager of the Fulham Road Pizza Express! Promise I get to play him.'

'OK,' Nell wiped her eyes. 'He's all yours.'

Sita looked at her. 'Will we really do it?'

Nell smoothed down the sheet of paper. 'I'll phone the Chiswick Arms tomorrow and book a date and then we'll have to, won't we?'

'I guess so.' Sita began scribbling stick figures on a set. 'I've always wanted to use that Clint Eastwood music, you know, at the beginning of *The Good, The Bad and The Ugly*? We could have cowboy hats and guns, and whip them out when the customers are rude.'

'I love it.'

'I love it too.'

'But will we still be dressed as lobsters?'

'Possibly . . . ' Sita stood up and began pushing back the sofa. 'Or,' she was panting, 'one long strip of Velcro and we're free!'

Location Wars

Dan could hardly contain his excitement. 'You can come too,' he told Jemma. 'That's the beauty of it. They'll pay for you to fly out. And Honey.'

'Really?' Jemma stood very still. 'That's amazing.' He could see that she was struggling. 'It's an actual offer then?'

'Look, you don't have to come for the whole time.' Dan peered into the Moses basket where their daughter lay, a centrepiece of exquisite fascination on the kitchen table. 'Fly out in the middle, for a month, or a couple of weeks. Whatever you want.'

Jemma nodded, but she didn't speak.

'Come on, Jem, I haven't worked since February. I turned down that ITV drama because they couldn't promise to release me for the birth. And I know it's not great, location-wise, with Honey so little and everything, and it's winter there, but . . . ' he needed her to understand. 'It's a properly exciting job, something relevant, and anyway, I've already said yes.'

There was silence while Dan filled the kettle.

'So,' Jemma lifted their sleeping girl and held her against her shoulder, 'what's it about, then?'

'It's set in the Gulf War. The SAS. Hard men, behaving heroically, or not so heroically at times. I expect there'll be lots of young actors, flexing their muscles. I thought I'd grow a moustache.'

'No women?'

'Just one. I don't know who they've cast yet.' He turned away to pour water into a cup, scalding the tea bag so that it swelled and floated to the top.

Jemma was swaying from side to side, her head turned to stare into Honey's squashed asleep face. 'I'll have a read of it later,' she said softly.

'OK, but I'd better warn you. I get captured, and tortured. And there's . . . ' he sloshed in milk, 'a bit of sex.'

'Really?' Their eyes met. They hadn't managed sex yet since the baby, or, in fact for some long months before, and just saying the word felt fraught. 'Tea?' he offered, realising he'd only made one cup. Jemma nodded quietly.

'So, what . . . ' she began once she'd taken a precarious sip. 'You're beaten and in prison and they smuggle this woman in to you, or how does it work? Or are you having homoerotic sex with the other inmates?'

'No,' Dan laughed. 'I'm having a perfectly straightforward affair, back at base camp, with Sergeant T.P. Miller, and she's the one who sends out the search parties, and then of course there's the reunion . . . ' Dan blushed in spite of himself. 'Read it if you really want,' he shrugged. 'I'll get it for you before I go out.'

'Where are you going?' Her voice rose in alarm.

'To the gym. Where else? And by the way, from today I'm on a diet. Nothing white, and nothing that grows underground.'

'Oh, come on. Fat, puny people have sex as well, you know.'

'Maybe. But not in the SAS. And anyway, what are you saying?'

Jemma laughed. 'Dan, that's the most ridiculous diet I've ever heard of. Not even carrots?'

Dan stared at her supercilious face. 'Not even carrots. Not even radishes. Not even onions.' He felt prepared to fight for his diet to the last.

'What else is there?' She flung open the fridge.

'I don't know.' All he could think of was salami. 'Spinach,' he offered gratefully. 'Lentils. Don't worry, I'll do some shopping on my way home.' Dan grabbed a towel from a pile of washing and stuffed it into his bag. 'Don't worry about it.'

'Can you buy Pampers? Newborn,' she called as he headed for the door, 'or are they too white?' and then a moment later she was in his arms. 'Sweetheart. I'm sorry.' She stretched up, tearful, for a kiss. 'Congratulations. Really. It's great. I'm glad you've got work.'

★　★　★

That afternoon the gym was full of actors, and whereas last week Dan had imagined them watching him, pityingly, his presence there proof that he was unemployed, now he felt euphoric. He nodded to Declan McCloud, who he'd last seen at an audition for a new detective series which neither of them had got, and stepped on to the running machine. 'Why don't you jog round the park?' Jemma had once asked him, but he didn't like jogging round the park. He felt bored by it, and self-conscious, aware of his imperfect technique, whereas on the treadmill, with the music playing and the screens alive, he could slip into a pounding kind of trance. He wondered if Declan had been up for his job. He'd have been perfect for one of the parts. He'd have been perfect for *his* part. He glanced across at Declan now, his neck straining, his biceps bulging as he lifted an inordinately heavy set of weights above his head. He hoped he had, and hadn't got it. Or maybe Declan was already busy. Maybe he'd been offered it, and turned it down. Dan ran faster. Maybe everyone had been offered it. Was that why the producer was so pleased when he said yes? Sweat darkened his T-shirt. He was panting, running for his life, keeping his elbows by his side, his hands like scissors, hareing like James Bond across the tarmac. Stop it, he told himself. It's my job now. And as he readied himself to leap into the open door of a helicopter before it soared away, he had one last flashing thought: now all he had to do was be the best.

★ ★ ★

Alice Montgomery wasn't a name Dan knew. The director had seen her in an independent film and decided she was perfect for the part of Sergeant T.P. Miller. Strong, charismatic, and totally unselfconscious. But Lenny, Dan's agent, had better news than that. He'd heard that the

194

director had a new baby, born around the same time as Honey, and his wife was planning to be out on location for at least some of the shoot.

Dan burst in with the news.

'Born the same day?' Jemma looked amazed, and Dan tried to remember exactly what Lenny had said.

'The same week. The same time. That's good, isn't it? You'll have someone to keep you company.'

'Yes,' Jemma agreed. 'That is good. Look, I've decided. I might as well come out with you and make the best of it. I'm sure their winter isn't actually that cold. And at least we can travel together.'

'Really?' Dan looked at the pages of the script, spread over the kitchen table. 'Are you sure? It'll be pretty barren. The location is doubling as the site of the Gulf War, don't forget.'

'That's not what you were saying this morning.'

'What do you mean?'

'Well, I got the impression you wanted me to buckle down and get on with it. I mean people must live there. Real people. With babies, and nappies, and kettles.'

'No. I just meant, let me go out there first and get settled. Then come out, maybe a couple of weeks later, when I know what I'm doing.'

'And the journey? With bags and a pushchair and Honey.' She picked up a stray page of the script and began to read. 'I mean. Is the flight straight through? Or will I have to change?'

Dan longed to tell her it was straight through.

All she would have to do was get herself on the plane, and he'd be there to meet her at the other end, but he knew she'd have to change, wait for eight hours at Johannesburg airport, and then take a smaller plane west over the mining land to Upington, where she'd arrive twenty-four hours after leaving Britain.

'Look, it's brilliant that you're coming out,' he put his arm around her, 'but let me see if there's a schedule. See what scenes I'll be doing the first week. And then we'll sort out the practicalities. The arrangements for travel and everything. All right?'

Jemma stood stiffly beside him. 'All right.' She knew what he was saying. 'So . . . have they cast everyone yet?'

'Not sure.' He kissed the top of her head.

'Have they cast your Love Interest?'

'Umm,' he moved away to unpack the shopping, 'there's a shortlist, I think. No one I've heard of. Right. Sea bass. Brown rice. Salad. Shall I make supper?'

'OK. But I have to point out, unless you've moved on to a new diet, fish is white.'

Dan unrolled the dense paper packet, releasing the slimy dark grey scales of the fish. 'Not on the outside, it isn't.'

'True. But you're not planning on eating the skin.'

Dan shot her an irritable look. 'It's only for a couple of weeks. As soon as I arrive on set I'll be living on location food with the odd strip of biltong. So let me do this. The trainer at the gym says it works brilliantly.'

'Fine.' Jemma set the table. 'Maybe I'll lose some weight too.' She thumped down a glass, and just in time Dan remembered: 'Don't be silly. You look great. And anyway, Honey's only six weeks old, you're meant to be a little . . . bigger.'

Jemma filled a jug of water. Dan could see her smiling to herself as she put the salt to one side.

'Would you mind,' he said when they were halfway through their meal, 'if I went to a film later? There's something this director thinks I should see, and it's only on for a couple more nights. I thought it might be helpful, you know, get an idea of his style . . . '

Jemma looked over at Honey, a brand-new smile lifting the corner of her sleeping mouth.

'Maybe,' Jemma slid her finger into the curl of their daughter's tiny palm, 'we could all go. She's been so good today. She might sleep through.'

Dan bit his lip. 'We could . . . But I think it's quite a violent film. Vietnam. I'm not sure if her ears could take it.'

'Or mine.'

'Sorry. It's just . . . '

'It's fine.'

'I'll try not to wake you when I get home.' And he turned his full attention to his fish.

★　★　★

The film was actually set in Tuscany, at the house of an English professor, and could have done with some bombs and a few helicopters to liven up the action. He felt uncomfortable about

197

lying, but then it was him who had to show his arse — literally — to millions of people, and he'd never have been able to concentrate with Jemma there.

The girl, Alice, who was to be T.P. Miller, reminded him of a white version of Charlie. She was tall and angular and there was a light in her eyes, sly as a fox. The professor and his son were both in love with her, and she played them, one against the other, with enviable skill. Late one night, after a scene of competitive charades, she peeled off her dress and dived naked into the pool. Her body was lean, an arc in the moonlight, leaving barely a ripple on the surface, and as the two men tore at their own clothes, both struggling to be the first to leap in after her, she clung to the rail at the side of the pool and watched them, her eyes glinting, her mouth curved in an impenetrable smile.

Yes, Dan thought. She's good, she's very good, and he began to play the scenes they were in together over in his head. Alice Montgomery in army fatigues, leaping into jeeps, barking out orders, unfazed as the enemy approached.

Towards the end of the film, the professor's son caught sight of her in the shower, head thrown back, water pouring off her lint-white body. Dan sank deeper in his chair. He alone in that small cinema had a future with her. He, of all the other faceless men in the seats around him, would soon hold that fierce, slippery woman in his arms. He would have to kiss that mouth, stroke her hair back from her face, wrap his arms around her slender body when the trials and strictures of the SAS became too much for her. Yes, he imagined himself in character, for ever in uniform, his body toughened by training and the challenges of war. That's it, he murmured to himself, and for an instant, he knew who he was.

⋆　⋆　⋆

'Right,' he told Jemma the next day, 'I've got the schedule and we're actually going to be in the desert, in a different location for the first two weeks, and then again at the end. It's very remote, we'll be sleeping in tents, apparently, it's where we'll be shooting the combat scenes, but then in the middle we'll be in a small town, and we'll be based in a hotel. I've asked for the biggest room they have,' he didn't stop for questions, 'but I don't know what that really means. And the director's wife will be coming for the middle bit too, so they'll probably get the biggest room, if there is such a thing, and we'll . . . ' he'd done it. 'We'll just have to manage.'

That night they lay in bed, Honey stretched like a starfish between them. Dan put his arm across and felt for Jemma. 'Will you be all right?'

'When?' she asked.

'On your own, here?'

'Yes,' she paused. 'I'm not sure what I'll do for eight hours at Johannesburg airport though,' and Dan squeezed her hand and held it there until she fell asleep.

Dan lay in his bed in the narrow hotel bedroom, the cot already set up in one corner, and fumbled for the off-switch on the alarm. A faint grey light crept in around the edges of the curtains, but outside it was silent. This time tomorrow there would be a little hump of baby in that cot and Jemma, leaky and inquisitive, would be beside him. As if in practice for their arrival he tiptoed to the bathroom, showered with the door shut, and then, still in darkness, pulled on his clothes. He'd have breakfast in the dining tent on set, the smell of rope and canvas and fresh air obliterating the usual fried odour of food, and then, most probably, he'd wait around for several hours before he was used.

It was still dark as they drove towards the outskirts of the town, past the signpost to Namibia, which always made him smile, and out into the desert. The set was an encampment of its own, with trucks and jeeps and army camouflage everywhere you looked. He felt a keen stab of excitement. There was nowhere he'd prefer to be. To be working, to be part of a unit, a cog in the wheel of something exciting and new.

'Bloody freezing today,' the make-up woman, Hilda, shivered. She pulled a hand-knitted shawl over her shoulders. Through the door of the make-up wagon Dan could see the sun rising, the air lifting from the grit of dawn, burning orange as the whole sky lightened.

It was always cold here in the mornings. An ice

breeze that cut through the day, underlying even the brightest sunshine, deceiving you, hardening your skin. If you were lucky you could find a sheltered spot and bask in the bright sunlight, but usually they were out in the open, toiling through barren country, or crawling on their hands and knees over the bare terrain. They hadn't done any of their interiors yet. The capture, the torture and interrogation were all to come. They had filmed one sex scene, though. Outside, at night, against a wall, when T.P. Miller, or Tippy, as he called her in their more intimate moments, had caught up with him, and although his character was meant to be on duty, he'd lost control of himself and seized her in a frenzy, pushing her back, not unwillingly, against the splintered planks of the barrack wall. Alice had asked for a closed set. No extras hovering, no unnecessary assistants, stunt men or runners. But after the eighth take, when he'd grappled her, pulled open her flak jacket and unfastened his belt, those spare sparks who'd declared themselves invaluable wandered off anyway of their own accord. Dan had never been involved in a sex scene before. He'd kissed. On stage and on television, but never had to perform. He didn't mention this to Alice, in awe as he was at the way she had so effortlessly seduced both father and son (and the director too, if gossip was to be believed) in her last film. She'd done it all with such an air of professionalism that it seemed almost as if it wasn't her. But in reality she was jumpy. 'Christ,' she kept saying, 'I hate these scenes,' and he'd smiled manfully and tried to keep himself calm.

'Right,' the director approached them. 'Take her in your arms, move in against her, hand under her shirt. And thrust.'

Thrust? He pressed his body against Alice. She felt cold, her flesh retreating. Nervously he fumbled with her jacket. It wasn't so easy. Not the fluid movement of desire he had imagined. 'Faster. Right. Great. We'll go for a take this time.'

Alice's make-up woman dashed forward and dusted her with a coat of powder, while Hilda gave a quick tweak to Dan's moustache.

'Ready. Quiet on set.' Dan felt his heart thumping. He swallowed, tried to put the terrible thought of an erection out of his mind, although never in his life had he felt less aroused. But then the lights needed adjusting, and in a burst of sudden noise and movement everything came to a halt. 'Are you all right?' he whispered to Alice, the cold feel of her skin still lingering. Alice nodded, and took out a can of breath spray. She squirted some into her mouth. 'Bloody hotel,' she whispered as she offered it to him. 'I tried to sleep this afternoon but there was a fucking baby crying.'

Dan made a sympathetic face. Did Alice know it was the director's baby? His wife had arrived a couple of days before and he'd seen her, hovering on the edge of the set, the baby in a pink bonnet against the sun, a dummy in its mouth to keep it quiet. Twice she'd approached him and asked when Jemma would be arriving, and he'd admired her baby, asked how old it was, what it was called, information he'd immediately forgotten and then failed to pass to Jemma in adequate detail in his calls home. 'Honestly,' Alice shivered, 'I can't wait for this job to be over. Bloody awful goddamn place. What are you up to next?'

'Not sure.' Dan looked around. He wanted to use this lull to make a plan. Strike up a deal with her. Should I grab your breast under the jacket? When we kiss, will we use tongues? But Alice kept on talking. 'I'm going to fly from here straight to LA to try out for pilot season. Have you ever tried it? I mean, LA?'

Dan shook his head. He'd heard too many stories of British actors lost out there in a sea of castings, demoralised, desperate, working as doormen, scrabbling together the money to survive. 'Great,' he smiled. 'Good luck. Have you got somewhere to stay?'

'OK. Ready to go. Silence.' The assistant director spread his arms and Alice's make-up woman was between them again, dusting and preening in the gloom.

'And . . . Action!' For a second Dan's eyes met Alice's and he moved in for a kiss. He held her head and pressed her backwards, the new moustache tickling his own nose, the spearmint flavour of their saliva mingling together as he fumbled with her jacket. Belt, he remembered, belt. He had his mouth still glued to hers, as he tugged at the belt, almost ripping the buckle off in his need to free himself and get through all the moves before the director called 'Cut'.

'And cut.' Gasping, Dan pulled away.

'Bloody hell,' Alice put a hand up to her face. 'When did you last shave?'

'This morning.' Dan hoiked his trousers up and re-fastened the buckle.

The make-up woman was patting the skin around Alice's mouth, blotting it with foundation. Dan put his hand up to his own face. His chin did feel rough. Of course. He should have waited and shaved this afternoon. Idiot — he cursed himself. But before he could apologise the set fell silent.

By the time they next broke Alice's poor face was blotched with red.

'What does your girlfriend say about that moustache?' She eyed him sceptically.

All he could remember was Jemma laughing as the sharp hairs tickled her face.

'I could never go out with a man with facial hair. Really.' Alice rolled her eyes. 'I'd have to give up my career.'

They broke for supper, although now it was one in the morning, and after a quick dash to his caravan to brush his teeth, Dan prepared himself to film the scene from T.P. Miller's point of view. The cameras were behind him now and Alice's eyes were lively in the light. Her hand went up and caressed his cheek, her leg slid between his and he realised momentarily before he was subsumed by his tasks how much easier everything was now that she was responding. Kiss, jacket, fumble. Her flesh was warm and willing. She even smiled as he jolted her up against the wall. He tugged at his belt buckle, 'Thrust', he heard the director in his ear, and aware of the camera, trained on his backside, he lifted Alice off the ground and holding her tight he moved in, grinding against her narrow camouflaged pelvis, eyes closed, panting, waiting for that most magical of words, 'Cut.'

Alice pulled away from him. 'Good work.' Her gaze was steady.

'Great,' the director called. 'Five minutes and we'll go again.'

★　★　★

'Did you get an erection?' Jemma wanted to know, and he told her in all honesty that it was the un-sexiest night of his life. 'I can't wait to see you,' her words soothed him down the line, 'I wish I was there,' and he closed his eyes and imagined her warm, yielding body, the smell of her, the fine gold chain that creased into her skin as she slept. 'Oh Jem,' he could have cried for something that was real. 'I wish you were here too.'

★　★　★

'So when's your family coming out?' Hilda asked him. She was still working on his scar.

'Today.' Dan looked at his watch. 'They'll be here about seven. They're flying now.'

'You've got a baby.' Hilda smiled, indulgent. 'How old?'

'She's . . . I think about twelve weeks now. All I know is that I've been away for a third of her life.'

'Wait till they get bigger.' Hilda shook her head. 'That's when travelling gets really tough.'

'Have you got kids?' He looked at the make-up woman with new eyes. Friendly, middle-aged Hilda, always ready for a chat.

'I've got a boy of twelve. It's bad timing for him, this job. I'm away his entire summer holiday. But I had to take it. A big film I was meant to do earlier in the year fell apart.'

'What happened?'

'Some of the investment disappeared, and the studio let it go. They'd already spent half a million on pre-production. It's beyond belief. And it would have been so perfect. All in London. Anyway . . . ' she shrugged, 'I'm doing this.'

'So who's he with?'

'My sister. And a few weeks on one of those Woodcraft camps. He'll be all right. He's a good boy.'

Dan nodded. He wondered where the boy's father was, but he didn't like to ask. Jemma would have asked. She would have opened her blue eyes in compassionate inquisition and found out everything there was to know. He smiled. By this time next week he'd be privy to the most intimate secrets of the entire cast and crew.

'Right,' Hilda straightened up. 'That's you done.'

'Thanks. See you later.' He moved along the trailer to where Pam from Hair was waiting to check his moustache against a batch of Polaroids to see if it had grown.

★ ★ ★

That morning involved relentless hours of surveillance. Dan and two soldiers stood with binoculars, looking out over the glaring sand. The other actors had been out drinking the night before and the alcohol wafted off them poisonously. They talked between takes about a feud building up between the British and South African actors, about a local girl, Chantelle, who was throwing herself at Steve, who played an officer. In lowered tones they discussed Matt Wilkinson, who was up at five every morning, lifting weights, doing press-ups, and when he had to make an entrance, he insisted on running twice around the perimeter of the set so that he could arrive genuinely out of breath. 'Drama Arts,' one of the soldiers scoffed, and Dan secretly worried that Matt, who'd been two years below him at college, would transpire to be the real star. Matt had remained loyal to Patrick and Silvio's teachings, and when Dan watched him he could see the spark of genius — or was it madness? — in everything he did. There'd been one scene where he and Dan had had to fight, and as they'd wrestled, Dan had looked into his eyes and seen nothing there but hate. 'Pervert,' Matt had hissed once he'd pummelled Dan's character unconscious to the ground, and eyes closed, breath still, Dan had felt a gob of spit land on his cheek. A searing heat rose up in him. 'You fucking moron,' he'd leapt up, cursing himself for accepting the more passive role, and he'd grabbed hold of Matt Wilkinson's shirt and

207

punched him in the ear. Matt responded no less viciously, in or out of character, Dan never knew, and they'd grappled and thrashed, and thrown punches at each other until three members of the crew had had to wrench them apart. They'd avoided each other since then, much as their characters were inclined to do, and the night before when things began to get raucous, Dan had slipped off back to the hotel. It wasn't just Matt, Dan told himself, he didn't want to risk being hung over the day Jemma arrived, and he imagined her now, getting off her plane in Johannesburg, Honey up against her shoulder, the pushchair folded into mechanical knots. His heart tightened. He hoped they'd be all right. He glanced at his watch to see how long it would be before he could get back to the trailer to check his mobile phone in the unlikely event that she would have called. He'd only bought a mobile a few months before in case Jemma went into labour when he wasn't there. But now he couldn't imagine how he'd managed without one. No more dashing in to check the answerphone, no more calling his agent at the end of every day. It was a liberation and he loved it. But Jemma was against one, for herself. We can't afford it, she insisted, and anyway she wanted to be left alone, to work on her Russian coursework — she was in the second year of a degree. 'And who would call me anyway?' she challenged. 'I don't have an agent, remember?'

'I would,' he told her.

'Sure. Call me at home. I'm usually there.'

But when Dan did get back to the trailer just

before lunch, to his surprise there was a message. She must have negotiated the myriad complexities of a foreign phone box, changed money, found the right coins.

'Hi darling. We landed. All fine. I'm at . . . ' there was a pause while she turned to talk to someone, 'I'm somewhere in Johannesburg, on the outskirts. Don't worry. I met this nice man on the plane and he said we could spend the day with him. I was just so tired. I had to find somewhere to lie down. He's going to drive me back to the airport later when I've had a sleep. Don't worry.' There was a small muffled shriek from Honey. 'I'd better go. See you later. Bye love. Oh dear.' There seemed to be some kind of scuffle. 'Bye.'

Dan's heart beat so hard he had to double over.

He flicked to missed calls to trace the number but it hadn't registered. No number, it said. He pressed it anyway, hoping that it might connect, but the line was dead. Fuck. He stared at the phone. He felt like throwing it down and stamping on it. It was only twelve o'clock and he'd have to wait another seven hours to know if they were ever going to arrive. He replayed her message. 'Hi darling . . . All fine. I'm at . . . Somewhere in Johannesburg. On the outskirts . . . ' What was she thinking? Going off into one of the most violent cities in the world, with a *nice* man. He sat down on the floor. Kidnappings. Car chases. Honey's neck jolting dangerously as Jemma fled down an empty road.

'You all right?' It was the runner, come to

fetch him for his next scene.

'Sure.' Dan smiled grimly. He'd forgotten, momentarily, they were about to do the stunt. At least he had no lines. He splashed his face with cold water and then remembered makeup and stared into the mirror. The water ran off the greased surface of his skin, dampening his collar, distracting him, if briefly, from thoughts of Jemma.

Dan had offered to do his own stunt. 'Are you sure?' the director asked him, and Dan insisted he knew what he was doing. They'd done a fight workshop at Drama Arts in their second year: flinching away from the point of contact, working with your partner to make the moves convincing, rolling and reacting as the boot went in. He remembered Pierre's thin arm shooting out and catching Eshkol on the nose. There had been blood and foundation and some hysteria, and the fight teacher who'd been drafted in for the day had stood back amused as girls ran to and from the toilets with tissues.

Dan mimicked what the stunt man had done in rehearsal, standing on the flatbed of the lorry, jumping forward, twisting, landing on his back, while three extras moved in for the attack, kicking the ground around his body, their boots stopping just short of his groin. 'Great.' The director nodded, and Dan stood up, and waited while wardrobe, hair and make-up dusted him down. 'We'll go for a take.' The cameras rolled, the truck started and Dan leapt to the ground. But this time there was no holding back. The first man got him in the stomach. Bloody hell,

Dan was too winded to protest, and anyway he was down now, his face in the dirt, and the kicks were coming at him quick and sharp. Fuck! A boot caught him in the arse, and another, sharp across his shin, but he didn't dare raise his head to call for help. 'All right, boys. Cut. I said CUT.' A murmur of chatter broke out around him. 'You all right?' Someone was bending down.

'Yeah, sure.' He tried not to wince as he stood up. 'I think so, anyway.' He looked over at the men, smirking as they leant against the truck.

'It's the stunt man,' Steve said, as Dan examined his wounds. 'He's pissed off because you took his job. Now he won't be paid his rate.'

'What?' Dan shifted his weight. 'Someone could have warned me.' His coccyx was bruised and it was painful to walk. 'Bastards,' he muttered, and he checked his phone again. Jemma would be on the plane soon, if she was getting on it, if she wasn't someone's prisoner, if she wasn't . . . He closed his eyes and mumbled a prayer. Please, he directed his thoughts towards the harsh blue cloudless sky, beyond which he hoped a white-bearded God was listening. Please let them be all right. Look after my baby, and I promise . . . what would he promise? That he'd never take another job away from home? That he'd . . .

'Dan?' It was a woman's voice. Dan snapped open his eyes. 'Sorry to interrupt but I just wanted to let you know, it's fine to take the Land Rover if you want to pick Jemma up from the airport yourself.' It was the director's wife and she had her baby in a pushchair. 'Here are the

211

keys,' she dangled them for him, 'and tell her, well, I'm just along the corridor from you, so I'm sure we'll meet.'

Dan nearly put his arms around her. 'Thanks so much.' He took the keys. 'I can't believe . . . I mean . . . it's hard to imagine them actually arriving. You know what I mean?'

'I know,' she laughed. She bent down to adjust her baby's bonnet. It was white today with an embroidered trim. 'Sometimes I can't really believe we're here.'

She pointed across the tented city. 'The car's over there. The green one. I put a baby seat in the back. See it?'

'Yes.' Dan thanked her again. He'd have liked to have stayed talking but he couldn't think of anything else to say. He couldn't tell her about the phone call. Didn't dare see her reaction in case it was bad. 'What?' Her eyes might fly open, and his bruised body would turn to jelly and his hands, already trembling, would begin to shake.

★   ★   ★

The car jumped forward when he turned the ignition. Some idiot had left it in gear. He tried to breathe, steering the four-wheel drive slowly past the maze of other vehicles, tanks and props and trailers. Eventually he was out through the gates and on to the dirt track that turned to tarmac and led onwards to the airport. It was half past six and the town was already closed. The shops, which seemed mostly to sell furniture, cheap wardrobes and three-piece suites, were all shut up. There was nowhere to buy clothes, or food, that he could see, and only three places to eat. A glass-and-steel coffee shop that sold fizzy drinks and waffles, a dingy pizza place where he'd waited an hour once while they defrosted some fish, and one smart restaurant where every dish came with a 'panache' of vegetables and a 'drizzle' of extra virgin olive oil, and even the bread was baked with paprika and garlic. Maybe he'd take Jemma there, and they could laugh over the menu. Maybe . . . There were very few cars on the road. He was still in his uniform. He hadn't had time to change, but it felt good to drive without a camera trained on him. Maybe he and Jemma could hire a car one Sunday and set off on a trip. They could get a baby seat of their own and head out across the desert. Dan turned off the road and pulled up in the car park. There were a few other cars already there and a scattering of people waiting in the oblong building. The runway stretched before them and he remembered how surprised he'd been four weeks before, getting off his plane and finding the mini-van that was there to collect him parked just yards away. He breathed in the sharp air. Dust and cold and space. Africa. He could feel the vastness of the continent stretching away on every side. A speck appeared in the distance. Everyone tensed, squinting, shading their eyes as it turned into a plane. Soon the roar of its engines could be heard as it rattled through the sky. Its wheels were out, its nose pointed earthward, and for a moment the plane seemed to be racing towards them, suicidal, as they stood huddled together at the glass. But just in time it landed, screaming as it hit the ground.

Dan forgot about his bruised leg, the possible cracked rib, the ache in his coccyx as he rushed out on to the runway. The staircase was attached, the door was opening, and the passengers began to appear. Three African businessmen, a big raw Boer, a family with teenage children and then Jemma, Honey in a sling, her eyes fixed on the metal steps as she climbed down.

Dan stood where he was. He saw her look around, take in the dome of the darkening sky, the low arrivals hall, their bags already being unloaded onto the ground. He took a step forward, but she didn't recognise him. 'Jem,' he called, and he saw her start, and imagined for a moment what she must be seeing. A soldier in brown camouflage, his face smeared with real and fake blood, the edges of his moustache hanging down like a bedraggled moon. 'Dan?' And she was in his arms.

'You're all right,' he held her. 'Thank God, you're all right.'

'But you . . . ' she put a hand up to his face. 'What happened? What happened to you?'

'Shhhh.' He kept her close, their baby's warm, padded body between them, and they stood there on the tarmac as the last of the passengers trailed by.

Slow in Summer

Charlie stood in front of the bathroom mirror and examined her face. 'Oh God,' she murmured, peering closer, but there was no denying it, there they were. Three spots pushing up under her usually smooth skin. One on her chin, one on her jawbone and worst of all, one in the middle of her cheek.

'Why, why, why,' she howled, but quietly, because she didn't want to wake Ian, the lodger, who might stumble out of his room and witness her humiliation.

She leant into the mirror again and, knowing she shouldn't, she attacked the biggest spot, squeezing it hard, rubbing it, and then when it only darkened and grew larger she changed her tactics and doused it with cold water. The others she stared at, turning her face right and left to catch the light, frowning, smiling, pouting, but whichever way she looked, they were still there. 'Fuck!' She felt like sobbing, but instead she took a deep breath and began applying foundation. She added mascara, lipstick, and then taking a wad of tissue, she smudged the lipstick off again. Shit. She stared at herself coldly; it's only six in the morning, and anyway, once she reached the film set, Lauren, the make-up woman, would scrape back her hair, wipe her face clean and reveal the truth.

215

'It's nothing to worry about,' Lauren said dutifully. 'I hardly even know what you're talking about.' She peered into the mirror at Charlie, already in costume as Melina, a girl from the South Sea Islands, brought into the country as a slave, but now, through her own ingenuity and astounding beauty, the wife of a country squire.

'I just don't understand it.' Charlie felt despairing. 'I've always had good skin. Why this, now?'

Lauren swivelled her round so that she could stare with professional scrutiny into her face. 'Little outbreaks like yours,' she conceded, 'they're not at all uncommon. Acne can be caused by any number of things. Food allergy. A change in cosmetics. Genetics. Stress.'

Charlie shrank away from the word 'acne'. Honestly. She only had three spots! 'I don't know,' she hesitated. 'I guess I am quite stressed about this part, I still don't really know who Melina is.' But then a new job was always stressful. Not that the alternative of no job was any better. The best moment in an actor's life, Rob had once told her, was the day the work was offered. After that it was all downhill.

'The good news . . . ' Lauren was still squinting at her, 'is no one will ever know. You wouldn't believe the repair jobs we have to do on some people, really, some of the problems we see.' And as she worked, smoothing and moulding, fluffing and patting, she lowered her voice to tell Charlie about rashes, cold sores, spots and boils on the most celebrated faces.

With every new story Charlie felt increasingly alarmed. *And you'll never guess what I spent all morning doing* . . . she could imagine Lauren whispering to whoever took her place in the make-up wagon next . . . *covering up Charlie Adedayo-Martin's appalling break-out. Like the surface of the moon, it was* . . .

'There, my beauty,' Lauren patted her. 'All done.' And Charlie thanked her dolefully and moved along three seats to where Jilly was ready with her wig.

★ ★ ★

Later, her auburn hair wound into a loose bun, Charlie picked up her long skirts and stepped through the early morning sunshine to her caravan. As she pulled open the door she held her breath against the smell of the bright blue disinfectant they used to douse the toilet, which permeated every synthetic fibre of the built-in furniture. The caravan was large — a sitting room with a pull-down double bed, a kitchenette, a loo and separate shower — and as a sign of her elevated status, it was just for her. *I'd have happily lived here a few years ago,* she muttered when she was first shown round, although it wasn't long before she noticed it was smaller than her co-star's caravan — Ben Trevelyn, who, although he had half her lines, was being paid roughly twice as much.

Charlie slammed the door shut and looked at herself in the full-length mirror. Not just at her face but at the line of her body in her pleated skirt and waisted shirt and the hair pulled softly up to show off her neck. 'He'll just have to film me in long shot today,' she shrugged, remembering the director's appreciative glances, and she shouted, 'Come in!' to Matty, the runner, who was knocking on her door with a polystyrene cup of coffee and a bacon roll.

★   ★   ★

'Cut!' It was early afternoon and the director and the lighting cameraman were in conference, heads bent together, gesticulating, concerned.

What's the problem? she wanted to ask Lauren, who had run forward, a finger ready with a dab of concealer, but she couldn't bring herself to say it. She already knew ... The problem was her. Eventually they started up again and shot the same scene from another perspective. 'Get as much cover as you can,' she heard the director hiss, and then, an hour earlier than expected, she was told she wouldn't be needed any more that day. They were going to get some landscape shots while it was still so bright.

'You all right, sweetie?' The director approached. 'You don't seem very focused today. Big scene tomorrow, though.' He patted her arm. 'OK?'

'OK,' Charlie said cheerily, 'see you all in the morning,' but she felt her stomach lurch.

On the way home she sat silent in the back of the car, warding off conversation with her driver — every detail of whose life she already knew

218

— by pretending to sleep. But she wasn't sleeping. Her eyes were open, just a fraction, enough to see the men and women on the streets, at bus stops, in cars, pushing babies, all of them, although they didn't need it — didn't even care — with perfect, unblemished skin.

★ ★ ★

When Charlie arrived home, her lodger, Ian, was in the kitchen, making himself a nut roast. Two weeks before he'd been offered an advert, and now he was on a diet. Having never dieted before and knowing nothing of the myriad choices available to dieters, he'd simply opted to miss out lunch and buy a three-week supply of instant nut roasts from the health food shop under the bridge. He'd given Charlie the impression that he'd been asked to diet, that the producer of the commercial (a woman) had told him that he'd be expected to walk bare-chested along an Algarve beach, and even though the advert was for a sickeningly sweet breakfast cereal, she still hoped to see him svelte and defined in his trunks.

Charlie watched him pour boiling water into the mixture and turned away to avoid the smell, but however disgusted she was with this repetitive meal and Ian's dogged observation of it, she couldn't help but admit that it was working. When she'd rented him the room, only a month before, he'd been a heavy-set, unexciting man in jeans and a sweatshirt, a lodger she thought she could safely rely on for a weekly influx of cash without being in any way distracted, but now, with his jeans hanging a little more loosely, his faded T-shirt flat against his stomach, she found herself uncomfortably aware of him.

'Hi,' she said, coolly, tugging at her hair in an attempt to hide the already hidden spots. 'How's it going?'

'Fine.' Ian slid the foil baking tin into the oven. 'Beautiful day today.'

'Yes,' Charlie nodded. She'd spent most of it in the drawing room of a country house near Watford, attempting to avoid the shafts of light that fell through the half-drawn curtains, arguing archly with an admirer who was imploring her to run away with him. For every one of her tart replies he became more genuine, more passionate and desperate, offering his heart to her, his very soul, if she would only consider him, so that it seemed by the end of the scene that they were speaking two different languages, were standing on either side of a wide, intricately carpeted divide.

Ian checked his watch. Charlie knew from the night before, and the night before that, that his nut roast would take fifty minutes. Fifty minutes! She was irritated and impressed by his organisation. If she was hungry, she'd pull something out of the fridge right there and then, and if she wasn't, she probably wouldn't bother to eat at all. And what if someone called and invited her out at the last minute? All that planning, and chopping. It was hardly worth the bother.

'Oh, I forgot . . . ' Ian frowned, his hand already on the door. 'A man called for you . . . Rob, I think it was.'

'Thanks,' she yawned, but as soon as he'd retreated up the stairs she picked up the phone. 'You rang?' she said, imperious.

'I did indeed.' Rob's voice was low and teasing. 'I'm coming into town tonight, wondered if you fancied a drink?'

Charlie hesitated. A drink meant many drinks. His hand on her arm, a tussle on the pavement while she tried to resist his kisses and then, giving in, a thrilling, thrashing film-star fuck up against the wall of the hall with the door slammed hard behind them.

'Do you know what?' Charlie caught a glimpse of herself in the mirror. 'I can't tonight. Filming at the crack of dawn. Sorry.' She yawned to show how tired she was. 'Another time maybe?'

'Baby . . . ' Rob said enticingly. 'Just one small drink?'

'Sorry. No.' She held fast, savouring her power.

'Hmmm.' Rob paused. 'So what's the story? Got someone new?'

Charlie gasped in mock outrage. 'I'm tired, that's all. And I've got lines to learn. Some of us take our careers seriously.'

'It's that new lodger, isn't it? I expect he's cooking for you right now, while you take a bath and slip into something comfortable.'

'Hardly. He's only got one thing on his mind and that's an advert for Munchy Mix.'

'Tasty.' Rob laughed. But her cruelty had

221

infected her and she asked coolly after his latest girlfriend, a regional theatre director with a ten-year-old child, the last in a long line to have lured Rob away.

'OK, OK,' he said huffily. I just wanted to catch up, that's all. Another time. Sweet dreams.' And he put down the phone.

★ ★ ★

Charlie lay in the bath and worried about Melina. She knew she could write a back story for her, dissect her actions, imagine for herself every intimate detail of her life, but she'd always claimed to despise such methods. 'Have you never heard of Acting?' she liked to quote Laurence Olivier, with whom no one was inclined to argue, and she'd looked on scornfully as her fellow students sat ensconced in their research. But Melina was tricky. She was so hard, so relentlessly cold. If I was her, she thought, I'd have run off with the gorgeous Colonel by now. Or at least abandoned myself to him behind the topiary, and then, although she'd promised herself she wouldn't, she began thinking about Rob. The magnets in the pads of his fingers, the electric current that shocked her each time they touched.

Fuck it, she decided, I'll call him back. So what if I look hideous? We'll go somewhere dark. And she leapt out of the bath, and grabbing a towel, she flung open the door just as Ian appeared on the landing. 'I'm sorry,' he stammered, his eyes widening, his neck flushing deep red, and shaking her head, Charlie retreated into the bathroom. 'Bollocks,' she said, although she was grateful too for being saved, and she splashed back into the water, where she lay, her long brown body submerged, the smell of nut roast, nauseating, drifting in under the door.

★   ★   ★

The next morning her skin was worse. There was a fourth spot, and a raised ridge of tiny white pimples in the crease of her chin. She peered at herself in disgust.

'What am I going to do?' she said to Lauren, silently beseeching her to say that it was nothing — but Lauren took her face in her hands. 'I suppose you could see a doctor.' She was sombre. 'Get some antibiotics or topical lotion of some sort.' She began to mix a mud paste of foundation. 'Before it gets any worse.'

All afternoon they worked on an exterior shot of the garden. Melina bending gracefully in long shot to gather armfuls of white flowers, meandering between the box hedges, sniffing the occasional rose. But as she neared the camera her self-consciousness rose up and strangled her, and twice, just the thought of her lumpy face swimming into focus made her stumble, and they had to start again. 'Cut!' The director was flustered. 'I've told you, no emotion! No one should know you care.'

★   ★   ★

As soon as she was safely in the car Charlie scrolled through her list of contacts. 'Nelly?' she managed, turning away from the driver. 'It's me. Something . . . ' and then, unable to control herself a second longer, she began to cry.

'Oh my God.' Nell was alarmed. 'Sweetheart, darling, what is it?'

'It's . . . umm . . . it . . . it's . . . ' but she couldn't get a hold of herself. 'I've got . . . oh it's so terrible . . . ' Her tears turned to painful rasping sobs. 'I've got spots!' Now she'd said it she was laughing. Sobbing and laughing, and wiping her nose.

'You what?' Nell, relieved, was laughing too. 'I thought someone had died!'

'They have. Me. And the new spotty Charlie Adedayo-Martin has been reborn.' Charlie sniffed and without looking up, took the box of tissues offered by the driver.

'Sweetheart,' Nell soothed. 'Honestly. Do you want me to come over?'

'Would you?' Charlie felt her eyes well up again. 'I'll be home in forty minutes. I'm warning you I look horrific.'

'Likely story,' Nell snorted, and she promised to be there by seven.

★ ★ ★

Ian was sitting at the table eating his nut roast when Nell arrived. 'Hi,' he looked up, still chewing, when Charlie introduced them. Nell had brought a bottle of wine and Charlie set about opening it. 'Do you want a glass?' She turned to

224

Ian, but he shook his head, and pointed to his tumbler of water. 'Nothing impure shall pass my lips.'

Charlie carried the bottle through to the sitting room and Nell followed with an ashtray and two glasses. She pushed the door shut behind them and they grimaced at each other. 'Where did *he* come from?'

'Some friend of a friend of Dan's. He's here to help pay the mortgage.'

Charlie poured the wine and went and peered at herself in the expensive gilt mirror above the fireplace. 'See?' she turned to Nell. 'Look what's happened to me.'

Nell came closer, creasing her forehead and screwing up her eyes as if she'd have to search for years before finding anything. But even though Charlie knew she was pretending, she was grateful all the same. 'Well, I do see a few small . . . blemishes.' Charlie's heart sank. If even Nell was prepared to admit she looked like a monster, then what hope was there? She wished she hadn't rung her. She wished she hadn't come. 'But I promise you,' Nell carried on, 'unless I was this close, staring at you, searching for something wrong, I'd never notice. Truly.'

'Really?' Charlie loved her again. 'It's so strange, for the first time in my life I don't want anyone to look at me. And this job doesn't help. I'm meant to be a flawless beauty. Able to transcend impossible social barriers by the sheer irresistible gorgeousness of my looks. Yesterday they shot my whole scene from the point of view

225

of the servant. All anyone will see is the back of my head.'

Nell laughed. 'I don't believe you.' And Charlie, her hand up to her face, feeling for the little bumps along her jawline, agreed it wasn't entirely true.

★ ★ ★

Charlie and Nell curled up at either end of the sofa.

'So how are *you*?' Charlie remembered to ask.

'Not bad.' Nell poured herself more wine. 'You know we're taking *Two Lobsters and a Prawn* to Edinburgh. To the festival.'

'That's great.'

'We've got these brilliant posters. Me and Sita with our guns, and once we're there we're going to go out flyposting. There won't be a person north of the border who doesn't know our show is on.'

Charlie had never seen Nell so happy. 'Maybe I'll come up and see it, if I get a few days off.'

'Yes, that would be great. But the place we're staying . . . ' Nell looked worried. 'It's a friend of Hettie's and she said if we didn't mind we could kip down in the kitchen . . . '

Charlie laughed. 'I'll stay in a hotel. But I'm not sure anyway. I don't have my schedule yet. I may not have time.'

'If you can . . . ' Nell drained the last of her wine. 'Bloody hell, this bottle's finished already! Shall I run out and get some more?'

'No. I'll go. Stay right here.' Charlie snatched

226

up her bag and ran down the stairs to the front door. As she stepped out on to the street she came face to face with the man who paced daily back and forth, shouting and cursing, his eyes darting sideways as if it may not have been him. Sometimes it seemed that Charlie never opened her door without confronting him, his stick raised, his mouth open in a roar. She waited a moment until he was ahead of her and then darted across the road, round the corner and past the chip shop to the off-licence. She chose a chilled bottle of white and waited while the man in front bought three cases of lager.

'All right,' he winked at her as he stacked them into his arms and she smiled her most unfriendly smile.

★ ★ ★

'Ian's got a crush on you,' Nell whispered delightedly once they were back on the sofa.

'Don't be ridiculous,' Charlie shook her head — she'd found them chatting together in the kitchen — but all the same she went and looked at herself in the mirror. Her cheeks were flushed from the wine, and the spots had darkened to maroon points under the concealer. They felt itchy and sore. 'What makes you say that?'

Nell looked at her. 'Just the usual signs. Blushing. Stammering. An inability to stop mentioning your name . . .'

Charlie flung herself back down. 'He's all right. Just one more insecure actor, that's all.'

'You know what's happened to me?' Nell's

eyes were sparkling.

'No? What?'

'I've met someone.'

'You're joking. Why didn't you say? Who is he?'

'He's . . . well, the really amazing news is . . . he's *not* an actor.'

'My God . . . there are such people!?'

Nell was excited. She knelt up on the sofa. 'I did this thing. I read about it. I made a wish list. Apparently if you write down everything you want and put it in a drawer, it all comes true. So at the top I put 'A Boyfriend — But No Actors'.'

'What else?'

'A job. A flat of my own. With a view.' She looked round wistfully at Charlie's large sitting room which she'd helped paint in a ragged distressed yellow. 'Children. Umm. What else. A waist . . . smaller tits.' She was laughing. 'Anyway, three days later, literally, I went to see a play at the Finborough Theatre. You know Samantha was in *The Maids*, again. And I got talking to this guy.'

'And did you warn him?'

'What? That I'd sworn off actors. No. Well, not until I found out he was a stage manager.'

'What's he like?'

'Well.' Nell went dreamy. 'He's good at moving furniture around.'

Charlie kicked her.

'No, he's lovely. He's about 5.10, curly hair . . . Green eyes.'

'Sounds like Dan.' Nell kicked her back. 'I hope he appreciates you, that's all.' Charlie was

228

already prepared to hate him. She wouldn't admit it but it suited her when Nell was single. 'So, not a hopeless loser like all the others?'

'You can talk!'

'True,' Charlie agreed and she reached for the wine.

'I'm starving now,' Nell said hopefully. 'Do you have anything in?'

'Sorry.' Charlie shook her head. There was nothing in the house except fifteen boxes of nut roast mix and they weren't even hers.

'You don't look after yourself,' Nell told her.

Charlie put a hand to her face. 'Maybe it's all the location food. It is particularly disgusting this time.'

'You know, there's a brilliant Chinese doctor round the corner from here. He cured a friend of my sister's who had eczema. I'll get you the number. Or a nutritionist. Or maybe you should see one of those homeopaths that tell you about your allergies.'

'Yes,' Charlie sounded unconvinced.

'Well, if I'm going to get the bus . . . ' Nell looked round for her bag, 'I should get going.'

'So where's the gorgeous stage manager tonight then?' Charlie asked as she hugged her goodbye.

'On tour. I'm going to stop on the way to Edinburgh and see him.'

'Have fun.'

'I'll ring you with those numbers. As soon as I get them.'

'Thank you. And thanks for coming round.'

'Bye.' Nell trotted down the stairs, her lovely

homely body swaying with wine and the knowledge she was useful.

'Bye,' Charlie waved. 'Bye.' And she was gone.

* * *

Charlie was woken by the bell. Who could that be? Today was her day off, and no one visited at ten in the morning. She waited, hoping Ian might rise from the cave of his room and answer it, but assuming, rightly, that no one ever called for him, he didn't stir. The bell rang again. Sharp and insistent.

Charlie wrapped herself in a long wool cardigan and went downstairs. Two smart, black Jehovah's Witnesses stood on the doorstep. 'Hello,' they beamed, and the man's aftershave hit her like a wave. 'Do you believe in God?' He spoke in a strong West Indian accent.

'No,' Charlie told him.

The man rebounded. 'NO?' He looked aghast, although he must have heard the word a thousand times. 'Did you ever believe in God?'

'No,' she lied. There had been a time, she supposed, but her Catholic boarding school had put an end to that.

'What do you believe in, then?' The man moved closer.

Charlie looked from his gleaming face to the woman's, a little more reserved, her eyes already retreating. 'What do I believe in?' Charlie put her head on one side. 'I believe in . . . ' She knew she didn't actually have to answer. 'I suppose I believe in myself.'

The man widened his eyes, the woman pursed her lips.

'I believe,' Charlie continued, 'in people being big enough to say sorry. I believe in . . . hope.'

The man shook his head as if that was the wrong answer, but the woman looked interested. She rummaged around in her bag. 'We believe in hope too,' she said, 'and one day there will be the end to our hoping when good will conquer evil, and we will be rewarded.' She held out some photocopied pages with several lines underscored.

'No thanks.' Charlie shook her head.

'There will be an almighty battle. A heavenly war. Only the good will prevail.'

'But where will this war happen?' Charlie looked round to check no one was listening. 'In heaven?'

'No,' the man boomed. 'Here on earth. And then peace will reign.'

'But you can't have a war without guns and bombs and people dying, and that's why I don't want anything to do with God.'

The woman looked genuinely shocked. 'But there will be angels . . . '

'So what happens when someone sets off a bomb? What about all those people in Omagh, the woman pregnant with twins, out shopping with her mother? Were there angels there then?' Charlie began closing the door.

'If God created the earth,' the man tried a last different tack, 'then there's hope, and if he didn't . . . what is there to hope for?'

'Sorry,' Charlie said, diminishing him to a slice.

'Think on that,' he called.

'I will,' she called back, and she went upstairs and watched them from the sitting room window, scouring the houses, wondering which bell to try next.

Ian was in the kitchen making tea. 'Who was that?' he asked and Charlie laughed, more at herself than them, as she repeated the conversation. 'Tea?' he offered, and Charlie sat down.

'So when do you start this advert?' It was rare, she realised, that she asked him a question.

'The week after next. I'll be gone for five days.'

'And then?'

'Nothing then.' Ian wilted. 'My agent says it's a slow time. Slow in summer. But I haven't worked since January. Slow in winter. Slow in spring.' He laughed wryly. 'Actually I'm thinking of packing it in.'

'No!'

'And retraining.'

'Retraining as what?'

'A lawyer.'

Charlie was amazed. 'How long will you give it?'

'Not sure. One more year.'

'I don't know what I'd do if I stopped acting.' She felt a chill of alarm run through her. 'I don't think there's anything else I could do.'

'But you're a success,' Ian gazed at her. 'You won't need to. What was that film I saw you in? *The Haven Report.* And *Celestina.* You were brilliant.'

232

Charlie blushed. 'Hardly.' But she felt a glow of pleasure all the same.

'And *Giant Small Steps*. That was the best thing I've seen on TV in years. Have you got anything lined up, after this film you're doing now, I mean?'

'Not really,' Charlie shook her head. 'I've been offered a tour. Rosalind in *As You Like It*, but I don't know if I can face it. All those dreary northern towns in winter.' Too late she remembered Ian was from Birkenhead. 'And anyway, I don't know if the production is *themed*. Once I was offered Juliet at the RSC and I arrived to find that the Capulets were all of African descent and we were expected to be half-naked, playing the bongos at every opportunity, tearing into strips of meat.'

Ian laughed uproariously.

'My agent swears that this is a *colour blind* production, but I'm going to wait and see who else they cast.'

'Well, I hope it works out.' Ian was still chuckling, gratifyingly. 'You'd be perfect.'

Charlie sipped her tea. 'Maybe.' She could feel Ian looking at her, stealing glances while he had the chance, and she kept her head tilted, showing her best side, the lace trim on her slip just visible beneath the grey wool of her wrap, and then she remembered. Of course, he wasn't admiring her at all. He was looking at her spots. Setting down her tea she ran upstairs. Maybe there is a God, she felt like wailing as she peered into the mirror, and he's decided it's my turn to be punished. She mixed a pool of foundation in the palm of her hand and smeared it on, reminding herself she was one of the lucky ones — if she could take a bigger view — she was one of the luckiest people in the world.

★ ★ ★

'Well, it's hardly life-threatening.' Dr Helik smiled, blushing a little as he had done ever since he'd made the error of mentioning he'd seen her in an episode of *Sisters of the Night*, in which she'd appeared dressed only in the skimpiest of underwear, brandishing a whip. 'But then again, in your profession . . . ' he conceded, frowning, shaking his head. 'Presumably,' he had to ask, 'the problem is only on your face?'

Charlie nodded tersely.

'Right.' Dr Helik scribbled on a slip of paper. 'These antibiotics are very mild and won't take effect immediately. Come and see me again in three months and we'll . . . um . . . review the situation.'

Charlie stared at him. I'll be dead by then, she wanted to say, or too busy retaking my A-levels, but she stuffed the prescription into her pocket and sauntered across to the chemist.

She took the first pill as soon as she got home, and although she knew it was ludicrous, she ran and checked to see if there was any change. 'What am I going to do?' She bit her lip, and unable to think of anything else she lay on her bed and flicked through some of the scripts Maisie had sent her. *Mika, exotic beauty . . . Gloria, strong, charismatic career woman.*

Loretta. Sultry, sexy mistress of Philip.

Charlie sighed, pulled the quilt over her head and slept.

⋆ ⋆ ⋆

That night Charlie made a plan to stay in. It wasn't that she'd never had a night in alone before, she had, but she'd never actually planned one. She bought vegetables from the stall at the end of the road and some fish from the fishmongers that until now she hadn't noticed was there. She even took down a cookery book her mother had once given her. A book she'd never opened, not even to read the inscription which she now saw for the first time.

'To my beautiful daughter, stay well. With love always. Mummy.'

Charlie flicked through the pages. This doesn't look so hard, she decided, but she had to run out twice, once to buy a lemon and then again for bay leaves. When she had everything she needed she put on an old Country and Western tape. 'Joleen, Joleeeeeen,' she belted along with Dolly Parton, and for a moment she felt supremely happy.

She sliced courgettes, celery and aubergine. She dipped tomatoes in boiling water and peeled off the skin, and as she sang, and twirled and chopped, she imagined Ian might come through the door and be amazed to see her. Not just a talented actress but a goddess in the kitchen as well. But the time for Ian's nut roast to go into the oven passed, and then the time at which he

235

usually ate it. Charlie sat down at the table, with her slice of grilled cod elegantly perched on a bed of ratatouille, alone. Not bad at all, she nodded, and she ate it, ravenous.

After she'd eaten, and left the dishes in the sink as proof of her productivity, she sat with her back against the sofa and switched on the television. But it bothered her to see the actors playing parts that should have been hers, or playing parts badly, or worse, with style and grace. It made her uneasy, and reminded her she still didn't understand Melina, and had no idea how to approach tomorrow's scene — a confrontation with her husband, her children hanging on her skirts. She switched off the TV and put on a CD, a Bach sonata she'd bought once to impress Marcel on his first and last visit to this flat. He'd been on his way to New Zealand, where she'd been planning to join him for a month of travel, kayaking with dolphins, catching river taxis along the Marlborough Sound, but before she'd had a chance to book her ticket he'd called to say he was sorry, he'd fallen in love with a documentary filmmaker who was making a film on the making of his film. He didn't know how it could happen, the girl was half-Maori, had only recently graduated from film school . . . and the attraction, it was . . .

'No,' Charlie stopped him, 'please, don't, don't . . . ' and afterwards she'd lain on the floor, curled up against the pain, and thought, so this is how it feels — and she'd prodded the pulpy bleeding muscle of her broken heart.

Charlie let the music swell around her. It was

too late to switch it off. And wondering what she could possibly do now she remembered a packet of white organza on a shelf in her cupboard where it had sat since the week that she'd moved in. She'd planned to make a lace curtain for her bedroom window several years before but had never found the time. She retrieved it and tipped it out on to the floor. The material was fine and creamy, a little dusty from lying folded for so long, but she ironed out the creases and then turned the top over in a pleasing double hem and pinned it. The curtain wire was coiled in the packet too, and as she was threading it, pushing it inch by inch through the hem, bunching and straightening with a caterpillar's progress, she heard a crash outside. There was some muttering and cursing and the scratching of a key at the front door. Charlie frowned and continued threading, hoping it was someone from the flat below, but then her lodger's unmistakably heavy steps began ascending.

It took Ian some time to fathom the intricacies of the next lock, but eventually he was in, and she could feel him standing looking down at her from the hall. 'Charlie,' he spluttered, helpless, 'meet Charlie,' and she glanced up to see he had a traffic cone in his arms.

'What about your supper?' She couldn't think of anything else to say. 'You missed it.'

'Oh that,' he stumbled forward and still holding the cone, he slumped on to the sofa. 'I met up with a friend, we went to the pub and I thought, fuck it, fuck the advert, fuck Munchy Crunchy mix. It won't get me anything I want.'

He looked at her mournfully, his eyes so shiny they were wet.

Charlie continued with the threading. The material was all bunched up now and she had to ease it along the wire with great care so that it didn't slide off. 'Could you take one end?' she asked, thinking she could measure it against this window, identical to the one above, and Ian leapt up to help her so quickly that he stumbled over the cone and fell. 'Charlie,' he moaned to the cone, 'I'm sorry, baby, I'm so sorry,' and the real Charlie stood and looked at him, her face closed. It occurred to her that she was haughty as her character, cold and admired and absorbed by domestic deeds. 'Don't worry,' she said when Ian dropped the wire for the second time, 'I'll take it, I'm going up to bed now anyway,' and still in her role as nineteenth-century paragon of woman-hood she gathered the white organza in her arms and aware how much it suited her, how the nape of her neck looked as she bent over it, she walked quickly up the stairs.

★ ★ ★

Once she was in her bedroom she realised she'd forgotten the little screws that needed twisting into the wooden window frame, but she couldn't go back down. She abandoned the material in a pile and pulled off her clothes. This is ridiculous, she thought, it's only ten o'clock, and it occurred to her she hadn't seen a single person that day, apart from the doctor. If Ian comes up, she thought, and if he waits for long enough outside my door, I'll let him in. He's not that bad. She opened her script and looked over the next day's lines. Just to have someone's arms around her, a man's hot beery breath against her ear, but the minutes passed and there was no sound from him. It's for the best, she told herself. Just think of the next morning. A small tear trickled down her face. We'd have to eat breakfast together like some horrid suburban couple, and with Melina's lines circling in her head she fell asleep.

* * *

The next day at six a.m., her face made up, her skin still blotched and lumpy, she came downstairs to find Ian asleep on the sofa, the traffic cone beside him, his arm clutched tight around its base. Charlie looked at him, and then she went and found a blanket. As she draped it over him he reached up and caught her hand. 'Sorry,' he mumbled, his eyes still closed, and for a moment she allowed herself to sink down beside him. To feel the warmth of his touch, the pressure of his fingers, smell the male hay and sweat smell of his skin. 'Charlie,' he moaned, 'sorry about being an idiot . . . ' and as he tightened his grip she remembered herself, and who she really was, and disentangling her fingers she turned impassively and walked away.

The Tour

Outside the theatre Nell stopped for a minute and caught her breath. She was only ten days into an eight-week run but already the thought of setting eyes on Bernard made her queasy. The bullet shape of his head, his stomach taut under his rollneck top, the mean shape of his mouth as he heaped scorn on everything the company said or did. Nell made herself concentrate on the rest of the cast — Chrissie, who played Bernard's wife, solid, sensible Gavin. And Saul, quiet and watchful, who'd read with her at the audition.

Nell heard raised voices even as she ran up the stairs. 'This tour,' Bernard was saying as she opened the dressing-room door, 'is a poncy load of rubbish.' He had a list of the venues in his hand and he was staring at it in disgust. 'You said we'd be playing working men's clubs, political centres, union halls. But no, we're off to the Ambleside Women's Institute, and from there we'll be at . . . wait for it . . . The Lake District Ramblers' Association.'

Matthew, their director, a pale man, prone to attacks of giggles, swallowed. 'We will be going to Southport. That's only an hour from Liverpool. And we're still holding out hope for York.'

Chrissie put a hand on Bernard's arm. 'Whoever's in the audience, they're still important. Think of the service you're providing. The inspiration.'

'Inspiration my arse,' Bernard shook her off. And Chrissie retreated, wounded, to her allotted space before the mirror.

There was a pause while Matthew gathered up the courage to give notes. 'So,' he took a short shallow breath. 'Nell. Not quite sure what you were doing last night, but good. Maybe a tad quicker? And funnier if you can? Gavin, you're losing the laugh at the end of Act I. Take your time. Stay with it. Now, Chrissie.' He sighed. 'Energy.' He made a swooping movement with his hand. 'It's not *Swan Lake*. And was your apron on backwards? I see. Interesting. Keep it.' Saul, as ever, was perfect. 'So, Bernard . . . ' The others all looked up. What would he say to Bernard, who'd mangled his last big speech to such an extent that the sense had all but disappeared. 'Bernard,' he said. 'That was . . . ' Matthew closed his eyes and opened them again. 'Unique.'

'Cheers!' Bernard raised a tumbler of what everyone hoped was water to his lips. 'What would you do without me, eh?' And draining the contents of the glass, he went down to the stage to check his props.

★ ★ ★

'Oh my God,' Nell called Pierre from a phone box in Keswick. 'He's getting worse. Tonight he cut my cue, then skipped to the end of the scene, so, I promise you, I walked on, and then without saying a word, ten minutes later I walked off again.'

Pierre cackled with laughter. 'I'll have to come up and see it. Unless of course it transfers to the West End.'

'The weird thing is . . . ' Nell was reluctant to admit it. 'Some nights he's sort of brilliant.'

'Maybe Bernard's actually a genius.'

'He certainly thinks he is. But the truth is he's probably a sad old drunk.'

'Darling . . . ' Nell could hear the buzz and beep of switchboard phones. 'I'd love to talk, but I'm meant to be in a managers' meeting in . . . Christ, twenty-five seconds. Call tomorrow?'

'Sure. Bye then. Bye.' Nell stood with the receiver to her ear, breathing in the last echoes of a familiar voice. She could try Charlie, but Charlie wouldn't pick up if she saw an unknown number, and Sita was in Bristol, in a hospital drama, providing the subplot of a nurse forced into an arranged marriage. Anyway, Nell thought, looking at the darkening hills. I'd better get going. For one brief moment she considered calling her father, who was in Scotland, not so very far away, but the thought that his new wife might answer and ask who it was, stopped her from dialling. Instead she stepped out into the late afternoon, glancing at the peak above her where all day fog had been collecting. As she walked towards the theatre, white tendrils began spiralling down, cloaking the already silent town in quiet. Who would their audience be tonight? she wondered as she hurried through the empty streets, and she tried to imagine who might venture out on an evening like this to see a play about the evils of capitalism, even if it was billed as a farce. But then again, what else was there to do here? Nell peered into the window of a boutique, already closed, displaying an assortment of heather-coloured capes. There was a newsagent, shut too, and a pub with gritty, rendered walls, the silhouettes of a few early drinkers passing blurrily behind its mottled glass. But for all Nell knew, tonight there might be someone in for whom this play would be the bright spark of their lives. Someone changed for ever. Set on a different course. As a child she'd been taken to see a touring production of *The Playboy of the Western World* and from almost the first scene she'd felt her heart expand until she'd thought it might be going to burst. I'll do anything, she told herself, as the actors laughed and fought and danced, I'll dress up in sacking, play an old woman, sweep the stage, if it means that one day I can be like them.

'Good show tonight,' Bernard said later as they climbed into the mini-van, half an hour later than usual. 'Really excellent performance, if I say so myself.' And in lieu of last orders which they'd all now missed due to an improvised dance routine inserted by Bernard into the second half, he lit up the stub end of his cigar, and took a swig of whisky from his hip flask.

★ ★ ★

But even so, no one expected, for a minute, that Bernard would desert them.

'Where is he anyway?' Matthew asked as they assembled in the vast dressing room of

Southport's Theatre Royal.

'Don't worry, he'll turn up.' Chrissie was handing round brightly coloured mugs of tea. 'He's turned up late before.' And it was true. Bernard had arrived more than once after the half, sauntering in, unrepentant. 'Places to go, people to see,' he'd winked, and he'd waved his furled-up newspaper in their faces. Nell often wondered where he'd actually been. She tried to picture him sitting in his B&B, his shoes kicked off, his gut spilling over his suit trousers, fathoming out the crossword, just waiting for the day to be done.

But the half came and went. 'Where is the bastard?' Matthew fretted, having failed to get him on his phone, and he threw one weak shoulder against the wall, causing the mirror lights to flicker. Just then the stage manager thundered up the stairs with the news that Bernard had been seen, earlier that day, hitching towards Manchester. 'God knows where he'll be by now.'

'No!' Chrissie looked as shaken as if her own real husband had abandoned her. 'What are we going to do?'

'We'll think of something.' Gavin began massaging her shoulders. 'Don't worry. Just stay calm.'

Nell remained silent. She was playing Bernard's noodle-headed daughter-in-law, and she'd learnt from experience that any comments she made were usually ignored.

'OK,' Saul was drumming his fingers against the formica of the dressing table. 'Matthew, how about you go on with the book, and then we get a few days off anyway, and we can find someone who'd be able to take over.'

'The show must go on,' Chrissie said weakly.

Matthew didn't look remotely relieved. 'Fantastic idea,' he said. 'I'll get someone to start calling round right now,' and paler than ever he went through to Bernard's dressing room to try on his voluminous costume.

* * *

Nell stood in the wings, her hand over her mouth, too frightened to laugh as she watched the play unfold. Matthew's pork-pie hat was perched at an unstable angle, the cigar, Bernard insisted on smoking, trembling in his hand. As he spoke Matthew waved his sheaf of photocopied script, but he didn't refer to it at all. The audience, as usual, looked stunned. Go on, don't stop, Nell willed him on, as he fumbled for the lines, and then mercifully Gavin climbed through the window in his policeman's uniform and began chasing him round the stage.

'How's it going?' Saul was beside her in the dark. Nell inhaled his warm and smoky smell, so familiar from this moment of proximity, repeated every night. 'Not bad,' she kept her eyes on the stage, 'but he's not sticking to the script.'

They stood side by side, listening to Matthew as he scrambled from scene to scene.

'Bloody hell.' Saul tensed, his cue hurtling towards him. 'I'm on.'

'Have fun,' Nell whispered as he glided away

245

from her, too superstitious to risk Good Luck, and she watched for the moment when he and Matthew came face to face. There was a tiny terrifying pause as neither of them spoke. Instead they stood, rigid, their eyes glued to each other's, the corners of their mouths twitching, hilarity dancing in their throats, but then Saul bit hard into his lip, turned away and with a visible effort of control, spoke his first line.

'What's happening?' Chrissie was beside Nell now, and before she could answer, they heard their own cue, three pages early. 'What shall we do?' Chrissie gasped and Nell, catching Saul's frantic look, grabbed her hand and rushed her on.

Matthew didn't notice. He flapped his unused script and raged and roared into his big monologue while the rest of the cast stood in a line, their eyes on the floor, waiting to find their way back in. Nell stood beside Saul, the only time in the entire play when she did, and as she listened for her cue, she forgot about her Action and her Activities, the rhythm of her Inner Attitude, her decision never again to get entangled with an actor, or for that matter, a stage manager, and instead drifted into day-dreams — Saul, choosing the seat beside her as they travelled in the mini-van, Saul, draping his arm around her as they slept. Nell snapped open her eyes. Twice now she'd been so caught up in these reveries that she'd forgotten to come in with her line and Saul himself was forced to reach out and nudge her, sharply, in the side. 'It wasn't me, Inspector, honest, it was those

246

bastards upstairs,' she shouted, still, amazingly, evoking a laugh, and Matthew, seeing the end in sight, gained confidence, even attempting a small routine with oranges that he'd warned everybody he'd most likely omit. But he managed it, almost, catching one orange in the crook of his arm, another flying into the third row, so that the play ended in a burst of applause with the five actors bowing low down to the floor, beaming, while Matthew's script was hurled high into the air.

That night the drinks flowed. 'Cheers. Well done, mate.' Even Gavin, usually so serious, sat grinning at their table. 'What a relief, we don't need him after all.' He held up his pint, and they agreed that life without Bernard was infinitely superior.

★   ★   ★

Philip, Bernard's replacement, was a small, neat man. He'd played the same part at Taunton only eighteen months before and he'd spent his train journey re-acquainting himself with the play, so that by the first rehearsal he already had a better grasp of the lines than Bernard ever had. They spent all of Sunday rehearsing, and Monday too, and by Monday night the play was just about ready.

'Break a leg,' 'See you on there,' 'You'll be great,' they all told him and each other, and during the performance the only alarm that sounded was when Nell drifted into her daydream and forgot to come in with her line.

'You dope.' Matthew sat down beside her. 'What's going on in that dreamy head of yours? I'm watching you, and I see it, you go all soppy.'

Matthew was like a girl. He loved to talk. He loved to gossip and surmise, and once, before a show at Wigton, they'd stopped at a tearoom and he'd eaten three cream cakes in a row. 'Come on . . . ' Matthew wasn't letting it go, 'you can tell me in confidence . . . you know I'll never breathe a word.'

'Stop it.' Nell shushed him. 'You'd be the last person I'd tell.' And just then Saul appeared and she took a quick gulp of her wine.

Matthew winked and raised his eyebrows, and the next night on stage Nell almost cut him off, she came in so quickly with her line.

★ ★ ★

It took a few days before anyone could bear to admit it, but Philip wasn't funny. True, he knew his lines, didn't branch off into spontaneous improvisation or cut someone else's speech, leaving them open-mouthed and stranded, as Bernard had often done, but even so, there was something vital missing.

Philip was impervious. 'Good show tonight, don't you think?' he said as he sat neat and amiable at the bar.

'I have told him,' Matthew was quick to waive his responsibility, 'but he insists on doing it the Taunton way,' and the others shook their heads and ordered more drinks and drifted into favourite tales of their own and others' escapades

248

on other nights, in other productions, in other theatres and plays.

What none of them had realised was that it was Bernard who'd held the company together. His awful jokes, his petty complaints, his outbursts on and off stage had united them as a group. But now that they had Philip, with his hiking boots and light all-weather clothing, they found they had nothing in common. Splinter groups formed. Nell and Chrissie spent an afternoon looking round Scarborough. Gavin and Saul attempted to find a pub that showed the rugby, but soon, it was Nell, Saul and Matthew that sloped off most regularly together. Gorging themselves in teashops, wandering round deserted seaside towns, drinking past last orders, hoping to come across a nightclub in Stockton or Penrith. One night, just as in Nell's fantasy, they arrived at their bed and breakfast late and finding no one up, and Nell's room locked from the inside, they piled into Matthew and Saul's twin room. Matthew lay down first, not bothering to undress or even climb under the bedspread, and Nell, suddenly both cold and sober, watched as Saul tugged the covers out from under him and tucked him in. They stood there, then, uncertain, and Saul offered to sleep on the floor. 'No, don't be silly,' she said, and so he pulled off his jeans and climbed into the narrow bed, and with that same shy smile with which he greeted her each night in the wings, he looked up at her now. 'Getting in?'

Nell slipped out of her own jeans and crept in beside him. There was no room to be aloof. She lay against his side, her skin slowly warming with the heat of him. 'Night then,' he whispered, and she lay there, her heart racing, breathing in the familiar smell of smoke and sweat. This'll never work, she thought, but gradually she felt Saul's body soften, and the rhythm of his breathing lulled her into a wakeful, restless sleep.

★　★　★

'Well,' Chrissie plumped down beside her in the mini-van, her voice rich with delight. 'What happened to you last night?'

Nell looked away. She knew it was cruel, but she couldn't bring herself to offer up what was expected. 'I didn't want to wake you,' she said. 'I kipped down with the boys, that's all.'

'Oh,' Chrissie looked deflated. She began to rummage in her cavernous bag and when she found what she was looking for, a packet of digestive biscuits, she didn't offer one to Nell. Be like that, she seemed to say, and once they reached the theatre Chrissie stared into her own reflection in the dressing-room mirror, spending an inordinate amount of time arranging her make-up, pinning up her cards. On stage, professional that she was, Chrissie was warm and twinkly, but as soon as the interval arrived she turned her face away again and didn't speak. Nell made a bed of chairs and closed her eyes, and allowed herself to relive the moment when Saul had appeared beside her in the wings. 'How's it going?' he'd asked, and he'd slipped his hand under the hair at the nape of her neck and held it there. Now she imagined leaning back and being held for ever, and she thought of those first lonely weeks of rehearsal when the red tower of the phone box, the only colour in the endless grey and green of the Lake District, filled her with such longing for home that she'd sometimes pull back the heavy door of the booth and stand inside, breathing in the ash and dust smell, even when she had no one to call.

⋆　⋆　⋆

That night's bed and breakfast was on the outskirts of Newcastle, and after the pub they travelled there together in the van. 'Hey,' Matthew put an arm round her shoulders as they stumbled in. 'Come in here with us. You don't want to get mixed up with those hill walkers.' Blushing, Nell tried to quieten him.

'Come on. Let's stick together,' he insisted.

Nell glanced across at Saul, but he didn't catch her eye.

'OK, just for a minute.' But like the night before, as soon as he was in his room Matthew collapsed on to his bed.

Nell stared down at him, his shoes still on, a snore already rumbling in his nose. 'Is he OK?'

'He's gone to pieces since Bernard left. His job's on the line and he knows it.' Saul tucked him in. 'That, or he's got some pretty disgusting habits. Unlike me, of course,' he grinned. 'I'm perfect.'

Nell grinned back. He was perfect! She'd thought that the first time she'd seen him. With his ragged clothes and Doc Marten boots, and the quiet way he smiled. 'Hey,' he put out his hand to her, and when she took it, he led her to the other bed. ' 'It wasn't me, Inspector, honest,' he whispered as they lay down, 'it was those bastards upstairs,' and as if he'd always known what was in her mind, he wrapped his arms around her and covered her smile with his own.

★ ★ ★

The hotel was silent when Nell woke. A pale grey light fell through the curtains and the smell of old bacon hung in the air. Nell craned to see her watch on the bedside table. It was after twelve, and Matthew's bed was empty. Very carefully she slid free, untangling herself from the weight of Saul's limbs, mindful not to look at him too closely as he lay, mouth open, black stubble already shadowing his chin.

The water in the bathroom was cold. Nell let it run, hoping to feel it warm, but when it wouldn't, she filled a basin and began to wash, soaping her armpits, rinsing between her legs, letting her mind run over and dissect the awkward, hushed and furtive choreography of last night's sex. How bony Saul's body was, how urgent his desire, the terrible moment when Matthew seemed to wake, half sitting, before he fell back with a snore. Nell shivered. The water ran in rivulets down her sides, collecting in grey suds on the floor. 'Lovely girl,' he'd breathed into her ear, and now as she allowed herself to feel his hands on her again, the sweet searching

252

of his mouth, the painful, exhilarating moment when he pressed himself inside her, she felt the air catch in the bowl of her stomach and she leant over the basin, her legs weak, and moaned.

There was a tap at the door. 'Can I come in?'

'Wait!' She panicked, grabbing a towel, wrapping it round herself.

Saul was already dressed. 'Morning,' he said, looking much the same as always, and he leant over and splashed his face.

Nell's own face looked pale and bare, and she hadn't risked borrowing a toothbrush in case it was Matthew's. 'I'll see if I can get into my room,' she told him, and holding her clothes in her arms she ran along the corridor and tapped at the door.

Chrissie smiled coldly. 'Hi.' She blew on the fingers of one hand where new red polish was drying.

Nell unzipped her bag, and pulled out fresh clothes, aware of Chrissie's eyes on her. Aware too that now, through her desertion, this was Chrissie's room. 'What are you up to today?'

'Nothing much,' Chrissie was applying another coat of varnish.

Nell pulled on jeans and a silk blouse. Her clothes felt loose, her body slimmed down with the constant travelling and the regularly missed meals.

'I think I'll have a pampering day here,' Chrissie stretched out. She had on a pair of feathery pink slippers, very much like the ones her character wore in the play, and beside the bed was a large packet of chocolate biscuits. For one moment Nell imagined lying down too. Telling her everything. Painting her own nails. Winning a biscuit as reward.

'OK,' Nell said. 'I'd better get going . . . I'll see you back here, or at the theatre.'

Chrissie looked up at her, and Nell remembered what it felt like to be lonely. 'Bye,' she said, forcing herself away, and she ran back along the corridor to where Saul was waiting in his room.

★ ★ ★

Saul and Nell walked away from their Bed and Breakfast, through near-empty streets, passing the occasional bare-legged girl, her heels clacking, pinpricks of cold mottling her skin. 'Any idea where we're going?' she asked, and Saul said yes, this was the way to the centre, the quayside, they'd find somewhere there where they could eat.

'How do you know?' she asked, admiring.

'We drove this way last night.'

He took hold of her hand, and they walked on, the smell of the river sharpening the air, gulls wheeling above them, cawing, heading back out to sea. 'What do you fancy?' Saul peered into the dark interior of a pub.

'Maybe there?' Nell pointed to a café, a hot white fug of steam flowing from its door. They pushed their way in and sat opposite each other. Pie and mash, sausage sandwich, ham, eggs, beans. Nell wanted everything. She ordered a cup of tea. 'I'll have liver and bacon,' Saul decided and Nell looked up at the waiter, a large man with a tea towel draped from his pocket. 'Shepherd's pie and peas.'

'Reet you are.' He hollered their order through to the kitchen, and he swept up a teacup and a stack of egg-stained plates and carried them off on one brawny arm.

It was warm in the café. Nell and Saul sipped their hot drinks and stared out of the window. 'So, um,' Nell started. There were so many things she didn't know. All they'd ever really talked about was the play. The play and the people in it, the unfolding drama of each day. She remembered Matthew telling them, excited, in rehearsals, how this play was a sensation when it first appeared in London. The audiences had responded to its themes of social injustice, of class division and corruption, and they'd stood up at the end and roared. But now, a decade later, the response was never more than polite. 'They eased their consciences by voting in New Labour,' Bernard had snarled, when they still had Bernard, 'and now they're happy to spend the rest of their lives shopping in IKEA.'

'Sorry?' Saul leant towards her. 'What were you saying?'

'Oh yes, I was wondering . . . in London, Peckham, is it? What kind of a place do you have?'

'Small,' he told her. 'Ex-council. Not too bad.'

'Right. I see. Do you . . . ' she needed to know more. 'Do you live on your own?'

Saul lit a cigarette. 'No. I share. With Lorraine.' He blew out a plume of smoke and looked at her. 'My wife.'

Nell nodded quickly to show she was unfazed. But even as she did so she saw that he was smiling. 'It's all right. We got married one afternoon at drama school. We were best mates anyway, we just wanted to see how it felt.'

'How did it feel?'

Saul squinted. 'All right.'

All right? Nell felt her heart squeeze. But she thanked the waiter brightly as he banged down her plate of food. They ate in silence, the hot mush of food pinning Nell to the chair. They ordered more tea, and Nell dithered over pudding. Treacle sponge. Apple crumble. Custard with jam tart. She longed for them all, but at the same time she couldn't face it. Saul lit another cigarette. 'I wonder what Bernard's doing now,' he said, and Nell pictured him sitting in a restaurant, as she'd once seen him in Kendal, a napkin tucked into his shirt front, waiting to be served. He'd been alone, with his newspaper and cigar, and Nell couldn't help but feel impressed by how seriously he took himself.

It was nearly three by the time they wandered out into the drizzle. What shall we do now? they asked each other as they walked aimlessly towards the Tyne. At the top of the road was a phone box. 'Ahhh.' Nell hurried instinctively towards it. Her phone was out of credit again.

'Use mine if you want.' Saul called after her, but Nell already had her fingers hooked inside the iron groove of the handle. 'It's OK,' she needed to talk to someone from home. 'I won't be a minute.' But as she swung open the door she saw a small orange wallet sitting on the metal

256

shelf. She picked it up and there inside was a wad of ten-pound notes. Fifty, seventy, ninety pounds. 'Look,' she held the door for Saul. There was nothing in the wallet except money. It must belong to someone very young, and Nell imagined a girl just back from collecting the dole. No bank cards, or travel cards, or library cards. Nothing.

Saul counted out the notes. 'What do you want to do?'

Nell looked along the street both ways. What she wanted, and also didn't want, was that someone would come tearing round the corner to claim it. 'What if we handed it in to the police?'

It seemed a ludicrous idea. Would anyone think of going there to ask for it? And would the police be honest enough to hand it back? Not if they were anything like the policeman in their play, corrupt and heavy-handed, and if their play was to be believed, they were the good guys, she and Saul, and all establishment figures were rotten.

'If we left it,' Nell mused, 'the next person who comes along . . . ' and for some reason she imagined Bernard, his mean round mouth, his beer belly and dainty legs, taking the purse off to the pub.

'How about we divide it up?' Saul hesitated. 'But only if we spend it before the end of the day.'

'That's it. That's brilliant.' They rushed on, their eyes straining for any suitable shop — passing wholesalers, ironmongers, bathroom showrooms full of fixtures and fittings. Eventually they came to a department store. Nell pulled the purse out of her pocket.

'Surely there'll be something,' she handed over fifty pounds. 'You take that.'

'No,' Saul protested, 'it's got to be fair,' and he unravelled a torn five-pound note from his pocket and pressed it on her.

At first they wandered through the shop together, subdued by the hush of its interior, the scent of perfume, the array of scarves, cushions and dried flowers. Nell stopped by a stand of necklaces. Round balls of different-coloured glass, or was it plastic? 'Nice,' Saul smirked, and embarrassed, Nell turned away.

There was an escalator and a sign for Ladies Fashions. Nell knew she'd never be able to choose anything with Saul beside her, and now that she was here she felt an overwhelming desire to buy something, anything, as if that was the sole purpose of life.

'Shall we meet by the main door at five?'

'Sure,' Saul agreed, 'right,' and he wandered off between the stands of neatly folded T-shirts, woollen V-necked jerseys, bath mats, towels.

Ladies Fashions was a sombre affair. Dark cardigans with gold buttons. Dresses with moulded shoulders and built-in slips. She looked at the underwear but that seemed wasteful. To spend so much on something that only someone who was already pretty damn interested was going to see. Anyway, when she got close, the underwear was frightening.

Padded leopard-print constructions, pants the size of the moon. She raked through knitwear, but everything had one unnecessary detail — a bow, or a flounce, or a row of buttons, that needn't have been there. Her own clothes, when she caught sight of them, seemed oddly perfect in comparison. But there was one skirt that wasn't entirely horrible. It was navy, as was almost everything, with very fine bright yellow stripes half hidden in the gather. As she tried it on, an announcement boomed from a grill in the wall, the shop would be closing in ten minutes. She looked at herself in the mirror. The skirt was all right. She pulled up her shirt to reveal the waistband on her newly narrow waist. Yes, she decided and she rushed out to hand over the money, almost exactly the right amount, before it was too late.

Saul was waiting in the street. He'd bought himself a pair of shoes, not the Doc Martens that he usually wore, but black and pointed, with an inlay of suede.

'Great,' they said, examining each other's purchases. 'Nice.' But as they walked towards the theatre Nell felt deflated. It's as if we've committed a crime, she thought, we should have given the money away, to a beggar or a single mother, and she glanced at Saul, and wondered if he too felt soiled.

The show that night was half empty. 'Matthew's gone to London,' Chrissie told her coldly, from her seat beside the radiator. 'We're up and running now, I don't suppose we need him to be here, every night.'

'I see.' Nell turned away, quickly, before the subject of the night ahead, Saul's empty room, ballooned between them. Instead she pulled out the new skirt. It wasn't really very nice. Or if it was, it didn't suit her.

'Splashing out?' Chrissie eyed her, and Nell, in a sudden fit of inspiration, turned towards her. 'Would you like it?'

'Me? Chrissie patted her stomach and laughed. 'It wouldn't fit me, are you kidding?' But later, when she made the tea, she asked Nell if she wanted a cup.

⋆ ⋆ ⋆

'How's it going?' Saul murmured as they waited in the wings, standing close, his sinewy arm beside her.

'Fine.'

'Listen,' he leant in to her. 'I've got someone in tonight. It's a bit awkward, it's . . . it's Lorraine, I didn't know she was coming. I guess she wanted to surprise me, and now she's suddenly turned up.'

Nell didn't look at him.

'So if I don't see you afterwards. The thing is, we'll probably go and get something to eat. An Indian or something.'

'Right.' Nell kept her eyes on Philip, who never missed a line.

Very lightly Saul put his hand on her shoulder.

'That's you,' she said, as they heard his cue, and he glided away from her on to the stage. Nell stood and watched him, breathing in the last traces of his smell, and she wondered how Chrissie would hide her amusement when later that night she knocked on the door of their shared room and asked to be let back in.

The Dream

'Really?' Jemma's eyes lit up. 'New York?'

'The play starts rehearsing in April,' Dan squinted as if he could see April, just there, in the future, 'then runs to the end of July.'

'Broadway . . . ' Jemma seized a small pink sweatshirt from the ironing pile and pressed down on it so hard that it scorched.

'It might be *Off* Broadway,' Dan wasn't sure.

'Oh but Dan, can you imagine? Four months in New York! I knew good things would happen this millennium. I'm so in the mood for an adventure.'

'They're seeing other people too.'

'Who else?'

'Five or six others, I'm not sure.' His agent, Lenny, had told him, but he decided not to say. It seemed just possible that by refusing to name the competition he could ignore them, for a while at least. 'Scarlett Johansson is coming over to read with everyone next week.'

'Scarlett Johansson! Is that really true?'

'Yes.' Dan had been as excited as Jemma a moment before, but now, faced with her elation, the reality hit him — he probably wouldn't get the job. 'I wonder,' his faith was wavering. 'Is Scarlett Johansson actually right? I mean, when did she ever do any theatre?'

'Of course she hasn't done any theatre.' Jemma folded a miniature pair of pants. 'If she'd been touring round the country for the last two years she'd never have been cast. These days they need a film star in the leading role to fill a Broadway theatre.'

Dan opened the fridge. There was a white net tiara sitting on the middle shelf. He reached past it and pulled out the jam. 'They're sending a copy of the play over this afternoon.'

'Who's it by? Is it a new play?'

'It's adapted from a film. Set during the Napoleonic era. Did you know there are more books about Napoleon than any other man that ever lived?'

'Wasn't he a midget?'

'No! Honestly, Jemma. Anyway, the lead part is a sort of Iago figure, a sexy, devious character, of any height, who Josephine takes for a lover only weeks after she and Napoleon are married.'

Jemma swung herself up on to the worktop. 'Sexy and devious, eh?' She slid the fingers of one hand around his neck, distracting him as he rifled through the bread bin. 'That doesn't sound like you.'

Dan laughed. 'It's been on once before. With John Malkovich and Julianne Moore, but now it's being directed by a Brit, and there's some deal with Equity which means they have to cast the male lead from here.'

He pulled out a loaf of bread and sniffed it. 'Is this old?' He turned it over and found a ring of green mould furring on its base.

'Sorry.' Jemma eased it from his hand and slung it into the bin. 'But just think, Dan. If you got it we could rent an apartment. Take Honey

263

to Central Park. Eat out in diners. Even breakfast. Maybe we could get somewhere downtown. Near Ruthie. I'll ask her. I'll ring her now. No, wait, it's five in the morning. Just think . . . New York City in the spring!'

'Shhh. Calm down. I might not get it.'

'But you might,' Jemma bent forward and pressed her face against his. 'They'd be lucky to have you. Who could be better?' She nuzzled him. 'Who?'

'You know what?' Dan wished he hadn't said the words 'John Malkovich' because now how would he ever get that menacing, pigeon-toed performance out of his head. 'If we do go, we should stay in Brooklyn. Steve lives there now, you remember Steve? He says it's a real community. And it's cheaper. Look, if this job happens there's not going to be a lot of money in it.'

'Brooklyn?' Jemma frowned. Dan could see her, attempting to adjust to the sudden relocation when, a moment ago, she'd been skipping through the air vents and glamour of Manhattan. 'I've never been to Brooklyn.'

'Nor me.' Dan looked out of the side window, at their neighbour's extension, the pipes that ran along the wall, the green stains from the overflow, where, the year before, and the year before that, fallen leaves had blocked the guttering. In Brooklyn they'd have a Brownstone, overhung by a pale-leafed maple, and every afternoon when he set off for the theatre he'd wave to the neighbours out on their stoop, all making good new beginnings in the bright,

264

new city of New York.

'Right,' Jemma shook herself free. 'I'd better get Honey from nursery. Do you think you'll have to do a French accent?'

'No!' Dan was appalled. 'I'm sure I won't. Well, no one's mentioned it. I can't see Scarlett Johansson doing . . . '

'I'm meeting Mel in the park.' She'd stopped listening to him. 'We'll give the kids lunch in the café if it's not too cold. Fancy it?'

Dan sat down at the table. 'I'll probably work, or go to the gym,' but once Jemma's coat, her gloves and scarf had been pulled on, the empty pushchair wrested from the hall, the door slammed shut, Dan opened the newspaper and bent his mind to the crossword as if solving its fabricated puzzles was the most pressing task in the world.

★ ★ ★

The play didn't arrive till late that afternoon. It was delivered by a courier who stared, unspeaking, at Dan through the window of his motorcycle helmet. A courier had once smiled and said how much he'd enjoyed his performance in *Rainstorm*, a series he'd done when he'd first left college. 'Fucking tops,' he'd grinned, before handing him a pen, but today this man said nothing, simply watched him, balefully, while Dan printed his name and signed. Several years ago, in a horrible moment of awkwardness, he'd thought he recognised Gabriel Grant peering out at him through the

265

visor, but when Dan moved towards him, arm outstretched, the man stepped back, alarmed. 'Sorry . . . ' Dan murmured, 'I thought . . . ' But he didn't go on.

Dan used to play football with Gabriel Grant. Gabe had organised a group of actors, boys from RADA and Central, a couple from Mountview, most who'd been out of college a year or two, some who'd started working, others who never had. They met up on Saturday afternoons on Hampstead Heath, just above the running track, and Gabriel had even brought along a sack of coloured bibs. Friends and girlfriends came out in support, standing along the sidelines, chatting, but the first time he played, Jemma arrived with Honey, a baby in a sling, just as Gil Bisham was being carried off the field on a stretcher. 'What happened?' she gasped, still blowsy and easily moved to tears, and Dan told her it was just bad luck, an accident, Gil would be all right.

'Poor kid,' Gabriel joined them, 'what a disaster. He starts rehearsing at the National next week, and it looks like his leg is broken.'

Jemma's eyes spilt over with tears.

'Hey, it's all right,' Dan reached for her hand, but she bent her head as a wave of sobbing convulsed her.

'Hey, he'll get there, there'll be other jobs,' and Dan had to arc his body around the pouch of their baby in order to console her.

The next time Dan played, two actors got into a fight, mocking and lashing out at each other, and then just before the finish Gabriel had tackled him so ferociously he fell and sprained

266

his thumb. 'What are you lot trying to prove,' Jemma had shouted furiously from the sidelines. 'Scared someone might think you're a bunch of poofs?' and she'd stomped back to the car.

It was a year at least since Dan's last game. He missed it, the camaraderie, the drink afterwards in the pub, but if occasionally he got a call, he was either working, or he wasn't working, and either way, he couldn't take the risk.

★　★　★

Dan carried the thick brown envelope upstairs to the bedroom, away from the noise of Honey, beating her spoon on the table, from Jemma, singing raucously to a tape ' . . . Heads, shoulders, knees and toes, knees and toes . . . ' as she prepared Honey's tea.

He could feel his heart beating as he slid out the sheaf of photocopied paper and flipped open the first page. *Battle to the Heart*. He ran his eyes down the list of characters. Josephine de Beauharnais. Albine de Montholon. Pierre Augereau. A flush of fear washed over him as he attempted to pronounce their names. 'Jem!' he shouted. He'd been brought up in Epping, for God's sake. He'd left school with three O levels and not one of them was French. He'd only ever seen France from a train, except once when he'd spent a weekend there — Jemma didn't know this — she must never know — but he'd gone to Paris with Charlie in the first term of their third year. It had been her idea. She'd whispered the plan to him one wintry afternoon while they

267

were rehearsing a play by Pinter. 'Research,' she'd mouthed — they were illicit lovers in *Betrayal* — and so as not to lose momentum they'd taken the Tube straight to Victoria, the train to Dover, and boarded a ferry. They'd arrived late and waited in the station while a woman from the tourist board rang round for a hotel. '*Non*,' she kept shaking her head, but eventually she found them a room, far out towards the end of the Metro, somewhere cheap, and drab, but still French, and they'd drunk brandy and fucked, and when they'd finished fucking, some time around the afternoon of the next day, unable to think of anything else to do, or say, they'd almost smoked themselves to death. 'Jem!' he called again, but it was clear she couldn't hear.

Dan remembered Charlie's long, strong, caramel-coloured body, the ridge of her breastbone, the beautiful jut of her hip. He could almost feel her silky lips, fluted as a sea shell, and the tickle of her kinked hair.

Josephine de Beauharnais. Dan sighed, speaking the French name with more confidence. Pauline Bellisle Foures. He imagined these women, their sloping shoulders and white necks, the soft folds of their pleated dresses, thinking of nothing except sex. His character, Hippolyte Charles, was described as charming, dangerous, capable of damage. 'That's me,' Dan determined, his blood stirring, 'that's my man.' And he closed his eyes and conjured up the figure of Josephine, who'd given herself so willingly to him.

'DAN!' Jemma was calling him now.

He risked another minute before answering. 'What is it?'

The tape must have started again. 'Heads, shoulders . . . ' He could hear Honey screaming. 'Don't worry.' Her voice trailed up the stairs. 'Forget it.'

'Really?' He listened hard, and when she didn't answer he flipped over the page.

The casting director had marked three scenes. He read them through, taking all the parts, his spirits lifting and plummeting again every time he stumbled on the lines. Damn. He needed Jemma to read with him, but that wouldn't be possible now until Honey was in bed. He traipsed down to the landing and put his head round the bathroom door. 'How you doing?' Honey's hair had been lathered up into a beehive and she was standing, admiring herself in the mirror. Sponge letters were scattered on the floor, pools of water lay in quivering puddles. Jemma looked up from where she was crouching, her arms on the edge of the bath. 'Come in, love, and shut the door, you're letting in a draught.' Dan stepped forward and felt cold water seep into the toe of his sock. 'Do you know,' he said, retreating, 'I think I'll just nip out for a drink, I'll be back in a bit. Do you want me to get anything?'

Jemma looked at him, affronted, as if this was the first time. Dan ignored her, easing the door shut as the tip of Honey's hairstyle drooped over and spiked her in the eye. 'I won't be long,' he called, over a prolonged wail of agony, and guiltily, he ran down the stairs.

It's not as if I can do anything to help, he shrugged as he slunk away. Honey had taken against him recently, and unless Jemma was actually out of the house, she wouldn't even allow him to read her a story. 'Mummy read it!' her lip would quiver if he even suggested such a thing, and she'd rush to Jemma, and curl like a cat around her legs.

'Hey. Sweetheart. I'm really good at telling stories, that's my job.' He'd crouch down, but his daughter only narrowed her grey eyes at him. 'Mummy does Made Up stories, and she sings.' She looked triumphant, half hidden by her matted curls.

'Does she now?' Dan tried to smile.

'It's because you were away so much last year,' Jemma attempted to console him, embarrassed, but also, he was sure of it, gratified by so much adoration. 'Kids are like animals, they want what's familiar.' But even Jemma became exasperated when Honey wouldn't let Dan fetch her a glass of water, and then when he tried to ease the pushchair from Jemma's hands as they struggled up Kite Hill, Honey whipped round as if she'd been stung. 'NO!' she yelled, 'Mummy push. Mummy's the boss, not you!'

Dan felt himself flush. 'I am the boss.'

'No.' Honey's eyes were blazing. 'Mummy's the King. And you. You're not even the Queen.'

'I am the Queen.' He spat back at her. 'I *am* the Queen!' and then noticing several passers-by slowing to stare, he muttered something, unintelligible even to himself, and abandoned the pushchair to Jemma.

'Maybe I should go away for a few days,' Jemma said, tearful, and Dan, although he knew it was childish, walked on ahead.

'Or maybe I should.'

★　★　★

Dan sat in the Duke's Head and read through the scenes. He wiped the froth of lager from his mouth and turned away from the other, mostly solitary men so that they wouldn't see his lips moving as he whispered the words.

'How you doing then, mate?' It was Sid, a regular Dan knew from his own regular visits. 'Fancy a refill?'

Dan looked at his empty glass. 'I shouldn't really, but . . . Go on then. A pint of Fosters. Cheers.' He put down the sheaf of papers and waited for Sid to return.

★　★　★

It was after ten by the time he got home. 'Sorry!' He opened the door too vigorously and let it slam into the wall. 'Sorry.' He imagined a leather whip slicing across his back. Jemma was sitting at the computer, frowning at the screen. She raised her head as if to speak, and then looked down again.

Dan leant over her. 'Hello, my darling.' He recognised the title of that term's essay and the Cyrillic script of the text. 'I bumped into Sid. We talked about the play . . . you know he was

271

Napoleon once in a platform performance at Stratford?'

Jemma kept on typing. 'If only you could get a job in St Petersburg or Moscow, then I could do my year abroad, and finish this degree. Imagine, with a Russian degree I might be employed by an oligarch, or put in charge of a multinational business.'

'Sure,' Dan watched her fingers, mesmerised as the mysterious letters bloomed, 'but what happens if I get some glamorous job filming on a beach in the Maldives, or even jetting off to Broadway? You wouldn't be able to come with me — you'd have to report to your boss at the Grozni Deli and beg for a long weekend.'

'True,' Jemma sighed, and she shut down the screen.

★ ★ ★

They had to sit close together in order to read. Dan put the gas fire on and pulled the lamp a little closer so it cast its golden glow over the sofa. They read the first marked scene. Josephine was confiding in him — her lover — that she found the physical presence of Napoleon repulsive. '*He is so attentive I can hardly breathe, and now I must lie with him each day and night so that when he returns from Italy I am certain to be carrying his child.*'

'*But Madame, surely it is worth a little discomfort. When you think of the benefits, for yourself, and your deserving courtiers.*' Dan felt his tongue loosened, his voice smooth as sauce.

272

'A soldier will fight long and hard for a length of coloured ribbon. Is that not so?'

'That I wouldn't know. And you. What would keep you fighting?'

'I might need more than a promise of ribbon.'

'A promise of what, then?'

'Ahh . . . But first answer me this. Did you give your word to be faithful during the long months of the campaign?'

'The best way to keep one's word,' Josephine was quick to respond, 'is never to give it.'

'It's good.' Jemma nodded solemnly.

'And you,' Dan told her. 'You're good.' She'd always been a skilful sight reader, and tonight she read with ease and grace. 'Is Honey asleep?' He stood up and adjusted the curtains.

'Of course. What are you doing?'

'Nothing.' Dan stretched out on the floor before the fire. 'I'm cold, that's all.'

'But surely the danger is too great, for me to take my pleasure elsewhere,' Jemma continued. 'And then, without pleasure, soon I shall shrivel up and fade away.'

'You know,' Dan looked up at her, 'there was an eighteenth-century theory that blondes were inherently more modest and respectable than any other species of girl, which is why Josephine, a brunette, was so very popular. But,' he began to crawl towards her, 'I know otherwise.'

'Hey,' she said, 'I thought you were in a hurry to read through the rest of the scenes?'

'The audition's not till next week.'

'True.'

'So plenty of time for getting it right.'

'I see.' She bent her head to the play. 'But think, how much fun would it be to go to New York? To have an adventure?'

Dan took hold of her free hand and ran his thumb across the palm. 'Aren't we having an adventure here?' Jemma placed the page before his eyes. He looked at it for a moment, and then easing the sheaf of papers from her hand, he flung it to the far side of the room. 'Dan!' she gasped. 'What are you doing?' But she didn't resist when he pulled her down with him on to the floor.

Jemma's skin was softer than any woman he'd met. She'd put on weight since Honey, a fact she railed against, although, as far as he could see, without making any visible effort to lose it. Dan said nothing, in part because her conviction she looked monstrous seemed unshakeable, but mostly because he liked the way she was now. Curving roundly at the hips, her shirt straining, her clothes hiding secrets waiting to unfold. Jemma's shirt was half unbuttoned and he slid it down over her shoulders. Her arms were pale as a painting, her breasts high. 'So Madame,' he grinned. 'What do they say about your modesty now?'

'It's not my modesty that's in question,' she was laughing, 'it's my choice in men,' and giving in, she bent her neck and kissed him.

★ ★ ★

That Sunday they went to Jemma's friend, Mel's, for lunch. It was Mel's birthday and the kitchen was full of family and friends. They'd met Mel and her husband Tim at a series of classes for expectant parents when Jemma was pregnant with Honey, and Dan had felt bound to them, and also vaguely repelled, when Jemma told him how Tim had taken it upon himself to partner her and Mel alternately at the 'positions for labour' class that, due to filming, he'd been forced to miss.

'Oh come on,' Jemma coaxed him when he voiced reluctance. 'It's only round the corner. We don't have to stay long, and there'll be other kids for Honey.'

Jemma and Dan helped themselves to food and stood in the window talking to Mel's sister, who worked as a midwife. Mel's sister was telling them about a new phenomenon — patients who were so obese that an extra pair of hands was needed — usually hers — to hold up the flab during a Caesarean section while the surgeon rooted around to find the womb. 'I'm on call again at six tomorrow morning. Flab holder. What kind of a job is that?'

'We'll think of you,' Jemma was attempting to press a spoon of couscous into Honey's averted mouth, but Dan found himself staring at the cheerful, worn face of the midwife. 'But doesn't it make you feel good? I mean, to know that you're doing something worthwhile?'

The woman put her head on one side.

'At least you're not dressing up in tights and a codpiece,' Dan continued, 'or having a cast of your head taken, not for medical science, but in order to perfect your likeness to an alien.'

275

The midwife laughed. 'But you're making people happy.'

'But not intensely, life-changingly, like you.'

'I don't know.' She paused. 'Think of those people who go to *Les Misérables* once a week. Or whose lives revolve around *EastEnders*? But there are times . . . ' she conceded, 'when it is a miracle. Actually, I cried the other day for the first time in years. This birth was just so beautiful. But I promise you, it's often easy to forget.'

'So what are you saying?' Jemma took Dan's arm. 'You're thinking of re-training as a midwife?'

'Maybe.'

'Dan!' Tim was upon them with a bottle of beer. 'What are you up to at the moment, anything exciting?'

'Well,' he began, and unable to resist Tim's expectant face he told him about New York.

⋆   ⋆   ⋆

On the morning of the audition Jemma and Dan read through the scenes. They stood in the kitchen among the mess of breakfast, while Dan tried to imagine himself drinking champagne in Josephine's private salon. He read quietly, casually, throwing away the lines in what he hoped was an offhand, gallant manner. 'Do you want to run through them again?' Jemma asked, anxious, betraying the fact the words had come out flat and lifeless, but he shook his head. 'No time.'

'All right, then.' She followed him into the hall and watched as he pulled on his coat. 'Take care.'

Dan laughed. It wasn't as if he was setting out into the snow to trap a wild beast to kill and skin for supper. 'OK,' he shook off a last embrace. 'I'll see you later.' But as he walked towards the Tube he felt unpleasantly nervous. Lenny had told him he was the second actor on the list and as the train sped south he allowed himself to say the other men's names, accepting finally he had no power over whose fortune rose and fell. Not even, of course, his own. Greg Hawes was in first. Dan could imagine him pulling it off, although he wasn't as right for the part as, say, Declan McCloud, who was going in after him. If it came to it, Declan was his real competition, he'd lost two jobs to him in the past year. He tried to focus on exactly what it was Declan had that he didn't possess, apart from ridiculously white teeth, and then, without warning, nerves overwhelmed him. His throat tightened and his stomach grew loose, and shakily he stood up and fought his way off the train. No job for a grown-up; he breathed shallowly, but his eyes felt gritty, and his face was numb. He ran up the escalator and breathed in the cold, welcome city air, and checking his watch, he set off through side streets, dodging the people, avoiding the busy roads, running past the marooned stone lions of Trafalgar Square.

Everywhere he looked he saw signs of hopelessness. A man asleep in a cardboard tunnel, another, shivering beside his dog. There

277

but for the grace of God go I, he muttered, as he bought a copy of *The Big Issue* from a man with no official permit, and pulling his jacket round him he pushed on, telling himself he had no time for this, not now. Instead he searched his mind for something to hold on to. Honey. His angel child, with her curls and deep grey eyes. Honey. But he couldn't shake off the image of her growling at him from the royal seat of her pushchair.

He could see the faces of the people on Kite Hill, watching him, suspicious as he defended himself, and a bubble of laughter burst up in him as he remembered. 'I am the Queen!' His shoulders shook, a mist of hysteria obscured his vision and he had to stop outside the theatre and wipe his eyes. 'I am the Queen!' and once inside he gave his name and still smiling, sank gratefully down on to a seat.

★ ★ ★

'How did it go?' Jemma called to him as soon as he came in.

'I don't know. All right, I think.' He stamped into the kitchen.

'When will you know?'

'They didn't say.'

'But you must have some kind of idea how it went.'

Dan couldn't help it, he grinned. He'd felt calm and strong when he was finally called in. The words, worried and stumbled over for a week, flew from his mouth as if they were his

278

own. Scarlett Johansson was radiant. Her eyes glittery, her skin translucent, her smile mischievous as he expected it to be. She carried herself lightly, but with a conscious grandeur. Had she been born like that? Or was it being a film star so early that had formed her? Dan watched her, never allowing himself to forget that, he, or his character at least, was her preferred lover.

'Let's read that scene again.' It was a challenge, and this time as they jousted, they kept their eyes fixed on each other until Dan felt a sheen of sweat across his back.

'Thank you,' she'd watched him, her head a little on one side, and he'd shaken hands with the director, before turning to catch her slim fingers in his own. On his way out he'd nodded bountifully to Declan McCloud, pale, still waiting for his turn, and flashing one last unnecessary smile at the casting assistant he'd pushed the door open on to the street.

'Sweetheart,' he looked at Jemma, 'there's nothing I can tell you. We'll know when we know. It doesn't start till April, they're under no pressure to decide.'

All the same, with every hour that passed, he expected a call. At ten to six he couldn't bear it any longer. He phoned Lenny.

'No news as yet,' Lenny told him. 'But if you say it went well, that's great.'

'Just thought I'd check in.'

'Sure, sure, no problem. I'll call you as soon as I hear. Talk soon, all right?'

'Yes, all right. Talk soon.'

Jemma knew him too well not to be hopeful. He heard her on the phone to her sister the next day. 'Dan thinks Brooklyn, but Ruthie says we should find a place near her, down in the village . . . maybe you could come out and visit us, maybe June, before it gets too hot.' He heard giggling and high spirits, and later, Jemma singing as she ran out to get Honey from her nursery.

Dan waited two more weeks before calling Lenny. 'Any news?' he asked, 'on *Battle to the Heart?*'

'Right,' there was an ominous pause. 'Very frustrating. I was going to call you. They decided to go in a different direction. Although you did get down to the last two.'

'So, who,' Dan swallowed, 'did they go with?'

'A surprise choice, actually. Do you know Laurence Ryan? I'd never heard of him, but that's who they went for in the end. Not long in the business, came from university . . . did a marvellous Benedict, apparently, at the West Yorkshire . . . ' but Dan was so relieved it wasn't Declan McCloud he'd stopped listening. 'Now,' Lenny caught his attention again. 'You may not be interested, but I've got you an interview for a part in a *Miss Marple.* What do you think? Shall I send it over? It's another killer, I'm afraid, but it's all filmed here, in London.'

Dan paused. He could hear the blood in his head roaring. 'No,' he decided. 'I'll hold out.'

Lenny was waiting. 'Right you are,' he said eventually. 'I'll be in touch.'

★　★　★

A week later, after Jemma had throw up two mornings in a row, Dan called him back.

'You know that *Miss Marple*, I've been thinking . . . ' he held the sharp edge of a red electricity bill pressed against his palm.

'Ahhh,' he heard Lenny's intake of breath. 'That's gone, I'm afraid. Declan McCloud. Odd choice for him, but then they do well in the States. But . . . now, hold on a minute, there's a play on at the Bush, no money obviously, but it's a new play, sexual abuse in competitive gymnastics. You've nothing against playing a suspected kiddie fiddler, have you?'

'I'll look at it.' Nauseous himself, Dan slid the bill into his pocket. 'Bike it over. I'll be in all day.'

'Sure. How're your cartwheels?'

'Not bad,' Dan grimaced, 'as long as I don't have to do the splits.' And he sat quite still, wondering how he would introduce this new subject to Jemma.

PART THREE

2003 – 2006

The Other Girl

Nell scribbled the details on a pad she kept by the phone. *Mary Peacock. Stabbed and killed husband. Australia on a convict ship. Set up own refuge for women.* 'I should warn you,' Nell's new agent added, 'they're seeing everyone, the world and his wife, or should I say husband?' He coughed, embarrassed. 'The thing is, they don't know what they're looking for. A *quality* apparently, so just go along and . . . meet.'

'They're seeing everyone, apparently,' Nell repeated the news to Sita when she came in from work.

'Well, they're not seeing *me*.'

'True,' Nell bit her lip.

Sita was temping as a receptionist for a software company specialising in games. She'd been working for this same firm, on and off, for a year, and although she insisted it was boring, it was clear to Nell she was unusually content. Sita emptied the contents of her carrier bag on to the table, — apples, satsumas, and a string bag of mixed nuts — hazels, walnuts and brazils. Their shells clinked seasonally. 'Do we have a nutcracker?'

'Probably,' Nell pulled open a drawer. 'Look, why don't you call your agent and ask straight out, why you're not being seen?'

'I know why.' Sita reached for the scissors and snipped through the taut diamonds of the orange

285

string. 'As far as the whole bloody business is concerned, I'm Asian, and no one wants to look beyond that. Anyway, the boss at work has asked if I can do maternity cover for Belinda. I'll have to do a training day and commit to a minimum of six months.'

'Six months!' Nell retrieved the nutcracker from a dusty corner where it had lain since last Christmas, undisturbed.

'I know. But then I thought, why not?'

Nell made tea and set it on the table. She still had the black-and-white polka-dot teapot Charlie had never bothered to reclaim. As soon as she'd become a film star Charlie had bought everything brand new. New furniture, new cutlery, new clothes. True, she wore the same flint and khaki outfits, casually thrown on, but instead of cotton, frayed and creased, now they were spun from cashmere and silk. If *she* ever made any money . . . Nell looked around the kitchen and sighed.

'Maybe . . . ' Sita pulled out a chair. 'I'll let fate decide. I've got one more week before I have to commit, and if my agent hasn't called by then . . . Can you imagine how my Dad will react when I tell him I've got a proper job? He'll probably burst a blood vessel and die from sheer relief.' Happily, Sita dug her nails into the skin of a tangerine.

Nell watched her. 'None of this has anything to do with that guy Raj in Accounts, has it? I can just see it, after all your years of rebellion, you're going to find a nice Hindu boy, get a reliable job and settle down.'

Sita's eyes were shining. 'You know what I will do if I take this job?' The peel had come off in one soft piece, spongy as a starfish on the table. 'I'll book a holiday. An actual holiday. One where I'm not worried I'll miss out on the chance of a lifetime the minute I arrive in the Algarve.'

'Remember the time I gave in and went to Spain with my Mum and missed the audition for *Twelfth Night*? The director had asked for me specially, I'd done a workshop with her at the Actors' Centre, and I know it's stupid but I still think, that could have been it.' Nell felt sickened, even now, just thinking about it. 'But maybe it's never like that. Maybe there is no such thing as a lucky break. Maybe you do well, or you don't do well, and that's how it is.'

'Maybe,' Sita shrugged. 'But then there are always those stories about someone who didn't work for five years, and then, just when they were about to go and train to be a plumber, it turns out they're the only person in Britain who's right to play Paul McCartney, and suddenly they're in a West End musical, out at the Ivy every night, their wedding paid for by *Hello!*, going, 'Oh, yes, I do have various projects in the pipeline, but I'm not sure which one I'll do next.''

'So how do people ever give up?' Nell chose a hazelnut and with all her strength pressed down on the flimsy silver ends of the nutcracker. 'There should be a support group — we could start one — Actors Anonymous.' The nut slipped from its vice and flew across the room. 'It would be so popular. In fact it's probably why so many actors in LA go to AA. Most of them don't even have a drinking problem. They're actually looking for tips on how to give up acting.' Nell sat back in her chair. 'Sita. Do you remember when we were in youth theatre, and we did that improvised play about a women's hostel, and that mad director, what was her name, made us all go off and spend the weekend at a battered wives' home?'

'Sure. But they're not called that any more.'

'True. It's just this part, it's for a woman — a victim of domestic abuse — who set up the first ever refuge in Australia. It's a film about her life.' Nell had a vision of Sita, as she was then, sixteen years old, sitting with the others in the basement kitchen of the hostel. She had her hair tied high up on her head, as if her mother might have done it, and she was wearing bright make-up, pink lipstick, and eye shadow of variegated blues. They'd all sat around that kitchen table, cradling their mugs of tea, turned away politely from a tall thin woman, newly arrived. The woman was dressed smartly, in dark trousers and a short belted coat, a doctor's wife, they found out later, and she'd stood by the barred window, a handkerchief held up to her nose, her handbag tucked under her arm, and quietly cried.

'Honestly, what were we thinking?' Sita frowned. 'Those poor women. Can you imagine? You finally escape your violent relationship only to find seven teenage members of a youth theatre looking you over and taking notes.'

'We should never have gone.' Nell could still feel the chill of her discomfort, watching the women on cooking duty, stirring metal pots of mince, drifting in and out of the steam of the potatoes boiling, ghostly, preoccupied, sad. 'I mean, if we could have done anything to help, that would have been different, if we could have made them a meal, or . . . I don't know, entertained them, sung some songs. Remember Binny? She was brilliant on the guitar . . . '

'*No more, no more*,' Sita began to sing, '*no more . . . beating.*'

Nell had forgotten there'd been songs, but unable to resist she joined in on the next line. '*Women are not made for . . . hitting.*' Their voices swooped and chimed like Japanese. '*Woman are not made for this.*'

'But what if it was good?' Nell reconsidered. 'If it made some kind of difference? Even if one person : . . '

'I suppose that's what we hoped,' Sita agreed. 'Someone saw it and thought, no, I'll stand up for myself. Get help. Do you remember that girl who'd had to leave her baby?'

Nell had seen her, standing in the hall, holding on to herself so hard her fists were claws.

'Is that hostel still there, do you think?'

Nell didn't know. How strange to think it might have been there all these years, with its scarred front door, its empty windows, the silent hull of its basement kitchen, while she'd done A levels and struggled through drama school, played a penguin over one entire winter of five a.m. starts, won and lost agents, driven to Edinburgh, the mirror ball sparkling on the back seat of Sita's car, performed fourteen sold-out shows at the festival, had an affair with a comedian. She'd endured ballet classes, tap classes, diets, jogs around the park, productions in cellars and above pubs all over London, and then they'd taken her and Sita's show back up to Edinburgh, where, mysteriously, it had failed. 'I hope it is still there,' she decided. 'I just hope it's nicer now, that's all.'

★ ★ ★

Nell expected nothing from the audition.

'They're seeing *everyone*,' Hettie told her when they bumped into each other on the steps. 'I was only in there for five minutes. The casting man looked girl-blind.'

'How are you?' She had on a purple coat with a fake fur collar and she looked more than ever like a little girl, dressed up.

'Good,' Hettie smiled. 'I'm doing panto. *Jack and the Beanstalk*. I love this time of year, at least I always work. And you?'

'Yes.' Nell nodded. 'All good.' She didn't elaborate. She didn't mention she was still doing shifts at Pizza Express. 'Have you seen any of the gang?'

'Umm. Let's think. Samantha. She's not been working much. But she's married. Unbelievable. They moved to Brighton. Jonathan's not too bad. He's helping out at the Terence Higgins Trust. It's a miracle really. These new drugs he's on. And Pierre. My God! Who'd have thought he'd be such a big shot at business? Have you seen his new offices? You know he's done a deal

290

with Saudi Arabia. He's virtually in charge of all the telecommunications in the middle east.'

'Yes.' Nell beamed. 'And Dan?'

Hettie clapped a hand over her mouth. 'Did you not hear? Jemma's pregnant again. With twins!'

'No.' Nell frowned. 'But didn't they just have another baby?'

'I know. It was an accident, apparently. They went away without the children. For the first time in God knows how long, and . . . well . . . they must have got carried away because when they got back . . . last time I spoke to Jem she was in tears . . . but then she cheered up and said at least there'd be lots of people to visit them when they're old.'

'True.' Nell had a pang, as she always did, at news of Dan. And then, as if the hurts had merged together, a vision of the stage manager rose up before her, his mortified face and desperate protestations when she'd misguidedly taken the train to visit him a week earlier than promised. 'I'd better go.' Nell forced a smile. 'Lovely to see you. And good luck with the panto. Where is it? Maybe I'll come.'

'Basingstoke.' They kissed. 'But honestly, don't worry.'

'I'll try. I'll bring my nephew.' Nell ran up the steps and in through the door of the building. She gave her name and waited with a row of other girls to be seen.

Mary Peacock. Nell took a breath and pulled out her scribbled notes. *Stabbed and killed husband. Australia on a convict ship.* She could

291

see Mary, a young woman in nineteenth-century clothes, a worn grey petticoat and a shawl. She imagined her life, up at dawn, cleaning out the grate, stirring porridge, keeping the children quiet while her husband slept. She was most likely limping, or wincing with the pain of a cracked rib, but Mary knew better than to complain. It was always this way. Or had been since a year into their marriage when their first child, a boy, was born all twisted round and wrong. An idiot, the baby was declared, with half a brain, and her husband had fixed his cold accusing eye on her. Now he turned vicious whenever he was drunk. Jibes and taunts, flashes of raw fury if any small thing was out of place. Mary Peacock had three more children, although the youngest, another boy, was weak as milk. She'd sat up late with him, soothing and rocking, until they'd both fallen asleep before the fire. 'Will you drive me mad!' She was woken with a kick, and after hours of soothing, the child began to cry. 'Please,' she begged, 'have patience, I'll build the fire up again,' but he dragged her from the chair and flung her back against the wall. It was then, it must have been, that her blood rose so high it choked her, and blind with it, she seized the knife from the table and wheeled around. Nell felt her heart swell. What must it be like to take revenge? To lose yourself so completely in the moment that nothing else is there? She thought of Harold Rabnik and his wine-soaked tongue. And with Mary Peacock, she flung herself forward and plunged the knife into his chest.

'Nell Gilby.'

Flustered, Nell stood up. 'Yes. That's me.' She scrabbled for her notes, and her heart beating, her cheeks flushed, she walked into the room.

'Right.' The casting director had found her photograph, the new one her new agent had asked her to have done. 'So.' He looked at her, patient, already a little bored, but just as he was about to speak a police siren exploded in the street below. Nell, fresh from her scene of violence, started. 'That's me they're coming for, most likely,' she laughed, and she saw something light up in the casting director's eyes.

★　★　★

Nell's agent was staggered. 'The director wants to see you. Tomorrow, first thing. So it went well?'

'I think so. It was odd. We started talking and . . . I don't know . . . ' Terror overcame her. Now she'd got this far, all there was left to do was mess it up.

'So, same place. Go along at 10. They'll probably put you on tape. I'll fax over some pages.'

'Apparently,' Sita warned her later, 'it's the first eleven seconds that are crucial. It's not to say it can't go wrong after that, but if you're going to get the job, you're going to get it then.'

That night Nell couldn't sleep. 'That's me they're coming for, most likely.' The line that had saved her swam round inside her head, but she couldn't use it, not again. It seemed so tantalising that only yesterday there was nothing to lose. Now there was everything. 'That's me they're coming for,' she twisted in her bed, clutching at the cool hot water bottle. 'That's me.'

Sita brought her in tea before she left for work. 'Remember,' she took hold of Nell's hand in both of hers. She had beautiful hands, fine and strong, with white gold rings on every finger, given to her by her father for each significant year. 'They need someone to play the lead in this film or it won't get made.'

'Yes,' Nell nodded. Fear still gripped her. 'I see what you're saying,' and she promised to stay calm.

★   ★   ★

Nell scanned the faces of the people on the Tube. There was one girl, with auburn hair and clear pale skin, whom Nell felt sure was going to the audition too. But then she remembered how on her first day of college she'd been convinced that every person she passed was going to be in her year. Nell closed her eyes and thought about the women's hostel, and how in the middle of that first night she'd been woken by a scuffle. She'd lain there, paralysed, convinced that someone was trying to break in. It had happened before, the youth theatre director had told them. A man had come to the house, claiming to be an electrician, sent by the council to mend the heating, but when the door was opened, he'd pushed his way inside. He'd run from room to

294

room, howling for his wife, and when he found her, he'd dragged her out on to the doorstep and stabbed her in the stomach.

But that night, there was no man trying to break in — just a woman, pleading to be let out. 'Leave me alone!' There was a gasp, and Nell heard Pat, who ran the place, grumble and then swear.

'I'm sorry,' the woman sobbed, 'but I left the children. I have to get home.' The front door shuddered open, and Nell crept from her bed. She crawled past the sleeping bodies of her friends, reaching the window in time to see the doctor's wife step out into the night. Nell looked along the street, expecting the woman's husband to jump out from behind a bush, ready to attack her, expertly, so it wouldn't show, but there was no one there. The woman looked surprised too. She whipped round, and seeing no one, stalked off along the empty road.

*   ★   ★

'Nell!' The casting director looked genuinely pleased to see her. 'Let me take your coat.' The director was there too. He shook Nell's hand and looked her over with hungry, hopeful eyes. 'Take a minute to read through this scene, it's just come through.' He adjusted a camera on a tripod, tilting it to point straight at her chair.

Nell read the new scene through so fast the words blurred before her eyes. Mary Peacock was in court, pleading for her life, while a judge summed up her crimes. 'Shame,' someone called from the public gallery, and Nell felt her blood rise. Shame on *you*, she would have yelled back, but the script dictated she stay quiet.

'Ready?' The director smiled at her when she looked up. He was tall, and palely handsome — shadowy, as if he'd been inside too long. The casting director took a seat beside her. 'One minute.' The red light of the camera blinked. 'OK. When you're ready you can start.'

Mary Peacock was defending herself. There had been no agreement that she should, but as the judge raised his hammer to proclaim the sentence, she pushed herself forward in the dock and begged to be allowed to speak. Nell imagined herself to be the doctor's wife, lunging round in terror in the empty street, and she wondered what had happened when that woman arrived home, whether for the sake of her children she'd endured her punishment, or whether she'd taken a knife from the kitchen and treading upstairs, soft on the soft carpet, she'd plunged the blade into her husband's heart.

Nell knew she was fighting for her life. Her voice was low and desperate, her eyes wild, and she kept in mind the hovering knowledge that even if Mary saved herself from hanging she'd lost all chance of seeing her children again.

'Very nice,' the director mused, and the casting director patted her on the arm.

They read another scene. Mary was in Australia now. She was older by some years, and after several entanglements of a violent sexual nature, she'd found a saviour who'd taken her in. He'd conveniently died not long after, leaving her his house, and Mary had turned this building into a refuge for any woman who had been abused. But now, not for the first time, the house had been mistaken for a brothel. A group of men were baying outside the window while Mary pushed a chest against the door. There were three other women, one older, two hardly more than girls, but it was Mary Peacock who yelled down to the men to get off home or she'd come out with a shotgun and send them on their way.

'You're a lot of ignorant, disgusting pigs,' she hollered after them, as she took aim from a window, and even after they'd turned tail she kept throwing insults into the night.

'Very nice,' the director nodded, and he looked at her, searching, before asking her to read again.

★ ★ ★

As Nell walked towards the Tube, head down against the biting wind, she had an irresistible desire to call Charlie. She hadn't seen so much of her this year, as Charlie had been based in Manchester, playing a detective opposite an actor she considered second rate. She'd made the mistake of seducing him before they'd finished filming the first series, and after that, as she'd told Nell in various dejected late-night calls, she despised him more than ever.

'So how are you?' Nell asked her now, and she slowed to take in the flow of woe and vitriol that poured into her ear. There'd been a perfect job, in America, playing some big star's girlfriend, but at the last moment the producer had insisted on another girl, a white girl, and as from today she was out of the running. 'My agent says the producer's racist, but I'm not sure. I've lost my looks, that's the thing.'

'Don't be silly,' Nell tutted, sympathetic, disbelieving. They'd had this conversation before.

'And you?' Charlie asked, distracted.

Nell took her voice down to a casual tone as she replied, 'Actually, I've just been up for a film.'

'Really?'

'I saw the casting director yesterday, and he wanted the director to meet me. Ciaran Conway. He made that . . .'

'Yes.' Charlie was impatient. 'I know Ciaran. I saw him a month or so ago for dinner. In fact I must find out what hap . . . It's not that post-apocalyptic thing, is it, tribes of lost souls wandering through a desert?'

'This one's historical. But it is set in Australia.'

'Not *Mary Peacock*?'

'Yes.'

'Bloody hell!'

'I know.' Nell felt uncomfortable. Guilty almost. 'It's starting straight after Christmas. Can you imagine being in the middle of the Outback for New Year?'

There was silence. 'Fuck. I was still waiting to hear about that other thing.' She sounded winded. 'I guess that's not going to happen now.'

Nell pulled her coat round her. 'Well, I've no idea what's actually going on. I think they've got to send my tape over to America.' She turned her back into the wind, which was cut with splinters of sharp rain. 'I'll tell you what. I'll call you later. When I know more.'

'But Nell,' Charlie wasn't ready to let it go.

'What?'

'You're not up for Mary, are you?'

'I think so . . . yes.'

There was a quick intake of breath. 'That's brilliant. I'll tell you what, I'll phone Maisie for you now and see what's going on.'

'Great,' Nell frowned. 'Good idea.' And she ran into the shelter of the Tube.

★ ★ ★

Nell resisted phoning her own agent. She knew he'd be in touch if there was any news. She made herself lunch and looked over her Christmas present list, flicking satisfying ticks beside the names of those people she already had gifts for, and scribbling notes and question marks beside the more impossible members of her family — her father, her brother-in-law, her mother's boyfriend, Lewis. What could any of them possibly want? She sighed. Maybe that was the problem with men. They didn't need anything. At least, they didn't need anything from her. The phone rang, and her heart flipped. But it was only her mother. 'I was just checking, you're not a vegetarian or anything at the moment?'

'No,' Nell rolled her eyes.

'And I was wondering, too. Will you be bringing anyone with you for Christmas? I'm imagining not, as you haven't mentioned it, but before I get everything organised I thought I'd better check.'

'Actually, Mum,' Nell felt her heart quickening again, 'I'm not sure if I'll get home for Christmas now.'

There was a silence, into which Nell felt all her mother's hopes and aspirations tumble together in confusion. 'Is it . . . do you . . . ?'

'Oh Mum, it probably won't happen. But I'm up for a film and if I get it . . . ' Her mother squealed. ' . . . if I get it, I'll have to be in Australia by the twenty-eighth, and everyone says it's better to stop, somewhere like Japan, on the way, so you're not so jetlagged, so I don't know if I'll have time . . . '

'Don't worry,' her mother cut in. 'It doesn't matter at all. Wait to see what happens and if it's at all possible, well, that will be a bonus. You know, someone, maybe even Lewis, could always drive you to the airport on Boxing Day.'

'Oh, it probably won't happen.' Nell dreaded the thought of spending three hours in a car with Lewis, with his whistling and his attempts at celebrity gossip, and the polite need for a goodbye embrace which had never felt the same since one late night in the kitchen on a trip home from college, when he'd made a drunken grope for her. If only, she thought, she had the courage to become a lesbian, then the whole lot of them could go and fuck themselves. She let out a breathy gasp of laughter and her mother paused in her plans.

'Nell?'

'It's nothing. Look, I shouldn't have said

300

anything. Really. Assume I'm coming, on my own, gagging for turkey, and I'll let you know if anything changes.'

'OK, my love.' Nell felt her mother smile. And she thought not for the first time how much they both needed her to succeed.

Nell sat with the phone in her lap. How did she know she wouldn't be happier with a woman if she never tried it? She felt again the swirling, melting lick of fire, as Charlie's narrow tongue pushed into her mouth. But she'd never wanted to be kissed by any other girl. And not really even by Charlie after that. In her dreams it was a man she longed for. Someone without the inquisitive chatter, the endless intricate memory for who did what and when. A stranger was what she wanted, mysterious, unknown. She dreamt quite regularly about this stranger. How he'd lay his body over hers, draping himself across her feet. I love you, I love every part of you, he'd repeat through her sleep, and Nell would wake, filled up to the brim. Once she'd dreamt about Sita, the two of them, their bodies entwined, their fingers tracing patterns on each other's skin, but that was only after the stage manager had asked if they'd ever had an affair. 'No!' she'd laughed, and she'd attempted to explain how deeply, passionately, girls could love their friends.

The next time the phone rang it was Charlie. 'Right.' She was matter of fact. 'I've spoken to Maisie and what she says is this. There are two actresses in the running and they're both unknowns. The execs in LA will watch their tapes, and then they'll decide.'

'Really?' Nell glanced at herself in the mirror. 'The money men. Is it really up to them?'

'Not always, but sometimes. Or occasionally the director likes to make them feel they've made the decision. But usually he'll push forward his favourite.'

'By when, did Maisie say? I mean, when will they decide?'

'Soon, I imagine. Maybe today.'

'Oh my God.' Nell gasped to catch her breath. 'I wish I knew who she was. The other girl.'

'There's always another girl,' Charlie said wistfully. 'Although, occasionally, the other girl is you.'

★ ★ ★

Nell sat for a while in the chilly flat, and then, pulling on her thickest coat, she slipped her mobile phone into the pocket and went out for a walk. The street outside was quiet and grey. A car sped by, racing over puddles, sending out an arc of filthy spray. Nell kept close to the cropped hedges, releasing a shower of chandelier droplets each time her shoulder nudged against the hidden twigs. At the roundabout she ran across the open plains of tarmac, trudged up and down the humpbacked bridge, thinking as she always did of Billy Goat Gruff heading for the meadow, and as if she really had evaded the ogre, there ahead of her was the green oval of Queens Park. It was bordered by large houses with bright painted doors, curlicues of white wooden detail

302

on their eaves. There was a playground in the park, which must have always been there, but which Nell had only noticed as her thirtieth birthday loomed. There was a café too, from which she bought a takeaway cup of tea. She wrapped her hands around the cardboard cup, and ambled on under the great bare trees, glancing across the road as the houses grew even larger, imagining their warm wood interiors, the mess of Wellington boots and toys, the smell of fish fingers, cakes cooling on a tray. In one doorway a woman was haranguing two small girls, buttoned up in woollen coats, their faces tilted in mute bewilderment. 'I don't want to say it again,' she scolded. Nell turned away, unwilling to have her fantasy interrupted, and walked on round the perimeter path. There was her favourite house, a dolls' Regency villa in one window and in another a stained-glass nativity scene made from tissue and black card. Light from a lamp illuminated the colours, the gold of the star, the red flames of the fire flickering between brown twigs. That's what I'll do, she decided, I'll decorate the window of our flat, and stopping at the newsagent at the end of her road, she used her Saturday night waitressing tips to buy a stack of tissue paper and some card. As she left the shop she checked her phone. There was one missed call, how could that be possible? But when she pressed on it she saw it was only her sister, acting, she imagined, as their mother's envoy for more news.

Nell laid out the card on the kitchen table, and carefully sketched a palm tree, a camel and a star. She attempted a baby in a manger, but it looked like a banana, so instead she drew three kings with crowns like castle turrets, their bodies draped in capes. Slowly she began to cut, and as she sliced into the card she dreamt up her new life. She'd move from here. Leave behind the draughty bedroom, the condemned boiler in the bathroom, whose words of warning she'd read so often they'd lost all sense of threat. She smiled to think of her landlord's surprise when finally, after all these years, she'd tell him she was going. Would he apologise for not making the promised repairs, never replacing the mouldy carpet or mending the leak in the roof? Maybe he'd offer to reward her in some way for the floorboards she and Sita had spent a weekend painting after they'd pulled the carpet up themselves. More likely than not he'd insist that they replace it. Nell glanced up at the pale-blue kitchen, the cloud effects they'd sponged on to the ceiling, the stencils of fruit and vegetables they'd sprayed on to the cupboard doors. But maybe Sita wouldn't want to move? Maybe she'd want to keep the flat on, split the rent with Raj?

Her mobile rang and she nicked her finger in her rush to answer. 'Hi,' she said, and she tensed her whole body for her agent's news.

'Right.' He sounded neither exuberant nor mournful. 'You're in the running. That's the good news. But there are two other girls.'

'Two?' Nell mouthed hopelessly.

'It's ultimately up to the director to make his choice, but the money men have to agree it. They don't need the girl to be well known, they've got a big Australian soap star, Wayne Hull, playing the male lead, and a grand Dame of the theatre — Judi possibly — doing a cameo.'

Nell pressed the phone against her ear. 'So . . . will . . . when do they have to decide by? I mean, do they want me to go back in, read again or anything?'

'Maybe. But not for the moment. Let's just sit tight.'

'OK.' Nell was too stunned to ask him anything else.

'We'll talk later, all right?'

'OK.' Nell took up her knife again and sliced out the first king, giving a jagged ridge to his crown, leaving a sliver of light the length of his staff. She tore off a corner of tissue and pasted it over the star, and deciding it was insufficient, she glued on two more layers. She held it against the window to admire her work, and realised with a shock that it was dark. She was due to start her shift at half past five. Hastily she piled everything up at one end of the table, changed into her uniform of black skirt and red T-shirt, the material of which she'd come to hate. *No news yet.* She scrawled a note for Sita, and she ran out of the door.

It was only when she reached the Tube that she found she'd forgotten her phone. Alarm coursed through her, and she had to reach out and steady herself as if the phone was as integral a part of her as the joints in her knees. Should she go back? She could do it in ten minutes if she ran, but she was late already, and the thought of being reprimanded by the manager Sadiq

— until last week a waiter himself — made her baulk. I'll call when I'm there, she decided, and she stepped on to the escalator.

Sadiq eyed her dispassionately as she rushed in. 'We've got a party of twenty booked for six fifteen,' he said. 'I've put them in your station, so you better get going.' The tables were empty. No knives and forks or napkins, just sprigs of flowers in thumbnail vases. Honestly, she thought. It was already five to six. She'd lay up and then ask if she could use the phone, say it was an emergency, her mother was ill. No, she couldn't risk her mother's health. She didn't even feel willing to hex Lewis, much as she despised him. She clattered down the cutlery, and flew round with a pile of napkins. Her grandmother then, who was already dead. She was setting out water glasses when the group of twenty appeared at the door, coats and hats and umbrellas dripping, laughing and talking, released from the office early. Nell approached the manager. 'Can I . . . ' but without waiting to hear her he thrust a pile of menus into her arms. 'Get their orders fast as possible, this table needs to be free again by 7.45.'

Nell turned away. There was probably no news anyway. What did it matter? She'd be working here for the rest of her life, she might as well accept it, and smiling the length of the long table she handed the menus round.

The worst thing about large groups was that no one could remember what they wanted to eat. 'Calzone,' they'd linger over the menu, 'or salad Niçoise? But twenty minutes later, although they'd opted for the calzone, there was not a single nod of recognition when the food arrived. 'Calzone!' Nell would shout, the plates hot and heavy in her hand. But there was only a babble of talk and a bank of flushed and blinking faces. Occasionally a meal had to be taken back to the kitchen, unclaimed, and it was only when everyone had been served and one customer sat forlornly at an empty place, that they'd finally remember — the word dawning on them like a brand-new thought: calzone.

Nell didn't get a break till nearly ten. She took her salad and a glass of diet Coke to the steel table at the back of the kitchen. 'How you?' Dragan, the Croatian washer-upper, asked. Politeness dictated that she respond with a question of her own, but it always seemed cruel to torment him. His English, even after all this time, was almost non-existent, and when he did finally manage to make a sentence, the news he had to impart was usually sad. 'My girlfriend, she gone home,' he managed. 'My baby. She not well.' Nell scrunched her face in sorrow and crunched a lettuce leaf with Thousand Island dressing. What if she never did come to work here again? She looked round at the white tiled walls, the tall tin prep tables, the towering piles of crockery. At the open kitchen, their faces to the diners, the chefs performed in their pirate-striped T-shirts, spinning dough and sprinkling cheeses, arranging olives, sliding pizzas in and out of the furnace of their ship.

It was after twelve before the last customer was ushered out, the tables cleared and wiped, the tips divided. Nell pulled on her coat, and as she was about to step out into the night she turned and ran through to the kitchen where Dragan was loading coffee cups into the machine. 'Goodbye,' she said, and seeing his surprise at this unnecessary exchange, she wrote her mobile number on a napkin. 'Just in case you ever need advice or anything . . . to talk to someone . . . you know . . . '

Dragan didn't attempt to reach for the well of words that usually evaded him. Instead he smiled, and with a solemn dip of his head, he tucked the napkin into his pocket and turned back to his work.

Outside, the temperature had dropped. Nell took in a deep cold breath of air and lifted her face into the night as one white, star-shaped flake floated down towards her. 'It's snowing,' she said to two men heaving drunkenly by, and for a moment they took hold of her arms and the three of them swung along together down the street. Nell laughed and disentangled herself. There were more flakes now, soft as feathers, melting as they neared the ground. She wrapped her coat around her and hurried towards the Tube. Outside, she bought an *Evening Standard*, her attention caught by the photograph on the front page — a gaunt, bearded Saddam Hussein, looking up at the uniformed legs of American soldiers from a hole in the ground. Everywhere she looked people were staring at the image. A tyrant brought low. How long had he been hiding in that hole? she wondered, and she had to fight off the impulse to feel sorry for him.

When Nell got out at her stop the snow had thickened to a blizzard. Fat flakes swirled and settled, picking up again, gusting on to rooftops, lying still. The grey streets were transformed. Roof tiles made beautiful with icing, window ledges sweet as gingerbread. Nell kicked her way along the road, smiling at anyone who passed her, assuming a temporary truce in the malevolence that was usually brewing at this hour of the night. Her footsteps fell silent, her face tingled, and occasionally she caught a wafer-thin offering of snow on her tongue.

At home the lights were out, all except the one lamp Sita left on for her if she'd gone to bed, but even from the foot of the stairs she could see her phone on the hall table, blinking out the news of a missed call. She laid her hand on it, and fumbling with her gloved finger, she pressed the message. 'Must have missed you.' It was her agent, breezy, cheerful. 'Call me back. Soon as you can.'

Her heart pounded. Her face scalded, red, and then the cold that had been collecting froze her blood. She listened to the message again, straining for meaning in every inflection. Was that actually excitement there? Or was it simply his professional determination to continue now that they knew the worst? Nell tiptoed along the corridor to Sita's room. The light was off, but even so, she stood hopefully outside her door. Just as she was about to turn away, she heard Sita's sleepy voice. 'Nellie, is that you?'

Nell inched her door open and crept into the gloom. She sat down on the edge of the bed.

'What do you think?' Sita held the phone to her ear.

Sita sat up. 'Must have missed you.' Her agent's voice vibrated between them. 'Call me back. Soon as you can.'

Sita frowned and examined the phone as if its small stout body could reveal the truth.

'Have I got the job?' Nell winced, when Sita didn't speak, and Sita laid her head back on the pillow.

'I actually, honestly, think you might have.'

The two girls screamed and clutched each other's hands. 'But I'm only guessing, it's just why would he phone like that if you hadn't?'

'I know, that's what I was thinking.' Nell hadn't allowed herself to think anything of the sort, or if she had, just for the smallest second. 'Soon as you can,' she echoed. She leapt up and tugged at the blind. 'Have you seen?' A cotton-wool curtain of snow fell vertically down.

Sita took up the phone again and pressed it to her ear.

'What are you doing?' Nell asked.

'I'm calling.'

Nell wrestled it from her hand. 'It's one in the morning,' she was laughing, 'and anyway, it's an office, there won't be anyone there.'

'But it's so exciting,' Sita insisted.

'I know.' Nell climbed into the warm bed beside her. 'Or it might be,' and they chatted and planned and watched the snow plunging past the window, inching themselves towards morning and the moment when, officially, Nell's life might be about to change.

Rice Cakes and Starbucks

When Dan and Jemma arrived in Los Angeles it was raining. Not drizzling, or even pouring, but streaming down outside the glass doors of the departure lounge in thick, grey sideways slices. Water sluiced along the airport roads, tumbling in the gutters, spinning in the wheels of the taxis that splashed up to collect the lucky people at the head of the queue. 'Blimey,' they said, almost in unison, and Dan put his hand up to his mouth and laughed.

'I'm cold,' Honey shivered in her T-shirt, and Dan knelt down to rifle through their bulging bags, removing as he did so, numerous insubstantial outfits which they'd packed with the expectation of the six of them lifted out of a grey London winter into an endless bright blue Californian afternoon.

Dan and Jemma had rented a house in the hills. The house had been recommended by a friend of Dan's, although at the last minute his wife had interjected: 'They can't stay up there! They've got to be by the ocean. In Santa Monica.'

'But Santa Monica's extortionate, and you don't even get a pool,' Dan's friend told her, 'and what's the point of LA if there's no pool?'

Jemma and Dan had listened nervously. They'd already said yes to the house in the hills, paid their deposit, filled in numerous forms for

311

the insurance, the gas, the electrics and the telephone, and so neither of them mentioned Santa Monica or the ocean again. Instead, they talked about the pool. 'The pool, the pool,' they repeated like a charm, and Honey and Ben tugged on their swimming costumes, blew up their armbands, and ran shrieking up and down the draughty, carpeted stairs of their north London home.

The higher they drove the more heavily it rained. It clattered on the roof of the taxi and washed in sheets over the windscreen, and when the driver stopped to call the number that they gave him for directions they could see the water rushing downhill over the cobbled streets. 'Got it, got it,' he assured their landlord, who was waiting with the key, but then almost immediately they'd become lost again, roaring up and down the narrow roads, catching glimpses of lit-up Spanish villas and rain-soaked ferns and the same few street names over and over again.

By the time they finally found the house, in a tiny cul-de-sac obscured by darkness and a large half-fallen bush, Ben and the twins were asleep, although Honey was still up, staring out intently at the night. 'Careful,' the driver warned as Dan stepped into a foot of gushing water, and the landlord opened the yard door and stood watching them from underneath a white umbrella as they struggled with their luggage and the warm weights of their children, unloading them into the chilled hush of the hall.

★ ★ ★

It had been Jemma's idea to come. 'Dan!' he'd heard her calling from the bathroom, and although she hated it when the children shouted to her from the top of the house, she was doing it herself now.

Slowly Dan walked upstairs and put his head round the door. 'What is it?' He waited. She was lying stretched out in the bath, her face flushed, her hair a straggle of damp curls, her breasts blue-veined and swollen from feeding the twins. 'Listen, I've been thinking. We could rent this house out, say for six months, put all our things in storage, and then before the children get too big, we could go to America and give it a chance. While your series is still on.'

Dan sat down on the toilet seat. 'Are you serious? With four kids?'

'Why not? We could get good money for this house, and we could use that money to rent somewhere out there.'

Dan looked at his feet. 'I suppose, in theory, we could.'

Jemma was busy calculating. 'I'll phone the estate agent first thing on Monday and see what they say. And we could look into the right time to go. If there's a good time, a good season . . . '

'I don't think they have seasons.'

'Don't they have pilot season?'

'Well, yes . . . '

Honey was shouting from the kitchen. A door slammed and Ben gave an almighty scream. Dan imagined fingers caught in the hinges, small creased digits sliced right off. He flew down the stairs. 'What are you doing?' Honey and Ben

313

looked round at him. They'd climbed on to the worktop to get at some biscuits and for a second they froze. 'No,' he snatched the biscuits away. 'It's lunch soon,' he told them, and then thinking that actually, with Jemma still in the bath and the babies sleeping, lunch may not be for at least an hour, he peeled back the shiny plastic wrapping and gave them a biscuit each.

'Just one,' he said, to impress on them this new unshakeable rule.

'Oh please, just two,' Honey made her eyes as round as coins, and giving up any pretence he was in charge Dan slid out two more and shoved them into their hot hands.

'Dan!' Jemma was shouting to him again and he ran back upstairs. 'What?'

'Shall we do it?' Her eyes were bright.

'I don't know.'

'Why not?' she challenged, and instead of telling her why not — so that he could blame her for ever for holding him back, for having four children when he only needed one, for making it impossible to realise his dreams when they all relied on him, all five of them, to be at home, he changed the inflection and shrugged. 'Why not?'

They looked at each other and Dan attempted a smile. 'I mean, the worst thing that can happen is they hate me, and then we can come home.'

'Well, not if we've rented the house.'

'True.' He bit his lip. 'Well, they'll just have to love me.'

'They do love you. Of course they love you. Didn't Finola say the show was getting great reviews?' and showering him with tiny flicks of water she levered herself out.

★ ★ ★

The house was immaculately furnished, with fragile lamps and highly polished surfaces, and although it had a den, a dressing room and a study, it seemed to only have one bedroom. 'But it does have a pool,' Jemma said brightly, and they pressed their noses against the black panes of glass and stared out into its choppy, rectangular depth.

All night it rained. Dan could hear it crashing against the glass windows of their cold white room while Lola and Grace kicked and snuffled in the bed between them and Ben and Honey shifted uneasily on lilos that they'd laid down in the dressing room next door. At three Grace woke and began to gurgle happily as if it were late morning, which of course it was, for her, and Dan turned on his side and pretended to be oblivious. Jemma fed her and shushed her and even pleaded a little with her to be quiet and then, when Lola woke, she sighed, got up and took them both away. Not long after, he heard Ben begging to be allowed to go in the pool, and then Honey screaming that she was mean, mean, mean for not letting them even try it. 'It's dark,' Jemma protested, remarkably cheerfully, and some time later, although it was *still* dark, he heard the garden door creak open and the sounds of the three of them, Jemma, Honey and Ben, squealing as they ran out into the rain to

315

dip their feet into the water. 'It's freezing!' Honey complained. 'You said it would be warm!' And he heard the slam of the door as they hurtled back in. Eventually, when he really was asleep, Jemma slid in beside him. Her body was chilled and she pressed herself against his back for warmth. 'The twins are having a nap and the others are watching *Sponge Bob*,' she whispered, and Dan tried to remember where he was. Oh God, it all came back to him, what if they don't like me? What if I can't get a single audition, let alone a job, and then by the time I get back to London they've all forgotten who I am? He felt so sick and weary that when the first baby woke, forty minutes later, Jemma had to kick him in the shins to rouse him.

But once Dan was in the kitchen with Grace under one arm, he was cheered by the sheer Americanness of everything. The size of the fridge, inside which was a two-litre carton of fresh orange juice and a giant bag of bagels, the size of the cooker with its industrial grey hob, and the width of the wide-screen television before which his children sat like puppies, their eyes round, their mouths open. He peered out at the pool. It filled every available space of garden and could be reached from French doors in the den. Once it stops raining, Dan told himself, I'll swim in that pool every day, one hundred lengths, until my body is hard and lean and irresistible.

★   ★   ★

But it didn't stop raining. 'Is this normal?' they asked the landlord, who appeared shortly after nine to tell them how to work the washing machine and the dryer, how to sweep out the gas-fuelled log fire and adjust the temperature in the pool when — if ever — that became applicable.

'Not normal at all.' He shook his head and he flicked on the television news to show them how some of the neighbouring houses, clinging to the hill by steps and stilts, were beginning to slide down the mountain. 'Four people already lost their lives,' he said. 'And this rain still ain't letting up.'

He lent them his umbrella and offered to drive Dan to a car-hire centre.

'I won't be long.' Dan turned to Jemma, who'd been mentioning since seven that it would be great to get out, somewhere, anywhere, for breakfast, or lunch, or whatever meal they were on now.

'Dan . . . ' she hissed, widening her eyes at him, but he pretended not to notice and quickly turned away. 'I'll be half an hour at the most.'

★ ★ ★

The car-hire centre was clean and spacious. There were gleaming saloons and magnificent four-by-fours. 'I need a family car, with two baby seats, and a booster seat . . . and . . . Do I get a discount if I take it for . . . ' he swallowed, 'six months?'

'You sure do.' The man smiled at him, his

317

teeth were so highly polished they were translucent. And by the time he'd chosen and filled in all the forms the car salesman, whose name was Duane, wished him not just a Nice Day, but a Fantastic Day, with such genuine enthusiasm that Dan felt quite uplifted. Once behind the wheel, he couldn't resist it, he took the car for a quick spin, and then finding himself driving past a supermarket he decided to stop and buy provisions. The supermarket was enormous, a whole aisle for sliced cheese, and after filling his basket with fruit and vegetables he became distracted by the hardware section where he bought cheap raincoats, a pack of cards and a bumper bag of teething rings for the twins. Then on the way back he forgot the street sign was hidden by the fallen bush and drove fast past it at least five times. When he finally arrived home it was after twelve.

'How is everyone?' He rushed in through the rain, shaking himself and stamping in the hall.

Jemma's face was stony. 'Fine.' She handed over Lola and slammed out of the room.

'What's up with Mummy?' he asked in a conspiratorial way, and Honey hung her head and said Mummy was cross because she'd taken Lola into the garden. 'I only dipped her feet in the pool up to her toes. I wanted to see if she'd like it.'

'And did she like it?' Dan laid the baby along the length of his knees and kissed the dense pads of her feet in their stripy skin-tight socks.

'Not really. I think it's too cold for her. She screamed and screamed and cried.'

318

'Right.' Jemma was back, with Grace in a cagoule. She looked as if she'd been crying too. 'Let's go. We need to get out of this house. Now.'

* * *

'For God's sake.' Jemma frowned when she saw the car. A great black seven-seater SUV that all four children had to be lifted into.

Dan raised his hands to show the decision had been beyond him. 'It's all they had,' he told her. 'And if it goes on raining we'll need something powerful to get up and down this goddamn hill . . . '

'Sure, sure . . . ' Jemma threw him a disbelieving look and climbed into the front.

'Honestly.'

The inside of the car smelt so new, so sleek and shiny that it made Dan smile. The windscreen wipers whipped back and forth, the lights on the dashboard twinkled. 'Hang on,' he said and he ran back into the house and returned with a CD which he slipped into the player. Green Day swelled and roared above the weather. The children squealed and even Jemma couldn't resist a smile. 'Where to?' he asked, as if everything, from now on, were up to her.

'Let's drive around and find somewhere nice to eat.'

There was a map in the glove compartment and Jemma stretched it over her lap. 'Sunset Boulevard,' she read.

'Really?' Dan peered out.

'No. I just had to say it.' She took a breath. 'Venice Beach.'

'You're confusing me.' Dan sped through a junction.

'Beverly Hills. West Hollywood.'

'Look, we're on Santa Monica Boulevard.' Dan pointed. 'Shall I keep going?'

Jemma stared at the map. 'It leads right to the sea. That would be fun. What do you think, kids? The ocean!'

An hour later they were still on Santa Monica Boulevard. The traffic stopped and started, grinding slowly forward in the rain. Dan kept his eyes open for a restaurant. Burger bars and fast-food chains lined the deserted streets. 'I thought everyone was meant to be so healthy out here.' Jemma squinted.

'Not everyone. Just Brad Pitt. Everyone else is fat as fuck.'

'Daddy!'

'Fat as a duck, I said.'

'How about there?' Jemma pointed, but it wasn't a restaurant at all, just an antique shop with a table laid for supper, rosebud crockery and a bowl of glass grapes. They drove on, the windscreen wipers working powerfully, Green Day playing over again.

The children were unusually quiet, stunned by the time change, the rain and the music. 'If we don't stop soon, they'll go to sleep,' Jemma worried. 'And we'll all be up again tomorrow at three a.m. Or some of us will.'

Dan turned off Santa Monica Boulevard and sped along smaller streets, crossing junctions and searching left and right until with a screech of brakes he pulled up at a sign for pizza.

But it was too late. All four were fast asleep. Dan and Jemma looked over at their children. Honey with her halo of gold curls, her black lashes lying like a fan against her skin, Ben, his thick mouse tufts unbrushed for several days, one ear bright red where it had folded back against the seat, and the twins in their own row, still bald, their faces unformed, a silver line of dribble hanging from each chin.

'Shall we go back to the house?' Dan said quietly. 'I bought some food. We could make lunch there and then wake them up.'

They glanced at the pizza restaurant. A row of men in beige security uniforms sat at the window on stainless steel stools. 'Or not wake them?'

Jemma slid her hand on to his knee. 'Or not immediately. We could recline these seats and have a quick sleep first.'

'Mmm, lovely.' And more slowly, with the music lower, they drove home.

★ ★ ★

It was a week before Dan had his first casting. His American manager, Finola, called to say that things were Great. They were going Really Well. A lot of people had seen his series on BBC America — a dark and chilly drama about police corruption at the highest level — and she'd been sending out his show reel, talking him up, and now, finally, he had a meeting with a casting woman from CBS. 'But how are you managing?'

she asked, concerned, 'with your little ones, and all this rain?'

'Fine, fine,' Dan told her. 'We're used to it.'

But it wasn't true.

'What's the point of this place if it isn't sunny?' Jemma shook her head, and Dan overheard her telling Grace, 'If it rains one more day, we're going home.' He didn't ask her how she planned to break the news to the Dutch osteopath and his family who'd rented their house for half a year, or to Finola, who swore she was working round the clock to get him seen. 'It wouldn't be so bad if it wasn't for the fucking pool. The children never let up for a moment, whining and pleading to be allowed to swim.'

'Just let them then,' Dan muttered, but he had to agree that it was freezing, the surface of the water awash with debris, palm fronds and the dried brown tendrils of a plant that looked like spiders.

★ ★ ★

The day of the casting Dan woke early. At first he imagined it must be nerves, but then he realised that it was silence that had woken him. The downpour had stopped and the window was filled with a thick grey rainless light. Miraculously, the children were still sleeping, Grace and Lola in newly assembled cots at the end of their bed, the others in the room next door. Very carefully, he tiptoed into the kitchen. He took a breath. It was the first time in a week, the first time since the car-hire centre, that he'd been alone. He opened the French doors and stepped out into the garden. The air smelled good. Musty and foreign. He knelt down and dipped his fingers in the pool. The water was still cold, but hopeful and intoxicating and above him hung one tall palm, its leaves a far-off flower.

Dan was startled by a shriek. 'We're going in!' There were Ben and Honey, tugging off their pyjamas, screaming and hopping with joy.

'Hang on, you two, it's only 6.45!' But Dan didn't have the heart to stop them.

'Don't move,' he said instead and he ran in and grabbed Ben's armbands, unpacked and waiting since the first day. As fast as he could he blew them up. Honey was in first. 'It's not cold!' she said defiantly, although her teeth were chattering. Ben screamed as he jumped, and then screamed louder and longer as he hit the water. 'It's not cold either,' he promised once he'd recovered from the shock. Dan pulled a chair outside and watched them, ducking and fighting and flicking water at each other until their lips were blue.

Jemma made porridge, although like everything, it tasted different — finer, softer, further removed from the original oat. Her face was creased and heavy with a rare night of unbroken sleep. 'I think we're over the worst,' she rubbed the children's towelled bodies to bring back blood and she smiled hopefully at Dan.

After breakfast Dan tried on his suit. Did men wear suits in California? He didn't know, but he couldn't help admire himself in the charcoal cut of it. He moved back and forth before the mirror, sucking in his cheekbones, sticking out his chest, checking the imperfect creases of his trousers. 'No hands! No hands!' he warded off the children as they rushed towards him, and he heard Jemma cluck disapprovingly.

'I thought the meeting wasn't till 12.'

'Yes. But I need to find it first. It's somewhere in West Hollywood and I thought I'd go for a coffee before . . . get my bearings. Take stock.'

Jemma handed him a muslin and then Lola, both of which he took reluctantly. 'Right,' she said. 'I'm going to get a shower.'

As soon as she was back she dressed the children and then began to pack a bag. Rice cakes, water, tangerines, bananas.

'Where are you going?' Dan asked, holding both twins now, hardly daring to take his eye from them in case they threw up, one over each shoulder.

'I thought we'd come with you. We can find a Starbucks or something and wait.'

Dan was appalled. 'No . . . really.' He imagined running from the flock of his children, scattering rice cakes and baby milk, muslins and frappuccino, arriving red-faced and dishevelled at the marble steps of CBS.

'We can't stay here all day.' Jemma didn't meet his eye. She didn't want an argument and they both knew she'd waver if she saw the fury in his face.

'Jem, it's why we came. For me to get work! It's what we decided.'

'I know. I know.' She bustled at the sink, putting the porridge pan on to soak, wiping down the surfaces. 'But I can't spend another day in this house . . . ' she swallowed. 'No school. No nursery.'

Dan put both girls on the floor, where they sometimes could and sometimes couldn't stay upright on their own. Grace sat for a second and then fell forward, her face squashing into a rubber mat. 'Sweetheart.' He took hold of Jemma's shoulders. 'I won't be gone all day. It's stopped raining now. You can take them for a walk or something.'

'Dan,' she looked at him and her face was white. 'What's more important to you? An episode of *Entourage* or finding your wife and children lying at the bottom of that pool?'

'For God's sake! The drama! Why did you give up acting again?' and he picked up Grace, who had found an ancient Oreo and was forcing it into her mouth.

'Because I was thrown out of drama school. Remember?' Tears sprang into her eyes. 'And in case you've forgotten they kept you on for one more year, to try and convince you you were gay.'

Grace spat the Oreo out down the front of Dan's suit. 'Bugger!' He put her down again and she began to cry. He wet the muslin and began to dab at the cloth, and then, accepting defeat, he walked into the den and shouted at the others to switch off Cartoon Network, NOW, and get into the car.

The Starbucks on Wilshire was huge. Dan sat in an armchair, the stain still visible on his left lapel, and read the *International Guardian* while

325

Jemma slumped on a sofa, eating a biscotti, and breastfeeding Grace, who had a scattering of crumbs over her ear. The children ran riot at the other end, climbing on to and then jumping off a horseshoe of chairs which were luckily deserted. Occasionally Dan looked up from his paper to check that the staff weren't calling the LAPD for reinforcements, but the noise was conveniently drowned out by the sound of the cappuccino machine whirring and buzzing for the line of takeaway orders. How did this happen? he thought to himself, but it was hard not to smile.

'Right.' It was 11.30. 'I'll be off.'

'See you back here then,' Jemma looked up at him. 'Give me a call when you're on your way. And sweetheart . . . '

He waited.

'Good luck.'

★   ★   ★

Dan walked twice round the block to shake all thoughts of his family off. Was it possible to be a great actor, and still be loyal to your wife? He searched round for examples and couldn't think of any. And then, to his relief, he remembered that Paul Newman had been married to Joanne Woodward for almost fifty years. They had three daughters and lived on a ranch in Connecticut where, as well as directing and starring in numerous films, he marketed his own brand of salad dressing and donated the proceeds to charity. And he'd still managed to win an Oscar. In celebration Dan walked round the block again. 'Hey there! Great to meet you.' He had five more minutes in which to practise his American accent. 'Fantastic day.' But when he finally came face to face with Pammy, the casting woman at CBS, he put out his hand and his greeting was as mild and British as an advert for Marmite. 'So nice to meet you.'

'And you,' she told him. 'Come. Sit down.'

Pammy had seen his show reel and was full of praise. 'I really think we could use you out here,' she nodded, and she began to outline for him a new series that was coming up. 'How's your American accent?'

'Good. Pretty good.' Dan knew if he had any guts he'd break into one right there and then. 'I was in *Streetcar*. I played Stanley Kowalski . . . in Sheffield . . . ' he tailed off.

'That's just great!' Pammy beamed. 'So you're out here with your family, I hear.'

'Yes.' Dan nodded. 'My wife and . . . we've got four kids, Honey, who's six, sweet as anything but a bit of a handful.' He pulled out his phone and showed her a photo — Honey, fresh, from her swim, grinning into the camera, her face a dazzle of delight. 'And Ben, who's two . . . ' Just in time he noticed her eye flicker towards the clock. He slipped his phone away.

'Well, I expect Finola explained this is a general meeting. As soon as there's something more concrete we'll have you right back in.' She paused as if remembering something. 'If only you'd been out here last month.'

'Really?'

'Well. Not to worry.' Pammy was standing up,

brightening. 'We'll see you again soon.'

'All right. Bye then.'

'Have a great day.'

'And you. Have a . . . ' he coughed, 'great day too.'

* * *

Dan stood out on the street. He took a deep breath and steadied himself, just for a minute. Maybe this is it, he thought, a lifetime of general meetings, one after another, and he imagined himself having endless great days, in his increasingly stained and filthy suit. Before calling Jemma he dialled Finola's number.

'How'd it go?'

'Fine. Pretty good. She talked about something called *Flamingos*.'

'Oh that.' Finola sounded disappointed. 'That's not ever going to happen. And if it does it's got Declan McCloud attached. But did she like you?'

'Umm. She seemed to. Yes. It was great.'

'Great!!!' Finola sounded reassured. 'Well, I'll call you as soon as there's more news.'

* * *

Dan walked slowly towards Starbucks. They could just about manage, he calculated, for three months, and then if nothing happened, they could always fly home, and . . . and stay with his mother in Epping. A car beeped and he spun round. He felt self-conscious, the only person walking, and he was sure that cars slowed a little to stare at him as they passed by. The day was warming up, the sun visible finally through the breaking clouds. I'll make it work, he told himself. From now on I'll swim a hundred lengths each morning and spend an hour a day with my language tapes working on my accent. And then behind him a car screeched to a stop. Dan's heart leapt into his mouth. His knees turned weak. So this is it? Murdered at the end of my first week in LA, and he imagined the news stretching back to London, the shock, the laughter (he was walking!), the quiet satisfaction of a handful of actors whose work he always took. 'Hey!' There was a shout, and he imagined Jemma waiting for him with the children, still there at three in the morning when Starbucks forced her out. 'Stop, you gotta stop!' and rather than be shot in the back, Dan turned slowly round. A young man was striding towards him, unshaven, arms spread wide. 'Hey,' he was squinting. 'It is you! It's You.' The boy looked almost tearful. 'You're the guy from *Rainstorm*. Doody. You was my inspiration, man, when I was a kid.'

What do you mean? Dan felt all fear receding, you're still a kid? But he allowed the boy to clasp him by the shoulders. 'That show. That meant the world to me. My Mom, she ran off too . . . and my Dad . . . ' For a moment he looked as if he might be going to cry, but he pulled back and looked Dan in the eye. 'I thought it was you. I drove round the block and had to stop. Hey,' he shouted towards the car in which sat a surly troupe of his friends. 'It's him. It's Doody!'

'Cool,' one of them shouted. And someone beeped the horn.

'They know nothing. They never saw it. Hey man . . . that scene when you broke into the house.' He laughed, remembering. 'They can't understand. It was you that kept me going.'

'Right,' Dan made a vague gesture. 'That's great. I'm glad. I'd better be getting on. Take care of yourself. And . . . you know what, mate . . . thanks.'

'It's OK.' He was still smiling, wide as his whole face. 'What a day!' And shaking his head he backed towards the car.

★ ★ ★

By the time Dan reached Starbucks Jemma was on the pavement, overseeing running races between Ben and Honey as if they were in a 1950s slice of black-and-white film.

'How'd it go?' she said.

'You know what,' he bent down to greet the twins who were strapped companionably into their double buggy, 'I've no idea how it went. Apparently CBS can *really use me*. But the chances are I'll never hear from them again.'

Just then Dan's phone rang in his pocket. 'Or maybe not.' It was Finola and he grinned at Jemma, his spirits soaring as he clicked it on.

'Hey listen, Pammy's just called. Apparently you mentioned you had a real cute six-year-old daughter, well, they're looking for a little British girl for the lead in this new thing, it's a mixture between *Running with Wolves,* and you remember that Amish film? Well, she just thought . . . would Honey be available for a casting later today?'

'Let me think . . . ' Dan swallowed. 'Actually, Finola, I'll have to get back to you about that. I'm just not sure. OK? I'll call you back.'

'What was that about?' Jemma was looking at him.

'Nothing.' Dan began to laugh. 'The land of opportunity and adventure, eh.' He put his arm around her. 'Right,' he shouted to the children who were squatting, professional as sprinters, on the pavement. 'Ready, steady, GO,' and he watched them charge towards him, their feet pounding, their arms outstretched, each wanting to be the first to grasp at the charcoal lapels of his good suit.

The Reiki Master

When Charlie woke she couldn't think where she was. She could make out the grey silhouette of a window, offering no clues, a high-backed upholstered chair entwined with vines, and then, as she moved her head, a poster of a boy band Sellotaped to a lilac wall. She closed her eyes, and heard her father's lilting voice. 'Charlotte? Are you up?'

Charlie, a child again, sank lower into the dip of her old bed, raising the ridge of one sharp shoulder, determined not to be disturbed. But the door eased open anyway and the sound of a teacup rattling on its saucer reached her ears. In an instant she remembered why she was here. 'Daddy?' She sat up.

Her father crossed the room in his dark suit, his white hair startling against the blackness of his face. 'Here,' he said. 'Drink up.'

Charlie glanced at the bedside clock, and saw it was exactly seven. 'Thanks,' she took a sip, imagining him, waiting, impatient to be allowed to wake her at what he considered this civilised hour. 'I'll be down in a minute. I'll have a quick shower first.'

Charlie saw her father stiffen. The hospital was twenty minutes away. No visitors were allowed in till after nine, but even so, she could feel him fretting that she'd make him late. 'I won't be long,' she yawned to hide her irritation, and slowly, he backed out into the hall.

The shower was new and powerful, the whole room, since she was last here, fitted out with a matching bathroom suite. Her mother had mentioned this refurbishment to her, even attempted to lure her in with a pretence of indecision over the colour of the tiles, but Charlie had refused to get involved. Now the decor made her laugh. A row of alternating limes and lemons stood out in relief around the bath. Why? Charlie could not imagine. And then, her hair swept into a turban, she leant in to try out the new mirror. From a distance the mirror looked sleek and caring, but as she leant closer it became apparent that a fluorescent tube had been set into the silver overhang, flooding the glass with unforgiving light. There were no actual spots, but one old scar was refusing to fade, leaving a patch of pigmentation that hollowed out one cheek. Shit, she cursed, reaching for a stick of concealer, and with one foot she slid the bathroom scales towards her. Several months ago she'd given up smoking, assured by everyone that this would help her skin, but instead, for the first time in her life, she'd discovered hunger. She'd always been uninterested in food, turning away, even as a young child, from the pale meals presented by her mother, so that pushing away her plate soon became a game of violent wills between them. And then at boarding school, the food really was disgusting, and by the time she left she'd already developed her passion for smoking, an activity that seemed so much simpler and more satisfying than the endless decisions about what to eat and when. What she hadn't realised was that her taste buds had been numbed by tar. Now they were emerging, snapping for new sensations, ravenous, so that in the last three months she'd put on more than half a stone. Everything tasted good. Fruit, chips, nougat — the silky vanilla taste of it as you tore it with your teeth — bread dunked into olive oil, chickpeas with cumin, even salad. Now as well as watching for her skin to flare, she had to be on guard against a constant desire to tear open a packet of pistachio nuts or heap cream cheese on to a cracker. Her stomach felt swollen, her skin was blotchy, and in panic she'd agreed to visit the homeopath whose number Nell had found for her. The homeopath, who was plump and mousy-haired, but undeniably serene, attached a wire to one toe, took a strand of hair, and after lengthy and expensive tests told her she was intolerant to wheat, dairy, chocolate, tomatoes, fried food, onions, alcohol, seafood and the orange seasoning on crisps. She typed the foods out in a long stern list.

For two weeks Charlie stuck to this restricted diet, sitting alone at home, eating vegetables and brown rice, until in a rebellious fit that included a bottle of red wine and a row over the phone with Rob, she threw away the list. Now she was smoking again, snacking on chocolate biscuits and chips, and she wasn't entirely sure that she felt worse.

★ ★ ★

Charlie and her father sat side by side in the hospital waiting room, leafing through magazines, staring round at optimistic prints of harvest time and sunflowers. They'd arrived too early, as Charlie knew they would, and she tried not to think of the coffee she might have brewed if her father had not already had his coat on when she came downstairs. The clocks, and there were many of them, hovered obstinately at half past eight. 'She'll be ready for you in just a little while,' the receptionist told her father the second time he went to the desk to enquire. 'Just take a seat and you'll be called.' She spoke slowly, patiently, as if he might not understand the language, and Charlie felt the stirrings of humiliation and rage that had dogged her as a child.

Eventually they were directed along a corridor, through swing doors, down a short flight of steps and on to a small, warm ward. Her mother was in a private room, in this private wing, but even so, with her hair brushed back, still obstinately blonde, and with a dab of lipstick on, she wasn't able to sit up. 'Dear girl, you don't look too bad.' Her father pulled up a chair. 'Not too bad at all.'

Not too bad! Charlie hung back. Couldn't he see the life that had gone out of her? The depleted figure, flattened in the bed, who must have been hiding all these years behind the intransigent, battling, obstinately cheerful mother that she thought she knew.

'Mummy?' Charlie moved round to her other side. Tentatively she leant down for a kiss. Her mother smiled, surprised, and reached for her

335

hand, and for the rest of the visit they stayed like that, Charlie's hip pressed against the bed frame, their fingers entwined.

★　★　★

'She'll be out in a few days,' her father told her solemnly as they drove home, and although Charlie knew it was true, her mother's prognosis was good, the doctor's had assured them she had every chance of pulling through, Charlie felt herself dissolve. 'Shhh now.' But she couldn't help it, she could feel the sorrow flooding through her, feel it stinging in the sinews of her heart and lungs. 'Come now, come,' her father tried again as she stooped, sobbing into her hands, but her head had turned into a spongy mass of loss. Her father pulled into a lay-by where he drew out the white handkerchief he kept folded at all times, and pleased to finally have cause to use it, he pressed it on her. 'Thank you.' She blew her nose in a satisfying stream. 'Thanks,' and she savoured one last shudder.

★　★　★

Back in London the next day, Charlie rewrote her list. Wheat, dairy, fried food, chocolate, tomatoes, onions . . . What else? Oh yes. She threw the remaining Silk Cut into the bin, and then after a few minutes fished them out again and hid them at the back of a drawer. Alcohol.

She had an interview that afternoon for the part of a head-mistress. Ridiculous, she muttered

336

to herself, as she flicked through her wardrobe. She'd said to Maisie that she wasn't interested, surely she was too young, but Maisie had made her feel somehow that she had to go. There was a tone in her voice, a warning almost, that if she didn't go up for this, there might not be very much else around. Charlie found a narrow skirt she'd bought cheap on the last day of a TV film. She struggled into it, matching it with a silk shirt and a pair of heels that made her feel like a giraffe, so that after almost falling down the stairs, she kicked them off and swapped them for plimsolls. Now at least she could walk, and then it occurred to her that if she left early enough, she could walk into town. She had nothing else to do, and after checking her bag for make-up and enough money for a taxi in case her strength gave out, she set off for Soho.

It was May, and London was alive with sunshine. Windows gleamed, and tired men smiled, and the grime of Ladbroke Grove felt glamorous as she walked under the bridge. Even the black enamel of the funeral director's looked classic as a film. On the corner, by the pub, the flower stall was blazing. Roses in veils of spray, tulips, tightly bundled, sophisticated in burgundy and white, their more lurid, ragged cousins razor-edged in orange. Charlie stopped to admire the twists of daffodils in bud, breathe in the perfumed frills of the narcissi. 'Can I help you, love?' the woman asked her, and Charlie sighed — she had no one to send flowers to. 'No, that's all right,' and she walked on.

Why was she even going for this interview? she

337

thought as she marched up the hill. She'd read the script and seen immediately there were only three decent parts — for girls, and she, of course, was grouped now with the older generation — the women. Charlie tugged down her skirt, and smoothed the already smooth surface of her chemically relaxed hair. It was five years since she'd worked with this director, and she braced herself against the shocked look in his eyes when he saw how much she'd changed. But when she arrived at the production office she was told she'd have to wait. 'If you'd like to take a seat . . . ' the receptionist said, 'we're running late today,' and she handed Charlie a flimsy page of script. Charlie found a seat and bent her head to the lines: '*If I ever have to listen to such impertinence again* . . . ' she read, but before she'd got any further a voice echoed back at her through the plasterboard partition. 'If I Ever have to listen to Such Impertinence again . . . ' The vowels were long, the rich tone, round, and then after a muffled interjection, they were offered again, longer, rounder, regal in their swoop.

Charlie stood up. 'How long is it likely to be before I'm seen?'

'Twenty minutes . . . at the least. I'm sorry.'

'If I EVER . . . ' The words were booming now ' . . . have to LISTEN . . . ' and as if to get away from the cascade of the next line Charlie nodded to the receptionist, mouthing that she'd be back, and set off at a sprint. She was still running when she reached Old Compton Street and only slowed to navigate the crush of people spilling over on to the road. She could stop for a coffee at Bar Italia, or at Patisserie Valerie for an éclair, but then she remembered the limitations of her diet, and walked on, crossing into Covent Garden, past the cheese shop with its great gourds of cheddar, and the dance studio where, before the idea of drama school occurred to her, she had once auditioned to be part of a dance troupe, entertaining passengers on a cruise. There was a health food shop at Neal's Yard she'd walked past a thousand times. Now she went in and bought herself a seed bar that looked unnervingly like dung, but which she had to admit, in her famished state, she found oddly delicious. As she chewed, she looked at her watch. If she turned round now she'd arrive back within the bounds of punctuality, but instead she found herself back inside the shop, buying a packet of dried fruit, and slowly, chewing on the hard heel of a pear, she walked on down Neal Street, passing the theatre on the corner, looking dreamily into clothes shops and hat shops and at the window display of crystals suspended on their threads of silk, splashing rainbows from their chiselled points. 'Coming in?' A man stood in the doorway, shuffling cards, and Charlie smiled in what she hoped was a mysterious way and asked the price of an amethyst.

'If you're interested,' he wrapped the delicate purple stone in swathes of paper, 'there's a tarot reading course, starting tonight in the shop.' He looked at her, quickly, closely. 'I'm picking up on something. I think you might have a feeling for it, a gift.'

Charlie laughed out loud. 'Bye,' she remembered to say as she reached the door, and she repeated to herself, astounded, hilarious, 'a gift. I don't think so.' And still laughing, reaching for another handful of dried fruit, she walked off down the road.

★ ★ ★

The next morning there was a message from Maisie. 'What happened?' Her voice was tight. 'The people at Opus were worried about you. Call me and we'll set up another meeting.'

Charlie lay in the bath and looked at the oblong of blue sky above her. A bird flew across the skylight, and then far above it, a plane. *If I ever have to listen to your impertinence again.* And she closed her eyes.

★ ★ ★

The homeopath, when she next visited, encouraged her to keep on with the diet. She diagnosed a yeast infection that needed to be treated, and after writing down the unappealing names of various herbal remedies, she suggested she get them at the Planet Organic shop, just opened, not far from where she lived. The shop was large, two floors of pulses, juices, whole grains and rice crackers. Upstairs was a pharmacy with an enormous selection of bath and beauty products, and a revolving pillar of books. *Depression, Sleeplessness, Anxiety, Addiction, Living with ME* . . . Charlie leafed through the imprints.

Bloody hell, she thought, I've got off lightly, and she visualised her Silk Cut, like a holy relic lying in the shrine of the kitchen drawer. As she spun the pillar round, she became aware of someone talking on the phone. 'Sure, but isn't that the problem . . . ' It was a man. 'Really? OK, try me. And this time, I promise, I'll actually listen.'

On the other side of the pillar the titles were more optimistic. *Visualisation. Meditation. Reiki. Yoga.* Charlie plucked *You Can Heal Your Life* from its wire rack and listened to the man listening. After a while, when the silence had gone on longer than most silences lasted, Charlie looked up. The man was young, a boy really, skinny and messy with bright blue eyes. He caught her looking and smiled.

'OK,' he said eventually. 'I didn't understand.' He took a breath. 'So let's meet. Let's sort it out.' Charlie moved towards the till. 'What? No, I mean now. I've got a break at three.' He laughed, and the person at the other end must have laughed too. 'Great. See you tonight then. Good. And don't forget whenever you're ready, I'll give you your next attunement.'

Charlie felt she was allowed. 'What's an attunement?' She looked at him, and his blue eyes sparkled. 'And if it's nice, can I have one?'

'Sure,' he said, taking her list, and scouring the shelves for what she needed. 'I train people, I'm a Reiki Master, and if you want an attunement, I'm doing one next Thursday. Do you know anything about Reiki?'

'No,' Charlie glanced at the stack of books.

'That's all right,' he slid her remedies on to the

341

counter. 'An attunement is where I pass on the power to start healing. No one knows anything when they start. I got my first attunement from a nun in Shoreditch. It was just chance. Or maybe,' he opened his eyes wide, 'it was Meant to Be.'

'OK.' Charlie scrabbled in her bag for a piece of paper. 'Tell me when and where and I'll try it.'

The phone was ringing and there was another customer waiting, but he bent over the paper and wrote down the details. 'I'm Bram,' he told her. 'I'll see you then. Look forward to it.'

'Charlie,' she said, and when she walked outside she realised she hadn't thought once about her skin.

★   ★   ★

Right up until Thursday Charlie wasn't sure that she was going to go. Maybe she'd be offered the headmistress job anyway, and be taken up with fittings for shoulder-padded jackets. Or her mother might suffer complications and be re-admitted to hospital and she'd have to dash back to Cheltenham and stand by her bed. But Thursday came with nothing in her diary but a question mark and the word 'Bram'. The address he'd given her was in Stoke Newington. What should she expect? A temple of some sort, with supplicants bowing before a shrine, or the nunnery he'd mentioned, with a light-filled room and one white bed? But in fact Charlie found herself welcomed into a perfectly normal basement flat, a futon racked up with cushions, socks drying on the radiator, tea offered in thick stained mugs. There was one other girl there, watchful like her, unsure what to expect. 'Hi,' she said, 'I'm Tasha,' and they sipped their tea while Bram asked them both to say why they were there and what they hoped to learn. The room smelt of incense. Three candles, their wicks alight in caves of wax, glowed palely on the narrow ledge above the gas fire. Tasha told them she was a massage therapist and wanted to heighten her skills, Charlie said she didn't know, she supposed she was just curious. Then for a while no one spoke. Music played quietly, not music really, but a series of sounds, burbles and gongs and sharp metallic chimes. A bird twittered, a car hummed by outside. Then Bram spoke quietly from where he sat. 'OK, now I can feel that everything is open and receptive I'm going to give you your attunement.'

He asked them to hold out their hands in a prayer position, and he moved across the room and, without warning, seized Charlie's palms from behind and drawing them up above her head, blew into them. Charlie tried not to laugh. His breath was cool and ticklish, his grip surprisingly firm. She took a breath to steady herself as he returned her hands, dipping them towards her forehead, her throat, setting them back before her heart. 'That's good,' he murmured, 'now I'm going to place my hands on your energy chakras.' Charlie waited for his touch, but she felt nothing. 'What the hell am I doing here?' she asked herself, but soon she felt heat spread out across her shoulders. She shifted. It felt good. Like the sun shining down on her. The heat moved up her neck, down over her head like a hood. Her brain stilled, her thoughts lulled, her eyelids drooped. For a long time she sat there, aware of where his hands were, drawing waves of energy she didn't know she had around her body. She could feel it like the tail of a Chinese dragon, undulating in a concertina dance, and then, as it moved across her chest, it stuck. There was a layer of resistance, as if her heart were sealed in a padded, heart-shaped box. 'That's better,' Bram muttered, as with a little tear the dragon tail shifted free, and he reached down for her hands again, blew into her palms, and moved away. Come back! she wanted to call after him, Don't leave me here, but actually she was full.

Later, Bram showed them the system of placing hands, over and over until they had the order. He told them that for twenty-one days they should give themselves healing, starting at their heads and working their way down to the feet. 'First you need to put energy into your hands,' he said, 'then focus on the parallel space between the hands.'

'Reiki, Reiki, Reiki,' he chanted, and he asked them to do the same. Charlie waited for a smirk to rise and overwhelm her, but there was something so straightforward about Bram, so charming and light-hearted, that it never came. 'Reiki, Reiki, Reiki,' she said, and she attended to the energy accumulating between her palms.

'That's great,' Bram encouraged. 'Now, before you start your healing it's nice to ask the person you are working with, or yourself, what it is they want. What do you want?' he asked Tasha.

'Strength and peace.' She sounded sure, and Charlie was relieved she hadn't suggested a lead role opposite Daniel Craig.

'Health and happiness?'

'Health and happiness,' Bram repeated, and as he moved his hands across the force field of her body, he told her that sometimes it was possible to get a sensation in your own body that directed you to where the other person needed healing.

★ ★ ★

That first night Charlie sat at home and tried out her new skills. She held her hands in parallel. Reiki, Reiki, Reiki, but the space between them remained empty and cool. She made a bowl of her palms and blew into it, asking herself what she wanted. Nothing, it seemed. There was nothing there. Instead she flicked on the TV and found to her horror that she was watching a repeat of the first episode of *The Inspectors*, the detective series she'd made in Manchester the year before. There she was, with that idiot John Bulling, as they ran from a burning house and took shelter in a warehouse filled with feathers. Her finger hovered over the remote, but she was unable to look away as, turning sharply to avoid John's embrace, she caught his arm and pulled him down into the soft mountain of a stack of pillows. She watched, nostalgic for the flicker of desire that still existed between them, cursing herself for ruining it one late bored night when

345

she set herself the challenge of seducing him. For the rest of that long series she had to meet his hurt and angry eye, and listen to the make-up women report on his increasing desperation, especially when, through some misguided notion of the importance of honesty, he decided to tell his wife, who promptly left him. 'Pathetic,' she muttered to herself, and the scene still playing, Charlie held her hands up to her face. 'Peace and Forgiveness,' she pleaded, and she felt the first warm tingling as her fingers responded.

Charlie practised every day that week. What do I want? She closed her eyes, and she held her healing hands up like new toys.

★ ★ ★

'I'm sorry,' Maisie called, 'the headmistress job didn't work out. There's some interest from *Casualty*, though. I'm not sure if you . . . ' she trailed off. 'It would be a guest lead.' Charlie put her hand over her heart to calm herself. 'No, that's all right, Maisie. I think I'll pass on that.'

Maisie laughed. 'What happened? I thought you'd tell me to bog off.'

'Bog off,' Charlie said. 'And by the way, I'll be out of London from tomorrow. I can get back if it's urgent. But not if I don't have to. Just for a few days.'

'OK,' Maisie sounded perplexed. 'Talk soon.' And she rang off.

★ ★ ★

The next day Charlie drove to Cheltenham. It always shocked her that it only took two hours, when sometimes months, or even once, a year passed, without her finding the time to visit. Her parents were waiting, as she expected them to be, in formal black-and-white arrangement in the lounge. There was tea laid on a tray before them, a circle of biscuits on a plate. Irritation rose like a habit inside her. Now there would be a row when she said no to shortbread, concern when she asked for tea without milk.

'My daughter, it is good to see you,' her father patted her shoulder and her mother, struggling, stood up.

'Oh Mummy,' Charlie rushed towards her. 'Stay where you are.'

Gratefully, her mother sank down again and Charlie took her hand. 'How are you?' A grey pallor had taken root, and the rings under her eyes were worn and creased.

'Oh, not too bad, you know.' Her mother smiled, and she bent forward to the teapot.

'No milk,' Charlie stopped her. 'Actually, I'm on a special diet. To try and sort out my skin.'

Her mother looked at her, and even her father came closer.

'What do you mean?' They looked outraged. 'You have lovely skin.'

'No really . . . '

'You don't need any special diets.' Her mother shook her head. 'Go on, have a biscuit. If anything you're too thin.'

Charlie shrugged her shoulders. 'I'd love a cup of tea, with lemon?' and relieved to have

347

something to do, her father disappeared into the kitchen.

'So,' her mother leant back. 'So tell me, what have you been up to? It's been a while since we heard any news of that nice young man, Rob.'

Her father returned with three thin slices of lemon on a saucer. 'Thanks, Dad,' she smiled at him and she settled back for an evening of surreal questions and disjointed conversation, broken up by her mother's occasional shudders of discomfort and her father's anguished fussing.

★ ★ ★

'Mummy, can I try something?' Charlie asked when there was nothing left to do but go to bed.

'What's that, dear?' Her mother had her feet up on a stool.

'It's something I learnt,' Charlie told her. 'If you close your eyes, I don't even need to touch you. Just put my hands like this.' Charlie held her hands out before her, and said Reiki, very quietly, three times to herself. She heard her father clear his throat, but then his chair squeaked as he drew it nearer. 'How would you like to feel?' she asked, wincing at the unfamiliar question, moving her hands to hover over her mother's head.

'Ohh,' her mother exclaimed, 'well . . . ' she laughed, as if it was neither here nor there. 'Well, I'd like to feel . . . comfortable, and . . . ' Charlie could almost hear her thinking, 'and optimistic. Yes.'

'OK,' Charlie blinked away a spray of tears.

'Right.' Warmth was spreading through her fingers, as if light was seeping into her veins. Slowly she moved her hands, resting them on the cushion of her mother's discomfort, following an invisible thread of pain. Her hands grew hot, and the harder she concentrated the brighter the light shone inside her, until she felt she was pulling her mother towards her, so unfamiliar, after a lifetime of pushing her away. Slowly, tentatively she let her hands hover over her mother's stomach, swollen, tender, setting up a corresponding throb in her own womb, but as the heat intensified, her mother's eyes sprang open. 'No,' she struggled to get up, and unable to manage it she vomited over the side of the chair. 'Charlotte Adedayo!' her father shouted. But her mother shushed him. 'It was too much,' she gratefully accepted the proffered hankie. 'It was too much for me, that's all.'

Charlie rushed to the kitchen, her cheeks burning, her hands suddenly cold. She filled a basin with water, threw in a cloth, stuck a roll of kitchen towel under one arm. 'I'll do it,' her father insisted, and for a moment they wrestled dangerously over the plastic bowl. Charlie gave in. She sat back on her chair and took a bitter sip of tea.

'It shouldn't stain,' her father said a few minutes later, paws planted, for all the world like a large, grizzled dog. 'Now you two, surely it's time to sleep. Go on up. Please. I'll finish off down here.'

★ ★ ★

Mortified, in her single bed, Charlie looked round at the shapes of the old furniture, at the bedraggled posters of actors and pop stars that had comforted her so much when she came home in the holidays from school. It surprised her that her parents, usually so pristine, had never got around to taking them down. Maybe for them, in their late sixties, time went so fast now, it was as if she'd just moved out.

She was tempted to ring Bram and admonish him for what had happened, but she didn't relish the sound of her voice, audible in the silent house as she recounted the story of her mother's mishap. She wanted to tell him too about the extraordinary feeling that had surged through her. Ask if it was appropriate. Allowed. The sensation of joy before it all went wrong.

The next morning Charlie slept late, and when she finally came downstairs her mother was in the kitchen, wrapped like a parcel in her pinstriped apron. 'Darling,' she drew a plate of bacon from the oven, her hair perfectly arranged, her make-up on, 'it's the oddest thing, but I do feel rather better today.'

'Really?' Charlie doubted it was anything to do with her, but she moved towards her mother and held her perfumed, toast and bacon-smelling body in her arms. Later, she decided, she'd go out and buy flowers, and she smiled to think how easy it was going to be to surprise her.

Nightfall

'No thanks,' Dan told Lenny, when he was offered theatre, 'I can't afford it. Are you crazy? I'm still recovering from last year's extended holiday in LA.' But that was before he was sent *Nightfall*. *Nightfall* was different. It was a new play, by a young Geordie writer, and when Dan read it, adrenalin coursed through his body, and the only reason he could see to turn it down was fear.

'What do you think?' He stood before Jemma, outlining for her the hours and the paltry fee, but before she could make any comment, he reminded her it was a short run, only eight weeks, and more importantly, it was the most exciting play he'd read in years.

'Really?' She looked worried. 'It will be hard, you being out every night, but at least it's in London, and you'll be home during the day. You could take Honey to school sometimes, now she's finally settled back in, and maybe on Fridays you could take the twins to that new music class up by the hospital. It's hysterical, there's this big silk parachute and they all throw their teddies into the middle and we fling them up . . .'

'I don't know how I'll do it, though,' Dan was too anxious to listen. 'I'm in every scene, and we've only got four weeks' rehearsal, it doesn't start for two weeks, but even so, my character's from Newcastle, and the accent, fuck, Geordie is well known for being virtually impossible. You should read it, it's brilliant. Very dark, the guy I play is a total maniac, and he's never off stage, literally, not for a minute.'

'But that's good, isn't it? I mean, what you hated so much about being at the Bush was waiting backstage, bored sick, with not enough to do.'

'True.' Dan could feel his heart thumping. If he said yes, he'd have to start work on the accent, now, today.

'And presumably you get previews. You wouldn't have to open straight into a press night?'

The words 'press night' left a sheen of sweat over Dan's entire body. 'I haven't felt like this about anything for ages.'

Jemma took hold of both his hands. 'Then you'll have to do it,' she told him. 'We'll manage. You'll see.'

The rehearsals were agonising. The lines refused to stick. There were just too many of them, and the accent was even more impossible than he'd feared. But the hardest thing to grapple with was the play itself. What had seemed electrifying on first reading, once investigated, broken down and dissected, appeared to be a dark and unremitting rant. The playwright sat silent at the back of the rehearsal room, refusing to allow them to alter a word, not even capitulating when Dan, in a fit of frustration, kicked over a chair. In desperation Dan went back to his old drama college notes, flicking through the scrawl of Silvio's equations, imagining the old, disappointed man, squatting frog-like in his lair. Nothing comes from Nothing, he could hear him now, his mouth turned down, his body drooping. Close. Flexible. Adrift. What character type was this man Gary? And he experimented with slashes and punches, dabs and flicks until he made even himself laugh. In an attempt to regain calm he sat up half the night and wrote out his back story, inspired in part by the writer's haunted presence, and something he'd let slip in one unguarded moment — the fact that all his stories had something personal at their core. The rest Dan invented. Gary's childhood, the cruelty inflicted on him by his mother, his father's absence, the discovery of his half-brother, also named Gary, who'd spent his life in care.

The director, on the other hand, was a jovial man. He regaled them with anecdotes of past theatrical successes, interspersed with stories of his own suffering at a minor public school, and often left it to Dan and his fellow actors — a nervous man called Brian, and a sweet young girl from Newcastle, who winced occasionally when his accent went awry — to call a halt to the informal chatting and get on with rehearsals. The first thing they did was break the play into sections, mark out the light and shade, form an arc to hold the rhythm of the drama, but the harder they worked, the clearer it seemed to Dan that the whole piece was nothing more than a bleak series of sermons — on fear, death, family dysfunction, abuse, cruelty and revenge. A two-hour ordeal that no one, surely, would want to pay good money to sit through. Sometimes he'd drift into a bleak fantasy, imagining the reviews, the critics mourning the loss of two precious hours of their lives, or, if by some miracle they liked the play, railing against the fact that a southerner like Dan Linden had been let loose on such an important northern role. 'Why *did* they cast me?' he asked the dialect coach, as they grappled with glottal stops and vowels, and he cursed himself for being vain enough to be swayed by his agent's insistence on his versatility. In future, he promised himself, when his heart started pounding he would recognise it for what it was — terror, not excitement. A signal to say no.

The night of the first preview Jemma sent him flowers. From the size of the bouquet, Dan worried she'd used up half his weekly wage. *You'll be brilliant,* the card said, *as you always are. Big Love, from your biggest fan.* But that morning she'd joked that if he thought he was nervous, he should think of her. She'd be the one hyperventilating in the middle row, and as he kissed her goodbye he felt her heart flutter against his, and he'd pulled away, anxious that she'd make him even more afraid.

'Now,' the director gathered them around him just before the half, 'this is a preview, no one expects it to be perfect. So use tonight to test the play, to find your levels, and don't forget to listen to each other, listen to the audience, find your pace.' He paused and they all watched his face, like prisoners awaiting sentence. 'You're all doing fabulously. Now go out there and amaze them.'

The actors hugged. Dan and Brian, clasping each other in a manly, stiff-upper-lipped embrace. 'My turn,' Michelle pressed herself against Dan, her skin goosebumps in her flimsy clothes. 'Tell me I'll be all right?'

Dan looked at her, surprised. She had everything for nothing. Youth, beauty, a genuine Geordie accent, and anyway, she only appeared in three scenes. 'You'll be great,' he told her. 'You are great. Really.' And she smiled at him with such gratitude that for a moment he forgot his own fear.

Dan was the first one on. He could hear the audience chatting, and he imaged Jemma sitting in the seat he'd booked for her, four rows back, a little left of centre. He'd made sure she wasn't sitting next to Brian's wife, he didn't want the two of them swapping tales of night sweats and despair. Thankfully there was no one else in that he knew, at least he hoped there wasn't, except for the dialect coach who'd promised to come and give her verdict on his accent. Dan ran over the first lines, telling himself he just had to get through to the interval, five scenes, the first one, the one he knew the best, and then four more, then three . . . He felt his courage slipping. Did he have time for one last trip to the toilet? No. The music had stopped. He hadn't known there was music until then, and the lights must have dimmed, because the noise of chatter subsided and then stopped altogether. Right. It was all up to him to make the first move, although he imagined if he didn't, a stage manager might appear from somewhere and push him on to the stage.

★ ★ ★

Dan laughed now, three weeks later, to think of himself, unrecognisable, as he sauntered towards the best part of his day. A week after that first preview, *Nighfall* had officially opened, and the next morning the first reviews came out. 'It's a rave,' Lenny boomed from voicemail when he finally switched on his phone, and not long after Jemma ran upstairs with a pile of newspapers and they went through them together while Grace and Lola bounced maddeningly on the bed between them, trampling the noisy sheets of paper, flinging the loose pages into the air.

'One brilliant one,' Jemma smoothed them out. 'One pretty bloody good, and one that loves you but doesn't like the play. So still good as far as we're concerned.' She laughed, victorious, and kissed him, and Dan lay back, relief washing over him as she read the best passages aloud. Later, he took a bath, ate a large late breakfast and went into the theatre for notes. The atmosphere was jubilant. Bookings were already up. He had friends in almost every night, people from college, actors he'd worked with, his mother, Jemma's parents, his great-aunt Anne.

That weekend there were more good reviews, which meant they were assured of an audience for the first month at least — London's theatre lovers who made it their mission to see all the successful shows — and others from across the country, some even from America and Japan. The most enthusiastic among them would wait afterwards by the stage door to congratulate all three members of the cast and have them sign their programmes. Dan's own personal followers, loyal since *Rainstorm*, hung back patiently, waiting for him to be free. They were an odd assortment, these fans — lone men, the occasional bobble-hatted woman, with digital cameras and photographs downloaded from the Internet, and never once did any of them mention coming to see the play.

'You'd think they'd want to see it,' Jemma said, 'gaze at you for two whole hours,' but Dan explained it wasn't the theatre they were interested in, not even really the shows he'd done on TV, it was collecting that stimulated them, one more autograph, another photograph, it had nothing really to do with him. He took Jemma's arm and whisked her into the bar, and he knew whatever she said, however irritable she might be that he'd not once managed to get up in time for breakfast, let alone that music class with parachutes, nothing could bring him down from the soaring, scissoring heights that he inhabited every night after the show. He knew that from then on he would be flying, his fears behind him, the knowledge he had lived through so much tragedy and survived, making him omnipotent. In the space of two hours he had laughed and fought, retched and wept. He'd attacked his cousin, the one member of his family he loved, and as a result of his subsequent remorse he'd inadvertently let slip his most guarded secret, releasing himself as he did so, making amends, and unexpectedly gaining as reward the beautiful Carina, who'd leapt, in her satin crop top, into his arms. 'Good show tonight,' he winked across at Michelle, and she raised her glass, luminous, the trembling of a few hours before absorbed into her blood.

★ ★ ★

They were a month into the run now, and he never wanted it to end. He felt lean and vital, had no need of the gym after the two-hour workout of the show and the adrenalin that took away his appetite, so that he existed on a late breakfast and a sandwich at five, and felt no need for anything more than that but drink. Most days he got up late, went into town for voiceovers, interviews or meetings, and when he was free he dropped in on Lenny, who always made time for a coffee, using his visit as an excuse to stand out on the fire escape and smoke. From there he would go straight to the theatre, find a café nearby to eat, mindful that from mid-afternoon onwards nothing would jeopardise the escalating intensity of his character's mood. Sometimes he played cards with Michelle, who came in early too, and he'd listen to her lovely grating voice as she told him about her boyfriend back in Newcastle, the fights he got into, the prison sentence he was serving, suspended for six months. There was no mobile reception in the dungeon of the dressing rooms, and only one high window on to the street, and once he'd climbed the stairs to make his obligatory call to Jemma, who was always busy right then with the kids, he'd settle in for the night. There was a green room, with several battered sofas, tea and coffee provided by the theatre, a microwave, a kettle. Occasionally stage management would file in and make a cup of soup. 'Who's winning?' they'd ask and it was always Michelle. 'I'm the champion,' she'd flex her pale arm, and she laughed so widely that her pink gums were revealed.

There were at least ten seats reserved every night for people from the business. Directors, producers, actors with influence, or so they hoped, who might phone through at the last minute and book tickets to see the play. There was hardly a night now when these seats weren't full. Dan made it a rule never to ask who was in, but afterwards in the green room Michelle would read aloud the names, listed in a ring folder, with accompanying notes as to their reaction, gleaned in the last act when she lay unconscious on the floor. Visibly moved. Non-committal. Tears.

★ ★ ★

'Don't you ever worry . . . ' It was Sunday and Dan had got up late.

'What?' He looked at Jemma, fiercely peeling carrots for the children's lunch.

'That one day I might leave you?'

Dan laughed, his mouth full of toast. 'What?' He took a gulp of tea, and then he saw that she was struggling to hold back tears.

'Hey,' he reached over to her. 'What's up?'

'What's up?' She clenched her jaw and looked out at the garden where Honey was tipping muddy cups of water over Ben's head. 'You're never here. You work two hours a day, and it seems to take up twenty-four. I mean, when did you last see the children?'

'What do you mean?' He felt confusion rise up and numb his brain. 'When did I last . . . I do see them. I see them all the time.'

Jemma curled her lip in disgust. 'Like when? By the time you get up, Honey's at school and Ben's at nursery, and by the time I get back from dropping the twins at Sacha's you're usually off somewhere . . . '

'Or at the matinée.' He felt aggrieved.

'Yes.' She glared at him. 'But only on Saturdays.' It seemed she'd been reminded of another hurt. 'I mean, when Honey finishes school, where are you? Don't you think it would be nice if just once a week you could take Honey . . . well, maybe that's asking too much . . . or at least collect her from school? Don't you care you never see them? Don't you miss them?'

'But . . . ' Dan felt trapped. 'It doesn't feel like that. It doesn't feel like that to me.'

'Well, it feels like that to me.'

'I see them on Sunday.'

'Sure. Sunday. But be honest, Dan, even on Sunday, you're hardly here.'

'What do you mean? I am here. Last week . . . ' What had they done last week? All he could think of was that Saturday's performance — not always such a good show, a weekend

360

audience was usually made up of tourists and people who felt overly entitled to be entertained, but that night something had happened between him and Michelle. They'd screamed at each other, as they always did, but this time at the height of the row, Dan had collapsed, weeping, and Michelle had come to him, held him in her arms, cooed the lines to him that only the night before had been harsh, and at the end of the performance, when the lights had finally dimmed there was a hush so deep in the theatre that even the stage management was awed. Maybe it was true. Maybe he was getting everything he needed from his job. He looked into Jemma's distraught face, but he couldn't think of a single helpful thing to say.

'The awful thing is I understand.' It was as if she'd heard him. 'But what do you expect me to do? Stay quiet? I've stayed quiet for the last six weeks and I can't stand it for one more day.' She looked round as if for something to slam down. 'Never once have you made time for us. It's as if we're not here. I've even started to wonder if you're having an affair.'

'Don't be an idiot.'

'It takes the joy out of it.' Now she'd started she couldn't seem to stop. 'Doing it all on my . . .'

'Fine.' Dan stood up. 'Why don't I take the kids out now? I'll take them all out, I'll give them lunch at the café in the park.' He slammed his own plate down in the sink. Why couldn't she have waited? Two more weeks, and the play would be over.

'Well, you'd better be quick.' Jemma abandoned the food she was making. 'It's nearly lunchtime now and the twins need their nap.'

Dan walked into the garden. 'Right,' he said. 'We're going out. Get your clothes on.' He looked at Ben, his face and tummy smeared with mud, and Lola, digging in the sandpit, her nappy sodden. Where was Grace? He found her emptying out a case of CDs, sliding them one by one on to the floor. 'Hon, where does Mummy keep those nappies?' and Honey, imperious, busy making a mud pat on the lawn, told him they were upstairs, in the drawer with tights and socks.

'But surely, she's got a secret supply . . . ' He couldn't face another glimpse of Jemma's bitter face, and so catching hold of Lola, he wiped her down with a dishcloth, and slipped her, nappiless, into her clothes.

It was another half an hour before he managed to get them out. Where were Honey's shoes? And the double buggy seemed to be jammed shut, so that as he wrestled it open, something snapped in the hood, leaving it hanging over to one side. Eventually they stood out on the doorstep. Dan took a deep breath and momentarily closed his eyes, and when he opened them, Ben, who'd insisted on bringing his scooter, had rushed off so fast on his small legs that Dan had to run, painfully, his head throbbing, to catch him up. 'I'm tired,' Ben decided when he recovered him, 'I don't want to scooter any more,' and so Dan folded the unwieldy metal contraption and attempted to slide it under the buggy, banging

362

his shin on the sharp-edged hinge as he set off again, his curse drowned out by the roar of Lola's protestations as the scooter wheel pressed through the canvas seat into her unpadded behind. 'Can I be carried?' Ben asked, and Honey began protesting that if he was carried, she should be carried too. 'No, you cannot. Either of you,' Dan snapped, and grimly they trudged on.

Later, guilty, he let the children order their own drinks, regretting it when they chose lurid cups of colouring and crushed ice, which left their eyes popping, their mouths bright blue, and their stomachs too full to fit in more than a few messy strands of spaghetti when it finally came. And it was all for nothing. When he got home Jemma was sitting at the kitchen table, leafing furiously through the jobs vacant section of the paper, the newsprint blistered and disintegrating with her tears. 'Why didn't you ask me to come?' she said. 'The children don't care, it's me that misses you,' and he held her in his arms and kissed her salty eyelids, and the sad wet bridge of her nose. 'Hey,' he soothed. 'We'll be all right. We'll get through this. Look, why don't you get a babysitter and come and meet me from the play?'

'Tomorrow night?'

'Any night. Every night.'

Jemma pressed her face into his shoulder.

'Let's not worry about the money. Who knows, a huge job might be just around the corner.'

'Yes,' she agreed. 'Who knows?'

* * *

The last two weeks of the play were sold out. People kept texting him, begging for tickets, and he arrived at the theatre earlier and earlier, pleading with box office, leaning over the counter, suggesting how they could juggle things around to free up extra seats.

We're going to be so broke when this run ends, he worried to himself when Jemma took his advice and booked a babysitter to come in four nights a week, and he tried to push away all fears of that year's encroaching tax bill, so out of step with what he was earning now. But after the show his worries floated away, and he was happy to see Jemma, free and single somehow, waiting in the bar. They stayed until the lights came on, pressed together on a banquette, talking over old times with friends — Hettie and Samantha, Pierre, Stuart, Kevin, even Charlie, surprisingly informative on the subject of Nell Gilby's meteoric success. Jonathan was there, looking well, with stories of how Silvio had finally retired, and Patrick was attempting to raise money to stage a professional production of *Hamlet*, a regional tour and then a short run somewhere in London. 'I'm surprised he hasn't been in touch,' Jonathan looked at Dan. 'Last time I saw him it was all he talked about. Wanting to put *Hamlet* on again. This time with you.'

Dan swerved his eyes in Jemma's direction.

'Obviously,' Jonathan continued, 'I was hoping he'd cast me again . . . but it's all about the investors these days, isn't it, and my name means nothing to anyone.' He laughed. 'If I'm lucky I'll get to play the Ghost.'

'If *I'm* lucky I'll get to play lords, attendants, guards and followers of Laertes.' Stuart sighed. 'Obviously, if he doesn't cast Samantha.' And even Samantha laughed.

'I think a toast's in order.' Pierre was quick to change the subject. 'To Dan and his excellent performance, here, tonight.' And he got up to buy them all champagne.

★ ★ ★

'*Has* Patrick been in touch?' Jemma asked once they were out on the street, waiting at a bus stop.

Dan shrugged. 'He wrote to me.' He might as well tell her. 'And asked if he could put my name forward, as part of the package, to raise money.' He felt Jemma's body cool beside his. 'Hey, what's the harm? He'll never do it.'

'You shouldn't even have replied. He's dangerous, really, the more I think of it . . . '

'Shhh . . . ' Dan saw the yellow light of a cab approaching. He hailed it and bundled Jemma inside. 'Not dangerous. Just a bitter, disappointed man.'

'You want to do it!' Jemma glared at him. 'You do, admit it.'

Dan sighed. What actor hadn't fantasised about having their name added to the immortal list of Hamlets? He might live for ever alongside Gielgud, Olivier, Sarah Bernhardt, Michael Redgrave, Jonathan Pryce, Kenneth Branagh.

'Don't worry,' he told her. 'I didn't promise anything, I just said, sure, mention my name, good luck, and I never heard another thing.'

'Strange he didn't come and see the play, though.' Her eyes flared. 'Or did he?'

'No! At least I never saw him.'

'The terrible thing about you,' Jemma slumped, 'being such a bloody good actor, I never know if you're lying.'

'I'm not. Really. Look, if he did come,' her compliment was warming him, 'he probably scuttled straight off. Chances are he hated it.'

'True. He was always hating everything. But Dan, promise you won't do it. I couldn't bear it, and apart from anything else, it seems wrong, like doing publicity for Pol Pot.'

'For God's sake,' Dan laughed. 'I'm not saying he wasn't a tyrant, but don't elevate him above his station. He was only a teeny weeny tyrant. He lied to me, he threw you out of college. He didn't massacre our entire village.'

Jemma was silent.

Dan reached for her hand. 'You could still try. You know that, don't you? If you miss it, acting, I mean.'

'No.' She frowned. 'I don't miss it. Not as much as I'd miss the kids if I was ever actually employed. And anyway, how would we manage if I went on tour? But one day . . . soon, I'm going to start translating again . . . I've found something that might even make a good play.'

He put his arm round her. 'Listen, I know it's mad, but you can understand, can't you, about

366

Hamlet, that it was sort of gratifying to be asked?'

★ ★ ★

The taxi drew up outside their house. The windows were dark, the street was dark. For a moment Dan thought there might have been a power cut and then he remembered it was one o'clock in the morning. 'You can jump in our cab,' Dan told the babysitter, opening his wallet, taking out the last £20 note. 'It'll drop you home,' and as Jemma disappeared upstairs to check on the children, he watched as she piled her A-level course work back into her bag. 'What are you studying anyway?'

'Maths, French and Economics,' she told him. And she smiled shyly. 'Good night.'

The front door closed with a click and the soft rumble of the taxi gathered power as it pulled out of their road. Dan listened. The house was quiet. The dense, warm quiet of small people sleeping. 'To be or not to be,' he murmured to himself, and, remembering he'd promised to finally get up and take Honey to school the next morning, he walked wearily upstairs.

★ ★ ★

The last matinée felt unreal. Every word rolled away from them, almost never to be said again. Occasionally they caught each other's eyes, just a fraction out of character, and afterwards they gathered in the green room and had a picnic tea.

367

The stage management joined them too, and they pooled the provisions they'd all brought, bread and cheese, small pots of salad, cakes, meringues and chocolate. There were tins of lemonade, and sparkling elderflower. They clinked glasses as if it was champagne.

The director looked in before the evening's show. 'What to say?' He held up his hands and for once it seemed he really didn't have anything to add. Later, in the wings, the actors hugged each other, as they had done on the first night, but now their bodies were so known they didn't need to speak. The music faded out, the lights came on, and Dan stepped on to the stage. He felt it instantly, the audience were different. They were breathing with him, sighing, laughing, mourning the passing of every word. He caught sight of the writer, glum as ever in the house seats by the aisle, and just to rattle him, he tried something different, a little teasing dance that almost caught Brian off-guard. But Brian picked it up, mirroring him, so that when Michelle came on she was laughing, her face open, letting them know she was ready to play.

Dan avoided his dressing room during the interval, standing in the corridor, swigging water, mopping his head with a towel. He'd already torn the cards down, packed his books and blanket into bags so that it wasn't his any longer, and he didn't want to be reminded of this now. The audience were more sombre in the second half, as if they were heading with him to the end, or maybe just waiting to express themselves at the curtain call, which they did, standing, their

368

raised hands clapping with all their strength. Dan's shirt stuck to him, his heart thumped and he clasped Michelle's fingers so hard she squealed. The audience laughed. The actors bent down for another bow, and when he raised his head, he felt as powerful as a lord.

Now he was glad he'd packed his bags. He couldn't get out soon enough. Toothbrush, comb, iPod speakers. He grabbed the orchid Lenny had sent him, scattering earth over the stairs.

The others were waiting for him at the stage door, their bags resting up against their legs. 'So . . . ' they looked at each other. 'Anyone for a drink?'

But Dan knew already that Brian had to be on the set of a film in the Isle of Man first thing, and Michelle's parents had driven down from Newcastle to take her home. 'Stay in touch,' they promised, and just then a man in overalls pushed past with a polystyrene rock. The shriek of drills and hammering echoed after him as the swing door swung. 'You'd think they could have waited,' Dan frowned, 'before they dismantled the set.'

Another man passed by, carrying a chair. Dan's chair. The chair he'd sunk down into only half an hour ago and cried. Brian patted him on the shoulder. 'It's been great.' His forehead was creased, his face looked sorrowful, and suddenly, with no script left, all three were lost for words.

Michelle put her arms round Dan and kissed him lightly on the cheek. 'Thanks for everything,' she said, 'it's been so special,' and turning to

Brian she did the same. 'I'll miss you.' There were tears brimming in her eyes, and picking up her overflowing bags, she ran out through the door.

Another polystyrene rock passed by them, and Brian's words to him were drowned out by an electric saw. In a couple of hours their set would be gone. By Monday morning the new set would be in place and the actors for the next play — a comedy — would arrive for their dress rehearsal and wander silently and strangely round it.

'Take care,' they shouted to each other, and unable to face a bar full of strangers, Dan headed for home.

★　★　★

Sunday wasn't too bad. It was his night off anyway. But when Dan woke on Monday it was as if someone had died. Jemma nudged him. 'Coming down for breakfast?' she said cheerfully, but he couldn't move. He went into town, had a coffee, dropped in on Lenny to find him uncharacteristically busy. 'Sorry,' he mouthed, his hand over the phone, and he went back to what sounded like some complicated high-powered negotiation.

Mid-afternoon his voiceover agent called him. 'How would you feel . . . ' she hesitated, 'about saying the words Erectile Dysfunction?'

'Ummm. I'm . . . ' Dan wasn't sure.

'It's going to be a big campaign.' There was only the faintest hint of hilarity in her voice.

Dan tried out the words, just under his breath,

spoken in a kindly, non-judgemental way. 'No,' he decided. 'I think I'll pass.'

'Arthritis?'

'Sorry?'

'I know it's a long shot, but they need someone young to head up an awareness campaign, but it's got to be someone who's actually suffering.'

'I could pretend . . . '

'Shame,' his agent sighed. 'That one really is going to be massive.'

And she promised to be in touch again soon.

★ ★ ★

That evening he sat at the table and watched the children eat. He helped Ben cut up his sausage, and wiped the ketchup whiskers from Honey's face. He stood out in the garden with the twins while they searched for snails among the mashed, bedraggled beds, and sat on the edge of the bath as, in batches of two, they bickered and splashed. He was exhausted and it was only seven. 'Shall we get them to bed?' All he wanted to do was lie on the sofa and stare at the TV.

Jemma scowled. 'If they go to bed now they'll be up at dawn. I try and keep them going till eight.'

'Right.' He stood in the doorway of their bedroom and watched while Jemma hoiked their damp pink bodies into pyjamas. They laughed and slipped away from her and she chased them, padding happily after them on hands and knees, growling, miaowing and roaring until they collapsed in a slither of squeals.

Dan smiled weakly. It was as if he was watching from far away. He stood up and stretched. 'Night then,' he didn't try and kiss them, fearful that they'd resist. 'I'll start our supper, shall I?'

'Sure,' Jemma looked away.

He walked into the garden and checked his phone. Nothing. Everyone in the world was giving him a day off. He scrolled down until he came to Brian. He let his finger hover over the name. No, he mustn't. Brian would be on set, still filming, or maybe sleeping off the long drive. Just then the phone buzzed in his hand. It was Michelle.

'Hello!'

'What time is it?' she asked him, laughing as she spoke.

'Why?' Dan glanced back inside to the kitchen clock. It was 7.42.

'It's the exact moment,' she told him, 'when we meet on stage.'

'It is.' He kept looking at the clock. Usually, right now, he'd be grabbing hold of her, snarling into her upturned face.

'I miss it all so much,' she whispered. 'I could die.'

'Me too,' he sat down on the plastic step of the slide and leant into the phone. 'So what are you up to?'

'Nothing,' she sighed. 'Maybe nothing ever again for the rest of my life.'

It felt as if it was the first time that day he'd actually been alive. 'I miss you,' he said, and there was a small pause on the other end.

'I miss you too.' Her voice was thick. 'If I came down to London . . . I mean, next week or something, do you think . . . could we meet?'

Dan looked up at the window and caught sight of Jemma, drawing the curtains. She waved at him, and then, a moment later, the four faces of his children, flushed and blinking, appeared above the sill. 'Daddy!' they pointed as if he were some exotic beast. 'Dad! It's him.'

'Sure,' he said, casually. 'Why don't we speak again in a few days?'

'OK,' her voice was small, confused. 'I'll think of you tomorrow at this time.'

'Me too,' he nodded, '7.42.' And hurriedly he clicked off the phone.

Royal Protocol

Nell ran herself a bath and looked at the sheath of silver satin, shrouded by plastic and looped by its hanger over the bathroom door. She'd been given ten tickets for that night's premiere of *Mary Peacock*, but, apart from Charlie, who had promised to accompany her, she wouldn't see the others until she reached her seat. Her mother would be there, her sister and her sister's husband, her aunts and uncle, and of course her mother's boyfriend Lewis. Poppy, from PR, had offered to come round and escort her to the cinema, but Nell said she thought she could manage the short journey in a chauffeur-driven car from Queen's Park to Leicester Square alone.

Nell rummaged through the suitcase which lay open on her bedroom floor. She'd bought Spanx to hold her tummy in and a balcony bra with detachable straps to wear under her dress. She'd found both these things in Austin, Texas on a weekend's break from filming on location in the desert, and they'd remained in their packets, and would have remained in their packets indefinitely, if it wasn't for tonight. The PR firm who were promoting the film had hired Tara Laurie to organise her dress. Tara had rung round the big shops, gathering together anything they had in her size, so that the day she arrived back in the UK she'd called to let her know that the dresses were on their way to her by cab. As they whisked through the London streets, Nell imagined she was about to meet a group of new and influential friends — austere, gushing, nondescript, casual, one flimsy green item, shy and demure. What if we don't get on, she found herself thinking, and she watched nervously as they were lifted up the staircase on their rail. Nell held her breath and tried them all, one after the other, keeping her highest heels on, swishing in and out from the bathroom for regular appraisals while Tara and her assistant Milly kept a constant beam of professional enthusiasm streaked across their faces. But right from the start it was the silver dress that Nell had hopes for. A floor-length swathe of mettle-dark satin, with nipped-in waist and one bare shoulder, which she imagined might transform her into the film star she was expected to become.

'Oh yes,' Tara mused. 'I think this is it. I really do.' And raising the bar on her enthusiasm, Milly gasped. 'It's perfect.'

The Romanian seamstress who'd accompanied them moved in with her bracelet of pins. The dress was a little tight across the hips, but if she hoiked it up and drew it in under the bum, not only would Nell look spectacularly curvaceous, she would also be able to sit down.

★   ★   ★

In the three days since she'd been back, Nell had been consumed by interviews and photo shoots, phone calls, fittings, schedules and question-naires. The London she'd left behind, a place of anonymity and indifference, of pavements pounded, buses missed, overcrowded Tube trains borne in silence, had transformed into a buzzing, swarming vortex of interest. In her. The people she met now were captivated by her, greedy for every detail of her life. They wanted to know about her early childhood, her parents' divorce, her move to London, her father's new start in the Highlands with his new wife, who refused to let them meet. Nell told them everything, uplifted by their attention, supplying names and dates and details, obedient to the last. 'And is it true,' one powdery woman leant close, 'that the director of *Mary Peacock*, Ciaran Conway, was so smitten with you that he's planning a sequel just so you can work together again?'

'No!' Nell protested, heat rising to her face, 'I mean, of course, I'd love to work with Ciaran again . . . ' And flustered, she attempted to explain the close friendships that could develop on a film set, especially when people were stranded in the middle of nowhere for months on end. But what she really wanted to ask was . . . Really? Is that true? And if so, how does anybody know? She felt her heart pounding as she remembered the last time they'd seen each other, how she'd stumbled from the wrap party to find Ciaran, standing, smoking alone in the black night. Three months of longing and a recent double shot of brandy, must have given her the courage she usually lacked, because she'd stolen up behind him and snaked her arms around his waist. 'This isn't what you need,' Ciaran had said, even as he turned to hold her. 'You don't want to get tangled up with me.'

'It might be.' She'd stayed in the circle of his arms. 'It might be what I need.' And they'd clung to each other as he whispered what she already knew. That he had one family, already broken, back in Ireland, and for the best part of that year he'd be in Australia doing post-production on this film. 'You have a whole new life ahead of you,' he whispered, and it was true, her bags were packed, a car booked to take her to the airport the next day to catch a plane to Moscow.

'I'll miss you,' she said, 'it'll never be the same, whatever else I do,' and he'd taken her hand and kissed it, and then, as if hardening his resolve, he'd lifted the canvas doorway of the party tent and shown her back inside.

Frustrated, Nell's interrogators moved on to the next film, listening intently as she described her time in Russia, the bleak grey sameness of the cities, the occasional romantic vision of a summer dacha glimpsed from the window of a train. But soon that conversation became tangled in the scandal of her co-star's attempt to throw himself from a third-floor window after being asked to repeat the same short scene for the twenty-seventh take. By the time they'd discussed her stint in Texas, an oddly peaceful three months playing a kidnapped pioneer, she forgot which film she was meant to be promoting. *Mary Peacock*, she wrote in large letters by the phone, and she stopped to place herself back in that winter morning, muffled and beautiful with snow, when this same telephone had woken her and spun her into a new life.

That first Christmas she'd spent flying. Reclining in business class with a small community of festive abstainers, she'd soared to the other side of the world. But the Christmas after, not wanting to be alone again, she'd brought her mother out to America to stay with her, and they'd worn cowboy hats and thick plaid shirts and eaten a BBQ dinner in a dusty windswept yard. A band had played, and later, fired with tequila, the heaviest, oldest, most awkward members of the crew had danced a square dance under a tarpaulin rigged up below the stars.

Dear Ciaran, Nell had written — postcards, emails, letters, describing the thrills and terrors of her new career, wanting him to know how she was using the skills she'd learnt from him on *Mary Peacock*. But she never sent them. She was too far from home to risk the chance of not getting a reply. And the possibility of that, if she allowed herself to think of it, was like a blow.

The only real person Nell had seen since she'd been back was Sita. Sita had arrived that first night with Indian food in Tupperware, cooked by her new mother-in-law, and with a bump, almost hidden, below her layers of clothes.

'Sita!' They'd embraced and Nell had felt the heat in her friend's body, the hard stretched skin of her belly butting out against her own. 'Why didn't you tell me?'

'I couldn't,' Sita looked distressed. 'Not over the phone.'

Nell hugged her again. 'I'm sorry. I'm just
. . . it's such a big thing, that's all.'

'Well, I *am* married . . . ' Sita laughed. 'I'm
thirty-two. If I'd waited much longer my sister
would be a grandmother before I'd begun.'

'It's wonderful. I'm so happy,' Nell sniffed. 'I
really am. Can I be godmother?'

'You can be Aunty. One of the Aunties. For
ever and ever.'

They laughed and sat down to eat, and as Nell
forked out aubergine and cauliflower and the
long green fronds of ladies' fingers, she asked,
'So is this it? I mean. Is it over for you. Acting?'

'It gave me up, remember.'

'But you were so good.' Nell didn't know why
she was doing this. 'At youth theatre. The best of
us all.'

'Not true. And anyway . . . ' She shrugged.
'It's not about that, is it? I'm happy for the
moment. I feel as if I've fallen out of love with
someone unavailable, someone quite unkind,
and found . . . well, Raj, who's lovely and who's
actually here.'

Nell took another forkful of rice. She felt
stubborn and unbending. 'Maybe now I'm back
we could do one of our shows.'

'Yeah, sure,' Sita tied her black hair into a knot
where it waited to unravel on the silk nape of her
neck, 'the film star and the pregnant receptionist.'

'What does your agent say?'

'Not much.'

For a while they looked at each other and then
they both laughed. Nell got up and put some

379

music on, the old blues tracks they used to play on Saturday mornings when they cleaned the house.

'Do you remember that time we went to Somerset?' Sita began to sway.

'Yes,' Nell said. 'How desperate were we? Me, I mean. You were always the cool one, of course.'

'Look at you now, though.'

'True. But look at you.'

Sita held out her hands and they danced, laughing, bumping up against cupboards, sweeping aside newspaper and magazine cuttings, scattering piles of party invitations to the floor.

'I wish you'd stay,' Nell said. She'd told Sita she could have the flat, share it with Raj, she'd probably hardly ever be there anyway, but on their marriage Raj's father had given them the deposit for a house in New Cross, with two bedrooms and a small paved garden of their own, and although Sita confided that she'd have preferred to stay here, renting, they both knew it was a lie.

★ ★ ★

Nell dragged herself up from the slick cooling water of the bath. She rubbed herself dry and wrapped herself in one of those luxuriantly thick white towelling dressing gowns every hotel begs you not to steal. But she'd been saved from such temptation by the unexpected gift of an identical one from the producers of the film, its title, *Mary Peacock*, in red letters embroidered on the back. How odd, she thought, when I could finally afford to buy it, and she started to see how much easier it was to stay rich once you'd begun. For a moment Nell lay down in the scramble of her bed. It was the first time in three days that she'd had a moment to herself and she allowed herself three deep breaths before picking up the schedule Poppy had biked over earlier that afternoon.

Mary Peacock. Royal Premier Call Sheet.
    Nell Gilby.
6.05. Car to collect you from home and
    transfer you to the cinema.
Dress Code. Black Tie. (Gloves need not
    be worn.)
Gloves? Nell looked around. Who ever
    mentioned gloves?

6.45. Arrive at cinema location where you
    will be met and escorted up the press
    line.
You will then be escorted to the upper
    foyer where you will be re-united with
    your guest and wait for the Royal Pre-
    sentation.

Attached was a second sheet:

Royal Protocol.

• As His Royal Highness The Prince of
    Wales and Her Royal Highness The
    Duchess of Cornwall move from person
    to person along the presentation line . . .

381

Just then the doorbell rang. My guest! she thought, and a flutter of apprehension flooded through her. If only she'd asked Sita to accompany her, but of course Sita wanted to go with Raj, and anyway, it seemed right that she ask Charlie. Charlie had asked *her* when *The Haven Report* opened, even if that was only because she'd rowed with her current boyfriend — how glorious that she couldn't now remember his name — and taking Nell had been part of her revenge.

'One minute.' Nell glanced into the mirror at the top of the stairs and gave her hair a quick scrunch. 'I'm coming,' and as she ran down to the front door in slipperless feet she appraised her perfect cherry-red nails as if she was someone else. But it wasn't Charlie, it was Melissa, the make-up woman, wrapped up against the cold, with a wheelie bag of equipment so large she had trouble heaving it up the stairs. 'I'd like a natural look, if that's allowed,' Nell said, and then remembering who she was now, she added, with more conviction, 'Natural, but utterly gorgeous please.' And she helped her into the kitchen.

Not long after, Tara Laurie and Milly arrived, shivering and blowing on their hands, although Nell could see the taxi they'd climbed out of, roaring warmly in the street.

'Bloody hell,' Tara swore, 'it's Arctic,' and looking Nell over, swaddled in her towelling gown, she warned her, not for the first time, that she must not, under any circumstances, wear a coat that night. 'You can wear one in the car, that's fine, but don't be tempted to keep it with you, even draped over your shoulders, or the dress won't get exposure. If the dress doesn't get photographed, the designer will become hysterical, and guess who'll get it in the neck? Yours truly. That's who.'

'OK,' Nell backed away, and she looked out of the window at the deep grey of the darkening afternoon.

★ ★ ★

Melissa was halfway through Nell's make-up when the doorbell rang again. 'I'll go,' Milly offered.

'No, it's all right.' Nell waited while her eyelashes were released from a medieval torture instrument that promised to add an inch to their length. 'I'll get it.' Her hair was bunched on top of her head, and her face was half made-up, but even so she ran down the stairs.

'Charlie!' Charlie stood before Nell in a parka with the hood pulled up. There was something different about her, but before Nell could decipher what it was, Charlie had hold of her in a hug. 'Careful, careful,' she warned, as the sticky sheen of her foundation smudged.

'It's all right,' Charlie said, 'I've got my dress in here,' and she held up a plastic bag.

'No!' Nell laughed, 'I meant of me.' And Charlie put her head on one side. 'You look great.'

'And you.' Nell stepped back to get a better look.

'What?' Charlie pulled down her hood.

'Nothing,' Nell blushed. 'You just look . . . I haven't seen you for so long, that's all.'

'Look what?'

'Your hair . . . ' Charlie's hair stood out from her head in an afro. 'Is it for a part?'

'No. I just thought I'd try it natural. Curiosity got the better of me. I haven't seen the real thing since I was fourteen.'

Nell led the way upstairs. 'I like it.' She turned to watch her. 'It's just a shock, that's all.' Now, as Charlie removed her coat, Nell could see that she was fatter too. Not fat — that was unimaginable, but her angular frame had softened, her face filled out into an oval, the new line of her jaw flowing softly towards her ear.

'Hi everyone,' Nell ushered her into the room. 'This is my friend, Charlie Adedayo-Martin.'

'Don't worry about me,' Charlie told them. 'I'll do my own make-up, and right now nothing makes much difference to my hair.'

'OK,' Melissa looked affronted. 'I'm here if you change your mind.'

'So what have you got in that fancy bag?' Nell placed herself back down before the sea of make-up and tilted her face for more, while Charlie drew out an ivory silk dress with creamy feathers in the low V of the back. 'I'll hang it up if that's all right,' and retrieving a hanger from the carrier she slung it from a high cupboard door.

'Are you sure you don't want to iron it?' Nell squinted at the jagged creases, but Charlie shrugged. 'It's OK, I've worn it before. Better

384

the crumpled look than the burnt.'

'I can press it,' Milly offered. She was already pressing Nell's dress, steaming its perfectly smooth satin through a series of wet cloths. Charlie was obstinate. 'I promise you. It's fine.'

Tara's phone rang and she barked into it, giving instructions, placating, laying down the law to a virtually silent colleague at the other end.

'So Charlie . . . ' Nell was desperate for news, but Melissa was outlining her lips with a small slick, ticklish brush. 'What . . . I mean . . . are . . . ' But the intensity of Melissa's face, working so close to her own, forced her to give up.

'Tea anyone?' Charlie put the kettle on, moving knowledgeably around the room, although in all the years Nell had lived there, she'd probably only visited twice. Nell was always the one who rushed round to hers, administering comfort, reassuring her with her own inferior life, so that however hopeless Charlie might feel about her lovers, her finances, her career, compared to Nell's it was never quite so bad.

'Give her up,' Sita had urged, exasperated. But Nell could never do it. Once, she'd even taken the train to Manchester after Charlie had hyperventilated on the phone, but by the time she'd arrived, Charlie had found solace in the arms of the lighting cameraman, and Nell had ended up staying in her rented room alone.

Charlie placed the old polka-dot teapot on the table. 'Anything else you need?' she offered, having set out mugs and milk, and Nell asked if she'd bring in a mirror. 'I can do that.' Milly set down the iron, but Charlie was already on her way. She reappeared with the largest, heaviest mirror, unhooked from the bathroom wall. She heaved it on to the table and held it with both hands. 'You look beautiful,' she said, serious, before Nell had a chance to look into it, and Nell breathed out slowly, dropping her shoulders, steeling herself for who she would see.

'Yes. That's good.' Her skin was glowing, her lips the cherry of her toes. Her eyes were smudged with smoky shadows, her cheeks moulded into hollowed planes.

'Enough?' Charlie took the mirror and propped it up above the mantelpiece. 'What time do we have to leave here?' She started on her own make-up.

'The car's coming at six, I think,' Nell said. 'There's a schedule somewhere.' Melissa was brushing and dampening her hair. 'It's on my bed.'

'I'll look.'

'Sorry about the mess.' Nell felt the blood spread warm over her neck. How strange to have Charlie Adedayo-Martin running around for her, and she thought of the premiere of *Celestina*, and how she'd sat up all night, stitching together panels of black lace, hopeful the result would create some old-world glamour to match the event. But on the night, surrounded by girls in tangerine crushed silk and bare brown legs, she realised she looked like an undercover body-guard, or someone's maiden aunt.

''Nell Gilby,'' Charlie read as she came in. ''Royal Premiere of *Mary Peacock*, in aid of the Actors' Benevolent Fund.'' She stood at the end of the table. ''Royal Protocol,'' she began, and then paused. 'Have you read this, Nell?'

'Some.'

'Oh my God.' Charlie composed herself, a smile hovering on her lips. ''As His Royal Highness The Prince of Wales and Her Royal Highness The Duchess of Cornwall move from person to person along the presentation line, they will be introduced to each person by their full name and title.'' She coughed and lowered her voice to give the protocol the weight it deserved. ''As Her Royal Highness hears your name, she will offer you her hand. HRH's hand should be taken lightly, swiftly followed by a bow of the head — men, a small bow, curtsey or bow of the head — women,'' Charlie attempted to do both, ''and one should say, 'Your Royal Highness' or 'Ma'am' (rhyming with Spam) whilst shaking her hand.''

Nell, Melissa, even Tara shrieked. 'Couldn't they have thought of something more sophisticated?' Charlie inspected the sheet of paper. 'Ham . . . Pam . . . What else is there?'

'Lamb?' Nell offered, but Charlie thought that might confuse the foreigners. 'Ma'amb, or even Maaaarm,' and Nell became so convulsed with laughter the hot tongs Melissa was using tangled in her hair.

'Well, I suppose Spam is fundamentally British.' Charlie raised her hand for calm. 'There's more.' She cleared her throat. ''When

387

introduced to HRH The Prince of Wales, one should shake his hand, swiftly followed by a bow of the head — men. A small bob (curtsey) or bow of the head — women. And one should say 'Your Royal Highness' or 'Sir' whilst shaking his hand. Please note,'' she paused for greater effect, ''that women have the option to curtsey — a small bob is sufficient — or to bow their head.' Now this is the really important bit. 'You should *not* initiate a conversation or ask Their Royal Highnesses any questions. Should Her Royal Highness ask you a question, answer naturally using the word 'Ma'am' (rhyming with Spam), e.g. HRH: 'Did you enjoy working on the film?' Reply: 'Yes, Ma'am, it was ... ' ''
Charlie's shoulders began to shake. 'I promise I'm not making this up. 'If asked a question by His Royal Highness,'' she struggled on, ''answer with the word 'Sir' as above. If spouses or partners are invited to witness the royal line-up they should remain behind the presentee and SHOULD NOT be brought forward into the line. Once TRHs have passed down the line, the presentees will be ushered to the stage, or to their seats.''

'Thank God for that.'

'So, Nell Gilby, tell me,' Charlie's royal accent was plummier than the Prince of Wales's, 'did you enjoy working on the film?'

'Yes, Sir,' Nell attempted a sitting curtsey. 'It was great fun. It was ... '

'Time's up,' she barked. 'HRH'll be on to the next one by now. Do you think he's got all night?' She turned to Tara Laurie, whose telephone had fallen finally from her ear. 'So tell me, did you enjoy working on the film?'

Tara looked starrily up at Charlie and grappled for a reply.

'Off to the Tower,' Charlie insisted. And Nell begged her to stop.

'Right.' Melissa released the tongs. 'Have a check and see what you think. We can always have a last go once your dress is on.' She blotted Nell's face with powder and touched up the mascara streak of her hysterical tears. There was a moment's silence when Nell stood up. 'Gorgeous,' Charlie breathed, and Tara moved in and fastened a pair of drooping diamond earrings to the lobes of each ear.

'Yes,' Milly sighed. 'Very lovely.'

Nell inspected herself in the mirror. 'Thanks.' She couldn't stop smiling. Her hair fell in glossy waves halfway down her back and her face was bright as a flower.

'Right then,' Tara gathered up the dress, pressed and damply steaming from the iron. 'Where do you want to get changed?'

'It's OK,' Charlie took it from her, unhooking her own dress from the cupboard. 'We'll call you if we need you.' And holding them both aloft she led the way along the hall to Nell's old bedroom.

'Did you see her face?' Nell shivered in her bra and knickers.

'She'll get over it,' Charlie said. 'Those women are tough as old boots.' She held the silver material as Nell carefully stepped in.

'So,' Charlie's hands fluttered across her back.

'How have you actually been?'

Nell looked round at her, closer to Charlie's height now that she'd slipped into her shoes.

'I mean . . . ' Charlie was serious. 'I know how lonely it can be on a film set. I was worried. I read something about Ciaran . . . '

Nell resisted her old habit of spilling out all her news. 'It can be lonely,' she agreed, and she sucked in her stomach to help Charlie ease up the zip, slowly, carefully, her fingers straining as they pulled the cloth in tight.

'You know,' Charlie breathed low over her shoulder, 'for the longest time now, I've wanted to say sorry.'

Nell felt her bare arms shiver. 'For what?'

'You know. For . . . ' Nell could hear her breathing, and then it was blocked out by the sound of her own heart beating, the rush of her insides, on fire. 'Not being a proper friend to you. At college, you know. And after.'

There was a break in her voice and Nell turned round. 'Hey,' she put up a hand to catch one slipping tear. 'What is it?' But Charlie only sniffed. 'I'm happy that you're back, that's all. I missed you.'

Nell felt herself quake. 'It's all right. I never thought that, anyway. I never minded, really. Well, not that much.' She laughed. 'I'm just glad that we're still friends. Even if you only want to know me now because I'm rich and famous.'

'At least one of us is,' Charlie wiped her eyes. 'I'll need someone to support me in my old age. It's either that or the Actors' Benevolent Fund.'

'Shut up.'

'No really. I've been working at the health food store at the bottom of my road.'

'You haven't!'

'Rearranging the vegetables to hide the mouldy organic brown bits. It's actually quite fun. You wouldn't believe the propositions I get in there. If I wasn't on a sabbatical from sex, who knows what I'd be up to.'

'Car's here,' Tara's voice called tersely from the kitchen.

Nell started in terror.

'Tell it to wait,' Charlie shouted. And she put out her hands and held them lightly over Nell's head.

Nell closed her eyes. 'What are you doing?' She felt a warm blanket wrap itself around her. She sighed. Even her shoes felt more comfortable.

'It's all right,' Charlie whispered, 'they always send the car too early,' and moving around her, swirling the energy, so that it roiled and pitched, she swept her hands in large strokes up and down Nell's body until she was calm. 'Thanks.' Nell's eyes felt soft and shiny. 'That was amazing.' And she looked at the tight curls of Charlie's hair, the rounded arm that hung from her new strong shoulder, and wondered what had happened in the time that she'd been gone.

It was only once they were in the car that Nell remembered that she'd forgotten to put on her Spanx. 'Shhh. It doesn't matter,' Charlie soothed her. 'You look great, although they may have been useful. If it snows you could have taken them off and used them as a hat.' Just then

Poppy, from the PR company, phoned. Her voice was strained. 'Where are you?'

'I'm not sure.' Nell peered out of the window at the inky streets. 'Where are we?'

'Five minutes away,' the driver spoke up from the front.

'Five,' Nell reported and Poppy shrieked. 'No, that's too soon, we need you to be last, you mustn't get here before Wayne Hull, drive around the block for a few minutes. I'll call you, but wait till at least quarter to seven.'

The driver pulled up in a side street off Leicester Square, and Nell and Charlie lay back against the padded leather of the car's upholstery and waited. If I could stay like this for ever, Nell thought, just on the brink, but she was ready, all the same, when Poppy called again.

For almost an hour Nell stood on the red carpet, pressed against the barricades, talking and signing and shaking hands with a crowd of well-wishers who had come to cheer her on. Poppy guided her, wrapped in a red coat, while Nell, for the sake of stardom and her designer dress, remained half naked in the icy February night. 'Nell, Nell Gilby!' young girls waved photos of her and shrieked, and Nell, caught up in their jubilation, moved from one to the other, signing her name on whatever they presented. She was too busy to notice the cold, not until she reached the entrance to the cinema where a man strode towards her, his lips blue, an expression of pitiful concern across his face. 'Nell Gilby,' he was speaking for the camera that would flash her image up before the waiting crowd inside. 'How does it feel tonight? The premiere of your first film?' Nell smiled. 'Wonderful,' she said, although in fact she'd lost all sensation in her feet and she was worried, if she took another step, she might simply topple over.

'From all reports it's destined to be a massive hit,' the man gushed, and Nell quivered, aware of several hundred beady eyes on her, grateful for the promotional words that were ready at her lips. 'An enormous amount of work and passion has gone into the making of this film . . . ' she began, and the two of them chatted, the wind gusting at her hair, his knuckles white where they clutched the microphone.

Eventually Nell was escorted inside, up the stairs to the foyer where the other actors and their guests, the producers from both sides of the Atlantic, and Ciaran, awkward in a suit and tie, stood waiting. 'Well done,' Charlie had a glass of wine for her, and her own coat to wrap around her. 'I'm sorry it's not hot chocolate,' and she took one of Nell's hands and attempted to warm it in her own. Nell glanced across at Ciaran. He was unaccompanied, at least she thought he was, and for a second it seemed as if he might be about to move towards her. But behind them through the wall of glass, the royal car was pulling into the square, driving up the red carpet to the cinema door. As fast as possible everyone manoeuvred into place, the front line sombre and expectant, the back row sniggering as if they were at school.

'Shhh,' Nell attempted to quieten Charlie, who was exchanging gossip with the producer's teenage girlfriend, and abandoning the coat she turned to watch The Royal Highnesses, who were moving along the line. 'Did you enjoy working on the film?' the Prince was asking, true to his script, his head bent in earnest anticipation of the replies, while Camilla sailed along beside him in a floor-length maroon dress. 'Sensible,' Charlie hissed over her shoulder, 'warmer than Spam,' but there was no time to respond, the royal entourage was upon her. 'Did you . . . ' a new idea had occurred to the Prince, she could see it dawning on his face. 'Did you find it very difficult, learning your lines?'

Nell was thrown. Not just by the question, but by the sheer delight the Prince took in producing it. 'Actually, well, no, not really . . . ' She felt a nudge from behind. 'Sir . . . But it was fun. Being in the film. I loved it.'

'Hello.' Camilla had caught sight of Charlie, peering over the top of Nell's head. 'What are you doing . . . ' she looked amused, 'standing back there?'

Charlie tried to duck. 'We're under orders. Ma'am. I'm not even meant to be talking to you.' She grimaced, and then curtsied. 'Pretend you never saw me.'

Camilla laughed. 'But I have seen you. Aren't you the girl from *The Inspectors*? Yes, I liked that. I thought you were awfully good.'

'Really?' Charlie frowned. 'I thought it was awful . . . but actually, thank you. I'm glad you enjoyed it. It means a lot.'

Nell and Prince Charles, the odd couple suddenly, stood nodding politely, trying to think of anything else to say. But then an aide was moving them on, a gentle hand at the Prince's elbow, and Nell too was steered away, down a flight of stairs, along dark corridors, into the secret bowels of the cinema to the wings of the stage.

Ciaran Conway stood before the curtained screen. 'And of course none of this would have been possible without my brilliant scriptwriter, the director of photography, the editors and producers who've worked so tirelessly, all of whom I thank from the bottom of my heart . . . ' There was a catch in Ciaran's voice, and his fingers trembled as he spread his arms wide, 'which only leaves me to introduce the cast, who dug so deep inside themselves to bring this story to the screen. There are many pitfalls in this business but there are wonders too, and we are honoured tonight to have so many of the actors with us . . . ' And having shaken off his usual shyness in favour of passion, Ciaran began to call the actors out on to the stage, hugging each one as they arrived, until Nell heard her own name. She took a last deep breath and walked out into his embrace. 'And now,' Ciaran kept one arm around her, 'it is with most humble gratitude, that we announce the Prince of Wales and the Duchess of Cornwall.' Above them, at the top of the stalls two trumpeters appeared, and with a blast of silver notes filled the auditorium with the medieval sound of victory. Tahdatadaaaaaah! The royal couple stood, heralded in state, while everyone in the cinema rose up in their seats and clapped. Ciaran took Nell's hand and squeezed it. 'It's so good to see you,' he spoke out of the corner of his mouth. 'I've missed you like hell.' The trumpeters blasted out another long, rich trill.

'Don't think,' Ciaran was still talking, 'that I'm letting you get away from me, ever again,' and Nell, dazed with happiness, looked out over the thousand starry faces, and seeing her mother, and in the row above, contrary to all expectation, her father, she pinched herself to check she wasn't in a dream. Further along the row was Pierre with his fiancé Robin, and Hettie, beside them, in some kind of feathered hat. Her sister was there too, with her husband, and Sita and Raj, their arms around each other. And there at the end was Charlie, luminous in her white dress, waving, blowing a kiss out over the crowd.

'Yes' was all Nell could say as Ciaran's arm tightened around her, and raising her free hand to her lips, she blew her own kiss back.

Acknowledgements

I'd like to thank the many actors who gave me inspiration and ideas for this novel, none of whom appear as themselves, but to avoid confusion I shall avoid listing names. But if I interviewed you, or cornered you at a party, or just watched you in admiration from the stalls, thank you, I couldn't have written this book without you.

I'd also like to thank my loyal early readers, Georgia Garrett, Alexandra Pringle, Xandra Bingley, Natania Jansz, Bella Freud and my husband, David Morrissey.

We do hope that you have enjoyed reading this large print book.

Did you know that all of our titles are available for purchase?

We publish a wide range of high quality large print books including:
Romances, Mysteries, Classics
General Fiction
Non Fiction and Westerns

Special interest titles available in large print are:
The Little Oxford Dictionary
Music Book
Song Book
Hymn Book
Service Book

Also available from us courtesy of Oxford University Press:
Young Readers' Dictionary
(large print edition)
Young Readers' Thesaurus
(large print edition)

For further information or a free brochure, please contact us at:
Ulverscroft Large Print Books Ltd.,
The Green, Bradgate Road, Anstey,
Leicester, LE7 7FU, England.
Tel: (00 44) 0116 236 4325
Fax: (00 44) 0116 234 0205